The Azaleas

Books by Katie Wainwright

Cuba on My Mind
Secuestro

*For Sue —
Best wishes,
Katie*

11/27/2013

The Azaleas

KATIE WAINWRIGHT

RED DUST PUBLISHING   WINDERMERE

The Azaleas by Katie Wainwright

Copyright © 2013 Katie Wainwright

All rights reserved. This book or any portion thereof may not be reproduced or used in any manner whatsoever without the express written permission of the publisher, except for the use of brief quotations in a book review.

Printed in the United States of America by Red Dust Publishing

First edition: September 2013
10 9 8 7 6 5 4 3 2 1

ISBN-13: 978-1492210917
ISBN-10: 1492210919

Book layout and cover design by Pattie Steib

This is a work of fiction. Any resemblance to persons living or dead is purely coincidental.

In memory of CTW

CHAPTER 1

Sundays before Katrina were bad, but after the hurricane they were the absolute pits. Café du Monde was half empty, the normal tourist crush replaced by haggard men and women wearing FEMA jackets and National Guards in camouflage and army boots. Across Jackson Square, worshippers trickled into the ten o'clock mass at St. Louis Cathedral, praying more for relief than forgiveness.

Glancing at the empty tables, Karla said to the Vietnamese waitress, "Not so good."

"It's a better. Some outta FEMA trailers soon." Li Wang placed a cup of café au lait and three powdered beignets on the table and wiped her sugary hands on a white apron.

"Thanks," Karla said. "You got your settlement?"

"Nah—no coming—ever. Fill out more paper. More paper."

"Who would've thought two years later?"

"You de lucky one—"

"Because the Quarter didn't flood and I don't own the apartment? Y'know what gets me? It's so quiet."

"Horn players coming back—black boys do tap dancing yestiday. Nice. Nice."

Most street lights were working, one-way arrows pointing the right way—signs of progress, of recovery.

"Yo' man, he come back?" Li asked.

In the French Quarter flooded with out-of-town gawkers, local residents formed a tight little community. Everybody knew everybody else's business.

"He's not."

"Good riddance."

Easy for Li to say— secure with husband and kids. Karla sipped hot coffee. A tidal wave of sorrow washed over her. Four years! Her best years, her prime, invested in a dead-end relationship.

Li moved to other tables while Karla wallowed in self-pity. Descending to the depths and touching her pain kept her sorrow fresh, tragic and beautiful.

She'd lost her significant other. She had no job. Half the restaurants and strip clubs were still closed. Her apartment roof leaked. The tub didn't drain. The city looked shitty and smelled like swamp mud.

The natural disaster atop her personal ruin brought tears to her eyes. She couldn't stop crying. How long she sat there, she didn't know. It must've been quite a while because someone waved a white handkerchief like a surrender flag under her nose, and said. "That's enough."

"Thank you." Karla blew, wheezed, blew again and offered the soiled handkerchief back to its owner.

"Perfectly all right—" The deep voice coming from behind the Sunday *Times Picayune* had the raspy quality of liquid sandpaper. "You keep it."

"I'm having a really bad day."

The man looked over the newspaper page. "You have a lot of company."

Uptown Albert! Karla should've known. He'd been drinking coffee at Café du Monde every morning for several weeks now, one of those people who periodically surfaced in the Quarter from the affluent uptown area. They found or didn't find what they were looking for, then returned to wherever they lived their daily dramas.

Uptown Albert with his rich, cushy, St. Charles Avenue life didn't have an inkling of Karla's pain and suffering. Her most recent tragedy occupied her life's center stage and spilled onto the aprons. She couldn't expel Richard from her heart or her head. She hated herself and hated him even more. Her anger far exceeded any she'd experienced before, a hot fury that erupted at unexpected moments into a red killing urge, eased only when the molten heat dissolved into tears.

"My boyfriend left me."

Albert finished Sports and glanced through Classified.

Didn't her plight merit skipping any section? "Did you hear me?"

"May I?" he asked, slipping into the empty chair at Karla's sticky table. "That way you needn't shout."

"I didn't shout."

"Yes, you did." He folded the paper and reached for his coffee cup. "Men leave all the time," he observed, "for a variety of reasons. You'll get over it."

"He got married! To somebody else!—"

"Ah! You're probably more humiliated than hurt."

A nugget of truth existed in that pronouncement. Richard graduated from Tulane, and suddenly Karla wasn't good enough for the doctor. The slap stung. He married high class with a pedigree. They had a huge wedding, seven bridesmaids—in Houston. New Orleans was too ravished, too sorry, too pitiful a place for 500 guests. Starving for normal news, the Times-Picayune society section ran a half-page spread.

"I'm not humiliated! I'm hurt and I'm mad." It stung that the bitch must've been planning the wedding the whole time Richard was sleeping with Karla. "Spitting mad—"

And destitute—rent two months behind, car repossessed yesterday and piano going tomorrow 9 a.m. sharp the man from Piano World said—"Richard took a big bite out of my life, then tossed me aside as if I were a bad apple or something. Do you think that's fair?"

Her lover had conveniently forgotten his promises. He swore as soon as he had that M. D. degree nothing but blue skies and pink roses for Karla and him. Instead of the anticipated good times, vultures were now circling overhead, picking her bones. "I'll get even with the bastard if it's the last thing I do."

With the folded edge of the newspaper Albert scraped powdered sugar into a white heap. "Life's not fair," he said, "and anger consumes energy better spent on positive things."

"Can't you understand? Richard wrecked my life!"

"Only if you allow it—"

Easy for Albert to say—he had money, position and Uptown status. He probably never got himself into predicaments that one of those three stations couldn't solve.

Yesterday Karla turned thirty– bad enough– but thirty, single and broke? She folded Albert's handkerchief, found a dry spot by the monogrammed AM and blew.

Albert said, "People who succeed in life don't depend on anybody for anything."

Great! Exactly what Karla needed—a lecture!

"Stand on your own two feet. Go to work."

"I do work."

"Playing the piano at the Parrot Bar–" *How did he know that?*—'is not a job. It's an avocation."

The nightly gig paid in tips only, and some nights there were no customers. "I work at a book store, too," Karla said defensively. That job was more main stream. "It's reopening soon."

"Ah, yes— Books by the Mile."

"Books-A-Million?"

"No difference."

For a while Karla had worked at the Librairie on Orleans Street until Jacques couldn't afford her pay. He was barely surviving himself. His musty-smelling hole in the wall specialized in rare and out-of-print volumes. The shelves were crammed from floor to ceiling with books fragile and delicate to the touch, their pages illustrated with lithographs and wood cuttings. The worn covers protected tales that outlasted time. Books-A-Million carried nothing comparable. Their books smelled new, the pages starched and crisp, best sellers: big fanfare today, forgotten tomorrow.

Albert said. "There's no point beating a dead horse."

What did this man know? Her horse still kicked. Married or not, Richard wanted her back in the worst way, and she wanted him, too. Why, just last night at the Parrot Bar he had whispered in her ear how much he missed her, how he couldn't live without her, words that caused her heart to soar.

"Richard still loves me. He's just been trapped into a situation–"

"Don't humiliate yourself by making excuses for him."

"God—you sound like Mimi!" Karla's fingers drummed on the table top. "Last night when we left the bar and started across the street to my apartment, Mimi stopped wiping circles on the counter and grabbed my arm. 'He's using you,' she said, all tight around the lips. 'Why don't you do yourself a big favor? Take the *l* out of *lover* and tell the jerk it's *over.*' "

"Now there's a smart woman," Albert said. "She knows your Richard won't be divorcing a socially correct wife."

Deep down Karla knew that was the undeniable truth. On a subterranean level, her mind understood the dead end of this affair, but her heart couldn't process logic. She wailed aloud. "What's to become of me?" and honked into Albert's handkerchief once again. "Just when I thought I had it made–" She stopped abruptly— "y'know Richard?"

"I know a dozen Richards," Albert said. "They fall madly in love with a flesh and blood girl then marry the paper doll debutante the parents picked out in kindergarten. They have no spine, no guts."

"You don't know my Richard! He's not at all like that—" wasn't he? Hadn't he done exactly that? "Oh, never mind! Leave me alone. Don't hassle me. You have no idea what I'm going through."

"I can imagine."

"How could you? You don't know the first thing about me."

"I know everything about you." He put the paper down and trained smoky gray eyes on Karla. "I ran a background check."

That stopped Karla cold. "What? You did what?"

"I want you to work for me, so I ran a background check."

She was on her feet. "You've got some nerve, Mister."

"Sit down, please. Hear me out. I'm searching for a bold and fearless salesperson, and I was given your name."

"By who?—"

"By whom?—that's not important. I know you have a GED high-school equivalency certificate, a lapsed real estate license and a year at Hasker and Blunt. You gave notice for no good reason and worked minimum-wage, dead-end jobs. You've never been married—quite unusual, I'd say—but you've tempered that statistic with a number of short-lived affairs."

Karla was momentarily speechless. She didn't know what stunned her more, the job offer or his delving into her checkered past.

He delivered his best punch. "I'm looking for somebody who needs to make a lot of money fast."

That certainly made Karla a candidate. "You're a real estate broker?"

"No—a lawyer—"

A light bulb thought pierced the cobwebs in Karla's mind. "Palimony suits? You do them?"

"I'm afraid not. The clients I deal with own property difficult to sell for a variety of reasons."

Selling easy property had been a hard enough job. "My license is in limbo. I don't have the money for the renewal fee. I'm sure by now there's a delinquent fine added to that. When you're down, you're always the target for that extra kick."

Karla's short-lived real estate career started when a slick recruiter tapped her on the shoulder in the Riverwalk Mall one Sunday afternoon. Every disaster in her life took place on a Sunday. The tarot card reader said it was because Gemini was in Pluto's path and formed a negative seven and she was star-crossed and Karla believed her. This recruiter promised the sky was the limit, and Karla was so far in the hole, daylight had to be piped in. She couldn't wait to sign up. Instead of blue skies, what did she get? Low ceilings heavy with atmospheric pressure—

Albert enticed her, low-key but persuasive. "I can activate your license, just like that." He snapped his fingers. "Gloria Stein said that if you'd stuck with it, you would've been the very best."

"Gloria said that? You know Gloria? Why don't you hire her?"

"She's carved her own niche."

"She's tops." Every Tuesday Hasker & Blunt's manager had a sales meeting where everyone bitched and complained, going at each other like stinging hornets—except Gloria. Above all that petty bickering, she consistently listed, sold and toted her money to the bank. She belonged to the industry's five-star clubs. By the time she wrapped up one transaction, she was deep into the next. 'If you have time to stop and count your shekels,' she once told Karla, 'you're not working hard enough.' "Gloria took me under her wing."

"She believed you had potential," Albert said.

"If the manager would've let me be, given me a little slack—I don't take to reins well — I could've done it. I almost had it down pat. *Almost* is so depressing, y'know? If you can't do it and you know it, that's okay. You make peace with it and skip to the next thing. But *almost* is like leaners in horseshoes—nearly a ringer, but it doesn't count. And the jerk manager was always lusting and chasing after me. It didn't take me long to quit. That's the way I am. Don't like something, walk away without ever looking back."

THE AZALEAS

"Exactly what I need, someone who will jump in, do the job and get out fast."

"You know what I've got to show for a year at H & B? A real estate license in limbo and $400 deeper in debt—Life sucks. If I had hospitalization, I'd crack up."

"Instead of having a breakdown, come work for me. I promise it'll be a lot more exciting."

He couldn't be hitting on her, all red-nosed and bleary-eyed as she was, so obviously he was nuts. Crazies abounded in New Orleans, the French Quarter their prime spawning ground. These characters could be dangerous. A real demon could be lurking inside the impeccable gray suit and silk ascot, the way a priestly collar hid a well-known Quarter pervert.

"So what kind of property are you talking about? Big white elephants?—"

"Worse than that—" He shrugged. "A dwelling where someone was murdered, a building under surveillance for whatever reason, a safe house that's no longer safe, a place believed haunted, an estate with forty-two owners who won't agree to sign a deed—sticky situations."

Karla scrutinized the man making this ridiculous proposition. "Sounds dangerous—"

"It is." He tamped tobacco into a slim pipe and the sweet-smelling smoke rose and curled over his silver hair. His well-shaped ears had a pale cast, translucent like a sea shell. A trim white mustache protected the bemused smile. His cheeks were soft and pink like a baby's—overall a weak, colorless face without sharp angles or strong lines. Karla guessed his age past fifty. He looked distinguished, with an air of a diplomat to an important country. Still, she hedged. Looks could be deceiving in a Mardi Gras city where everyone wore a mask.

He waited patiently without moving or fidgeting while Karla chewed the end of a yellow ringlet and took in her fill of his looks, his smell, his vibes. Finding them all positive, her focus slipped back to herself, but with a different twist, conscious, suddenly, knowing she looked a fright, nose like an over-ripe tomato, swollen lips tasting salt, cheeks tear-streaked and every dime-sized freckle popping. Her pony-tail was coming apart, and the humidity corkscrewed her hair in all directions.

She was drowning in her misery, and this man she knew only by sight and reputation, a man she'd never said more than good morning to, threw her a life line. Catch it and she'd be dragged back to the world of the living. Wallowing had its comforts. A certain relief existed in giving up, in not caring any more.

Crossing her arms over her pink tank top, she hugged her chest and rubbed the butterfly tattooed on her right shoulder. "This place you're supposed to sell," she asked, "what's wrong with it?"

"I don't quite know yet. I'm to meet the owner here—" he checked his watch—"after ten o'clock mass. Thirty minutes."

For the next few minutes they sat quietly and watched more national guardsmen stream into Café du Monde. The men bit into square doughnuts; powdered sugar fell in little white showers, sweet dust coating brash laughter.

Karla's gut told her to play safe and reject Albert's proposal. This deal wasn't on the up-and-up. It didn't have legs. "Thanks," she said. "You've been very kind, but the job isn't for me."

"Please, my dear." Albert raised a restraining hand. The diamond horseshoe on his finger reached the knuckle. "Don't be hasty. Think of this as an opportunity for us both. You need a job. I need sales help. You have complete freedom to manipulate, to reach the goal, no reins, no restraints, and the money is good."

Bills, bills and more bills; no health insurance; behind in the rent—Mimi had urged Karla to apply for food stamps and she'd wrestled with the prospect, but thinking about long lines, red tape and endless paperwork deterred her. Anyhow, food stamps and SSI validated failure. She hadn't sunk that low yet, thanks to an unexpected Red Cross disaster relief check made out in Auntie Emmy's name that arrived in the nick of time. "How good?—"

"Depends on the property and the sales price, but I don't handle ordinary places. I can safely say the commissions would never be less than $30,000 per transaction."

He let the number float like a trial balloon. The figure sucked up Karla like the tornado did Dorothy. She aspirated one single word: "Dollars?"

"Paid only if you produce—"

"And if I don't?"

"That's your gamble."

Karla was no innocent. This was a new bait-and-switch game. "Thanks, but no thanks."

"You can make $100,000 a year, easy. More, if business is good. It depends."

THE AZALEAS

Her antenna vibrated. "Who's gonna buy a million dollar house in New Orleans? Open your eyes! Look around. Everybody is leaving, you got that? Leaving! And if the pay is so good, how come sales people aren't beating your door down for the job?"

"I employ only one agent at a time. You're the first woman."

"How many men?—"

"A half dozen—"

"Why did they quit?"

Albert's unflinching gray eyes met Karla's. "Some made enough money and went on to more conventional, less stressful work. One had a heart attack. The last one had an unfortunate accident."

Whatever else he might be, this lawyer wasn't a liar, reason enough to be even more suspicious.

"The job is dangerous," Karla said, convinced now beyond doubt.

"Yes. High risk—nobody has lasted longer than two years. That's why the pay is so good."

Karla rubbed the shoulder butterfly, assessing the situation. She'd lost her confidence, had no ambition. Her sole focus was her bitter and consuming anger. Keeping that flame stoked took all her energy. "Your offer is tempting, but I pass."

"Have you ever seen a waterfall?" Albert asked.

Karla shook her head. Where would she find a waterfall in a flat land with no hills? New Orleans was surrounded by water, swamps and bogs.

"When the falling water is harnessed, the leashed force generates enough power to light entire cities."

She stared at him blankly. What was he talking about? But what the hell! Thirty thousand dollars could go a long ways toward brightening her life.

"You can accomplish whatever you want." Albert spoke with quiet authority, like a high school principal holding a report card, checking the A, B, C, D, F's of a student's life— "What you make of yourself is entirely up to you and nobody else. There's nothing wrong with making a mistake—"

"Richard wasn't a mistake!"

"A wrong turn, then. We all take wrong turns. To be pierced by misfortune's daily daggers and keep on living takes real courage."

Was he assessing her cowardice? Well, she hadn't fled to Houston or Atlanta or Chicago. She was still here in the same neighborhood, the same apartment, walking the same streets.

At times in her life Karla reached crossroads that changed her life for better or for worse: the morning she woke up in the boarding house bed alone, her mother gone; her senior year at McDonogh High when she quit before graduation; the day Auntie Emmy died; when Richard moved in; when Richard moved out; and now, when this pale old man sitting at her table, a total stranger, casually offered her a brass ring. Why? She swallowed the why. Who knew why? Life was all questions, no answers. But she couldn't stop herself—"Why me?"

"Let's just say I have my reasons and let it go at that."

He probably had only one reason and he carried it between his legs. "I've sworn off men completely, so don't think you're going—"

His laugh was insulting. "You need a few days to think it over?"

What for? Who was there to consult or advise her? Mimi at the bar?—the pervert priest?—the tarot card reader?—a séance with Auntie Emmy? The job paid mega bucks. Then again, it might pay nothing. But when Richard knocked on her door, she would be gone, working, gainfully employed and not moping around, waiting. A little distance between them right now might be the best thing, the right thing.

She couldn't do it. She wanted Richard. *She couldn't live without Richard.*

Stifling monumental doubts, she replied, "No need to think it over." Whatever Albert's corrupt reasons, $30,000 was a virtual fortune she couldn't pass up. "As long as you clearly understand I'm not sleeping with you and I haven't the foggiest idea what I'm doing, I'll do it."

"That's good enough for me. I can live with that." He looked up and saw a man and a woman crossing Decatur Street. "There she comes," he said, "the owner of the property."

CHAPTER 2

"Mary Bravelle!" Albert called.

A woman wearing a wide-brimmed black straw hat decorated with grosgrain ribbon and wisps of veiling rushed across the curb and stepped into Albert's outstretched arms, an enthusiastic embrace that knocked her hat askew. She looked at him with magnificent dark eyes. Her melancholy smile captured his undivided attention, cut the moment out of the surrounding noise and bustle, and the two were alone, bound by memory and circumstance.

"My dear—my dear!—" Albert held Mary at arm's length and looked her over as if she'd been delivered by UPS and he was checking for damages before signing the receipt. She had a model's coat-hanger build, no bumps, no angles. Her skirt hung straight and even. "You look marvelous. How are you?"

"Fine, considering—" her feathery voice matched her slight body. Everything about Mary was childlike, as though her development had been arrested at a youthful point in life. She had that waif quality every man felt compelled to protect.

In a little girl whisper void of Southern drawl and infused with a foreign lilt, Mary introduced her heavy-set companion who stood to one side, diffidently holding her hat. "Pierre Rousseau, my fiancé."

Pierre's bristly mustache brushed Karla's fingers. The moist lips gave her goose bumps that started at her wrist and spread up her arm to the butterfly on her shoulder. Some people had a sixth sense, intuition, ESP. Karla had goose bumps, an in-built radar system that blipped a warning. This Pierre trolled water like a submarine with a raised periscope.

Pierre said, "My pleashure, mam'selle."

Albert made the introductions. "Karla Whitmore, my colleague."

Colleague—the word had a nice ring to it—high-class—and the *"my"* put Monsieur Rousseau on instant notice. Albert was a pretty shrewd cookie. Nothing got past him.

Albert offered Mary condolences and a chair. He appropriated an empty table next to a woman holding a baby. The infant looked over his mama's shoulder and gurgled.

"Isn't he adorable!—" Mary extended a hand toward the baby and his chubby little fingers reached for Mary's. "You're so cute." For the next several minutes she became totally involved with the baby, playing with his hand, patting his cheek, tousling his hair. Finally, the daddy or significant other appeared and the mother, obviously relieved to get away from Mary, moved on.

"Your dear mother!—" Albert said, once Mary's attention returned to the table. "We will all miss her." He sounded like an audible Hallmark card. "When did I last see her? Must be two years—time goes by so fast—yes, two years. I helped her with her will, mostly by phone. She didn't get out much."

"She'd become a recluse," Mary replied, removing her nubby black jacket.

The diamond and pearl cluster on the lapel screamed money. Of course she had money. Poor people didn't own "hard to sell" property. Poor people didn't have "easy to sell" property, either. The lackey Pierre hung the jacket on the chair.

Mary smiled sweetly. "Thank you, darling," and then to Albert, "Mama battled depression. She was despondent most of the time, surviving on prescription pills. I worried constantly about her, and in the end there was nothing I could do." She heaved the sigh of the aggrieved daughter forced to become the parent.

Karla knew this role-swap well. Often as a child she had pulled off her mother's red sling-back pumps and helped her climb into bed, fetched aspirins for the headaches that never went away, and placed damp wash-rags over the painted face.

"The memorial service was nice," Mary said. "Father Berteau did it. He was Mama's priest."

Pierre's hand touched Karla's knee under the table. His shoe rubbed her shin. She shifted away her leg.

THE AZALEAS

Mary dabbed her eyes and recalled her mother's last years. "She refused to leave the house or have friends over. She didn't want to be bothered with anybody. I begged her to come live with me in Paris, but she wouldn't do it. She couldn't stand André, that's no secret. Actually, after a few years," a girlish giggle escaped her lips, "I couldn't stand him, either." Her pale hand flew to her mouth, amazed at what she'd said. "The truth is," she continued sadly. "I caused Mama so much grief. Her death was my fault. She was so bogged down in the past. She wouldn't let go and move on. I feel so guilty!"

"Don't be too hard on yourself," Albert said.

Mary looked away, sadness and regret shadowing her eyes. "Sometimes I wonder if her death was—but it couldn't be. I'm sure it wasn't."

Karla butted in. "Did she die at home?"

Mary sighed as if the sad event was more than her little heart could bear. "Why, yes."

"The coroner came?" asked Karla.

Until Katrina in Louisiana when a person died at home without a doctor or nurse hovering over the bed, the undertaker couldn't take the body away until the authorities arrived and signed the death certificate. After the flood it was different. Nobody could find the authorities. The Guard and the Rescue Units removed unidentified corpses from their watery graves and transferred them to the LSU football field in Baton Rouge, dry and above sea level, a temporary morgue.

Mary nodded assent. "Yes. He came."

Karla said, "He found no foul play, just an empty pill bottle on the night stand next to the bed. He signed off death by natural causes."

Mary's eyes twitched as if Karla had hit the optic nerve. "How did...how did..."

"Happens in the Quarter all the time—somebody gets addled and pops the wrong pills, forgets and takes the whole bottle, or mixes alcohol with Oxycontin."

"Mama didn't overdose if that's what you're implying," Mary replied stiffly.

"Probably not on purpose, but accidentally—happens lots of time. Did you request an autopsy?"

"There was no reason."

"Well, it's too late, but you should've. Now you'll have those nagging doubts all your life."

Truth could be swallowed, digested, transformed into nuggets of wisdom and passed on. Doubt ran constantly like diarrhea, impossible to shut off.

Albert didn't stop Karla's prying. She was asking all the questions he wanted to know but was too gentlemanly to ask.

"Did she have insurance?"

Pierre suddenly lost interest in Karla's legs, leaned forward and rested a big, hairy hand protectively over Mary's slim fingers.

"One small policy," Mary replied in her little girl whisper.

"Are you the beneficiary?" Karla asked.

"I'm the only child."

"What else did she leave you?"

"Her jewelry, household silver, china—that kind of thing—and of course, The Azaleas—" In response to Karla's raised eyebrows, she explained, "A plantation in St. Francisville I have no use for."

While Karla's piano was going out the apartment door for lack of a couple of hundred bucks, Mary Bravelle stewed over what to do with a plantation she didn't want—life at the height of its unfairness.

"This is the property Albert will sell?"

"Yes. The Azaleas has a lot of bad memories for us. Mama should've sold it years ago."

"And why didn't she?"

"Because of Aunt Agatha—when the plantation sells, Mama will get even with Aunt Agatha from beyond the grave."

Karla wondered what big feud Mama and Aunt Agatha had. Then again it might be nothing. Families had a way of falling out over the pickiest little things.

Karla's probing had touched a vulnerable spot. Two big tears spilled from Mary's dark brown eyes. Karla started to offer her Albert's handkerchief and thought better of it. Mary ran her fingers over her lashes, smearing the mascara.

Albert crumbled as Karla knew he would. Men couldn't handle tears. They walked away from bawling, but those silent drops sliding down an upturned cheek stopped them dead in their tracks. He offered Mary a fresh white handkerchief. Did he carry an unlimited supply? Pierre patted Mary's hand reassuringly. She melted into a puddle of helplessness, and the two men fawned over her. Karla watched with grave interest, wondering exactly what it took to achieve this state of terminal Jello.

THE AZALEAS

Albert consoled Mary. "Now, now—everything will be all right. We'll take care of the plantation for you. Just put all those worries out of your pretty little head." Karla thought she'd puke, but then he asked, "Did Agatha come to the memorial service?" and they were back on track again.

"Oh, dear, yes. You should've seen her! She walked right past me and never said a word. Not one word. You'd think she'd say one grateful word." Mary's eyes brightened, the tears temporarily contained. "After all, Mama did let Aunt Agatha live on the plantation rent-free." Mary's voice broke and she struggled anew with the catch in her throat. "Aunt Agatha thinks she owns the place, that she's entitled to it." She played with Pierre's hand, an unconscious, nervous gesture. When she spoke again wistfulness filled her voice. "Aunt Agatha was like my second mother until…until…I really thought she cared for me. At one time we were very close. Then when all that happened," Pierre's arm went around Mary's shoulders and she leaned into him for protection and solace.

Karla felt a jealous pang. *Oh, to be able to melt like that and have somebody take care of me!*

Mary burrowed her face into Pierre's coat and in a muffled voice said, "Yes! Yes! I will sell the plantation and put it all behind me. Finally!—" She raised her head and reluctantly turned to practical matters. "Will a sale take long?"

"Depends," Albert replied. "On how quickly Karla can find a buyer."

Damn! Lay the whole trip on her! What a copout. Hire her to sell the plantation, and when she couldn't do it, pass on the blame. Neat trick if he could get away with it. "Listen, Albert—"

"Have you driven to the plantation?" Albert asked Mary.

"I intended to, but when I got the cold shoulder from Aunt Agatha, I changed my mind. Maybe it's best. I have no business there. It's nothing but a run-down old house! The constant tug of war with Aunt Agatha drove Mama crazy. I won't let that happen to me." She sighed audibly as if the plantation were a weight that would sink her while the thought struck Karla that if *anybody* left her *anything* she'd take it gladly, in sickness or in health and not bellyache about it. "I had mixed feelings about The Azaleas, but I've sorted through them." Mary smiled wistfully, every gleaming tooth an orthodontic perfection. Karla's tongue darted out to cover the gap between her two front teeth.

Pierre gave Mary's shoulders a possessive little squeeze. "*Mon cherie*, perhaps it would be good for us to have a look at this plantation."

The plural possessive didn't get past Albert or past Karla, either.

"Pierre's advice is to sell The Azaleas immediately and sever all ties with the past and invest the cash," said Mary.

The word "cash" brought a champagne sparkle to Pierre's eyes. He raised Mary's hand and nibbled her fingers.

"Your mother tried to sell the plantation once before," Albert said.

"Yes," Mary replied. "There was a buyer, but he had a car accident of some sort. I believe he was killed. I can't recall exactly. Anyhow, any potential buyer Agatha couldn't run off, Felice did."

Once again Karla reassessed the situation. Chasing rainbows was tempting, but unreasonable. Mary dissolved into tears at every turn, Pierre prowled like an alley cat, and Albert was a puzzle with a key piece missing. At some point, she was bound to lose her cool and tell them all to stuff it where the sun didn't shine. Only a miracle would make this situation work and she didn't believe in divine intervention. Better to end this business before it ever got started. "Albert—"

The conversation had turned to more pleasant subjects. "Did I tell you I saw Walter in London?" Mary asked.

The three of them discussed friends and mutual acquaintances, leaving the unfortunate dead buyer and the mysterious Felice dangling like question marks.

Pierre did most of the talking and name-dropping. He and Mary had gone sailing with Count So-and-So in Spain. *La-dee-dah!* They'd been to Prague, the "in" place now. Such cheap prices! Better, much better than Turkey. Pierre had forced Mary to purchase a Khorassan rug. "So reasonable!" he said. "She should've bought two. Have you been lately?"

"No," replied Albert, "I haven't."

"But you were in Switzerland," Mary said. "The girl at your office told me."

"Yes. I have an on-going interest there, my niece."

"Of course—of course!—" Pierre agreed with a wicked twinkle in his eye. "Everyone has a niece, right? As soon as Mary finishes this business we plan a skiing vacation in the international banking capital of the world! Money, money, money everywhere!—"

THE AZALEAS

Karla scraped back her chair and stood. This business was not in her league. She didn't have a regular bank account, much less a Swiss one. "Excuse me." She'd made quick exits before. Disappearing didn't take superhuman effort, just a casual trip to the john and a quick bolt the back way.

Albert blocked her path. He looked lumbering, but he was swift on his feet.

Pierre checked his watch. "Have we finished here? Twelve o'clock, Mary! Time for our Quarter tour!—" He pointed toward the empty buggies and carriages lining Jackson Square. "You told Jeremiah Jones we'd meet him at noon. Let's not keep the Judge waiting."

Mary hung back, twisting Albert's handkerchief into a pretzel. "Albert, please come with us?—" an urgent invitation, and the quick afterthought: "And Karla, too—"

Gather a crowd and find safety in numbers. Karla wondered what had Mary running scared. Wanting no act in this circus, Karla quickly refused the invitation. "Thanks, but I have a hundred things to do—"

Albert said voice unctuous as olive oil, "All that can wait."

"I have a lunch date."

"Break it." He offered his cell, leaving Karla no choice except to call or make a scene.

She snatched the phone and punched in the Parrot Bar's number and told Mimi she couldn't make it for lunch, and Mimi asked what the hell are you talking about?

"I'll explain later," Karla replied, snapping the phone shut, kicking herself for being so not in control of her life. She hissed under her breath, "I'm not going on a dumb Quarter tour."

"Of course you are," replied Albert.

"And I've changed my mind about this whole business. I'm not selling anything and that includes plantations."

"You're having a moment of anxiety." His firm grasp on Karla's arm propelled her forward. "It'll pass."

On the Square, mules harnessed to carriages and buggies twitched their ears, swished their tails and flicked away flies. Although late September, the days were still warm, the temperature in the high 80s, the air thick and heavy. The sub-tropical heat steamed the manure on the pavement and an acrid odor rose. Tour drivers nodded drowsily, looking hopeful when anyone came along.

A sidewalk photographer propped his camera on a tripod and waylaid a family of passing tourists. He stood Mama, Papa, and little girl precisely, so that each snapshot showed Jackson Square and St. Louis Cathedral in the background, local color that distinguished New Orleans from Paducah, Kentucky.

Tourists, food and music—exercises in normalcy—the New Orleans way of coping with hurricanes, floods, corruption and high murder rate.

"We've been to the Ninth Ward," the woman said. "We're so sorry."

Visitors wanted to see the desolation that had dominated the national news for weeks. Tour companies had to overcome the slack somehow. They sent their vans and mini-buses to drive through the destroyed areas, $35 for a first-hand look.

The photographer overheard. "We're coming back. Nutin' can keep us down."

Mary gazed intently at the black-headed little girl. "She's adorable." A deep longing vibrated in her voice. "Adorable."

Karla's mental archive filed all kids under B for brat. "You have children?"

"No. I lost my only one at childbirth."

"Oh. Sorry."

Mary's incredibly sad eyes touched a chord, and Karla turned away. She'd gotten over her induced loss, but every now and then a look, a word—

Outside St. Louis Cathedral, an elderly man in a wheelchair waved. "Hello! Hello! Over here!" He fanned himself with a wide-brimmed hat. "Are we ready?" A green jacket draped his knees. A bizarre yellow tie dangled loosely; limp, damp shirt. Humidity fogged his horn-rimmed glasses. "It's a scorcher. Maybe high noon wasn't such a good time."

Mary avoided a tarot card reader who blocked the sidewalk and gave the man a clumsy hug— "Nice to see you, Judge."

"I hate for the occasion to be such a sad one—Seems the older we get, wakes and funerals are the only social outings left."

"I saw Aunt Agatha at the memorial."

"Well, you know Agatha. There's no changing her mind."

"It's been ten years."

"She has a long memory and she carries that chip on her shoulder like a badge of honor."

THE AZALEAS

Karla listened to the rancor. Albert, though more discreet, was all ears, too. Did Karla need this new entanglement? Not one blessed bit.

"Help me up, Sam," the Judge instructed the big hulk standing behind him, "We taking this buggy ride or not?"

Like an upright Smokey Bear, Sam lumbered forward, grinning stupidly. The Judge draped an arm over the broad, sloping shoulders. In one sweeping, practiced move Sam lifted the crippled man into the tour buggy.

The Judge settled in, hands crossed on an ivory walking cane. "How long will this take?" He questioned the carriage driver in the authoritarian tone of one accustomed to addressing a jury. "When will we be back?"

The driver slouched in the front seat looked over his shoulder. "One hour," he said, "unless you pay extra. We'll be back in front of the cathedral at one o'clock sharp."

"One o'clock, sharp," Judge Jones repeated. "You heard, Sam? Go wherever pleases you, but remember this buggy will be back here at one o'clock sharp. You got that?" In spite of his crippled body, the Judge gave no impression of helplessness. He came across as a crusty old colonel, who snapped his fingers, raised an eyebrow and things got done.

"I hears you, boss." Sam bowed and scraped and raised his hand to his forehead in a pseudo-military salute. The idiotic grin never left his face. Dribbling spit dampened his broad, flat chin. With awkward, clumsy movements he folded the wheelchair.

Karla had enough stresses of her own without taking on extra-curricular problems belonging to rich people who hated each other's guts. Her life might be miserable, but it was her misery and she had adjusted to it.

Pierre helped Mary into the buggy. Karla swung up on her own steam. The five squeezed in, shoulders touching and legs tangled, Pierre sandwiched between Mary and Karla on the rear seat, Albert and the Judge facing them. The mule pulling the buggy clipped-clopped along the Quarter Streets: Decatur, Chartres, Royal, Bourbon, Dauphine.

The young driver wore cut-off jeans and leather sandals. An orange stripe like a highway dividing line parted his black hair and tumbled into a messy pony tail. "My first time doing this—" he turned and said. "Rig belongs to my uncle, and nobody can find him—been looking high and low since the storm. He's either dead, or started a new life somewhere else." He flicked the flower-encrusted whip and the mule took a step. "Ain't got no work and this cart sitting under the carport doing nobody no good. I'm waiting to get my old job at Harrah's. I'm a dealer, but until we get more tourists, more'n half of us ain't working." The mule turned a corner. "Knows the route by memory," the driver said. "I just give him his head."

The carriage clattered past the closed Praline Shoppe with the politically-incorrect black mammy, red bandanna tied around her head, still guarding the silent entry. Most antique shops remained shuttered. Waiters, hoping for customers, clustered in restaurant doors. Barkers made half-hearted efforts to lure sidewalk strollers into the few open honky-tonks.

"Come on in! Right in! Ladies and gentlemen! Candy! Candy is back in town! Come on in! You don't want to miss—" the spiel echoed down the half-empty street.

When the mule rounded the St. Louis Street corner, the driver-tour guide said, "There's Antoine's," and motioned toward the scrolled iron balconies. "It's supposed to reopen soon, but who's to say. It's a fifth generation restaurant. Everyone from Mark Twain to the Duke and Duchess of Windsor ate there." A few blocks later as the carriage turned on Royal Street he pointed to a pink stucco building: "Breakfast at Brennan's, a tradition. The flaming Bananas Foster—" he brought his fingertips to his lips and blew a kiss in the air. "Wonderful."

Karla doubted the driver had ever been inside Brennan's. She couldn't afford breakfast there, and odds were he couldn't, either.

At the intersection, Karla caught the eye of the white angel frozen in place and waved, knowing Claudia wouldn't blink acknowledgment. She was much better than the silver Tin Man on Chartres Street. Any little distraction caused him to shift.

The mule pulled the buggy past the closed Bead Shop where Lila once strung beads to match any outfit. Before Katrina, at the Perfumerie, Joella created individual scents to blend and enhance personal body odors. Next door, Benoit from the Loom Works wove rugs to anyone's bad taste. Bookstores were wedged into every block: The Acadian, French-language books; Crescent City, rare and scholarly works; Faulkner House, trading on the Mississippi author's fame and name; the Librairie where Karla worked sometimes, helping

Jacques dust the shelves—old books that never sold. In most establishments one could shoot a gun and hit nobody.

"All those balconies—" Pierre pointed to the iron lacework overhanging the street.

Ferns, red geraniums, and entwined ivy formed bright colored spots in the otherwise drab surroundings. Green and purple Mardi Gras beads, remnants of a reveling past, dripped from the railings.

"It's hard to think of New Orleans without the madness," the Judge said, "Bars that never close and go-cups in the street. Here raunchy is okay. Nobody cares. Nobody judges. In my heyday, every young man experienced New Orleans as part of his education." He looked to one side, then the other. "The whole city is so subdued."

"New Orleans will never die," Albert said philosophically, "It is more than a city. It's a state of mind."

Mimi's husband, Bilbao, a merchant marine who bartended at the Parrot Bar when on shore leave said that, too— each time he sailed away from the port, he left New Orleans, but New Orleans never left him. "It's the way we enjoy livin', y'know? The taste we got fer good food—the ear fer music. And we can make a big party with a lil' nothin'. Just you show me a mid-westerner or a New Englander, or one of them Mormons from Utah who knows how to live it up the way we do."

The sure-footed mule plodded steadily through the light traffic, making the complete round and returning to the starting point.

"Where's that Sam?" the Judge grouched. "Didn't I tell him to be back here at one o'clock? I have witnesses!"

"I'll find Sam." Albert stuffed dollars into the driver's waiting hand and said, "Hold up a minute." He jumped from the carriage and walked away.

Karla spotted Lebron working the lucrative spot near St. Louis Cathedral, tap-dancing to the rap coming from the boom box, thin legs jerking up and down, elbows flying in and out, feet grooving to the music. His head bobbed right and left, green Miller Lite baseball cap on backward. His odd-colored hazel eyes squinted in concentration, his mouth a wide grin, teeth gleaming white like teardrop pearls. The tap-tappity-tap-tap-tap his dancing shoes transported him to New York, Radio City Music Hall, Broadway or Hollywood, escaping the need and the lack, the way piano notes lifted Karla above her misery.

The pious church-goers, fresh from conversations with Jesus, ignored the lanky little boy and the nearly empty cigar box sitting on the hot sidewalk.

Karla jumped from the buggy. Clink, clink—two quarters—her last—thrown at Lebron's feet brought him back. With a quick swoop, he scooped the coins: "Yo, Miss Karla! Thank you ma'am—" He winked broadly, touched his fingertips to his lips and threw her a kiss.

Karla waved. That rascal— he was a survivor, too. "Where's Joey?" she asked. Most days and nights Lebron and his older brother danced the streets together.

"He got taken away, so now I'm the man." He hooked his thumbs under the red suspenders and snapped the elastic, all the while tapping figure eights with his feet.

Karla couldn't help but laugh at the cocky little boy. "Where'd they take him?"

"L...T...I—" a tapppity-tap-tap rhythm accompanied each letter.

Louisiana Training Institute. "Stealing again?"

"Umpteenth time—all the peoples doin' it, takin' cigarettes and beer outta the Quick Stop, only this time Joey's got a gun, and the National Guard don't know him from Adam and they locked him up again. The probation officer says Joey's gonna end up in Angola, sharing a cell with Willis. He says there ain't no mo' he can do. Not one blessed thing." The Coca Cola caps imbedded in the soles of Lebron's shoes tattooed the pavement.

"You take a good look at Joey, y'hear? And your step-brother, Willis, too—" It hadn't taken Willis any time to graduate from LTI to Angola Penitentiary. Joey was following his footsteps. "Don't you end up like your no-good brothers—how's your gramma takin' it?"

"Gramma don't even know the time of day. She ain't missed Joey, yet. Ain't risen from her bed in a month, mebbe more—" a passing couple stopped, watched, reached in their pockets and threw in excess—"Thank you, ma'am. God bless you, sir. Every time there's a knock on the door or the phone rings she say, 'Willis? Is that my Willis? Is he here?' Nobody have the heart to tell her Willis ain't coming back for fifteen years, long after she be dead and gone." He vaulted into the air, flipped and landed on his feet, never missing a beat.

"Violetta come to check on her?"

"She don't give a shit 'bout us."

THE AZALEAS

"Don't you go hungry, y'hear? Come by and—"

A spontaneous combustion—fists and too much alcohol—erupted by the cathedral front door. Guys wearing orange tee-shirts scuffled. Lebron hugged the cigar box that held his earnings for the day close to his chest. A white-robed priest emerged from the church, face distorted as if he'd been sucking a sour lemon.

The Judge squinted angrily and peered from his buggy perch, ready to pass sentence. Mary, a fearful look in her big eyes, quickly stepped down, Pierre right behind her. The pair stood flash-frozen awaiting Albert's return, waiting for Sam to arrive with the wheelchair and help the Judge from the buggy.

The orange shirts—Phi Kappa Something— pushed and shoved, swinging their fists. Parishioners leaving the cathedral stepped back and gave the men fighting room.

"Here comes Breaux! Hey! Breaux!" Lebron yelled. "Over here!"

The overworked cop hurried over. Too many *beignets* had settled around his middle and he huffed as he zigzagged through the crowd. The French Quarter was his beat. Lately, it had been a quiet assignment.

Kawok! Thud! Mary's knees buckled and she sagged against Pierre.

The noise and confusion spooked the mule and with wild, bulging eyes, it bucked, hind legs kicking high, coming down, striking cobblestones. The Judge hung on with one hand and waved his cane over his head with the other. His hat sailed through the air.

"Whoa! Whoa!" The greenhorn driver cried.

Kawok! Lebron's head jerked back. He pitched forward. The cigar box lid popped open. Nickels, dimes and quarters spilled onto the sidewalk.

Breaux's leaden feet sprouted wings and he was suddenly everywhere, swinging his Billy club and yelling into his walkie-talkie.

"Whoa! Whoa! Whoa!" The panicked driver pulled the reins and beat the mule's rump with the flower-entwined whip. The mule bolted onto the sidewalk. The buggy tipped over, dumping both the driver and the Judge.

The driverless mule lunged. The iron-rimmed hooves came down heavy, sparking flint on the sidewalk. A kick landed on Lebron's ribs. A collective *ooooooohhhhh* rose from the spectators.

Reality became sound—shrieks and screams and clattering hoofs, yells and wailing sirens, blaring horns and saxophone blues. The strident noises trapped under balconies shook the iron railings.

Sam pushed the Judge's wheelchair through the curious onlookers. With powerful arms he lifted the crippled man. "Oh, Judge! Ohmegod, Judge! Are you hurt? Are you shot?"

The buggy driver was on his feet, dusting his knees. "The old man's okay. He's okay. The woman—"

Mary bent double, coughed blood. Pierre held a handkerchief to her lips.

The Judge was red-faced; his glasses smashed. "Set me down, dammit! Set me down, Sam!"

Albert surfaced. He turned sluggishly like a roulette wheel running out of speed, his face lifted toward the cathedral roof. He squinted against the bright sunlight, looking at the church spires. Karla followed his lead and saw nothing but dormers, steeples, shuttered windows and blue sky.

Two backup cops arrived, spilling authority. "Move back! Step back!" Crowd control was second nature to New Orleans police.

Karla squatted next to Lebron. Blood dripped down his face. It matted his kinky hair. Where was his green cap? On his dirty white tee like a rubber stamp dipped in red ink, a horseshoe slowly emerged. His leg twisted sideways. He no longer cried. He didn't whimper. He made no sound. Was he breathing? Karla reached for his hand.

"Don't touch that kid!" Breaux, flushed and panting from running and exertion, yelled at her as if she were some Yankee tourist instead of the person he saw every afternoon at the Parrot Bar when he stopped for a beer after his shift ended.

Sirens wailed. Attendants leapt from the ambulance before it came to a complete stop. They moved quickly, efficiently doing their job. They had enough practice. The paramedic bypassed Lebron—white female first.

Karla clutched the medic's green shirttail. "Listen, you son of a bitch, you're letting that little boy lay there and die and I'm holding you personally responsible—"

"Fuck off, woman! Let me do my job." He jerked loose. "Bobby!" he hollered, "See to the boy over there."

In minutes, the green-clad team had the victims on stretchers. Mary lay quiet and still, eyes closed, face death white, a dark stain spreading on her jacket. Her shoes made twin peaks where the paramedic tucked the blanket over her feet. Next to her, Lebron's body looked small and crumpled.

THE AZALEAS

The Judge refused medical attention, waving away help with a slash of his retrieved cane. "I'm all right, I tell you. I'm all right."

Albert touched Karla's shoulder, "How about you? Are you all right?"

"Go away! Leave me alone." If they would've skipped the stupid buggy ride, Lebron wouldn't be on that stretcher, half-dead. Or Mary, either.

A paramedic was loading Lebron into the ambulance. Karla sprang forward: "Where you taking him?"

"Charity Emergency—"

"It's open?"

"—Sortta—Trauma only."

She reached for the door handle. "I'm riding with the kid."

"Who are you?" Badges and certificates gave him authority to question.

"I'm his mother."

He gave her blonde hair and freckled face an astonished, disbelieving look, shrugged and let Karla climb aboard.

KATIE WAINWRIGHT

CHAPTER 3

Rain hit the hot pavement and vaporized into a steamy haze. Humidity trapped the smell of beer and wine, back-alley urine, and from several blocks away, the fishy stink of the oyster packing plant. Shadows alternated with bright splashes coming from open doorways. Diagonal yellow slashes shone through half-open shutters and striped the sidewalk. A familiar figure leaned against a lamp post, waiting in a light puddle. He tipped his hat when Karla went by. A lone woman in a black leather mini and sequined halter trolled the street, her perfume adding a cheap scent to the oppressive night.

A loud "Pretty Woman," blared from the Parrot Bar juke box. Under the glowing green neon parrot, the musicians huddled outside the door, laughing and talking friendly, nobody inside to play for. Their glowing cigarette tips bobbed like fireflies.

"Hi, guys," Karla said from across the street, and they hi'd back.

"Missed you," Hooey said.

"Been a rough night—"

"How's Lebron?" Bilbao, Mimi's merchant marine husband, leaned against the door jam, his hand clasping a Dixie beer can. He played a mean second sax with the combo when his ship was in. Hooey, initially reluctant to admit a white face into the tight, black circle of local jazz, later grudgingly allowed Bilbao played good enough to "be one of us," a back-handed compliment Bilbao didn't find easy to accept.

THE AZALEAS

Karla brought them up to date. "Lebron's going to make it. It'll be tough, but the doctor said he'll pull through."

The neon parrot turned the clustered black faces an eerie green and purple. Bilbao's red hair glowed as if on fire.

Norbert, the trumpet player, said, "Thank the good Lord for that."

"You know why he's pulling through?" Quarter tradition dictated sharing inside knowledge with the neighbors.

"Why?" Opie, the drummer, tapped the word on his knee. "Why?"

"Because there's not an ounce of fat on him—doctors got down to the bones right away."

"Bless my soul." Opie crossed himself. "And who was it said starvation ain't got its finer points?"

"I hear you," Norbert rumbled deep in his throat. The others joined with heavy, rolling sounds, a combo that meshed and jived. The men lived blowing and sucking on their trumpets and trombones, clarinets and saxophones. Their collective notes were a bugle call, sad and lonely and at the same time profound and reassuring.

"He's in Room 948," Karla half-mumbled, fatigue overwhelming.

"We'll amble down to Big C in the mo'ning and take a look see." Hooey threw down his cigarette and ground the stub with his shoe. "Violetta with him?—"

"Whadaya think?" Karla's fingers punched the security code numbers and her patio gate swung open to chimes playing Beethoven's Eroica.

"Bitch!—" Hooey spit the word.

"We'll see to him." Bilbao said.

"You bet your sweet ass we will." Norbert had fathered six children by four different women. He took diligent care of his offspring and fought with the neglected mothers.

"Yeah, right," Karla said. "We'll all see to him."

"Amen." The word caromed across the street borne on the vibrations of the men's laughter, communal prescription for survival. "Amen, brother."

Karla slipped through the gate into the patio's enveloping shadows. The streetlight's reflection floated across the shallow pool. A silky banana leaf brushed against her cheek. Every ridge and dent in the flagstone walk was familiar. She could've followed the path blindfolded.

Today had been a forever Sunday, a day that went on and on and didn't know when to quit. Hunger gnawed her ribs. Her cupboard was bare. The last stale bread slice went to the pigeons this morning. Oh, for a hot bath. Not a chance. The water heater had been off for days, economy measure. She'd left her bed rumpled and unmade. Too tired to deal with any of it, she closed her eyes. Maybe she'd sink into a black hole and wake up tomorrow. Tomorrow things had to be better.

Her key turned the door lock. She stopped in her tracks. A delicious smell filled the air. Someone had picked up the living room. Mimi? Not likely. Earl, the landlord?—her gut froze as though she'd swallowed an ice-cube. Two months behind on the rent and the landlord had a passkey. Opening and entering? Preliminaries to eviction?—God, she hoped not. Where would she go?

Red roses in a cut-glass vase (not hers) sat on the baby grand piano (hers until tomorrow). Did Earl send the flowers? If the landlord was kicking her out, why send roses? Was he so callous as to think a bouquet would soften the blow? She always left open the doors and drawers on the Louis XIV armoire that belonged to Richard's grandmother and that he no doubt would soon reclaim— easier to get to her stuff that way. The armoire was closed tight.

"Here, kitty, kitty, kitty." Sir Gato wasn't perched on the window sill waiting for her. He wasn't curled in the easy chair. "Here, Gato...Gato...Gato." Who let out her cat?

Any walk-in closet was bigger than Karla's kitchen. She stopped in her tracks. No dirty dishes in the sink! A clean plate, silverware, goblet and napkin on the table! A pot on the stove! She reached for the lid. Shrimp floated in thick red sauce. Scampi! —Her favorite. Maybe God did send an angel when a person needed one.

In the bedroom the bed was made, pillows fluffed; clothes off the floor and neatly folded on the faded blue chair. She pulled the tank top over her head and unzipped her jeans. Pants half-way down her hips, a muffled noise coming from the bathroom made her jump. She eased back soundlessly, inch by inch, hitching her jeans, talking to herself, pumping adrenalin, crouching, reaching under the bed for the NOPD Billy club Breaux gave her when he found out she didn't own a gun and didn't intend to get one. The neighborhood cop said you couldn't live in the Quarter without a gun. Well, she lived here and she didn't own a gun—yet.

The weighty wooden club imparted courage. She'd bash the intruder's head, crack his ribs, break his legs and mutilate his goddamn balls. Creeping forward as silently as Sir Gato stalking a bird, carefully avoiding the board that creaked, she swung the Billy club and pushed open the bathroom door. "Freeze!—"

"You've been watching too many bad movies," Albert said without looking up or raising his voice. Perched on the rim of the footed tub, he ran his hand through the water. "It's hot enough now. The heater was off, did you know?"

"What the hell are you doing here? Who let you in?" Thank goodness the intruder was Albert and not the landlord. Albert could harass and aggravate, but he didn't have the power to evict.

He turned his head and the appreciative look in his eyes brought Karla to her senses. She dropped the Billy club and hugged her naked top.

Albert said, "I'm running you a hot bath. Earl let me in." He left the postage-sized bathroom, squeezing past Karla, careful not to touch her bare skin. He pushed the door to, leaving a crack so they could talk.

"Earl has no business letting a stranger—" Richard's aura still filled every room, and she wasn't ready for another man to come in and drive out Richard's spirit. As long as the smell of Richard's clothes lingered in the closet, the whiff of his Kona Gold clung to the drapes, and the scent of his sweat bathed her pillow, a chance existed that he'd come back and re-inhabit their cocoon. "If Richard ever—"

Albert snickered. "Richard is gone and this morning you wanted to kill him, remember?"

"Richard may be gone, but don't be so presumptuous as to think you're taking his place. Nobody is. Nobody can ever take Richard's place in my heart—" Tall, lanky Richard with strong arms and the surgeon's gentle hands and feathery touch.

"Take your clothes off—"

"Get the hell out. I'm calling Earl—"

"I told Earl I'm your new employer and you were expecting me and running late. By the way, I paid him the rent."

"You did *what?*"

"Consider it an advance against your earnings. You must devote your undivided attention to this sale and not be distracted with side issues." Rent had never been a side issue with Karla. It had always been a major obstacle. "If you don't get in the tub soon, the water will turn cold."

Naked in the bathroom with a pervert or transvestite or control freak—her life could be at stake. Albert could hack her to death in the tub the way Anthony Perkins knifed Janet Leigh in the Psycho shower scene. Men turned weird sometimes.

"I have no weapon," Albert said, moving further away from the door, sitting on the blue chair.

Karla dropped her jeans and slid quickly into the tub—bath salts and bubbles, warm violet-scented water. "What? No rose petals?"

Through the partly open door, his shoe soles reflected in the mirrored wall behind the tub. He had his feet on Karla's bed.

"How's Lebron?" he asked.

"Bullet hit his rib cage, tore through and came out the other side. Can you imagine? He has two perfectly round holes, one here," she poked her right side, "and one there," she touched her left side. "His skull has a hairline crack from the fall. Lots of bruises, course he's so black you can hardly tell. His right hand is questionable. The buggy rolled over it and crushed his fingers. A total mess— I'm really worried about him. Doctor said he'd pull through, but at Big C, who knows?"

"I'm sure the doctors know what they're doing."

"The hell they do. The doc who talked to me looked twelve years old, an intern from Canada or someplace. Said he came down South after Katrina to help out. It's unbelievable, Albert. Emergency is on the fourth floor. On the other floors the mud and crud are gone, but everything is still brown. They can't erase the water lines. They're soaked into the concrete forever."

"You want to move him somewhere else?"

"And what would he pay with? The quarters in his cigar box?—"

"I'd see to it somehow."

"Well," Karla replied, too tired to make any major decisions, knowing for sure she didn't want to get indebted to this man and be forever beholden. "Let's see what happens tomorrow. Mary?" The ambulance had taken her to Ochsner, the paying hospital where the rich people went.

"The bullet went in below the right clavicle and out through the axilla. Very painful, I'm sure. And she has a slight concussion. They're keeping her overnight. The police will find the culprit."

"You have more confidence in the cops than I do."

"They know the sniper shot two .223 caliber bullets from the cathedral roof using a bolt action rifle with a silencer."

"How did he get a rifle up there?"

"The cops are working on that. They'll figure it out, I'm sure."

"Don't hold your breath." Karla closed her eyes and slipped deeper into the sudsy water. Sometime later, she awakened to an empty mirror. When did Albert, silent as a cat burglar, sneak away?

Her relief at getting rid of him didn't last long. The tip of a polished black shoe pushed the door open further. "Don't go to sleep in there. You could drown and we've had enough excitement for one day. Here." He handed her a wine glass and casually leaned against the door frame, watching her, a cat-and-mouse look in his eyes. He hadn't impressed Karla as being a big man, yet his body blocked the doorway. "*Pouilly Fuissé*, 1986. Not the best, but a tolerable year."

Karla waved a careless hand over her head. "My thoughts exactly," she replied, taking a sip. "Albert, I've been thinking—"

"That's a healthy sign."

"Oh, never mind."

He tossed her a towel. "Time to get out," he said in an easy voice.

She stood in the footed tub, her back to him, toweling herself dry, angling for the hard to reach spot between her shoulder blades.

Albert reached across the space between them, took the towel from her hands and with hard, clean strokes wiped her back dry. When Richard did that, her blood surged. This man, who suddenly occupied front and center of her shattered life, elicited not one tingle. He held up a white terry cloth robe and she ran her arms into the sleeves, tied the belt around the waist, and leaned into him, surprised to feel thick, taut muscles under the effeminate silk shirt.

"Someone wants your client dead," she said.

His arms tightened around Karla "What makes you think that?"

"The college boys with the orange tee shirts with the Greek writing—" she turned around to face him.

Interest swirled in his smoky gray eyes. "Phi Kappa—" he said.

"They created the disturbance in front of the cathedral."

Albert arched a silver eyebrow. "College kids bumming round the Quarter bombed out of their minds."

"Uh uh— No bars in the cathedral block. A barroom brawl breaks out on Bourbon or Royal, but in front of the cathedral? I don't think so. I gave the situation a lot of thought while I waited for Lebron to get patched up. Those guys weren't really fighting. They pushed and shoved and swung their fists without punching anybody. And of course Breaux ran after them like they anticipated and we all turned and gawked in the direction they fled. They faked that brawl. I'd stake my life on it."

"The police arrested a few orange shirts and took them to jail."

"You know as soon as those drunks can touch a finger to their nose they'll get a court date and be immediately released. The man on the cathedral roof—"

"Why a man?—"

"A woman who wants to kill somebody gets in the person's face with a big knife or a dose of arsenic—in a rage, in a passion—"

He chuckled. "First-hand knowledge?"

Karla ignored the interruption. "This was cold-blooded, premeditated. The only accident was that the first bullet didn't kill Mary and that the second one hit Lebron. That sniper couldn't hit the side of a barn—definitely not a professional."

Albert stepped back and moved toward the closet-kitchen. "Come eat before the scampi gets cold and the pasta soggy."

"What's your connection to Mary Bravelle?" Karla asked.

"She is Danielle Turner's daughter. Danielle was my client."

"And Pierre?—"

"As far as I can determine, he's a useless count who roams around Europe from one chalet to another. He's probably inherited a palace he can't maintain and a position in life he can't afford." Albert ladled shrimp onto a plate.

"I think he's after Mary's money," Karla said.

"You may be right."

"I don't know what she sees in him—must be something beside his bulldog looks. Was her first husband handsome?"

"André Bravelle? How would I be the judge of that?"

"Here's a choice. Did he look like Quasimodo or more like Gérard Depardieu?"

Albert furrowed his brow, pretending deep concentration. "Depardieu, I suppose."

"Then he was good-looking. Why did she divorce him?"

"The Frenchman had an addiction."

"Drugs?—"

"No, women—it's often worse and just as deadly."

"Were you her divorce lawyer?"

"One of several—"

"Did she sock it to him?"

He made a wry face. "What exactly do you mean?"

"Did she take him to cleaners? Wring every penny out of him she could?"

"Well. She definitely didn't walk away destitute." He refused to elaborate further.

"Pierre isn't any improvement. He's a skirt chaser, too."

"What makes you say that?"

"Women know. I could have him in my bed anytime I wanted. Isn't it funny how where men are concerned women are always attracted to the same type? We make the same mistakes over and over." She blew on the shrimp and tasted a mouthful. "Did you cook this scampi?"

"A favorite recipe of mine—"

"You're not going to eat?"

"I'm dining later, thank you." He dined. She ate supper. The differences between them were as wide as the Grand Canyon.

"Lots of people milling about and the woman who inherited a plantation is shot. What are the chances of that? One in a million?— don't you think that's too much of a coincidence?"

"I'm no Sherlock Holmes, my dear. I leave all that to the police and so should you."

"Unless—" an odd thought occurred to Karla— "the sniper was after you."

"Me?' Albert snorted. "Preposterous!"

"Nobody climbs halfway to the moon to shoot a stray bullet. A stray bullet comes on New Year's Eve or St. Patrick's Day from a balcony or a street corner or the river levee, not from a cathedral roof. It took planning and coordination to get up there. It wasn't accidental. Surely, you can see that."

"Purely speculation and I never speculate." Albert looked at Karla through long, silky lashes a woman would die for.

Long eye lashes and silk shirts—was Albert a transvestite? Some absolutely stunning men-women lived in the Quarter. Maybe—Karla stopped herself. "How did the sniper get up there?" she asked. "Think about that. He had to be inside the church and know his way around the altars and pews and belfries and priests. How did he get down and away with cops all over the place?" With the last slice of garlic French bread, Karla wiped the plate clean. "Delicious. You should open a restaurant."

"Heaven forbid! Have to deal with the Board of Health and hired help and chefs temperamental as ballerinas? Never!—" He took Karla's empty plate to the sink and busied himself rinsing it, a meticulously neat man.

"Albert, how many people connected with The Azaleas knew Mary was in New Orleans? Particularly in the Quarter?—"

"Lots: the plantation staff; three or four cousins from the father's side; a few elderly women who remembered the family; Sheriff Watson; Jeremiah Jones—"

"Judge Jones told me he owned the neighboring plantation and that he and Agatha went way back. There isn't any love lost between Mary and Aunt Agatha, is there? Why?"

"A typical family feud that never gets resolved and drives a big wedge between relatives—"

"What kind of a wedge?" Gleaning information from Albert was like pulling alligator teeth.

"I plead attorney-client privilege. I'm not at liberty to discuss their business."

"You're sending me into that boiling fester. I'd like to know the situation. If they're knifing each other, I don't want to get in the way. How come you and Mary are so chummy?"

He put his fingertips together and tapped his mouth as if to keep any confidences from slipping through his lips. "Mary was a headstrong youngster. I got her out of a little scrape in 1996, then again in 1997."

"And I suppose you can't discuss that either."

He nodded. "Young people do things without giving the consequences much thought. I did my job and took care of matters.

After that Mrs. Turner—Mary's mother— asked me to keep an eye on her daughter."

"How convenient—like giving the hen to the fox—"

"You mean letting the fox in the hen house." He had a nice smile, perfectly white and even front teeth like in toothpaste advertisements.

"You had an affair with her?"

"My affairs are also privileged information."

"But, hopefully, you do have them."

"Always hopefully—" He smiled wryly but his eyes let her know she'd pushed that envelope as far as he allowed it to go.

"Pierre insisted the group take the buggy ride, remember? Is it possible he knew about the sniper? Does Pierre have anything against you? A grudge?—" One more little twist wouldn't hurt. "Did you try to steal his girlfriend, maybe?"

Albert smiled wickedly. "Give it up."

"It's not funny, Albert. The whole thing is screwy. I don't have a good feeling about it."

"If you're not comfortable with this job, don't do it. Back out right now before you invest any time and effort," he replied without any big concern, like opening the door to let the cat out. No big deal.

He'd lured Karla with a fat commission and she'd struck at the bait. She was impulsive by nature, headstrong by will, prone to snap judgments followed by endless wrestling with second thoughts. She'd drowned in more consequences than she cared to admit. Auntie Emmy often warned her that one day this impetuous nature would lead to her downfall and ruin.

Did this idiotic man patiently waiting, looking at her with serious, calculating eyes, think he could dangle opportunity in front of her face then jerk it away? "I'm doing it." What harm trying?

A dozen lists organized themselves in her mind. She hadn't sat next to Gloria, H & B's zillion-dollar saleswoman, without learning. Gloria didn't get as dirty as a coal miner, but she worked her mother lode every bit as hard. She'd be on the phone, barreling down a tunnel to a sale, hit a dead end, slam the receiver down, curse, smoke a cigarette then attack again from a different angle. She didn't "farm" her prospects; she dynamited them, put a charge under their slow asses and blew them sky high. If a buyer demurred, she'd say, 'this property will be gone by tomorrow, so obviously you're not interested in being a player. I'll remove you from my list.' She had platinum, gold and silver lists, and investors knew it. Depending on their performance, finances and ability to act quickly, the names entered in Gloria's Palm Pilot slid up and down from one category to another like roller coaster cars at the amusement park.

"I'll need the floor plan, history of the house, layout of the land. I want to know the builder, what materials were used, when the house was renovated, zoning, school districts and local ordinances. I want a list of the neighbors, of who has been through the house, of anyone and everyone who has ever worked there."

Albert looked quite pleased. "I'll take care of the paperwork. You get a good night's sleep." He helped her to her feet and led her by a hand into the bedroom, folded down the covers and tucked her in as if she were a child.

"Jeez! Are you going to listen to my prayers and kiss me good night, too?"

He reached down and his mustache tickled Karla's cheek. Her arms went around his neck. At that moment she found something warm and comforting about Albert Monsant. Hours later, awakening from an absurd dream, she rubbed her cheek, unsure whether Richard's or Albert's lips caused the warm and tingling sensation.

CHAPTER 4

Four days went by and Karla didn't hear from Albert. Did she dream the whole business? He'd paid the rent. That was no illusion. Was she employed or not? If not, how to pay back two months' rent? She didn't want to be obligated to this exotic bird. She hung around Café du Monde, hoping Albert would appear and clarify the situation. Nothing—she stacked books on BAM's shelves. The days dragged. She started reading the most influential book of the 20th Century and couldn't make heads or tails of *Ulysses* until Cheryl, the after-school clerk, punched in *Ulysses for Dummies* in the Internet and the explanation printed out chapter by chapter.

"Nobody," Cheryl said with the superiority of a sixteen-year old, "understands *Ulysses*. That's what makes it so important."

Nights Karla spent at the Parrot Bar playing college songs during the musicians' break for the few tourists who dropped in.

Sunday marked one week since she had the close encounter of the strange kind with Albert. Time dimmed the situation; the event faded like a Mardi Gras float rolling past—big splash and then life as usual.

The ringing phone jolted her awake, heart pounding like an underwater swimmer who surfaces too quickly. She reached across the rumpled bed. The glowing green numbers on the bedside clock read 2 a.m. The hospital calling Lebron's next of kin? He'd died. He didn't make it out of Intensive Care. "Hello?"

"Three o'clock Friday afternoon. One Shell Square, 51st floor." Karla recognized the voice before the line clicked dead.

The remaining dark hours she argued with herself. Go. Don't go. This was a scam, a cloak and dagger one at that. Stay away. Where else could she make $30,000? She'd get paid only if she sold the property. That was a bitch. And what if she didn't sell it? Don't go down that path, girl.

Karla rode her Salvation Army Schwinn to One Shell Square. The intimidating white tower, the tallest building in the city rose 51 stories. Albert's office was at the top. Built to last, the building came through the hurricane intact.

The polished brass plaque on the mahogany door said Albert Monsant, Attorney. The order and quiet hush in Albert's office reminded Karla of St. Louis Cathedral. Gray walls, plush gray carpets, dark blue couches and chairs, glass-topped desks and tables—coordination to the nth degree—and not a single dead leaf on any potted plant.

"Miss Karla Whitmore is here." The receptionist whispered over the intercom. As the heavy door panels slid open, she asked, "May I take your helmet?"

"No, thanks—that's all right." Karla clung to the helmet's leather strap, her tether to reality.

Albert sat at his desk on a raised platform, the American flag draped on one side and the Louisiana state flag with the big pelican on the other. Karla's bare knee touched the floor. This audition with Prince Albert sitting on his throne was as close to royalty as she would ever come.

In her own digging she'd unearthed a few things about her employer. He came from old money which definitely meant he knew Richard's parents, New Orleans society being a small and closed enclave. If he knew Richard's parents, then he knew Richard, and maybe her ex-boyfriend son-of-a-bitch bastard told him about Karla, and the Sunday morning meeting at Café Du Monde wasn't as casual at it seemed. Albert owned a mansion near Audubon Park, but seldom stayed there. He frequently traveled abroad. He had an unlisted phone number. He sat on the NOMA board, a fact supplied by Ian Scott, the water colorist on the Square, who wanted Karla to pump Albert for a grant or sponsorship. Albert's office reflected his interest in art. He noticed Karla gawking at the paintings.

THE AZALEAS

"Hello, again," he said, rising. "Are you an art lover?"

A person couldn't live in the Quarter surrounded by artists, musicians, performers and would-be authors and not be pulled into the scene. The bars, lounges, cathedrals and haunted houses were for tourists. Sunday afternoon salons at Manda's, readings in the Faulkner House, performances at the Little Theater, art shows in Pirate's Alley were for the locals. No matter how strapped for money, the colors, the music, the poetry readings somehow lifted the Quarter residents above the poverty level.

Coming down from his hallowed perch, Albert stood before pink and purple water lilies on a green-blue background. "A Monet," he said. The painting probably cost ten times more than a heart replacement. "Over there," he moved in the direction of a pen and ink sketch of a Creole cottage, "a Degas from the artist's New Orleans period." He pointed to a cubed, orange and yellow woman with the left breast out of place. "Picasso has to grow on you." A red and black mobile hung near the door. "Calder," Albert continued, "is playful. Do you know that all great paintings have a touch of red?"

"No, I didn't know that." That detail had skipped her notice, though she'd spent many rainy afternoons at the Museum of Art. Usually she slipped in without paying by standing at the exit and when someone stepped out, making an excuse, "Oh, dear, I forgot my umbrella," then entering quickly through the door held open, retrieving a discarded entry tag, sticking it on, and touring the rooms in reverse order, from exit to entry. "Your office looks like a museum," she said.

"My treasures," Albert murmured. He had money and taste. Maintaining these digs must cost a mint. A secretary floated in like a feather caught in a draft. She placed papers on a glass conference table. He nodded curtly, "Thank you," and to Karla, "let's get down to business, shall we?"

The speed with which Albert arranged things made Karla dizzy. The new company name was Whitmore Realty. She now had a broker's license, though she hadn't taken the test. He handed her two checkbooks. The first, a real estate escrow account needed her John Hancock on the signature card. "Never embezzle that money," Albert warned. "It leads to grave and undue complications." The second, a Whitmore Realty Expense Account at Whitney Bank had a $5,000 beginning balance.

"But...but...how did you do all this?"

His mustache twitched. "It's my business to expedite matters. And it's yours to sell this plantation. As far as anyone is concerned, I have absolutely nothing to do with Whitmore Realty."

"Why not?" instantly alert— "Is this some kind of scam?"

"Not at all— I demand total confidentiality for reasons that do not concern you. Sign everywhere there's an arrow, please." He slid papers across the glass. The listing contract to sell The Azaleas was placed on top.

Karla had heard H & B's Gloria yakking on the phone about two million, four million, ten million, figures as incomprehensible as the national debt, vast sums that went in one ear and out the other without registering. Now an outer space number in black and white slapped her in the face. Price: $3,000,000 and 00 cents. No cents! She suppressed a giggle. What idiot would argue about pennies when millions were involved? Commission payable to Whitmore Realty, 10% of any sale amount—Karla looked up quickly. It didn't take a math whizz to figure out—

"A $300,000 commission," Albert interjected smoothly, as if he'd read her mind.

"You said $30,000."

"That's right. That's your guaranteed 10%."

"The standard is—"

"I'm aware—30% and if this transaction works out, there may be a big bonus that'll bridge the difference. Look at this as your learning curve pay."

"Am I getting screwed here?" She instantly regretted the question.

Technically, the paper work made Whitmore Realty hers, but in actuality it belonged to Albert. Only Karla's signature was on the bank card. When the plantation sold she could write herself a check, clean out the bank account and—

"The risk is mine isn't it? But I'm comfortable with that. I'm a gambler at heart."

He had to be, to take her on. She glanced through the paper work. "Wait a minute! One month to sell The Azaleas? That's impossible!"

The white eyebrows knitted. "Thirty days—through October 31st. We have a deadline, my dear. If The Azaleas doesn't sell by then—" the phrase hung in the air between them. "I'll need your signature here," he pointed to one line and then another. "Here and here."

THE AZALEAS

"Should I read what I'm signing?"

"Absolutely—everybody should read what they sign. I'll wait."

Karla skimmed the pages—a blur of fine print, bold print, filled in blanks, *whereases* and *herebys*.

"Oh, what the hell—" She scribbled her name, recklessly, with abandon, having no idea what she was getting herself into.

He flipped more papers— "And here and here."

She signed again, again, again, agreeing to everything, to $30,000, to freedom from debt, to a new future, to a new life—to nothing if the plantation didn't sell.

Finished, she recapped Albert's Montblanc pen. He handed her a key ring that weighed five pounds. "Agatha can tell you what doors they fit. I have no idea. She'll have a guest room ready for you."

"I'm staying at the plantation?"

"Either there or a motel, and I thought you'd be more comfortable at The Azaleas. If you're on the premises you can get the feel of the place and find a buyer quicker. Remember, speed is essential in this transaction. The flip side of that commission as you have been well informed is zero pay." He gathered the papers, tapped the pages on the glass top to even the edges, placed them in a briefcase and nudged the case toward her. "All yours—"

Karla surveyed the leather briefcase with her initials KW embossed in gold letters as if it were an alligator head. Did Albert intend for her to wear a blue power suit and pumps to match? In her wildest dreams she couldn't picture herself making a mad morning dash to any office. The image was so not her.

"Albert—" better to let him know right from the start that she was a wild card—

"People use briefcases because they're handy gadgets," he explained before she objected. "There's a place for papers—" he reached and unzipped a compartment. Karla surveyed business cards, pencils and pens engraved with Whitmore Realty. "This PC—you know how to use a computer? Instructions are included." A challenge lurked in his steel-colored eyes.

"I can use it." She'd teach herself tonight.

He placed several bills on the table— "Seed money. You'll probably need to get a few things for the trip."

"Like what?" She folded the five twenties in half and slipped the money into her sock. He looked amused. Maybe he led a bleak and boring life and she was his new entertainment.

"You'll think of something. Shall I drive to The Azaleas with you?"

Perish the thought. With no notion how to do this job, the idea of him looking over her shoulder, pointing out her mistakes and inhibiting her style was daunting. Twenty-four hours and she'd be fired, unemployed again. "Any particular reason why you should?—"

"Not at all—just trying to be helpful—" He removed a pipe from a rack, lit it and drew slowly on the stem. He replaced the doused match carefully in a little silver box. Expensive tobacco smell filled the room. "Here is a Sky Page, good anywhere in the world." He set a miniature phone on the table, along with an instruction manual. "My number is already programmed into it. Keep this with you at all times. You understand that?"

"What about if—"

He smiled knowingly. "At all times and that includes all what about ifs. Any questions?—"

Only a thousand, but not knowing which to ask first, she skipped them all. "Nothing I can think of right this minute."

"Then let's get to work. Can you leave this afternoon?"

A normal woman would turn cartwheels over this good fortune—a job, an opportunity, a way out of poverty, but Karla wasn't normal. She was quirks and odd twists, insecure bravado, courage with a yellow streak and trust swamped by suspicion. Someday when she could afford it, she'd hire a shrink to help her dig until she unearthed the tap root of her disastrous personality. She should kiss Albert's feet, this angel dropped from heaven to lift her from the gutter, instead of probing his motives and questioning his intentions. Why was he helping her? Why did his kindness scare her? Why did leaving the familiarity of her cramped Quarter digs for a grand plantation in the country terrify her? Why? Why? Why? The questions rattled her head. This pie-in-the-sky venture could be the biggest disaster of her whole sorry life.

Swallowing a sigh, she rose quickly, looking away so Albert wouldn't read the angst and indecision on her face. The windows of his swank office overlooked the Mississippi. The big bend in the river gave New Orleans its 'Crescent City' nickname. Tugboats, freighters, oil tankers, ocean liners and paddle wheelers plied the water, coming from someplace, going somewhere, steaming with purpose.

The overview of New Orleans sprawled between the river and Lake Pontchartrain was awesome and terrifying. From here Karla could clearly see where the 17th Street Canal levee breached, leaving a wide swath of broken homes. Weeds choked the yards. Those people weren't coming back. To the South, the Lower Ninth Ward no longer existed. Wind and water completely washed away that community. To the east and west the swamp encroached. Only the elite skyscraper cluster downtown survived intact.

Albert stood behind Karla, crept there in his silent way and placed his hand lightly on her waist. "It's beautiful, isn't it?"

At close range, Albert smelled expensive, of good tobacco and old whiskey. The trace of horses and leather must come from the aftershave.

Both stared at the city below. Albert reached over Karla's shoulder and with his fingertip traced the river's bend on the glass, slowly, lingering, as if following the sensuous curve of a woman's breast. "The Gulf, the lake, the river, the swamp—we're trapped. We're doomed. That's the crux of our *laissez les bon temps rouler* attitude. Let the good times roll. Live for today, there may be no tomorrow."

His breath felt warm against her neck.

The Katrina disaster had no foreseeable end. The Feds sent millions that were snagged in Baton Rouge. Governor Blanco and the legislature couldn't agree how to spend it. Nagin, New Orleans mayor, did a tap dance trying to get funds released for his dying city. Red tape and bureaucracy snarled reconstruction. The ongoing fight over who was in charge, who was the boss, who had the power, sapped everyone's energy. Meanwhile people slept in tents, lived in FEMA trailers, and the street lights didn't work.

Karla sighed and leaned back into Albert. His tensing arm muscles catapulted her to her senses. Was this spider spinning a web? If so, she didn't intend to get caught—"Gotta go. Lots of work to do—"

"I'll walk down with you." What could she say or do? He was technically her employer. He said to the anorectic receptionist with the thin voice, "I'm leaving for the day."

The elevator descended 51 floors, taking Karla's stomach with it. Albert didn't say goodbye in the lobby. He followed Karla across the marble foyer, through the revolving doors and into the street.

Snarled traffic lurched, stopped and inched along Poydras Street, cars swerving to miss rumbling buses and stopped delivery trucks. Preoccupied pedestrians hurried along, heads down—industrious, self-absorbed workers clutching briefcases, hustling to complete important agendas before five o'clock. The quicker Karla returned to the Quarter's narrow streets, the laid-back artists and bumbling tourists, the happier she'd be.

"Goddamit!—" A valentine red convertible, an insulting slung-back little car, was parked in the slot where she'd padlocked her Schwinn to a meter. "My bike's gone!—" She looked up and down the street, a sinking feeling in her stomach. There went her transportation. Where would she scrape money for another bike?

"No use calling the cops," she moaned. "They can't find a stolen car, much less a bicycle." If she didn't have bad luck she wouldn't have any luck at all. "Dammit! Dammit!" She kicked a fat Michelin tire. "Dammit!"

"Hey! Hey! Enough of that—" Albert pulled her away from the chrome hubcaps. "That's a Mustang Shelby '89. You must treat it with more respect."

"Respect hell! I'll bash the fenders! Scrape the paint! Smash the damned windshield! If I ever get my hands on the miserable sonofabitch who stole my bicycle, I'll strangle the sucker." She swung her arm with intent to damage. Albert wrestled the briefcase from her hand.

"It's a fine car," he said, "a classic. Look— new top and new cream-colored leather upholstery."

"I don't give a shit if the whole damned engine is new."

Albert crossed to the passenger side, opened the door and placed the briefcase on the front seat. Reaching in the glove compartment, he withdrew a manila envelope, dug in it and with a triumphant smile dangled keys that glinted silver in the sun. "Yours," he said.

"*What?*"

"You can't very well arrive at the plantation on a bicycle—"

"Why are you doing this? I don't want this car. I can't afford to pay for wheels and I don't want your charity. I can get to St. Francisville on the Greyhound bus—"

"That won't do. In this business illusion is more important than substance and image is everything—"

"Drive away this Mustang. Do whatever you want. I'm not getting in." She eyed the wheels closely and Albert was right—a fine, fine car.

"Get in." He sat in the passenger seat.

"You want me to get in? Okay, I'll get in. But I'm not touching that steering wheel."

"I've been checking the classifieds for weeks, you know. I finally found this little jewel in Biloxi. It belonged to a gambler on the Gulf Coast who lost everything in Katrina. Miraculously, a relative had borrowed the Mustang for a trip to Vegas, so it escaped the fury. An excellent mechanic, a good friend of mine, went over the engine and transmission, every nut and bolt, then sent it to the body shop for the paint job and upholstery."

"You like it so much? You drive it."

Albert looked sheepish. "I don't drive."

"C'mon, now!—you must be kidding." Everybody over sixteen drove. They might not own a car, but they had a license. Albert could have any car he wanted, but didn't drive, another odd feather in this weird bird's wings. "How do you get around?"

"Cabs, limos, public transport, friends—I was hoping you'd drop me at the Westin. I have an appointment there." He inserted the key in the ignition. Sensing Karla's resistance, he said, "The title is in Whitmore Realty, so through this convoluted arrangement of ours, the car is technically mine. You have use of it as long as you're working for Whitmore."

"In that case—" Karla turned the key. The motor purred smoothly. The Shelby slid easily into the traffic flow. Jealous looks hit her like green-edged daggers—young woman with her sugar daddy; reckless youth and middle-aged dreams. So what? Let the other drivers drool.

She stomped the gas pedal and the car surged forth. The big engine had ample horsepower for a quick getaway. A slight pressure on the steering wheel and the Mustang responded like a man seduced. From the corner of her eye, she caught the amused look on Albert's face. "How did you know I *love* red?"

"Loud and tacky—"

The insult spun her around. His arms were up, protecting his head. He was still laughing as he entered the Westin Hotel.

KATIE WAINWRIGHT

Next day Karla packed 2 jeans, 2 shorts, 2 shirts, 4 tees, 4 tank tops, 6 Victoria Secret thongs, 1 lace bra, black; 1 pair silk pajamas and matching robe, also Victoria Secret, lagniappe left over from Richard. She packed a Ziploc bag with make-up essentials, toothbrush; hair brush; another bag with tampons, aspirins, Immodium, NicoDerm and whatever else was in the medicine cabinet; Birkenstocks and pink rubber Crocs. She pulled down the canvas flap and zipped the bag closed, everything she needed inside.

When she told Earl, the landlord, she'd be away for a while, the old toad became suspicious. "Rent due first of next month. I'm not holding—"

"You think I don't know that?" He could croak all he wanted, but he couldn't toss her out. "The back rent is paid. Next month's will be on time."

"Same man going to pay it?"

A hot flush warmed her face. No goddamn business of Earl's who paid her rent as long as he got his due. "It'll be paid. This rabbit hutch you fancy up by calling it a *garçonnière*—"

"That is the correct term for the bachelor apartment of an unmarried son—"

"—isn't worth $800 a month, even if Tennessee Williams did write A Streetcar Named Desire sitting in the middle of the living room floor." Earl perpetrated that myth, retelling the tale so many times the lie became truth, and walking Quarter tours stopped at the wrought iron gate for a peek into the playwright's former patio. "It's extortion."

"You know I can get double since Katrina."

"I have a lease." She looked him straight in the eye, "and a lawyer."

News spread fast in Karla's block. Mimi popped in. "Let me give you a hand." Together they emptied the refrigerator, threw away half-eaten leftovers, wilted vegetables and milk that would sour. Mimi bagged butter, eggs and bacon. She'd make an omelet and feed the street kids breakfast tomorrow.

Mimi wrapped her arms around Karla's middle and squeezed—"Don't you worry none; we'll look after things. And Lebron, too—Bless his little heart."

THE AZALEAS

"They're moving him from ICU tomorrow. This morning he woke up and blinked yes and no. I hate going away and leaving him. Violetta's such a shit; both Joey and Willis in jail. His Gramma in never-never land. He's so pitiful—"

"We all live soap opera lives. We'll look after Lebron. You take care of yourself, girl. Find a man while you're gone, preferably good lookin' and rich."

"Thanks, Mimi. I already had one of them and he got away. But you're a good friend, anyhow— C'mon, Sir Gato." The cat arched his back and rubbed against Karla's leg. She scooped him in her arms and tickled his nose. "Hooey's keeping Gato for me."

Turning the key in the front door dead bolt made the mechanism click with a resounding finality. Sir Gato under one arm, the briefcase under the other, Mimi toting the canvas bag, the two trudged down the stairway and crossed the street to the bar.

"Hi, Bilbao!—Ship's in?"

"Sure— it's been a month."

"Time goes by fast when you're having fun," Karla retorted.

Mimi loved it when Bilbao was home. Between them they tended bar, waited tables, played music and provided entertainment. They yearned to buy the bar, to own their own business and fulfill the great American dream. The only obstacle in their way was their landlord, Earl. He wanted twice what the place was worth, normal for him. And no matter how hard Mimi and Bilbao worked, they could never put any money aside. Daily living gobbled their paychecks.

Karla set everything at Hooey's feet, reached in her sock and retrieved a $20 bill. "Watch after my place. Buy cat food if Sir Gato runs out."

Hooey took the money without hesitation and slipped the twenty into his shirt pocket. "Yes'm." Sir Gato squirmed in the old man's arms, trying to jump free. Hooey hooked a big knuckle under the rhinestone collar and stroked the black fur, reassuring both the cat and Karla.

"Keep up with how Lebron's doing and don't let him want for anything. Check Big Charity every day and if he needs something, call Mr. Albert. He'll take care of it."

"Yes'm."

"Watch this stuff for me while I go get the car. Okay?" Afraid to leave the Mustang parked by the street curb at the mercy of every car thief, she'd sweet-talked Evans, the Royal Sonesta parking attendant, into letting her sneak the car into the hotel's garage.

When she returned behind the wheel of the red convertible, Hooey said, "Ain't a bad trade, your bike for this car." Nothing surprised Hooey. He'd lived a long time and seen improbable things happen. He placed Karla's bag and briefcase in the trunk, closed the lid gently, breathed on the chrome and polished it with his shirttail. "I'll look after your cat. You take care."

Dusk filled the quiet streets, the lull before the hopeful onrush of tourists. One last look at her apartment and Karla swallowed hard—how terribly sad not to have someone special standing on the balcony waving goodbye, reluctant to see her drive away.

"Yoohoo!—Yoohoo!" Karla's slide into self-pity was interrupted by Albert walking on the sidewalk, drawing near. He stood by the Mustang, openly admiring his car. "I'm famished," he said.

The car was packed, ready to roll. "So?"

"Let's go to Central Grocery and get a muffuletta before you depart. You'll never get a good muffuletta in St. Francisville."

"Albert, I checked the map. St. Francisville is three hours away. It's not like I'm going to the moon."

"Well, yes, but you'll get involved in the sale and forget to eat, and anyhow those country towns don't know the first thing about making a good muffuletta. We'll walk over there."

"Can't you see I'm double parked? I really wanted to get on the road before dark—"

A forlorn expression came over his face. "Yes. That's quite sensible. In that case—"

"Oh, forget it. Let's go. Hooey!—" The old man stood an inch away from her, no need to holler, but yelling at somebody made her feel better. "Hooey, I'm leaving for a few minutes. Don't let the cops tow away this damned car."

"I'll watch it. Evening, Sir—"

Albert took Karla's elbow and kept his hand on her arm as they walked. Inside Central Grocery, they stood between cans of Rotelli tomatoes, jars of black olives, tins of Amaretto cookies and woven braids of garlic.

He ordered muffulettas. Standing in a corner next to the Community Coffee and Chicory display, they ate the big round sandwiches filled with ham, salami, black olives, onions and Italian salad. Done, they returned to the car, Karla taking two little running steps to Albert's loping one. She remembered how Richard—

Richard and she had this thing—they walked in sync—so much so, that on occasions he swung a hip, caught Karla's side and lifted her off her feet a la Fred Astaire or Gene Kelly. That little maneuver could only be done with perfectly coordinated steps. Albert's stride was longer than Karla's. By the time they reached the neon parrot sign, she lagged two steps behind.

Albert opened the driver's door. "Remember the seat belt." He hovered. "Maybe you should put the top up before you hit the road."

"The top stays down. Goodbye, Albert."

"Well, be careful. If you need anything—" Albert acted like a fidgety old man.

"The only thing I'm going to need is a buyer for The Azaleas." The words slapped reality in Karla's face. They turned the glass slipper back into an old shoe and brought an end to the fairy tale. She hadn't a clue how to go about selling a plantation. She had no backlog of waiting buyers and no idea of the pitfalls ahead. The sheer stupidity of this excursion panicked her. Not too late to—

"You can do it," Albert boosted her sagging confidence. "Take care of yourself. Be careful."

"If you tell me to be careful one more time—"

"Okay. Don't be careful. Be mule-headed and stubborn and stupid and idiotic and juvenile and impossible." The outburst caught Karla by surprise. "And careful," he repeated. "I insist. You understand me?"

She wrinkled her nose, made a face at him and stripped the gears shifting into first. The Mustang jumped away from the curve, tires squealing burnt rubber. She saw Albert in the rear view mirror, standing on the sidewalk, hands on hips. He was shaking his head and laughing.

KATIE WAINWRIGHT

CHAPTER 5

Karla followed the butler. The staircase to the Azalea's second floor was dimly lit. Chandeliers hanging from heavy chains cast eerie shadows reminiscent of *Gaslight*. "Here you are, Miss—the Andrew Jackson room." The butler opened the door. "The carved cherry Mallard bed is 200 years old."

Such a valuable bed! Worth a hundred times more than anything Karla owned. She stayed awake half the night, afraid to thrash about and collapse the satin quilted tester upheld by four graceful posts. Her feet hung over the edge. The bed was exactly two pillows wide, forty-eight inches, cozy or stifling, depending on the circumstances.

Before turning off the Tiffany bedside lamp, Karla read the full-color *"Spring Fiesta Plantation Tour"* brochure conspicuously laying on the end table. The house was built in 1854 by Henry Turner who left Georgia, stopped for rest and recuperation in Louisiana; married Felice Broussard and went no further. Originally the dwelling had no indoor plumbing, electricity or closets. The kitchen, now joined to the main structure by a colonnade, had once been a completely separate building. In 1865, at the end of the Civil War, Henry Turner died and Felice released 200 slaves who worked The Azaleas' cotton fields. Since 1992, Miss Agatha Turner, Henry's descendant, graciously allowed many weddings to take place at the plantation. (A list of prominent brides and grooms followed). With its glorious view of the front gardens, the Andrew Jackson room with the Mallard bed was a honeymoon favorite. Maybe that was why Richard walked in and out of Karla's dreams all night—arms around her, lips warm, body hard—he was taking her to the edge and she was falling...falling... falling...jolted into consciousness...panting.

She flung aside the sheet and bolted upright. Was the air-conditioner broken? Why wasn't Sir Gato at her feet? Where was she? Remembering, she curled into a fetal position, dragging the covers over her head only to slough them off a few minutes later, arms and legs kicking and flaying like a drowning swimmer fighting water.

Richard was gone, gone forever; married to the debutante with looks, brains and old money. An up-and-coming young doctor couldn't go through life joined to an unknown nobody whose shallow roots went back no further than two dead parents. New Orleans high society looked down their collective noses and frowned at such an unbalanced union. Four years of her life invested in this failure. She could've gotten a college degree, birthed three children, built a real estate career. She could cope with the pain—after all, Richard's leaving wasn't the first blow in her life, though his departure left the deepest scar—but the trap he proposed and she came within a smidgin of falling into, left her feeling cheap and tarnished and mad. Bastard! Goddamn bastard! Were they ever in the same orbit? On the same planet?—

A knock at the door interrupted Karla's frenzied thoughts. "Yes?" She quickly smoothed sheets and plumped pillows, apprehensive about the mussed bed, a new wrinkle for one who left her own unmade for days at a time.

The divine smell of fresh coffee and hot buttered biscuits filled the room. A young girl, twenty at most, dressed in a maid's uniform complete with white ruffled apron, said, "Morning, Miss."

She set a tray on the side table— a pink rosebud in a porcelain vase, orange juice in a champagne flute, bacon and eggs under a silver dome like those used by fine restaurants. "Wow! Thank you!" *Scarlett O'Hara, move over, honey.* "What a treat!"

"Miss Agatha's on her way up." The girl's tone held a warning note. She scurried away, quicker than a delivery boy on a skateboard.

A sharp rap and before Karla had time to say, "Come in," Agatha entered, manor queen with right-of-entry into every room. No lock existed that could keep her out.

"Good morning, dah-ah-lin'." Karla heard darling turned into a three-syllable word before, but this darling was so sugar-coated it could kill a diabetic.

The slight woman wearing a blue shift and pointed shoes didn't weight 100 pounds. Her blue hair was teased into a lacquered helmet fifties sitcom style. Immediately, she pulled open the drapes. The window shade rasped as Agatha raised it. Daylight flooded the room. The unexpected brilliance blinded Karla and she rubbed her eyes. The outside air drifted in, warm and humid and filled with unfamiliar—

Karla wrinkled her nose. "I smell—"

Every place she'd ever lived in had its own peculiar smell that faded with familiarity. Her first apartment on Rampart smelled of cats and dogs and musty carpets. The room above Papa's Pizza absorbed the onion and garlic smell from the kitchen below. Whenever she caught a whiff of charred wood and smoke she thought of Auntie Emmy's house. In her Orleans Street apartment, Karla splurged and bought cinnamon sticks and boiled them on the stove once a week. The sweet spicy scent overcame all others.

A straight-backed Agatha clutched the curtain folds. Through the window, she surveyed the estate. "I imagine you've never breathed unpolluted air—pine scent carried by the breeze, wind blowing over the fields, new mown grass—the swamp—" Agatha stopped and turned abruptly. She eyed the rumpled covers and asked, "Weren't you comfortable?"

On a one to ten rating Karla's comfort level never got past two last night, but it had little to do with the bed and everything to do with Richard and his new bride.

"What time is it?" Karla asked, careful not to spill coffee or drop crumbs on the quilted spread.

"Seven o'clock."

Holy cow! What did people do at this ungodly hour? As if in reply, a rooster crowed an enthusiastic cock-a-doodle-doo— too much; too perfect— Was Karla on a movie set with a director standing just beyond her sight?

Agatha came right to the point. "You've been hired by Mary Bravelle to sell my home."

"The Azaleas, yes—"

"Hasker and Blunt couldn't sell it and they sent their best sales people here." Gloria! Had Gloria tried and failed? "You might as well forget that business." She deep-sixed the sale with a casual hand wave. "With all those earrings in your ears, nobody is going to take you seriously, so we don't have much to worry about, do we?" Her flat, horizontal smile didn't lift her cheeks.

Karla fingered the gold hoops and studs. "Should I take them off, you think?"

"It's none of my business what you do." The frozen edge on the soft drawl let Karla know only one piercing per ear was acceptable in this area.

Agatha had the key to the front door—to every door, actually. Karla must win her over or she'd be struggling uphill from day one. "I'm sorry about the death in your family." Condolences should be a good starting point. "I met Mary Bravelle Sunday morning after the special prayer service for her mother at St. Louis Cathedral."

"They can pray until their knees are raw, it won't do any good."

After that comment there wasn't much Karla could say, but she stumbled on. "Mary said her mother's ceremony was beautiful and touching. Did you think so?"

"Not at all," Agatha snapped, leaving no doubt that the family relationships weren't rosy pink and lovely. "As far as I'm concerned Danielle Turner died when... when..." whatever the cause, the pain still festered like an infected sore—"when she left The Azaleas."

"Did you hear about the accident later that afternoon? The shooting?—"

"Gracious! That's New Orleans for you— People always shooting one another—five murders in one day last week—made our paper here."

"Well—" Karla bolted upright, pulled the sheet to her chin, ready to share gory details. Nothing created stronger bonds than good gossip. "After the service, Mary, Pierre, Judge Jones, Albert and I went riding in this buggy—"

Agatha cut Karla short. "I have a busy morning ahead. Is there anything particular you'd like to know before I get on with my day?"

"Everything about The Azaleas," Karla muttered, properly rebuffed.

Agatha's guard went up as quickly as Maximus's shield in *The Gladiator*. "What's to know?"

Karla's mind ran on idle in the morning, not really cranking until noon. She dipped a dainty spoon in a little silver pot and dripped honey over a biscuit and mulled the question. What would Gloria want to know? The history—neighborhood—construction?—technical details such as square footage? She stopped—much too early for her thoughts to gel— "Which boards creak in the middle of the night?—" always a big concern of hers when she moved into a new place.

Agatha relaxed a little. "They all creak. This house is old."

"Y' know, Miss Turner—"

"Call me Agatha. Everybody does."

"Miss Agatha, if this house is going to sell, I'll need your help to do it."

Agatha raised a skeptical eyebrow and said nothing.

"I've never been in a mansion like this before. It's so—" Karla searched for a proper word. "Majestic."

A pleased look came into Agatha's eye and quickly faded. "There's nothing majestic about this old house. It is termite ridden; the roof leaks and the toilets rattle and gurgle all night. Plug in more than three appliances at a time and the fuses blow."

So that was the way Agatha intended to play the hand fate and Mary Bravelle had dealt her. Run down The Azaleas and scare away any potential buyer. Karla wiped her mouth with a monogrammed linen napkin frayed at the edges and pondered the problem. Tangling with Agatha at daylight was useless. There would be many more opportunities for that.

Last night, exhausted, she'd pulled off her jeans and tank top. The clothes lay heaped on the floor, exactly where she dropped them. She pushed away the tray, threw the covers aside, and swung her bare legs to the floor. Agatha took one horrified look at Karla's naked torso and faced the other way while she dressed.

"All these keys!—" Karla fished the big ring from her briefcase. "Does The Azaleas really have this many doors? Forty-six! Why, some hotels in the Quarter don't have anywhere near this many rooms!" The skeleton keys were straight from a Vincent Price horror movie.

"Where did you get those keys?"

"From Mary—the brass ones are heavy—"

"Hank's keys!—"

"I don't know whose they are or what doors they fit." Karla had to get cracking. Thirty days to sell this joint. No sale. No pay. Sure disaster.

Agatha said in a sub-zero voice. "Hank's keys belong here, on this plantation." She extended her hand. "I'd appreciate it if you'd give them to me."

Karla snatched her hand back. Agatha had her sympathy, but not her keys. "I'll talk to Mary," Karla said, "and tell her you want the keys and if she says hand them over, that's exactly what I'll do." Agatha's jaw locked. "I'd rather you take me through the rooms than go bungling around on my own. Can you show me?"

Karla wondered if this little helmeted blue jay would catch her drift. If Karla didn't get cooperation, then she'd explore the place on her own.

"Dorcas can show you," Agatha replied through clenched teeth. A nervous tic overtook her left eye.

"That's great, thank you. When's a good time? At her convenience, of course—" Karla feigned casual, keeping any urgency from surfacing. Too much pressure and Agatha would break through her shell and howl and blow like a hurricane cut loose.

"I'll have my people gather—"

Go down, Moses! Let your people go!

—"in the kitchen—" The soft Southern drawl smooth and velvety raised goose bumps on Karla's arms.

Sweet, hushed voices terrified Karla ever since Miss Thorney, her first foster parent, worked her and two other kids nearly to death, starving them in the bargain, all the time fooling the welfare system with her honeysuckle sweetness. And Richard's new candy-striper wife, a smile and sunshine girl with a soft voice and peppermint breath, took Karla's man and never looked back. Mary Bravelle of the feathery tone had everyone at her beck and call. Even Albert, the perfect gentleman, was suspect. Her gut feeling told her Albert had a hidden agenda and her gut was never wrong. Give her someone like Auntie Emmy who hollered and yelled and stirred the water with an honest paddle. Her actions were clear, her motives exposed, her goals spread like Monday's wash for all to see.

Karla could play Agatha's game. "That's very nice of you," she said, stretching every syllable like a rubber band.

She followed Agatha down the stairs. Last night she'd been too tired to notice the surroundings. The sweeping staircase led to a wide hallway. Male ancestors in Confederate uniforms and female matriarchs with creamy skin looked down from the walls. Rooms filled with antiques flanked the hallway. A red velvet rope, the kind museums used when they didn't want visitors too close to the displays, barred each entry. Karla followed Agatha across an enclosed colonnade into the kitchen. Within minutes the help arranged themselves around the counters.

"This is Karla Whitmore." Agatha commanded everyone's undivided attention. "She's here to sell the plantation. You're to cooperate in every way."

The servants, faces blank, immune to this upheaval, answered collectively, "Yes'm" The woman cooking muttered, "Again?"

Agatha presented the staff by rank and tenure: "Clem, our butler. Clem's been with us forty years." Last night he'd been lost in shadows. This morning the black man looked distinguished. *Wearing white gloves for God's sake! He could be in movies.* Agatha tapped the shoulder of the heavy set woman working the six-burner commercial gas range: "Dorcas." Karla shook a thick, fleshy hand dusted slightly with white flour. "Sam belongs to Twin Oaks—"

"Hi, Sam—" Karla hid her surprise. Sam had been in New Orleans with the judge the day of the shooting.

Sam acknowledged Karla's greeting with the big, senseless grin she recalled. Sam wasn't hitting on all cylinders. He had a sparkplug missing.

"Judge Jeremiah lends us Sam when we have heavy chores." Karla imagined Sam could lift a refrigerator without much effort. "And here comes Laura. You met Laura. She's Clem's and Dorcas's granddaughter." An old man shuffled in. "Frank, we've got a visitor." Without bothering to look, Frank shuffled out. Nobody stopped him. "As you can see, my help has been with me a very long time."

Keeping up an almost empty house required this many people?

Karla's gaze skipped over Sam and traveled from Dorcas to Clem to Laura. They worked and lived at The Azaleas. The sale would shatter their lives. Their disinterest had to be faked. They must be having a collective heart attack.

Had the help decided to take matters into their own hands and eliminate Mary Bravelle? With the owner out of the way, the plantation wouldn't be sold. Agatha would stay, there'd be no disruption, and life would go on as usual.

Whodunit?—the butler?—Karla stared at Clem. No way could that frail old man scale the cathedral roof. "Will you stay on when the place is sold?" she asked.

All vacant eyes turned to Agatha. She answered for them. "Sure. They'll stay. But believe me, they have no worries. I don't expect any of us will be moving any time soon." Her confidence in Karla's abilities was underwhelming. She dismissed the staff. "Get back to work now. This isn't a paid holiday," and to Karla, "Dorcas can show you the rest of the house now, except the Jefferson Davis room. It's rented."

How would Karla get into that room to show prospective buyers? Better judgment told her not to raise that question now. "I thought you didn't do bed-and-breakfast anymore?"

"Only on rare occasions—Mr. Randall in the Jeff Davis room is writing a book—" a loud buzz interrupted her— "and needed a quiet place. He also does our crop-dusting. He's the nicest man and no trouble at all—" the buzzing came again, persistent, three short, one long ring— "and the extra money is always nice." The caller had a finger glued to the doorbell. Agatha called out, "I'm coming! I'm coming! Laura! Laura! Bring coffee to my office. And Dorcas, make sure that Karla meets Felice." She left in a flurry to greet the impatient visitor.

Agatha's departure siphoned the tension from the room. Dorcas surprised Karla by setting two mugs on the table. She plopped her ample bottom into a chair. "Have some coffee." Kitchen tables were good. Solid, gutsy information came across a kitchen table, while gentry in the dining room made clever, polite conversation that meant nothing.

"Who was hammering the doorbell?" Karla asked.

"The Judge—he comes by in the mo'ning for his coffee. The two of them sit in her study and go over things."

"What things?"

"Well, they ain't wedded, but they should be, so they jis' go over the day's problems jis' like any old married couple. You think you'll be sellin' us anytime soon?" Dorcas blew on her coffee and made a face.

"Somebody'll buy The Azaleas. Why do you think it hasn't sold?" Karla asked mildly, pretending half-interest, all ears.

"Miss Felice don't want it sold, that's why."

"I want to meet this woman who runs everybody off." Karla's premonition was that Felice must be a deranged relative chained to a bed in the attic, destined like built-in furniture, to stay with the house.

"C'mon, I shows you."

Dorcas waddled down the colonnade into the main house. Karla followed, taking a closer look at the rooms as they walked past. The library had leather-bound volumes lining dark shelves, and wing-back velvet chairs before a fireplace. In the formal dining room the table was set with china, silver and crystal, the sideboards heavy with candelabra and footed urns. They walked past an elegant parlor, then a second parlor, more opulent than the first. Dorcas undid the rope barring the door. She walked across the cream-colored hooked rug with its border of pink azaleas and stopped before the fireplace. Above the white and black Italian marble mantle, the portrait of a formidable woman surveyed the room.

Dorcas addressed the painting. "Felice, I's here to introduce you to Miss Karla," then to Karla, "Say hello."

"That's Felice? A painting?—"

Dorcas looked serious. "Hurry!—Say hello. You don't want to make her mad."

"Hello, Felice. How are you?" *Talk about feeling stupid.*

"See the eyes?" Dorcas waved her hand. "Move to the left."

Karla did. Felice's sharp black eyes shifted, focused her way. "That's not possible." *This was crazy.*

"What do you mean it ain't possible? You seen it yourself, ain't you? And something else, if she gets unhappy, ain't no peace in this house."

Before Karla could ask, "In what way?" a feeling of suffocation came over her, as if someone had dropped a black shroud over her head. She had difficulty breathing. The fine hair on her arms lifted. The nape of her neck prickled. She took an involuntary step back.

"You see?" Dorcas asked. "Whosa gonna live with that?"

A coughing fit nearly choked Karla. She told herself to grab reality and think sensibly. Ghosts didn't exist. They were figments of overwrought imaginations, Halloween myths. "You're saying this woman's ghost roams the house?"

THE AZALEAS

Dorcas didn't need to answer. Felice's presence was palpable. She filled the room. She crowded Karla, pressing close. Karla retreated toward the door. *My god! How weird!* Her heart drummed in her chest. This couldn't be happening. It was happening.

"No thinkin' to it. Miss Felice ain't never moved out."

How to deal with this? Suppose Felice haunted prospective buyers the way she was haunting Karla? Yikes! She'd better gather her wits and make a plan. How to overcome this unseen but very real obstacle? What to do? What would Gloria do?

Show Felice's room first and get the trauma over? If she did that, the prospective buyer might cancel the remaining tour. Gloria had said—what had she said? Karla racked her brain. The discussion they had one day about the house where the owner died with AIDS popped into her mind. Yes, yes! Gloria said AIDS did not have to be legally disclosed. The rules said a buyer must be told everything about the house, nothing about the owner. 'When you go to a hospital,' Gloria said, 'the nurse doesn't tell you who died in the bed you're in.' Telling a buyer things about the owner like his sex, age, religion or color was discrimination. What rule did Felice come under? If the portrait was permanently attached to the wall and stayed with the house, Karla must disclose the ghostly fact. If Felice wasn't a permanent fixture, she could keep her mouth shut.

Karla had to stop Felice from intimidating her or her buyer, if she ever got one. She must make damn sure of that, even if it meant ripping the stupid portrait off the wall, slashing it with scissors, piling the pieces and making a bonfire.

Felice read Karla's battle plan. She retreated into her golden frame. Karla literally felt the woman gather herself and slide back into the portrait. Not until the bright red gown settled into the umber background did she give Karla back her breathing space. The experience was so intense, Karla's knees wobbled. She collapsed onto the piano stool, only to immediately leap as if stung by an electric prod.

"She don't like nobody sitting on her seat," Dorcas said.

The housekeeper pointed to the portrait. Felice stood with one long, slender hand resting on the piano, on her index finger a ruby ring big as a baseball. Her brocade skirt fell elegantly near a piano stool identical to the one in the living room—pink azalea needlepoint cover. "Felice loved her piano. She played by ear. Ain't never got no formal teaching."

"Well," Karla sighed, suddenly relieved. She could handle a fellow music illiterate. "Tell Felice we at least have that in common."

"I ain't saying no more. Never can tell how she'll take it. I wants her to stay put."

"I understand," but not really. Karla studied the portrait closer. She'd go under the knife to have an aristocratic nose like Felice's. Her lips were full and sensuous. Thick, black hair cascaded to bare shoulders. "Mary Bravelle looks a little like Felice," she said. "There's a resemblance."

"Yes'm. Mary's the great-great-great granddaughter. We ain't laid eyes on that girl since her mother took her away. Beautiful! She could've been a princess. She was our princess. Black hair and them big eyes, sixteen year old—everybody in love with her—Bale Franklin, in particular—hung around here like a puppy dog. Every time I turned around, there he was. Miss Mary ain't even come back to scatter her mother or say hello." Dorcas clacked her tongue against her teeth, making 'tch-tch' sounds, her lips screwed tight. "We loved that girl. She lit up the place. Ain't never been the same since—" she caught herself and stopped.

"Since when?—What?—"

Dorcas shrugged heavy shoulders as if shifting a burden to a more comfortable position and dropped the subject. "Let me tell you about Felice. You gotta know 'bout her if you aimin' to sell the place."

Felice was ancient history. The current situation concerned Karla more. Something was hidden, something no one talked about. Albert didn't discuss it. Agatha made a wide circle around it. Dorcas came close then shied away like a skittish horse.

"Felice weren't very tall—mebbe so high." Dorcas held her arm even with her shoulder. "Less'n five feet—" Agatha wasn't tall, either. Little Napoleons slept in short beds and caused troubles. "Husband died—German measles somewhere in Alabama, last year of the War and left her with three girl children, a fourth one in the oven and fields of cotton wantin' pickin'—po' girl only twenty-some years old. She gone through plenty misery—but she tough, smokin' cigars, doing what she got to do to survive—you seen the 13th step, Miss Karla?"

"I haven't gone through the house yet. You're supposed to give me the tour."

"Well, take a good look at the 13th step on that staircase. Blood stain never came out, even though Miss Agatha had Sam sand the spot more'n once. Couple of days later, there's that red-black shadow back in its place again."

"Whose blood?—"

"River boat gambler attempted to do away with Miss Felice. A party of 'em came up from New Orleans for a visit. Everybody knowed Miss Felice and how sharp she could deal them cards. She turned the gamblers' pockets inside out in a poker game and they left in a big huff—the very idea of a woman strippin' 'em clean! They come back to get even. She spotted 'em skulkin' near the house and perched herself with a pistol on the upstairs landin' and shot the first one charged in after her. He died on the 13th step. The rest took off like their tails was a-fire."

Karla stared at Felice, a premonition rising that in the sale of The Azaleas this dumb portrait would prove the biggest stumbling block of all. Raising a defiant chin, she addressed the canvas. "Miss Felice, ma'am, with all due respect and beggin' your indulgence and tolerance, this place is gonna sell." *Put that in your pipe and smoke it.*

"And that's the same step where Mr. Hank—" Dorcas caught herself and stopped.

"Who's Mr. Hank— what?"

"That's his room at the top of the stairs. It stays locked. Nobody can go in there."

"I've got the keys to every room."

"No, siree—not that room. No indeed! Never!—" She worked one hand against the other like Lady McBeth trying to rub out the damned spot.

Karla waited while Dorcas's anxiety eased. How many phantoms could one place harbor? Gloria from H&B said a good salesman always visualized the end result. Karla could only envision a murky road with no final destination in sight. 'If you reach a dead end, ask for help,' Gloria advised. 'You'd be surprised how many people will help if you lower yourself to ask.' Recalling that sage advice, Karla turned to Dorcas, "We work together and sell this place, you get a cash bonus."

Dollar signs sprang into Dorcas's eyes at the same time that a rising heat warmed the room. Felice sucked up all the breathable air once again, leaving Dorcas and Karla panting and heaving, lungs rattling as if they'd just climbed Mount Everest.

"I can't take no money," Dorcas whispered dramatically, eyes rolling in their sockets like ball bearings. "I ain't taking no chances."

What The Azaleas needed was an exorcism. With chants and potions, a good voodoo practitioner like Esplanade Doree could vanquish a wandering spirit back to its proper grave.

Felice must've read Karla's mind because invisible waves pulsed through the room—warm, warmer, hot. Perspiration beaded Karla's forehead. "I'm going outside," she said, fighting her way through the surging heat, "and look at the grounds."

Dorcas mopped her face with her apron. "You can feel her like steam rising when she's 'bout to come down from that wall. C'mon, girl. Let's get out of here. I'll take you to Preacher Frank. He'll show you around."

They rushed from the parlor and sprinted down the hallway. The screen banged behind them as they crossed the veranda, took the front steps two at a time and landed in the yard. They didn't stop running until they came to the alley of hundred-year old oaks dripping Spanish moss. Between the trees, gigantic azalea bushes, thick and dense with shiny leaves, gracefully spread billowing green skirts. When the azaleas bloomed in the spring, they'd turn into cresting pink waves.

Quickly, her heart beating fast, Karla looked over her shoulder, expecting Felice in hot pursuit. Instead, peaceful St. Augustine grass carpets gently sloped away from the house. Like a golden chain, fall chrysanthemums outlined the lawn perimeters. Day lilies sprang in starry drifts from the hollows and low places.

"She don't come past here," Dorcas panted, slowing down and pointed to a three-foot high rusty cross made from welded iron rebars stuck in the ground.

At a distance from the portrait, protected by the Voodoo barrier, Felice's menace faded. The encounter lost its threat and turned ridiculous. Karla looked back over her shoulder again, emboldened by the airy space between her and the portrait. The Azaleas mansion stood white and shining in the morning sun, elegant and aristocratic. "My God, she's beautiful."

THE AZALEAS

"Them old plantation owners didn't stint none when it came to their houses. And they got all that free slave labor, black mens in the swamp cutting cypress logs, black mens on the levee baking bricks from Mississippi mud, and white overseer with a big whip makin' shore they set the walls straight." Dorcas didn't sound bitter. She piped ancient history, before her time or Karla's. "Cost so much to run these places now, the ones ain't been bought up by Shell or Texaco for fancy headquarters are turned into bed and breakfasts or left to crumble. We barely hangin' on ourselves—"

"I can see it needs paint, maybe a new roof, but it's so grand. Why it's grander than any house on St. Charles Avenue. The design is so perfect." Three-foot square brick columns on all four sides; first and second stories with workable green shutters; casement windows floor to ceiling—

"Clem's done lots of carpentry and he says square houses easiest to build. All them curves and arches and different level pitched roofs complicates construction and costs more money. Felice drew the plan for the house on a napkin."

If the house was any reflection of Felice's personality, she must've been a fairly direct and uncomplicated woman. The interior had clean lines, one wide hallway down the middle, rooms on either side, downstairs and up. Six chimneys poking through the slate roof took care of twelve fireplaces.

"There's Preacher Frank." Dorcas pointed to a shotgun cabin shaded by oak trees. He sat on the sagging step of the unpainted shanty, whittling on a stick. His denim overalls, torn at the knees, were hitched by one strap. The undershirt had once been white. "I got to get back to my kitchen," Dorcas said.

"Thanks." Karla stepped over gnarled tree roots. "Hi, Preacher—nice morning—"

Preacher didn't stop whittling. At his feet two long-muscled, web-footed dogs with leopard-colored coats lifted their heads and raised a ruckus. Their tails swished back and forth like windshield wipers. They barked shrilly and glared at Karla with mismatched eyes, one bright blue and the other a white, haunting color.

When Karla was in the fifth grade, a governor declared the Catahoula the Louisiana State Dog. The McDonough Elementary principal posted Catahoula pictures on the bulletin board. Auntie Emmy was offended. "New Orleans and the whole state in an uproar over school busin' and integration, riots in the streets and National Guard in the schools and the only thing the Louisiana legislature frettin'over is that the state gits a State Dog to go along with the State Flower."

The Catahoula dogs settled down. From Preacher's open front door Karla saw straight through the three rooms and the swamp beyond. She and her mother had once stayed in a similar shotgun house for a few weeks until an insistent knock on the front door terrified Mama and they escaped through the back door. A shotgun's front and rear doors were aligned so the owner could stand on the front steps and shoot straight through the house without making holes in his walls. Landlords couldn't blast tenants anymore, but their heavy-handed knock hadn't changed a bit. Earl was a master pounder.

"You a real preacher?—" Karla asked.

The black community overflowed with powerful, sing-song orators who got the "call," and added "reverend" to their name. They gathered any little group willing to listen. Down the block from Auntie Emmy's duplex on Rampart Street, one reverend's congregation met in an abandoned warehouse. Over the door hung a hand-written sign, "Church of Power & Mite." Auntie Emmy didn't go there. She went across town to the African Methodist Episcopal Church, dragging Karla along. AME had a properly ordained minister and three choirs.

"Don't preach no more. My boy took over, then my granson. Hallelujah! Over there." Through the pine trees, on a high knoll, sat a little white church with a tall spire. "New owners ain't gonna put up with a black church right out their front door. Miss Agatha tole us that already—"

"How long has the church been there?"

"Hunnerd years—"

The lawn around the church house looked neat and tended to. Beyond the back steps, a wrought-iron fence enclosed a cemetery. The headstones, streaked and loosened by time, leaned at odd angles. They marched up a slight rise like lines of scraggly, defeated soldiers coming home.

"One of my great grandpappies—" Preacher pointed with his whittling knife to the butterfly on Karla's bare shoulder, "had a brand on him."

"This is a tattoo."

"His'n was on his cheek."

"Odd place—"

He cackled like rustling corn stalks. The dogs raised their heads and their cloudy, mismatched eyes followed Preacher's every move. "Not odd if you're a runaway slave. Miss Felice had a hot iron and any slave run way twice had AP burnt on his cheek." The dogs twitched their ears, as if they understood every word the old man said. He saw the question in Karla's eyes and cackled again. "AP. Azalea Plantation—you running from something?—"

"From lots of things," Karla said, rubbing her butterfly.

"Ain't do no good. It always come backs and gits you."

"I hope not." She sat on the step next to him. He smelled rancid, of mothballs, liniment, and woodsy smoke. The curious dogs, familiar with Preacher's scent, ignored him and sniffed Karla's legs, their noses cold.

The pair sat in silence while the little shavings fell soundlessly to the ground. "You got family?" Karla asked.

"Two wives, both gone—had six chirren with 'em, and more outside chirren than I can count." He seemed proud of that. "Some of my outside chirren treats me better than my real ones do."

"You were born on this plantation?"

"Right in this cabin, eighty-five years past— I done lived here all my natural life." He could hear well enough and didn't wear glasses. His teeth were gone, his face sharp bones and sunken cheeks. The skin on his hands was coarse and yellowish, the color of pork chitlings.

"Who owned the plantation when you were born?"

"Ole man Turner."

That helped a lot: "The first, second, third, fourth or fifth?"

"Hank's grandfather."

He'd be the third. "Hank Turner, Danielle's husband, what happened to him?"

"She drove him mad."

"What'd she do?"

"Do? Nothin' special, just what women do best—nag a man to death—"

"Words don't kill."

"Ain't nothin' made that French woman happy—one day she jis up and drove off with her girl. Packed up their things, piled them into the new Ford he just bought tryin' to please her, and away she went, Mary leaning out the car door crying, "Papa! Papa! I don't want to go! Please Papa!" and all of us rooted on the lawn like we was oak trees. We never seen hide nor hair of 'em, ever again. Mr. Hank might as well have died that day and Miss Agatha—well, Miss Agatha just kept runnin' the place and she ain't never goin' to forgive Danielle Turner."

"What did he die of?"

"By his own hand—"

"Suicide?—"

"Accident, accordin' to the sheriff and the cor'ner."

"You don't think so?"

"I knowed Hank well— I raised that boy. He had a lot on his mind. His soul was heavy."

"You think he killed himself?"

"That was a long time ago—I ain't thinkin' nothin'. I ain't sayin' nothin'."

"How come Mr. Hank wasn't buried over there?" I waved toward the church graveyard.

"That's for black folks. If you's white and gots money you gits buried in town, in one of them fancy tombs." He threw the ball into Karla's court. "Your pa from around here?—"

"No. He's dead."

"You got fambly?—"

Karla's turn to dig through her roots and present the tree—tracing heirs was a pivotal Southern conversation. Residents below the Mason-Dixon didn't feel comfortable talking with a stranger unless they knew the pedigree. Upholding her end was a familiar hurdle. "My pa and ma are both dead." Karla said.

"Is you got aunts and uncles?"

"No."

"Cousins?—Nieces?"

"No.

"Bless you, chile, y'all alone?"

"Basically—"

"Not even a husband?"

"No. No husband."

"Why, that's the strangest thing I ever heard. Everybody got somebody."

"Well. Yeah—"

Suddenly he frowned and looked at Karla with open curiosity. "You the one Miss Agatha tole us was comin' out to sell the place?"

"Yes, I am."

"Oh, boy—"

"Where's the courthouse?"

He jumped like a gigged frog. "Why you be needin' the cotehouse?"

"To check out legal documents—paper work stuff. Nothing to do with the law," Karla assured him.

He sighed like a tea kettle hissing steam. "Down the road a piece in St. Francisville."

"You ride with me tomorrow?"

The hand with the knife went still. "I ain't getting mixed up in this stuff."

"I'm not asking you to get mixed up in anything. Just come with me. I don't want to spend hours lost and I bet you know your way around that courthouse." This old man had lived here for eighty-five years. Everybody knew him. Bringing Preacher Frank was like having ID—no trouble at the door.

Karla's former courthouse appearances included a visit to Juvenile Court, where a Judge Hastings robed in black as though he were a priest banged a gavel, leaned over the bench and said that against his better judgment and because Auntie Emmy had presented such a noble argument, he awarded this white child to the care and custody of Auntie Emmy, who cried and hugged Karla to her bosom. Traffic Court to fight a speeding ticket and when the hard-hearted female judge found Karla guilty and she had no money to pay the fine, she threw Karla into a cell filled with drunken women, and some stoned blotto. City Court when she accidentally got caught in a sting operation rounding up Quarter prostitutes and had to prove she played the piano at the Parrot Bar, period, no extra-curricular activities.

"C'mon. I'll buy you a box of cigars—" Bribery, the most direct line between two points— "What's your favorite? El Trellis?"

He wavered. "What time is you plannin' on going?"

"Tomorrow morning—whenever you're ready—"

"Cain't go there tomorra—"

"Why not?—"

"Cotehouse ain't open Sunday."

Damn! "Monday, then—" She'd lost track of time. Sunday was a dead day. Twenty-four hours wasted and she hadn't a minute to spare. "What's the sheriff's name?"

"Watson. Jimmy Watson, Mister James's boy."

"Okay, Preacher. We'll go first thing Monday morning."

When Karla returned to the house Agatha sat on a veranda rocker. Next to her Judge Jeremiah relaxed in his wheel chair. Old pals, Jeremiah had said. The way they sat, companionably drinking Bloody Marys confirmed they'd known each other since the beginning of time.

"Why, hello, Judge Jones." Karla extended a hand. "Remember me? I'm Karla. We rode the buggy—"

"Of course!—Of course!—" He patted Karla's hand cordially. "Nice to see you again—"

"Are you all right, Judge? You took a nasty spill the other day."

"A little bruised and battered, but these old bones have so many aches and pains in place already, it's hard to accommodate new ones," he replied.

"What spill?" Agatha eyed the Judge. "What spill?"

The Judge eased her mind. "I told you about the unpleasantness at the Cathedral. In the confusion the buggy tipped over and I landed very unceremoniously on my duff. The spill didn't hurt anything but my dignity."

Certainly, the Judge had told his neighbor about the shooting as soon as he returned to St. Francisville. Like fresh fish, that news wouldn't keep. This morning in the bedroom when Agatha cut Karla off so abruptly, she already knew Mary Bravelle had been shot.

Agatha asked, "And what have we been doing, da'ling? Have we been exploring?" All the sweetness and cordiality in the world couldn't hide her curiosity. "What did Preacher have to say?"

No matter how hard Agatha pumped, Karla wouldn't talk. "Nothing much—we had a little get-acquainted visit. This place is a jewel—so beautiful." Karla meant the compliment. "The Azaleas is truly impressive." And in case Jeremiah Jones didn't remember the reason for Karla being present, she refreshed his memory. "I'm here to sell the plantation."

THE AZALEAS

"Oh, I know. I know." He removed new horn-rimmed glasses. "Frankly, my dear, I hope you fail like the others did. I don't want to lose my favorite neighbor." He reached in his pocket for a white handkerchief and wiped the lenses.

Producing a white handkerchief with the flair and assurance of a magician pulling a rabbit from a hat was the true mark of a Southern gentleman. "I have a brilliant idea," Karla said, "You buy The Azaleas, join the estates and form a vast empire."

"Your proposal comes forty years too late." the Judge replied. "We old people dislike change. We're set in our ways. We want life to rock along same as always."

"Old?" Karla flashed him her best smile. "You're not old! I have you down as my first hot prospect."

His lopsided grin revealed crooked teeth. "Hot, eh?"

"Sizzling," Karla replied, arching her smile, rainbow promising warmth and sunshine and all things wonderful. Certain moves—a smile, a bend to retrieve anything, a leg extended for whatever reason—worked magic if a girl used them right. Men were all alike. Neither age nor handicap figured in the equation. "See ya." Karla walked past him and swung her hips to give him added pleasure.

He giggled like a teenager. Agatha frowned and looked severe. Inside the door, Karla stopped to eavesdrop.

"Can you believe," Agatha grumped, "that Mary would hire somebody like that to sell The Azaleas? It's ludicrous."

"I'd worry about this one, Agatha. She might perform where those other ones didn't."

"That girl?—Why, you can tell a mile away she's nothing but white trash. Those earrings! Have you seen the tattoo?—a butterfly on her shoulder. Disgusting! And those tight tank tops and hip-hugger jeans!"

Karla came within a hair of yelling, "I'm not white trash! I'm from the city. Not a country bumpkin! Not a throwback to the frickin' fifties like you are!"

"A diamond stud in her navel, too." Jeremiah Jones said with a chuckle. "Did you notice that little touch?"

"Rhinestone, probably—what makes you even think a girl like that can sell The Azaleas?"

"She's got a flip those others lacked."

"Flip! Fiddle-dee-dee! I'm not worried about her flip. Felice will take care of her."

"Don't bank on the old girl. I'm telling you this Karla is different. Take adequate precautions."

"The whole thing is ridiculous!" Agatha groused. "A farce to aggravate me and make my life miserable—"

"Listen to what I'm saying, honey. I dealt with sales reps all my life. When one walked in the door, even before he opened his mouth, I could tell whether or not he would sell me something. It's the body language, the attitude, the drive. This girl has it."

Karla grinned. Good for him! He knew the merits of the contents and wasn't led astray by the packaging.

"She's never sold anything before. There's nothing to worry about," Agatha insisted. "She has no idea what she's doing."

"That's the best kind of salesperson. She doesn't know it can't be done so she'll do it. You understand what I'm saying?"

The only response to his warning was the accelerated squeaking of Agatha's rocker and the increased twittering of the birds in the oak trees.

Karla edged away from the door and tiptoed upstairs, her mind in turmoil. Her insecurities and inferiorities burnt like acid, spilling doubt and etching indecision. Agatha was right. She had no business here. If she had any sense at all, she'd pack and leave right now, this minute, before something terrible and disastrous happened that would ruin her miserable life forever.

Wasn't her life the pits already? Leave and go back to what? Longing for Richard? Avoiding Richard? Wanting and not getting Richard? Wishing and not having? What kind of a life was that?

Jeremiah Jones thought she could do it. He thought her dangerous and liked her flip.

Well, flip she would be. She'd flip right into a sale, make her commission, pocket the money and start over. She'd show that goddam Richard she had more brains and smarts than his high-society wife. He'd regret the day he cast Karla aside. She'd get even. Lord yes! Get even.

Safe in the Andrew Jackson room, she sat at the desk and caught her breath. As she wallowed in self-pity and self-doubt, little threads of information about The Azaleas wove their way into her thoughts.

THE AZALEAS

She knew a whole lot more about the situation this morning than she did yesterday. The place had a ghost. Owner Hank's wife Danielle ran off taking Mary, their daughter. Hank committed suicide. Agatha, Hanks sister, ran the plantation that legally belonged to Hank's widow, Danielle. Upon Danielle's recent death, ownership passed to Mary. Mary wanted to get rid of the place.

What precautions did Jeremiah Jones think Agatha should take? What part did the Judge Jeremiah play in all this?—time to sift through the mother lode, identify and tag each puzzle piece.

She removed her new laptop from the new briefcase and found the on-switch. The screen lit up, magically flooding her with an aura of professionalism and confidence. She would overcome all obstacles and sell this plantation. She only needed one very important thing—not a hundred, not a thousand—just one—a buyer—one single little itsy, bitsy buyer. Where could she find that special person?

The Azaleas, she typed with two fingers. *Day One*—

CHAPTER 6

On Sunday a quiet stillness like a religious hush enveloped the house. Saints and cherubim hovered over the priceless Mallard bed. Karla wondered if one of those winged creatures was her own guardian angel. Did she have a guardian angel? Auntie Emmy, maybe?—could she look down from the place where she went to find her "great reward" and see Karla?

A longing for the old woman enveloped Karla. She snuggled deeper under the covers and wished Auntie Emmy was here. Auntie Emmy would cut through all the bullshit and get right down to business.

How often Karla made her cry! One of Karla's greatest regrets (and she had many) was that she never appreciated Auntie Emmy until much later, and then it was too late. She was sixty-two when she fought the court and took in an orphaned eight-year old. An old woman deserving a few years of peace didn't have to do that. She had no obligation. Her voice came through the Sunday stillness. "I ain't gave up nothing but a little corner space for your bed and a few mouthfuls of food."

Karla's nose twitched. She smelled Auntie Emmy's Southern fried chicken, dipped in egg batter, dredged in flour, dropped into bubbling grease until the skin turned gold and crispy.

THE AZALEAS

Dorcas's voice rose above the clanging pots and pans. The delicious scent tickling Karla's nose was real. She hadn't died and gone to Heaven.

She bolted upright—she was hungry. On her way downstairs she eyed the solid, six-panel oak door next to the second floor landing, Hank Turner's off-limits room. Forty-five other doors in the house, but this one interested her the most. The brass plate had a long, skinny key hole. Which skeleton on the heavy key ring opened this mystery? Impulsively, she reached and turned the knob.

"Intriguing, isn't it?" said a voice behind her.

Karla snatched her hand back as if she'd burnt herself on a hot stove. "You live here?" she asked.

"At present," the man replied, extending a friendly arm. "Doing brunch?"

Together, Karla's hand resting lightly on his arm, she and the boarder descended the curving staircase. As her feet touched one step and then another, the scuffed Nikes turned into red satin slippers. Her jeans morphed into yards of rustling taffeta; the tank top turned into a low-cut bodice, revealing cleavage and smooth shoulders. Her shoulders straightened and her chin went up. She was Cinderella coming down from the attic; Princess Di arriving at a Buckingham Palace ball with her Prince before their lives crumbled; the Queen on the arm of Rex, King of Mardi Gras. Neither she nor her escort spoke.

When they reached the dining room, the man said, "I'm Roger Randall," and broke the spell.

"Karla Whitmore. Pleased to meet you—"

Roger started to pull out a chair, but the butler beat him to it. Karla shook the napkin onto her lap, with each shake dispelling the magical aura and re-entering the reality orbit. "Is this like extra, or does brunch come with the room?"

"Everybody brunches," Clem replied. "We don't let anybody go hungry. You missed breakfast—it's at six."

Clem retreated to the kitchen. Karla studied Roger: slight build and tousled brown hair, brown eyes, whiskers a couple of days old; average height, average weight, average everything. He could blend into any crowd, be hard to spot and impossible to remember. A closer look revealed gray at the temples and the general relaxing of taut, youthful skin brought on by middle age. He was older than he appeared, fortyish, maybe. Roger looked like an unmade bed, rumpled and comfortable.

Clem returned with bowls of steaming soup.

"Where's Miss Agatha?" Karla asked, taking a sip. "Turtle soup?—is this turtle soup?"

"Dorcas makes the best in the parish." Clem bragged on his wife.

"How'd you guess turtle soup with a splash of sherry was my favorite?"

He smiled knowingly, "We have our informers."

That should've been Karla's warning right then and there, but the words sailed over her head and she paid no heed to them. She had no past history, no previous clues, nothing to alert her to the wiles and customs of these strange people who inhabited West Feliciana Parish.

"The lady of the house has gone to mass in St. Francisville," Roger said, "and to a luncheon and tea afterward. She won't be back until tonight, or maybe in the morning. Sunday is a big receiving day around here."

Sundays in the Quarter were slowly creeping back to normal, filling up with festivals, street shows and tourists. The holy day was a part of the weekend package. St. Louis Cathedral across from Jackson Square drew more tourists than penitents; the tap-dancing boys were a bigger attraction than the white-robed priest standing at the altar.

How was tap-dancing Lebron? She'd abandoned him, left him alone in Big Charity's dismal ward. He was tough and street wise. He'd be okay. *Please, God, let him be okay.*

"I worked most of the night and overslept," Karla said.

"There are Masses all during the day," Roger volunteered helpfully.

"I'm not Catholic."

"Neither am I," he replied "lapsed Episcopalian. My wife keeps up the tradition," immediately hinting to Karla he was taken—good husband, well-trained. "She teaches Sunday school and all that."

"Good for her. My Auntie Emmy—a body couldn't miss church when she was around— she'd raise a mean ruckus. Now she's gone, and I don't even feel remorse when I skip." Sometimes that bothered Karla. She believed in God and Jesus Christ and St. Peter guarding the Pearly Gate, and the Garden of Eden and the parables and fables and the begetting in the Bible, but sitting in church listening to the preacher pound the pulpit and threaten hell's fire didn't do anything for her well-being. "Besides, I'm too busy right now."

"Ah, yes. You're here to sell The Azaleas right out from under us." Roger's pleasant voice had a teasing lilt. "And then where will I retreat to finish my manuscript?"

"Oh, you're the one Agatha said was writing a book. How's it coming?"

"Slow. Writing is always a slow job. I get too bogged down in research. I find everything interesting and spend much too much time on the details. When my wife reads the first draft, she red-pencils half the research. That hurts."

"What hurts your vanity probably enhances your wallet," Karla replied. "You're writing about?—"

"Text and photographs of James Audubon's years around St. Francisville—he produced his best work while living in this area."

"Audubon as in Audubon Park?—"

"The very one," Roger replied, "named in his memory. When we drive to New Orleans, we always go there. My children love it."

A wife and children and Karla bet he had a house and a dog, too. Should she tell him she knew every inch of Audubon Park? That now it lay within Richard's territory so she avoided going there and jogged instead in City Park which she didn't like half as much? "You have girls? Boys?—"

"Two girls, Bonnie and Carleen, sixteen and fourteen—that age drives parents insane and we're no exception. Right now they're in a phase where they like to pretend Myra and I don't exist." He extracted photographs from his wallet for Karla to admire. Two girls and a nice-looking woman, the three wearing shorts and leaning against a convertible.

"Which one is Myra?" I asked.

Roger laughed. "What a way to score brownie points! I'll have to tell her. She'll love it. Bonnie's on the left, and that's Carleen. Myra fought me all the way on this car, Bonnie's sixteenth birthday present, but in the end she gave in. I mean, you're only young once."

"I have a Mustang convertible."

"Then you appreciate this. Isn't Bonnie gorgeous?" Before Karla nodded assent, out came another photo—daughter Carleen decked in a basketball outfit, satin blue, number 13 on the jersey. The proud papa pointed to her long legs and couldn't help bragging. "Center on the varsity team— I don't plan to skip a game."

"I bet you miss them when you're away."

"Like an amputated leg— Myra and the girls—they're my life."

"Where do y'all live?"

"Lake Charles, not far—"

"Do they come with you sometimes?"

"I wish! It's hard. The girls are into after-school stuff. We don't disrupt their schedules if we can possibly help it. And I have a crop-dusting business. Between books and weevils I'm gone lots. I hate that."

"Books and weevils, unusual combination of jobs—"

"The crop dusting business was abruptly passed on to me when my father crashed. In reality, it pays better than the books, so I keep on with it."

"How long have you been away this time?"

"I got here last week. I hope to wrap up the writing in two or three weeks, although I can't tell exactly how long it will take—that depends on how fast the facts surface."

"I have a killer deadline to sell The Azaleas in thirty days. I tell myself every morning that it's possible. In the evenings I list the reasons why it didn't happen."

"Deadlines are good," Roger said. "They provide parameters. A clock tick-ticking keeps one going. No time to lollygag."

"Maybe we can help each other," Karla said. "You buy my plantation and I'll buy your book."

He threw his head back and laughed. "Scratch me from your list. I wouldn't trade my little bungalow for this place."

Karla bit into a juicy drumstick. "Well, you can't blame me for trying."

In the course of her short-lived association with Hasker & Blunt, Gloria advised Karla to ask anybody she came across if they'd like to buy a property. 'You can't make a sale,' she said, 'unless you verbally, orally, out loud ask for the order. Sales people think they've asked, imagine they've done it, when in reality they've never opened their mouths. They get erased from the blackboard quicker than yesterday's math lesson. Never presume,' she warned. 'That's essential.'

THE AZALEAS

Gloria loved to tell stories of salespeople who missed the big one because they assumed the person didn't have the bucks. The old millionaire farmer (not from cotton but from oil deep in his fields) who walked into H&B with a bankroll in his pocket the size of a Subway sandwich, and the rookie agent on duty ignored him; the tattooed man wearing a muscle shirt and leather pants, arriving on a Harley-Davidson, asking for someone to take him to see a $250,000 house on the river; every salesperson except Gloria found themselves suddenly tied up with clients who looked better able. She climbed on his motorcycle and showed the man the property. He removed a case from his cycle rack, snapped it open and began counting hundred dollar bills. "Not stolen, either," Gloria liked to add. Then there was the little Italian lady in a cotton print dress and furry slippers who offered "all cash" and brought a Christmas stocking stuffed with bills on closing day. Gloria had dozens of stories. "Never," she said, "judge a book by its cover."

Roger said cheerfully, "I'm not a good prospect. I'd never walk away from our little place. My wife and I built it ourselves. We did everything together. Myra helped me dig footings, pour foundations, frame walls, nail shingles. She slaved like a common laborer and never once complained. I tell you," a pleased look in his eye, "a man couldn't ask for a better helper." He couldn't say enough good things about his wife, a refreshing twist. Most men belittled their "old lady" until one wanted to cram their words down their throats and hope they choked. "Next summer I intend to build a swimming pool for the girls, and hopefully, if the book sells well, I'll pay somebody to do it. I'm getting too old for do-it-yourself projects."

Karla wolfed down fried chicken, licked her fingers and listened to Roger rave about his wife and daughters and his happy life.

"One more year and Bonnie will be going to college. Where does time go? She can't decide whether to go to LSU and party or to Harvard and study. She can go anywhere she wants. She'll get a scholarship. Her grades—" he stopped mid-sentence. "I apologize. When I get started on the girls, I just rattle on and on. I bore everybody."

"Not me. I think it's great to have a family."

"How about you?—"

Geez—her fault—she'd inadvertently opened the Southern family tree dialogue. "I'm not married," Karla replied, looking intentionally solemn and dedicated. His eyes didn't brim with pity at her singleness or sparkle with anticipation at the solo possibilities. "I'm devoted to my career."

"And how is that coming?"

"Presently stalled— I'm beating the bushes, but haven't found a buyer for this plantation."

"Maybe I can help you."

Coming from Roger, a pleasant, decent man, the offer sounded genuine, nothing suspicious or subversive about it. "Could you? Would you?"

"I'll do what I can. I'm good at research, although I don't know how much of that you need. But I do go all over the parish interviewing folks for the Audubon book. I can work the sale of The Azaleas into the conversation. Wouldn't be any hardship at all to spread the word for you—"

"I'd really appreciate that."

"My pleasure—"

What a nice guy! He had an inner security, an easy self-assurance. He had a family, a home, a basic nest filled with love and comfort. Roger Randall had in his grasp what everybody yearned for.

Roger excused himself and opened the St. Francisville Banner, Sunday edition. Karla read the headline, upside down, *Sheriff under Investigation*. Preacher Frank was taking her to see the sheriff tomorrow. Albert had said being on good terms with the head law enforcement officer of the parish was important.

"Why are they after the sheriff?" Karla asked.

Roger took his time reading the article, his eyes traveling across each line, drifting to the bottom. "The FBI is in town looking into political extortion, grand larceny and drugs. Huh. They've covered the gamut, haven't they?"

Karla leaned forward eagerly, stirred by the thought that tomorrow she'd be face to face with an FBI most wanted. "And?"

Roger turned the page with deliberate slowness. "Continued on A-2—" He rattled the paper. "Let's see—it says here the authorities discovered a money-filled envelope—"

"How much?—"

"Three hundred thousand dollars deposited in a trash can in the alley behind the courthouse."

"Whew! That's a hefty sum to pitch in the garbage."

THE AZALEAS

"And suddenly, that money belongs to nobody."

"Would you claim it?" Karla asked.

"I don't think so," Roger replied.

The sheriff had to be either brilliant or utterly stupid, depending on how much control he exercised over the premises. How many deputies going in and out of the building would lift the top of a stinking trash bin? How many gun-toting men were assigned to guard the garbage? Was the sanitation department in on the heist?

Questions popped into Karla's mind. Her anxiety index zoomed. Tomorrow she'd have to deal with Sheriff Watson. A man entangled in a federal investigation would hardly give a damn about a real estate sale. Going to see him could prove a colossal waste of time and she had no time to waste.

Clem refilled the water glasses. "Sheriff ain't worried."

"You're absolutely right, Clem," Roger agreed, passing the paper over to Karla. "The reporter quotes the sheriff as saying he's been investigated by the IRS, FBI, CIA and a whole alphabet of federal stooges and no one has ever found a single piece of hard evidence to back up the government's fraud claims. He says this is an ongoing vendetta that's costing the tax payers thousands of unnecessary dollars."

"So how does Sheriff Watson operate?" Karla asked, curious. "What has he allegedly done?"

"Supposedly anyone wanting a casino license in this area has to first cut in the governor then the local sheriff. Otherwise paperwork gets stalled in the pipeline."

"You've got to be kidding! That's it? This may be big stuff in West Feliciana, but in New Orleans this tempest wouldn't merit a teapot."

"Three hundred grand creates a storm anywhere," Roger said. "We're not talking chicken feed here."

"You think the Feds will indict the sheriff?"

"Who knows," Roger answered.

Clem removing the dinner plates grumbled something under his breath.

"What was that?" Roger asked.

Clem gave his unsolicited opinion. "Ain't nobody gonna indict our sheriff."

"What makes you so sure?" Karla asked.

Roger said, "The article says he's cooperating fully with the authorities."

Clem nodded his white cotton head emphatically. "He always do—"

"Always?—" I asked. "How many times has he been investigated?"

"A bunch—"

A bunch was the same as a mess. Both terms meant anything from more than one to thousands.

Roger said, "The Feds on one side and the Vegas people on the other might prove a bit of a squeeze for the sheriff."

"Mr. Roger—Beggin' your pardon, suh—there ain't nobody in West Feliciana white or black care if the sheriff is rakin' off Las Vegas gamblers. Ain't no sympathy wasted on them. Nobody wants them out-of-state people here, anyhow."

"You're probably right on the button," Roger said, rising, "and all of this is a waste of time and money."

"The Las Vegas people have expensive lawyers, big guns," I said. "The sheriff better watch his step."

Roger stood, held onto his chair and looked pensive. Maybe he was thinking the same thing Karla was. It wasn't smart to mess around with big time West Coast gamblers. The sheriff could end up at the bottom of the Mississippi River with concrete blocks tied to his ankles.

Clem stood his ground. "Sheriff ain't worried one whit. Martha—she cooks for the Watsons—says sheriff said no foreign lawyer ever won a case in Feliciana Parish."

Karla didn't care what happened to the sheriff after The Azaleas sold, but until then, she needed him alive. She raised her eyes and met Roger's. The dark shadow in their depths told her he had a score to settle, too, but she had no idea what.

CHAPTER 7

The West Feliciana Parish Courthouse located on Prosperity Street had a bronze dome with an ornate clock chiming 9 a.m. Karla and Preacher Frank circled the statue honoring the First Regiment of the Louisiana Cavalry and parked the Mustang high on the curb. They climbed the marble steps. Karla assured the nervous Preacher that everything was okay.

"You're not getting mixed up in anything. Just take me to the sheriff's office, that's all. Then you can leave and I'll find you when I'm done."

Preacher Frank knew his way around. They reached the second floor and went in a door to the left. One window said 'Sheriff.' the other 'Tax Collector,' different departments, same person.

A deputy in blue uniform asked, "May I help you, hon?"

Preacher shuffled his feet and kneaded the battered straw hat he held with both hands. "We here to see the sheriff—"

The woman smiled brightly at Karla. Pinned onto her blue shirt pocket was a shiny tin star and beneath it a flat bar with "Beauty Jones" in black letters. "Anything in particular?— Something I can help you with?"

"Beauty—" Karla replied, wondering if Beauty was the deputy's real name or some nickname her mother mistakenly gave her at birth.

"I'm Karla Whitmore, and I'm in town to sell The Azaleas. Y'know anybody who'd like to buy it?—"

No Southerner worth his or her salt would leave a loaded question like that dangling in the air like a loose balloon. Inbred politeness declared proper anchoring.

"I wish—three million—whoo!" The word had spread quickly. "It's gonna have to be some mighty rich person from somewhere else."

"I need a word with the sheriff about the taxes, assessments—that kind of thing."

"Clerk of Court can help you."

"I know, but I'd rather start at the top."

Karla's knowledge of the system impressed her. She turned on a radio gadget and spoke into it. "Someone to see Jimmy—is he in the courthouse?" A garbled voice affirmed that he was. "Tell him to get his ass up here." She pushed a button and the door marked sheriff opened automatically. "Down the hall to the end—"

"Thanks." Karla handed Preacher $5. "Go somewhere and get yourself breakfast."

When Karla was four, maybe five— before first grade, anyhow— her mama once worked in a sheriff's office in Caddo Parish, near Shreveport. She took Karla to work with her one day. Her mother's desk had a telephone, a typewriter she didn't know how to use and six nail polish bottles lined in a neat row. Years later, when Auntie Emmy was crawling all over Karla about dropping out of high school, she told Karla about the deputy who fell in love with Annie. He took her to North Louisiana, Baptist territory where nobody drank, gambled, or whored around, and got her a nine-to-five, trying his best to turn her into a respectable woman.

Auntie Emmy had grabbed a fistful of Karla's yellow curls and yanked her so close the old woman's eyes looked like bowling balls. "Yo' momma lasted ten days—the longest ten days of her life, she always said—before she packed up and took the Greyhound back here so she could run the streets again. Runnin' the streets is a sickness and you better not think I'm a-letting you come down with that same fever."

Maybe if this real estate gig didn't work out, Karla could get a job at this sheriff station.

THE AZALEAS

It seemed well staffed. Sheriffs hired relatives, first; political paybacks, second; friends, third. Karla's application would be way down the line. Everybody's main job was to scour the countryside come election time and gather votes for the chief. Karla's father, Joe Whitmore, after he had disappeared from the face of this earth and been declared legally dead, voted twice locally and once in a November primary for Lyndon Johnson.

Karla walked through the outer office. A deputy holding a coffee cup giggled at the morning joke the computer spit. She led Karla into the sheriff's inner sanctum.

"He'll be here in a minute, hon."

Framed photos and awards plastered the sheriff's private office. His Louisiana State University diploma, Doctor of Jurisprudence from Tulane University, citations from the Governor, commendations from the local 4-H Club, the NRA, Special Olympics, etc., all shared equal billing on his wall. Pictures with governors, dignitaries and average Joes marched horizontally across the room. They vied for space with photos of wildly successful hunting and fishing trips. The sheriff led an active, non-stop life. She heard him coming.

"G'mornin' Beauty!—"

"G'morning, Sheriff. Big night, eh?—"

"Get 'em, Tiger!"

"Whoooooo, there's a pretty little package waiting for you!"

The sheriff entered his office. His presence commanded the room like a lion tamer did the center ring. He extended his hand with the breezy assurance of one who holds the whip. A big paw enveloped Karla's hand in a firm, no-nonsense clasp. On his index finger was a big LSU ring with a purple stone.

"Jimmy Watson," he said. "It's a pleasure to have you here, Karla Whitmore. My office is at your disposal." Indian tom-toms couldn't have relayed the news of her arrival any faster.

Karla had psyched herself to deal with a Hollywood stereotype Southern sheriff, a pot-bellied, bald-headed, belligerent hay seed. Sheriff Watson was about her own age, tall and powerfully built, not an ounce of flab anywhere. His eyes, the color of yesterday's coffee grounds, sized up Karla with arrogance derived from authority. His suit was gray silk and expensive. The tie had a CM monogram, a brand she'd seen on Albert's tie, so it must cost a small fortune, too.

His cowboy boots were alligator skin. The sheriff was good-looking, bold and self-assured, nothing shy in his demeanor. Karla found herself admiring him already for having stolen enough money to have the Feds come after him. The meek might inherit the earth, but the brave and daring had the use of it.

"That's a real sweetheart Mustang you've got parked out front," he said, "vintage car and in great condition, too! I have a '64 Thunderbird myself, but I haven't spent that kind of bucks on it. Mind if I look under the hood sometime?"

"Be my guest—anytime," Karla replied. For not driving a car, Albert had certainly picked a winner. The Mustang endowed her with a carefree yet sophisticated aura impossible to achieve with an unremarkable sedan. The car defined her and made a statement. Had all of that—or any of it—entered Albert's mind when he bought the Mustang Shelby? "Take it for a spin if you like."

He pushed a button on the desk intercom, asked someone to bring coffee then turned to the business at hand. "Don't be disappointed when The Azaleas doesn't sell."

"I plan to give it my best shot," Karla replied. "It'll sell. I'll make it move."

"Your best effort doesn't have diddly-squat to do with it." He bit a cigar end and spit the tip into the waste basket. "The Azaleas won't sell because Felice won't allow it."

"Ah, yes, Felice. What would happen if I took down that portrait and you stored it here until the plantation sold?"

He winced and threw up his hands in mock terror. "No way could I do that. The old gal would burn down the plantation or the courthouse or maybe both."

"Has the house burnt before?"

"Sure has. One fire took down the kitchen, if I recall correctly. Another started upstairs in a bedroom a while back when Agatha was taking in overnighters."

"Insurance purposes, maybe?"

His lips curled with amused contempt. "The Fire Marshall couldn't prove arson, if that's what you're driving at."

Karla got the message: The sheriff of West Feliciana Parish was responsible for the welfare of its citizens. A prying stranger better not step on any eggs. Feliciana life was sunny side up and no one better flip it over.

THE AZALEAS

"I understand The Azaleas' finances are touch and go. People short on money do things they wouldn't normally—"

"Like burn the place down or kill somebody?" His slow, deliberate drawl was identical to Agatha's elongated, softly curling sounds. "Don't start messin' round here with wild-flung city notions. Agatha is too old to climb a cathedral roof."

Karla had hit a nerve. The sheriff was politely warning her not to stick her nose in their closed-captioned living.

Karla back-tracked quickly—"I wasn't thinking of arson or murder—if I were in a financial jam, that Mallard bed I'm sleeping in would be the first thing I'd sell."

"Oh—the antiques—yes, of course—those blasted antiques," he warmed to the harmless subject. "My deputies prowl around guarding beds and chairs. We have a historical society here that advertises nationally, lures people to come look, invites them into the plantation houses for cake and ale, then goes hysterical if a dinner fork is missing or we can't keep the traffic flowing." He tapped Karla's arm and his fingers rested there, sending forth warm vibes.

Getting information would be a lot easier if Karla went feminine. She propped an elbow on his desk, chin on her hand and gave him a quick eyelash flutter. "Is there a survey?"

"Certainly—The Azaleas started out 4,000 acres, but big chunks have been sold over the years. It's down to 640 acres now. What more can I tell you?"

"Any leases?"

"A pasture lease to Bale Franklin— Oil rights are leased to Shell. The Tuscaloosa Trend ran underground like liquid gold until the oil bust put an end to that."

Karla hadn't the foggiest idea what he was talking about. Nobody drilled for oil in the city. "I didn't see any rigs on the place."

"Because The Azaleas retained surface rights and the drillers couldn't take one step on the property. Shell's man screwed up royally. They horizontal drilled that piece."

Karla made another quick note. *Check leases.* She took a wild stab at sounding intelligent. "Who's getting the oil lease money?"

"The lease owner, naturally—"

Naturally—"What happens when the plantation sells?"

His quick frown told Karla she'd asked an elemental question. "Those leases will be negotiated. The seller may retain the oil rights, or sell them. It's their option."

"How come you have all this valuable information about The Azaleas at your fingertips?"

He leaned across the desk, closer to Karla. "Because it's my job to know what's going on in my parish and I knew you were coming."

"That's efficient. You could never work for the NOPD. They wouldn't know 'efficient' if it hit them like a bullet between the eyes."

"Between the tourists and the housing projects, NOPD has its hands full. I like it here in the country. It's quiet and peaceful most times." Statistics bore him out. Last year, according to an industry-attracting pamphlet Karla pored over last night, West Feliciana had zero murders, two rapes, two robberies, 19 aggravated assaults and 32 burglaries. New Orleans had ten times that in one day.

"And we've got Angola Penitentiary right up the road," the sheriff said. "Eighteen hundred acres, 6,000 inmates—keeps everyone on their toes and makes them mind their p's and q's." He didn't seem the least worried that the FBI investigation might land him in Angola.

"Ever have any trouble from inmates nearby?" The proximity to the prison might have a detrimental effect on The Azaleas's value.

He horse laughed, "No way! Angola is surrounded by the Mississippi River on one side, and swamps on the other. No inmate ever escaped and lived to tell about it." He shuffled a few papers on his desk. "Here." He handed Karla a brochure advertising the 'World's Wildest Rodeo' put on by the convicts every Sunday in October. "You gonna be around next Sunday? Consider yourself my guest. This rodeo is something you won't want to miss."

"Sounds like fun." Karla replied, non-committal, reluctant to make any definite plans too far into the future.

"Well, don't get lonesome all by yourself in that big old Andrew Jackson honeymoon suite."

Jesus Christ! The place must be bugged.

"You could come keep me company," Karla replied, dimpling her cheek.

He gave her a narrow look. "Best proposition I've had all day." He glanced at the big diver's watch on his wrist with two dials and several hands. "And it's only ten o'clock."

Karla gathered up her briefcase. "See ya later."

THE AZALEAS

"No point rushing off." He came around the desk and held onto her arm.

She smiled unlimited prospects. "Right now I've got work to do. Can you point me in the direction of the clerk of court office?"

He phoned somebody. "This young lady coming over—you be sure to help her with anything she needs."

Elsa, first assistant to the clerk, showed Karla how to search the public records. Before long, Karla became engrossed in abstracting, the method of checking ownership. The registered entries identified sellers and buyers. Each document had a number, date and time of the transaction and where it was recorded—Book 356, Page 154, 3:30 p.m. With that information, the original "instrument" could be found in the courthouse archives. Each succeeding transfer connected to the previous one, link by link forming a 'chain,' back to Queen Isabella of Spain or King Louis of France.

"If it's not recorded," Elsa said, "it never happened, doesn't matter how loud they scream about oral contracts."

Karla waded through land grants, divisions and subdivisions, bankruptcies and seizures, divorces and settlements, partitions among relatives, disputed donations, and information nuggets such as surveys that began *starting at a point west of the big live oak*.

"What if the live oak is no longer there?" she asked.

"That's a surveyor's nightmare," Elsa replied. "He approximates the starting point, the neighbor contests it and the dispute goes on generation after generation. Honey, we've got reams of arguments on file."

Luckily, The Azaleas had no 'clouds.' The sell-offs were pretty forthright. Elsa described the deed as 'clean.'

Elsa couldn't be nicer. She helped Karla gather data and took her to the archives where the big over-sized books were filed in sliding racks. She showed her the number sequence, starting with '1' against the far wall all the way to 1,000 on the opposite end of the vaulted room. She made certain any document Karla needed surfaced immediately. Clerks tripped over each other to be helpful. Maps, surveys, leases, mortgages—anything Karla asked for appeared in minutes, Xeroxed and in triplicate if she wanted. Everyone jumped at her beck and call, a heady feeling. The efficiency pleased her, made her feel important.

"You have everything now," Elsa said. "The complete recorded history of The Azaleas."

"You've been very helpful." Karla thanked Elsa. "But there's a question in my mind. When Hank Turner died, the plantation was on the verge of being repossessed. There's a clear record of the debts—they amounted to $300,000 more or less. About three months after Mr. Turner's death, these debts were paid. I understand the Turners had no money. Did Danielle Turner borrow from somebody to pay the creditors?"

"Hank Turner probably had insurance."

"No, he didn't. I've checked that. He had no insurance and was penniless. The $300,000 must've come from somebody or someplace."

"Maybe he had a rich relative."

"No, I've checked that, too—only Agatha, and she's struggling to keep The Azaleas afloat. Danielle must've borrowed the money. Wouldn't there be a record of that someplace?"

Elsa cocked her head abruptly. "All I know is what's been recorded. It isn't recorded, it doesn't exist." Phones were ringing and office machines clattered. "Let me catch that phone. I'll be right back." She hurried away.

"Could you help me here—" Karla asked a clerk. The woman walked quickly past, shunning Karla as if she'd developed leprosy. Incredible how one phone call, one measly little phone call— "Where's Elsa?"

"Gone to lunch," the girl at the counter said.

Someone with capital P power had put an instant stop to Karla's research. The sheriff or the clerk of court— only they could do that. She hadn't met the clerk of court, so that pinned the tail on the sheriff. Earlier, Jimmy Watson had been very agreeable. What or who changed his mind? Karla mulled the situation, retracing events of the last hour. The frosty air blew in when she asked where the $300,000 to pay the debts came from. Now didn't seem a good time to pursue the matter, but she'd certainly be back later.

If the sheriff wouldn't cooperate, somebody else would. She gathered the maps, leases, plats and copy of deeds and stuffed the documents into the briefcase. The papers' physical feel gave her confidence. She wasn't striking in the dark any more. She had something to go on and lots of work and research to do. She needed an overnight education in real estate. God, there wasn't enough time. She'd never make the deadline—three days gone already and no buyer in sight. No white hat coming over the horizon galloping to her rescue, riding a white horse with saddle bags filled with money.

What made Albert ever think she'd be able to do this? He might as well have sent her to NASA and told her to become an astronaut. The odds of Karla reaching the moon or selling the plantation were about equal.

Nothing more could she do in this deserted bunker where everyone had conveniently disappeared. No point fighting City Hall. Like Auntie Emmy always said, 'there's more'n one way to skin a cat.'

What she needed was a sharper blade.

CHAPTER 8

Preacher Frank dragged his feet like a balking mule when they headed back to the Mustang. He clamped the promised El Trellis cigar between his toothless gums, puffed his cheeks and blew. His grumble came through the smoke ring. "I gots my own works to do—" he groused under his breath, loud enough for Karla to hear, deep enough for her not to understand.

"What's that?"

"I done brung you to the cotehouse—"

"Okay. I get it." They'd made a bargain. He'd brought her to Sheriff Watson, fulfilled his part. Bale Franklin and The Hills on Thompson Creek were beyond his call of duty.

"I ain't getting' mixed up in this and I's got work to do and now the whole mornin' is gone and prob'ly afternoon, too, and I reckon Miz Agatha, she's lookin' for me and when she cain't find me nowhere there'll be hell to pay."

Karla made a U-turn on Freeland Road, drove him back to The Azaleas, and returned to The Hills alone.

The Hills wasn't for the meek in spirit or the poor in pocketbook. The clubhouse, grounds and mansions overlooking the golf course reeked money. The place had an attitude.

THE AZALEAS

The Clubhouse Grill, a stratosphere away from the Parrot Bar, lacked the comforting smell of stale beer. The furniture and fixtures were smooth and polished, not damp and sticky. A black man with a cotton head wiped glasses behind the counter. "What'll it be?" he asked in a clipped voice lacking Southern drawl.

"Margarita straight up—salt on the rim—"

"A woman who knows her mind," He removed a frosted glass from the refrigerator, placed it upside down in a shallow salt box and gave it a twirl.

"Where you from?—" Karla asked.

"Bermuda," he replied. "Prettiest little island in the whole wide world. And you?"

Karla licked salt and smacked her lips. "New Orleans."

"What brings you to The Hills?" He gave her a keen look. "Not golfing, I gather."

"You gather right. I couldn't hit a little white ball sober or drunk. I'm here to sell The Azaleas."

"Oh, so you're the one."

News sure spread quickly in these parts. "Beauty at the courthouse told me I could find Bale Franklin here. Is he on the golf course?"

"Wonder Boy Franklin doesn't have time for golf. He's at the new site," and in answer to Karla's quizzical look, explained, "The boss is on the other side, past the 18th green where the hotel is going up."

"Okay if I walk over and find him?"

"Mon, yah!—He needs a pretty lass to interrupt his day. He never stops working—always going from one thing to another like he's driven by the devil himself." He pointed toward the door. "Go out, take a right and follow the bluff."

Karla placed $5 on the counter. "That cover it?—"

He slid the bill back. "First one is on the house."

A bulldozer groaned and rumbled at a distance. Karla walked through a pine thicket that smelled like the bottled Pine-Oil disinfectant she bought in the supermarket, only not as concentrated. The scent was milder, refreshing. A dinosaur backhoe tracked back and forth, beep-beep-beeping, yellow jaws opening and biting the earth, swinging right, left, spitting dirt, building an artificial mountain. Bobcats moved like bright orange beetles, their blades flattening and shaping the earth, motors droning background static.

Karla emerged from the pine woods into a cleared area where the sun bore down without mercy on the upturned earth. The heat rose in shimmering waves, bouncing on the tin hard hats, bright against the eyes.

She stood longer than necessary, watching the dozer operator wrestle the raw land, transforming it into his vision, the way a Quarter potter turned clay into a graceful urn or a sculptor chiseled stone into form. The medium was different; the creative force, the same.

Abruptly, the machine's rumble and growling stopped. A man climbed from the cat seat and sprinted toward her. He was tall and angular, an Olympic runner. *Adonis in khaki pants and dust covered boots—* Nearer, Karla saw his rugged, sun-baked face, skin leathery and crisscrossed with squint lines. The sunglasses hid his eyes but not his boyish grin. "Can I help you?"

"That depends."

A blue truck with a gun rack over the back seat and a Confederate flag across the rear window slowed down. The driver tossed a drink can and the bulldozer man snatched it mid-air. "Depends on what?" he asked, removing a heavy canvas glove from his right hand. The fingers yanking the can's metal tab were big and freckled. A fizzy spray shot into the air.

"On whether you're Bale Franklin or not—" Karla plucked a business card from the case supplied by Albert. "The bartender said he's out here somewhere." Her gaze traveled beyond the heavy equipment, looking for a white shirt and tie, an executive in charge. "I'd like to talk with him." The bulldozer operator slipped the card into his shirt pocket without looking at it. "Aha. The seller of The Azaleas—" The whole town had the scoop, so his knowing didn't come as any big surprise to Karla. "I'm Bale Franklin. Sheriff said you'd be looking for me."

The communication pipe line stunned Karla. Nothing comparable existed in the Quarter, and the city was brash and quick. "What do you have in this parish? Instant messaging at Internet speed?—May I have a word with you?"

"Well," he answered brusquely, "you're not going to talk to me in this scorching heat." At twelve noon, the sun like an unerring pile driver pounded the shadows straight into the ground. "Let's go to the clubhouse." He raised crossed arms and in response to his chopping motion, men stopped the big machines—lunch break.

Karla followed him to his truck and got in. He moved a holstered pistol from the seat and placed it on the dashboard under dusty blue print rolls.

"Is that gun loaded, Mr. Franklin?" She asked, buckling the seat belt. She'd been much too close to a zinging bullet recently.

"No formality here. It's Bale to you, and you can relax. I'm not going to shoot you and have Jimmy Watson put me behind bars for life. Nothing would please him more, but I'm not giving him the satisfaction."

She put that last remark in her mental microscope, hoping to enlarge and dissect the words, turn them into something she could understand. Did this rhubarb between Bale and the sheriff have anything to do with the phone call that put an abrupt ending to the clerk of court's cooperation? Obviously the two men had spoken. Bale had expected her. "Why would the sheriff want to lock you up?"

"Greed—life's greatest motivator."

"And I thought it was revenge."

"A close second—" At the clubhouse he said to the waiter who snapped to attention, "Charlie, take Miss Whitmore to my table while I clean up a bit."

The dining room was empty. The boss's table next to a window overlooked the ninth green and the woods beyond, a bucolic view. A framed, matted, *numbered* Audubon print—a wild turkey canted forward ready to gobble crumbs—hung on the wall. A pink rose nosegay centered the white linen tablecloth.

The sheriff and Bale Franklin had a problem. Greed, Bale said—what kind of greed?—Sheriff Watson wanted The Hills?—the golf course?—the hotel?—the money?—prestige? Franklin didn't have a wife, so it couldn't be woman trouble. They both seemed perfectly okay guys, but who better than Karla knew that looks could be deceiving.

Bale returned in a few minutes. He'd splashed water on his face and head. The unruly cowlicks and curls were damp.

"Would you like a drink?" he asked.

Too much drinking addled the brain, and Karla had already had one Margarita. She needed to be sharp, keep her purpose in mind and not let distractions side-track her.

Bale shrugged at her hesitation. "Mind if I smoke?" pulling a Marlboro pack from his pocket and wiping his forehead with a shirt sleeve, all in one motion. He had Band-Aids wrapped around two knuckles and a thin dirt line under his fingernails. His hands were rough and calloused, working man's hands.

"This sun will blister you dead." He leaned across the table. He smelled earthy, woods and swamps and honest sweat. "Nothing is secret in this beautiful antebellum community." His wide-set green eyes reminded Karla of Sir Gato's. "The dossier on Karla Whitmore is on the street."

"Amazing— I've been here three days."

"These people are fast. Three days is more than enough time for them to ambush and destroy—" sounded as if he talked from personal experience.

"And why would anyone want to do that?"

"Because you're messing around with Felice's house—"

"Oh bullshit!—sorry!—"

His laughter drowned her apology "My sentiments exactly." He reached across the table and rubbed the butterfly on Karla's shoulder. His fingertips had a rough, sandpaper feel. She didn't move, enjoying the touch. "So," he asked, "Have you sold any other plantation with ghosts roaming about?"

"Nope—first one—and I don't believe in ghosts."

"Felice will make you a believer."

Karla shook her head. Straggling curls brushed her face. "Just let her try."

The waiter set down a big water glass for Bale and a Margarita.

"I didn't order—"

The waiter pointed over his shoulder to the man behind the bar. "Peter sent it."

"You'll have to settle for a sandwich," Bale said. "The dining room isn't open for lunch. What would you like?"

"Hamburger—"

"Usual for me, Charlie—tell the kitchen to cook some sweet potato fries. They're excellent."

When the burgers came, both reached for the ketchup. "You first," he said and watched as Karla turned the bottle upside down and shook it.

THE AZALEAS

A kinship existed among folks who slathered ketchup. They gave notice to the world that no matter how rich, intellectual, famous, or notorious they became, they didn't stray far from their gastronomical roots. They would never, *ever* give up ketchup for soy, sesame, jalapeno or extra virgin anything.

Bale ate with gusto, taking big bites and energetically working his jaws. He got right down to business. "You know Rainbow Corporation holds a $300,000 mortgage on The Azaleas."

That's where the money came from! "It's not on record at the courthouse."

"Maybe you missed it. The payment is due upon Danielle Turner's death."

"I went through every scrap of paper—all the way back to the land grants—no Rainbow mortgage."

He raised a quirky eyebrow not agreeing nor disagreeing, letting the silence hang between them. He had the wait-and-see attitude of a cat who knew eventually the mouse must emerge from its hole.

Karla said, "And if there is a debt, Mary Bravelle will pay off the mortgage."

Bale called Karla's bluff. "With what?—Frequent flyer miles?"

Karla used her recently acquired knowledge. "This isn't the first time the Turners have come to this crossroad. When Hank Turner died, the bank was ready to foreclose."

"That's right. Agatha convinced Danielle Turner to use Hank's life insurance money to rescue the plantation from the creditors."

"Ah! But there was no life insurance. I've checked and double-checked that. The question is where did Danielle get $300,000 to settle debts if there was no life insurance?"

Bale shrugged and looked away.

"And how did Rainbow take a mortgage on a property so debt-ridden it was on the verge of repossession? Obviously, the money to pay off the bank came from Rainbow Corporation, but that transaction is not in the courthouse records. Did the corporation take advantage of a poor widow?" Karla asked not very convincingly because hard as she tried, she had no sympathy for Danielle Turner or her daughter. She changed tactics. "You need to buy The Azaleas and make it a part of The Hills. You've nowhere to expand except across the creek into Turner land."

"And pay through the nose when I'm this far—" he marked off an inch with thumb and forefinger, "of buying The Azaleas from Rainbow Corporation for ten cents on the dollar?" The hard look in the green eyes left no doubt Bale Franklin could turn screws without mercy when the opportunity arose.

"It'll never come to that," Karla replied. "I'll sell The Azaleas before the end of the month." At times when her mouth went into gear, she astonished even herself.

He threw back his head and laughed. "Sure, you will. And I believe in fairy tales, too."

She'd show him. By god, she'd show the cocky bastard. He didn't have the deed to this plantation in his back pocket yet. "Does Mary Bravelle know about this existing mortgage?"

Bale shrugged. "If she's the estate executor she'll learn about it soon enough."

"Does Agatha know?"

"Haven't you figured it out yet? We can have no secrets in the Felicianas."

Bale Franklin, developer of golf courses, residential subdivisions, shopping malls, hotels and office buildings had amassed more wealth than Karla had ever seen in her lifetime. Yet those riches didn't make him a happy man. What else was he after? "Would owning The Azaleas make you happy?"

"Not particularly. It would even an outstanding score."

"What would you do with the house?"

"Bulldoze that sucker." He saw the stricken expression on Karla's face. "The house is run down, termite infested and ready to fall apart."

The cold assessment stripped The Azaleas of its curtains, furniture, lamps; rugs. It negated the gentility enveloping the rooms, erased the Southern charm and left the plantation naked under the hot sun like a skeleton picked clean by buzzards.

He asked abruptly, "How about a ride through the woods to the property? You can get a first-hand view of the land. I've got Angus grazing on The Azalea pastures. I'll show you where the roads will go, one main boulevard with cul-de-sacs to the right and left—"

Appalling prospect, but Karla kept her thoughts to herself. "Let me get the surveys and maps from my car."

THE AZALEAS

At H&B, Gloria had a file cabinet crammed with maps. Under her supervision Karla had done nothing but study maps for one whole month. Gloria said a map was a real estate agent's best tool. It anchored one's vision, gave perspective to distances and form to the contours. Surveys gave boundaries, streams, fences, drainage ditches and right-of-ways. Section maps, one mile square, pinpointed properties and owners. Tobins, green with a thousand little red swirls described the soils, oil deposits, water levels. Highway maps placed cities, towns and distances in between. Each was useful in its own important way.

Bale walked through the clubhouse and Karla followed. This man would buy The Azaleas only if manipulated. She'd have to jam him into a corner where the only way out was to sign a check.

They skirted a swimming pool where three buoyant bodies floated like fishing corks. The hot sun made the water drops on their tanned backs sparkle like rhinestones. On the tennis court, a white-clad foursome lobbed glowing orange balls back and forth through the sluggish heat. Bale Franklin and Karla followed a gravel lane skirting the golf course, the land a green ocean gently rising along Thompson Creek bank, dipping into the hollows, dissolving into the pine thickets. Through the trees, Karla caught glimpses of white mansions tucked away in the privacy only money could buy.

The pickup bumped and rattled as they crossed over furrows no longer planted. Karla unrolled a survey and held it open on her lap, her finger tracing their progress across its surface. The property ran rectangular on the east boundary, then dog-legged into an L. They traveled parallel to a five-strand barbed wire fence in good condition.

The fiery afternoon sun edged silver the leaves, the grass, the lily pads on the pond. The warm landscape turned into a gilt-spattered painting.

Karla glanced surreptitiously at Bale Franklin. He had a determined set to his mouth. Thick, yellow eyebrows met above a hawk nose. A frown carved a straight furrow across his wide forehead. His arm accidentally touched hers. She edged closer to her door, away from imminent danger. Never again would a man sap her energy or divert her steps. The path before her was straight and narrow.

"All these cows belong to you?" she asked. Cows cooled themselves in shallow ponds, their reflections wavering in the brown water; lolled in green pastures, white egrets at their feet; stood still as statues in the shade of spreading oaks. They were big, intimidating creatures. The only animals Karla understood were small ones—dogs, cats and parakeets—people pets. On Sundays when she ran in Audubon Park, she cut across the zoo and saw caged monkeys, lions, zebras, but no cows.

Bale surveyed his peacefully grazing herd. "Black Angus—good beef cattle— I've increased the herd to five hundred. It's taken me a few years, but I finally reached the dividing line. The herd is making money—"

No wonder people called Bale Wonder Boy! Hotels, subdivisions, clubs, swimming pools, cattle! "The Hills was part of the original 4,000 acres?" Karla asked.

"I can see you're dedicated," he replied. "Yes—a 2,200 acre sell-off. I bought it after the '93 oil bust from the developers who'd acquired the tract earlier from Danielle Turner. Crude went down to $4 a barrel and everybody went bankrupt. I got the place at a bank auction. Didn't make me popular, but that's life. It was either me or somebody else. Everybody thought I was crazy putting in a golf course. When I mortgaged everything I owned to get Arnold Palmer to design it, they were convinced I was a certified loony. I needed a draw, something to attract people to the area. After the golf course was in, the place boomed. The Hills course is rated the best in Louisiana."

"And the first 1,160 acres?—"

"Way before my time—that's the site of the Feliciana Hospital, Dixon Correctional, Clinton Mental and the V.A. hospital. They're all clumped together."

"You're putting up a hotel?"

"Next phase in the master plan—"

They rode in silence across the pastures while Karla digested this new information. The pieces, somehow, had to fit together.

"And where did you come up with that number?" he asked abruptly, "Three million, my ass! What magician pulled that figure from a hat?"

Albert had determined the price for the plantation. Karla was sure he'd researched the area, ran comparables and studied the market. He was methodical. "You're the benchmark," Karla said. "You're selling an acre lot in The Hills for $60,000. Multiply that by 640 acres and what do you have?"

He looked away. He knew the answer. Not $3 million but $38 million, plus. Understandably, developing costs existed, but still when he split the land into lots he stood to make a big, big bundle.

"Wouldn't you hate for someone to come along and buy this land right out from under you?" Karla asked. "Then where would your development be? Locked up on one side of Thompson Creek— " She pushed a little. "When that happens you'll be kicking yourself and $3 million is gonna look cheap."

Gloria said that in order for a real estate transaction to take place the seller had to feel he made out like a bandit and the buyer had to think he got a steal.

"Three million never looks like chicken feed to me," Bale replied.

They were back to the math again, so far apart, the figures weren't even in the same orbit. Any further discussion would evolve into an argument. Arguments, according to Gloria, never sold anything.

Karla dropped the subject completely. They rode in silence, except for the truck rattling. They came to a big valve painted glowing orange. "What kind of gadget is that?"

"Safety valve for the gas line—See that cleared strip?" The brambles and bushes on a 50-foot wide stretch had been cut away, the grass clipped short. The lane looked like an airplane landing strip a drug dealer might carve in the middle of Nowheresville. "Gas pipe runs underneath. Nothing can be built on that ground. It's wasted land, and we'd all complain if it weren't for the royalty checks."

He stopped the truck in a shallow valley where pines grew tall and straight, forty feet. The woods were a good ten degrees cooler. The air smelled spicy like the lot on Esplanade Avenue at Christmas when it was filled with imported blue spruces and cone-shaped firs.

He climbed the truck bed and looked intently across the pasture where the black cows grazed. "Damn! Six missing!—the thirty in this pasture are scheduled for auction first thing in the morning."

The cows all looked alike. They stood still or moved in slow motion.

"You wait here. I know exactly where the missing ones have wandered to." He waved a hand toward the swamp.

According to the maps, the same dark and sinister muck that lapped at the edges of New Orleans, ran alongside the Mississippi

River and snaked through the Feliciana Parishes. The towns were built on the highest ground, the big houses on knolls. The surrounding pastures and fields eventually disappeared into the low lying swamps. Every plantation had its share of useless "bottom land."

Why would a man with so many employees personally chase after cows? A country ritual, the way city people preferred to walk their own dogs?

Bale pulled on hip waders. "I'll be gone twenty minutes. You'll be okay, city girl?"

"Can I go with you?"

"Maybe next time—you need rubber boots."

Karla watched him walk into the swamp, slush through the soft mud and disappear from sight. Twenty, thirty minutes passed. He didn't return. Karla examined dead bugs splattered on the windshield, opened the glove compartment and went through the papers, turned the ignition key and fought the urge to drive off. She got out and sat on the ground, her back against a pine tree. Forty-five minutes. Had Bale abandoned her? Did he forget her and go back to the clubhouse? She fretted and squashed bugs crawling near her feet. An ant regiment, each carrying a minuscule green snip, moved in a straight, flowing line. Two grasshoppers, chartreuse and bright—maybe they were locusts like in a Bible plague—rubbed their long green legs then jumped. A hundred creepy crawlers lived exciting lives in the green grass.

Could she find her way back? She could walk across the fields. There must be a trail or path she could follow to the clubhouse. How far?—A mile?—Two?—Ten?—Conditioned to sidewalk and block distance, miles made no sense. Ditch her in a dark alley and she could manage. Drop her in the middle of eight-lane Canal Street at rush hour and it wouldn't faze her. Send her to rub shoulders with hookers and hopheads and that was okay, too. But please don't leave her abandoned here in this endless un-trampled green space with air so sparkling and weightless it hurt her lungs.

Highway 10 wasn't that far away. She'd heard an occasional *whoosh, whoosh* of a passing car. She could make her way there, climb the fence, stand on the road and hitchhike. Somebody would stop and take her back to The Azaleas. Or she could hijack Bale Franklin's truck and let him worry.

THE AZALEAS

The quiet and emptiness of the uninhabited space made Karla aware of how much she liked crowds. What comfort she drew from anonymous people and unknown faces pressing close; from strangers touching and ignoring one another, wrapped in their private lives, living solitary traumas *en masse*. She liked arguing with a cabdriver, bartering with a fruit vendor at the Farmer's Market until he came down a dollar, looking up from the piano at the Parrot Bar and making eye-contact with a customer still sober enough to meet her gaze. A certain solace came from familiarity: diesel fumes, rotting garbage and yesterday's fish. The ear-splitting wails, the sirens and beeps of fire trucks, police cars and ambulances, all day, all night—civil servants at work for the public good. She understood city life. She liked people better than trees. Tripping across open fields like Julie Andrews in the *Sound of Music* didn't do it for her. So much open space wrapped in silence was seriously unsettling.

Had Bale stranded her on purpose? Had he disappeared like Elsa the court clerk? Gone to lunch forever? Did he want to scare her?

The relentless afternoon heat corkscrewed Karla's hair and sent sweat trickling between her breasts and down her thighs. Long shadows cast by pine trunks inched across the field.

Alone in this wilderness, not a house or another human in sight, no bar around the corner for a Margarita to bolster flagging courage—only land stretching in every direction— grass fields, pine thickets, dark green, pale green, chartreuse green reaching for blue skies. The vastness shrank her to nothing. She became nothing, no more important or necessary than a pebble, a pebble like all the other little rocks strewn on the ground around her. Never in her entire life had she been this alone.

Suddenly, as if from another planet, she heard a faint sing-song. She cocked her head and listened to the deep voices. The chant, eerie and other-worldly, brought her to her feet, heart thumping in her throat. She walked away from the soughing pines. The chant came again, sparking her already overwrought imagination. Ignoring better judgment, she ran across the open field, leaving in her wake a flattened grass trail and crushed yellow and purple wild flowers.

The chant grew clearer. The words of an old Negro spiritual were still and deep like a river current. *"I'm free. I'm free. Praise the Lord. I'm free."*

Auntie Emmy's church sang that spiritual at St. James AME. The choir sang it in the loft; the sinners sang it in the pews; those who got carried away stood and sang it, waving their hands over their heads and inviting Jesus to come down and set them free.

This unlikely choir sat on the highway shoulder, knees drawn to their chins and arms crossed behind their backs, dejection in the slumped shoulders and drooping heads.

"*I'm free—*" then a three-beat pause—how well Karla knew it! The notes vibrated in the pale wind and hung in the air the way a whispered hymn hovered over a grave long after dirt covered the coffin. "*I'm free!*"

Karla ducked behind a bush, peeking through leafy branches.

A blue van with revolving red lights and West Feliciana Sheriff written on the side was pulled to the side, rear doors flung open.

"Where's the goddamn jack?" A spare tire hit the ground with a bounce. "Sonofabitch—" The man digging flung wrenches and pliers. A white metal box with a red cross followed. The kit broke open and cotton balls spilled and caught by the breeze tumbled like snowflakes.

"Sonofabitch!" he said again.

The squatting men offered no help. They kept on singing: "*I'm free. I'm free. Praise the Lord, I'm free,*" totally disinterested in the deputy's problem.

A second deputy stood by the van without lifting a hand. He had a big gut, a silver belt buckle, a ten gallon hat, a handlebar mustache and a shotgun balanced carelessly on his shoulder. The weapon with the long shiny barrel looked like a prop on a John Wayne western. Karla pushed deeper into the protecting branches.

The six squatting men were black. One had a red bandana around his head; two wore baseball caps, two sported dread locks. The end one had an electrified Afro.

The one with the Afro jerked to one side and the other five swayed with him and the unity of their chant broke. The song lost its rhythm "*I'm free. I'm free. Praise the Lord, I'm free—*" The notes no longer in unison bobbled up and down like balloons cut loose from their tethers.

Another abrupt movement—*shackles!* Apprehension kicked Karla in the stomach. Tied together with a chain! No wonder they swayed and jerked. And handcuffs, too! Steel encircled every wrist. Convicts!

THE AZALEAS

Cool Hand Luke, alive and well, life imitating art. Go back or stay put? If she moved, the shotgun deputy would surely see her.

The deputy digging for the jack wiped his brow on his uniform sleeve. "Goddamn! Ain't no jack here, Bubba."

Bubba pulled his crotch and spit tobacco. "I reckon this new batch will have to lift the vehicle while you change the tire."

"Hell!" the other one fumed. "Use your cell phone. Call and tell them to send someone with a jack."

That seemed a reasonable plan to Karla.

Bubba gave his crotch an extra strong pull. "You forgot we're on probation, Tommy Boy? Whatcha think the sheriff's gonna say when he finds out we been drivin' all over the country with six convicts and no jack? Ain't that agin' some sort of regulation?"

"*I'm free—I'm free.*" The men didn't raise their eyes, but their shoulders shifted and their heads cocked to one side. Karla could tell their heart was no longer in the song, their interest diverted by the deputies' argument. *"Praise the Lord, I'm free."*

Deputy Bubba spun around. "You ain't free and you ain't never gonna be free, so shut yo' mouths and get up off yo' asses and lift this van." He waved the shotgun. "Now!—"

The inmates stopped singing and struggled to their feet, hunching shoulders to ears and staring at the ground as if probing for gold.

Karla held her breath so the leaves wouldn't tremble. She crouched quiet and still, eyes wide open, muscles taut, waiting. As soon as this group trucked down the highway, she'd streak quicker than a French Quarter thief back to Bale Franklin's pickup. She'd jump in and take off across the field, back to civilization. This country was much too weird for her.

The convicts hobbled and hopped about, getting to their feet. The end man, tall and bony looked like—*it couldn't be!* Karla rubbed her eyes. Was that Willis? Lebron's brother Willis sent to Angola for assault with a deadly weapon?

Not possible. Hadn't the sheriff said there were 6,000 men in Angola? There must be a hundred guys with Afros like Willis's.

"You want us to lift your van?—" Raspy voice gushing and gurgling like a bathtub draining. Auntie Emmy said Willis talked funny because he swallowed his tonsils when he was a baby. "We can do that. We can tilt it right over on its side."

Karla poked her head through the branches for a better look.

The end man took a shackled step and the other convicts teetered like bowling pins. He extended an arm. A blue snake complete with red flickering tongue coiled around his bicep. Karla clamped a hand over her mouth, stifling a shriek.

Believe it or not, her heart leapt, glad to see Willis, an old friend, maybe not her best or dearest friend, but somebody from the hood who knew the Parrot Bar; knew Sir Gato belonged to Karla; knew Ruthie walked her duck on a leash at four every afternoon; knew the PA walked the madman on a tether on sunny days; knew Central Grocery invented muffulettas. Details such as those created a bond, even if Willis had a criminal record, and she, by the grace of God and Auntie Emmy, did not.

The deputies must've been transporting the prisoners from the New Orleans jail to a permanent residence in Angola.

"Get them nuts loose, Tommy Boy," Deputy Bubba growled, his temper rising. The sun glistened on his bald head. "Time's a-wasting."

"Ain't found no lug wrench, neither." Tommy Boy took out his frustration on the van's rear door, slamming it with great force.

"Jesus!" Bubba swore.

"We can drive in on the flat." Tommy Boy was the man with the plan. If Bubba wouldn't let him call for help, then they'd limp into the station.

"Christ! And ruin the fuckin' rim? Y'know Uncle Jimmy is jus' waitin' for an excuse."

"Damn the sheriff."

Willis rasped, "Take these cuffs off and I can unscrew them lugs with my bare hands."

Bubba sneered. "How about your shackles?" he asked. "You want them off, too?"

Willis grinned and two gold stars flashed on his front teeth. "Suit yourself, man. But I'm here because that's my line of work."

Bubba spit a stream of tobacco that missed Willis by a hair. "You don't come to Angola for stealing cars."

"You know, that's the same thing I told the judge."

"I expect you shot somebody."

"Sometimes," Willis said. "Fools get in the way. You want me to take the lugs off or not?"

THE AZALEAS

The deputies put their heads together then Bubba reached in his pocket and brought out a key and walked like he was stepping on hot coals over to Willis and unlocked the handcuffs.

The shackled Willis rubbed his wrists and took a few steps toward the van, dragging the others along. He sat on the ground and put his ear to the tire like a doctor puts a stethoscope to a patient's chest. His arms and neck swelled. The horizontal muscles on his back ridged like furrows in a field. His whole body vibrated with the effort. "Damn!"

"You got it?" Bubba asked.

"Ain't budgin'—"

"Sonofabitch!—" Bubba poked Willis with the gun barrel. "You sonofabitch—"

Willis grinned and opened his hand. Karla was too far away to see. She stepped from behind the bush, crept to the barbed wire fence and leaned against a post.

Willis was at it again. His cheek hard against the tire, muscles pumped, face contorted. She saw him place the second nut in the deputy's hand, and the third, fourth.

"Now lift!" Bubba ordered.

"I ain't no superman," Willis said. "I can't lift this big van by myself."

Bubba turned to his partner. "Tommy Boy! Tommy! Come here and lend a hand. Tommy Boy! Get the hell over here!"

Tommy Boy heaved and pushed and couldn't raise the van. Willis could if he'd wanted to, Karla was sure of that. Once, in a fit of rage, he lifted the rear end of his girlfriend's Volkswagen and sent it rolling down the levee into the Mississippi. Maybe his adrenalin wasn't pumping. Maybe he wasn't mad enough to lift this van.

The tire-changing operation was at an impasse. The van rested on three good tires and sagged where the fourth went flat. Tommy Boy and Bubba cussed the convicts. The convicts stared back at them, a blank look in their eyes as if the deputies were talking Swahili and they understood not a word.

"You goddamn sonofabitch, you'd better put on that spare or I'll see to it you go straight to the hole," Bubba said.

Willis went from neighborhood bully to teenage delinquent. His reputation as a tough, mean dude with a hot temper and a quick switch-blade outgrew the Quarter streets and entered the data base of national computers. It wasn't a good idea to push or threaten him. "Change the fuckin' tire yourself," he said.

Bubba spun on one heel. "Say again?"

And Willis repeated each word clearly. "Change the fuckin' tire yourself."

Bubba smashed the side of Willis's head with the rifle butt. The black man staggered and raised his hands. His knees buckled. The convict shackled behind Willis grabbed him under the armpits, holding him upright. The panicked line came apart. The men cringed and swung their handcuffed arms, short, jerky motions. They barked quick, sharp yelps like the dogs in the Quarter when a sidewalk washer turned a high pressure hose on them.

"Now move! Move it!" Bubba yelled.

The convicts couldn't move unless the entire gang moved. Willis weighed a ton, as though consciousness was the water that kept his body buoyant and when it went, all his lightness evaporated. The men wrestled with Willis as the line struggled forward, an awkward operation, shackled as they were, and one dead weight among them.

Bubba grabbed Willis by the hair, his white hand like a bleached spider tangled in the wiry Afro. He snapped Willis's head back then gave it a shove.

Barbarian!—Big macho dude with a badge and a gun, hitting men who couldn't strike back. Willis's head hung down on his chest. Had the deputy broken Willis's neck? Bastard had no right—Karla would report him to the proper authorities immediately.

The deputy yanked Willis's arms behind Willis's back. When the steel handcuffs snapped, something went off in Karla's head, a panic that came to her at night sometimes, a dream, a rising terror, a fury that awakened her.

Before she drew a second angry breath, she had scaled five strands of barbed wire and catapulted over the fence. She heard her jeans rip when she belly-flopped into the scummy roadside ditch. The impact took her breath. Shitty tasting muck filled her mouth and nose. She raised her head, dripping slime, gasping for air.

Convicts and deputies froze. They stared at Karla as if she were the creature from the Black Lagoon.

"You fascist pig!—" Karla spit green saliva. "You have no right to—"

THE AZALEAS

Bubba recovered quickly. "What we got here?" He smiled slow and ugly. "A nigger lover?—" He drew near, a menacing swagger to his steps.

By rushing into the inmates' space, Karla had added a new dimension to their danger, their fate.

Tommy Boy came to his senses and hollered at Bubba. "Goddamit!—Ain't we got enough troubles already? Get back in the van before we get into some real fuckin' shit."

"Let me see if I can help this little bitch—"

Cold perspiration dampened Karla's forehead. Bubba should've never in his sorry life called her a bitch. Man, oh, man he made a mistake. A big mistake—

"What's your badge number? Who's your boss? If you killed this man, I'll report you to the sheriff—"

"Yeah?—Whatcha think Uncle Jimmy's gonna do? Fire me?"

"I'll sic the ACLU on you." She jabbed a finger in his face. "These prisoners have rights—"

Bubba grabbed Karla's arm in a crushing grip and twisted it behind her back, a practiced move. "Rights, my ass—"

"Let me go!"

"Jesus, Bubba! Turn her loose!" Tommy Boy yelled as he prodded the convicts with his steel-toe boot. "C'mon now— Get back in the van."

The chained men, Bubba and his shotgun, the van and the barbed wire fence—the entire surroundings took on a surreal *Star Wars* aspect.

Bubba twisted Karla's arm harder and leaned into her face. "You're a purty lil' thing," he leered. "You know that?"

"You heard your partner! Turn me loose!"

Bubba jerked Karla so hard her feet left the ground. "Where'n hell you come from?"

Karla clamped her jaw so he wouldn't hear her teeth clattering. "From The Azaleas—"

That got his attention and he let go with a shove that sent her sprawling. "You the one selling Miss Agatha's place?—"

Goddamn! Everybody knew! Was she the talk of the prison, too? Did the inmates make bets on the sale?

"Yes, I'm the one. And I'm checking the fences. The contingencies state that the fences be in good repair—"

"I don't give crap what your con...con...whatever— say. I don't wanna see you by this fence when I come by here again." Bubba's badge and hardware empowered the arrogant bastard.

"This is The Azaleas' fence and I'm perfectly within my rights to be on Azalea ground," Karla looked away so he wouldn't see panic in her eyes.

With the exception of the slumped Willis, every man looked over his shoulder. They hung on every word Bubba and Karla exchanged, as though their life depended on the outcome.

"C'mon!" Tommy Boy viciously kicked the end man, "Get in the van!"

Bubba backed off, leaving Karla shaking in her Nikes. Her twisted arm dangled painfully. Her thigh burned. A red stain spread slowly across her jeans.

On the roadside, the van sat lopsidedly like a beached whale. The highway carved a gray scar through the pines. Not another vehicle in sight. Not one living soul coming to the rescue. This would never happen in the city. The least provocation and a crowd instantly circled the casualty.

The convicts were back in the tilted van, waiting. The deputies stopped arguing when a pickup came around the curve. Bubba stepped into the road and flagged down the driver. A young boy jumped out and said right off the bat, "I weren't speedin'."

"Going ninety, at least," Bubba snarled.

"Aw, gee! Are you gonna give me a ticket?"

"I should, but lend me a hand here and we'll see."

With such incentive it was only a matter of minutes before the boy brought over a jack, shoved it under the van and mounted the spare. The van and truck drove away, disappeared round the curve, leaving Karla abandoned by the highway. What the hell was she doing here?

The phone vibrated against her hip. Her leg smarted and oozed blood. When was the last time she had a tetanus shot? She could become paralyzed and foam at the mouth. No, that was rabies. Tetanus turned your leg green and doctors cut it off. No, no. That was gangrene. Her fingers closed around the cell tickling her hip. "Hello?"

"Hi, Karla—"

Crap! Albert! Who needed Albert now?

"You must return to the city right away."

"What's tetanus?"

"A shot for lockjaw—any particular reason for asking?"

Karla clutched her jaw with one hand and worked her face about and the muscles moved properly. "Albert, you won't believe this. A prison chain gang just went by and the deputy hit Willis—"

"Hold it! Hold it! Who's Willis?"

"Lebron's brother. The one doing time in Angola. The deputy hit him on the head and I think he killed him. The others dragged him along, unconscious. I've never seen anything like it. I'm bleeding—"

"Calm down! Calm down." A whistling break in his deep, resonant voice— "Are you hurt?"

"I'm by the north fence and this crazy deputy—so I jumped—tore my leg—"

"My God, woman, what are you doing way out there?"

"Well, you see—"

"Listen to me. Get yourself back to the plantation. Have a doctor look at your leg, then return to the city."

Abandon ship? Not now. Not when she'd been to the front lines. Not with a possible buyer in her clutches. "I can't. I have a hot prospect. He's gone to—" Where had Bale disappeared to? "He went into the swamp and said he'd be right back, but he's been gone two hours maybe three and he's still in that awful place filled with alligators and deadly mosquitoes and—"

Albert cut her short. "Get a grip. Those country boys know how to get around in the swamp. Should I send someone for you?"

"No, no. I'm all right." Her thigh throbbed. She smelled like sewer. The whirling dervish inside her brain wanted to howl and scream and disconnect her employer, but she didn't dare. "I'm not leaving."

"You must. A problem has arisen."

"So? Don't you take care of everything? Take care of whatever has come up!"

"If you don't return voluntarily, I shall come get you."

"What in heaven's name for? Leave me alone and let me do my job." Prolonged silence at his end of line—the man had gone mute. "Are you there?"

"I'm here." Calm and in control—

"Leave early in the morning, and you'll arrive by noon." The terse voice left no room for arguments. "Do you understand? Is that clear?"

Why bother to answer? He held all the aces. He'd get his way in the end.

"Am I fired?" Karla aimed for defiant and got pitiful.

"Temporarily suspended—"

"Why?" Her ticket out of poverty torn in half—"I can do it. I swear, Albert. It's in the bag." She stopped herself. Damned if she'd beg. She survived before this gig, and she'd live after it ended. "Okay. I'll drive back to the city. No big deal."

CHAPTER 9

The note slipped under Karla's apartment door, written in Albert's left-handed slant said Windsor Court High Tea, 4:30 p.m.

Karla's guard went up. If Albert wanted to talk to her, the invitation wouldn't be to the ritziest place in New Orleans. They'd be meeting on a park bench in Jackson Square. She had half a mind to shock Albert by sashaying into that swanky tea and crumpet palace in tank top and jeans, but passed on the idea because "not proper attire" would get her turned away at the door by a snooty maître d' waving white gloves and speaking in a fake French accent.

She left the apartment at four. Initially, she borrowed a dress from Mimi since they were both size 8, but changed her mind, wanting something not tacky and better than Goodwill. She'd seen the red taffeta dress with the low-cut bodice and the long, tight sleeves in Lord & Taylor's window. The dress reminded her of Felice's brocade gown.

"For my niece," she told the sales girl. "If it doesn't fit, I'll return it tomorrow."

She paid with Whitmore Realty Expense Account check. She'd put the money back in the morning. Albert would never know.

Mimi had worked her magic. She'd hot-ironed Karla's curls into soft waves and painted and powdered her face as if she were a movie star. "Now, remember, sweetie, shoulders back, head held high.

You're as good as anybody there and ten times prettier." Karla had never been to Windsor Court. "Good luck."

The hotel had valet parking, but she didn't trust those dudes with her Mustang, so she circled the block three times and finally found a space in front of Mother's Diner and poked her head in there and asked Mother to keep an eye on the hubcaps. Eight quarters guaranteed two hours. That should be time enough for this gig.

When the doorman wearing red livery opened the door, her stomach muscles tightened. Entering the Windsor Court lobby was like traveling to another dimension, a rarified stratosphere, unfamiliar elegance. Two hundred white roses in a footed urn sat on a marble table in the foyer. She felt a petal—soft, velvety, *real*.

Anxiety rose from her gut to her brain. Remembering Mimi's advice, she pretended to balance a heavy dictionary on her head. Mimi said that particular stance gave one "presence," and Lord knew at this moment, as she approached the gilded cage filled with wealthy strangers who demanded good service and tipped well, she needed all the presence she could muster.

Albert always the cool, debonair one, dropped his jaw when he saw Karla. If his teeth had been false, they would've fallen out. He recovered quickly, instantly on his feet, nodding to the hostess, taking Karla's arm, drawing her toward the table where Mary Bravelle sat.

Mary wore a little black number set off by a zebra-striped sling cradling her injured arm. She looked as if she belonged on the cover of Vogue or Elle. Her Parisian flair came easy and natural, at home in the Tea Room. 'It's all in the quality and the cut," Madam Costeau, who owned a tailor shop in the French Quarter preached. 'And the right balance with the accessories.' Translucent makeup repaired any pallor caused by Mary's recent mishap. Sometimes when Karla walked through Lakeside Shopping Mall on her way to Family Dollar for a cheap lipstick, she lingered over glass cases home to Estee, Renee, Helena and Chanel. The vials and disks, pale green, pink, blue, liquid, pressed or powdered, smelling of money, could transform a toad into a princess.

"Hello." Mary greeted Karla. "Nice to see you—how are you?"

"Okay, I guess," Karla replied, gathering the rustling red Lord & Taylor dress around her. "How's your arm?"

"Dr. Benson said couple of weeks—good as new."

THE AZALEAS

The waitress approached. "Is everyone in your party here now?" She offered tea choices ranging from ordinary Earl Grey to imported Chinese. *Eenie meenie minie moe*—Karla picked something Indian. The waitress returned with individual porcelain teapots. She poured the tea through a little silver strainer into cups so thin the light shown through them. She went through the one-lump, two-lump routine. Mary's pinkie shot straight when she lifted her cup. Karla started to follow suit, thought better of it, and hugged the cup as if it were a mug.

"You look lovely, my dear," Albert said.

The dazzled look on Albert's face made the form-fitting outfit worth every dollar. Karla couldn't decide whether his gaze lingered longer on her boobs or on the leg showing through the slit in the skirt. The stilettos had little red straps—sexy.

Rattling the old fart lifted her spirits. Nice to discover he wasn't the iceberg he pretended to be. "Thank you." She hooked the borrowed necklace with one thumb and ran her tongue over the smooth, cool beads.

Albert couldn't pull his eyes away. "Nice pearls."

On a need-to-know basis, she had no reason to share with Albert that Mimi had lent her the pearls—real ones—her merchant marine husband, Bilbao, won in a crap game in Hong Kong.

"How's the injury?" Albert asked.

Polite inquiry or did he really care? What did he want with her? "Ten stitches. It'll leave a scar," Karla answered, reaching down and pulling up her skirt. "You want to see?"

His hand restrained her. "Not right now," he answered, face serious as a tombstone, eyes doing a tap dance.

"Totally horrible!—a chain gang!—I recognized Willis! When the deputy hit him with the butt of his shotgun, I lost it." She leaned forward eagerly. "Albert, you can find out if he is dead, can't you?"

Albert didn't laugh or blow off her concern. "I'll make a few calls."

"Thank you. Willis is Lebron's brother, you know."

"You told me," he replied.

"Can I visit Willis?"

"Are you kin?—"

"Kissin' cousins—"

His lower lip pulled down, holding back a smile. "Five days in the country has done marvels for you. Wouldn't you agree, Mary?"

"Lovely," Mary replied. Secure in her lofty position, she could afford to be generous. "You've met Agatha?"

"Yes—and Preacher Frank, and the staff, the sheriff, the house guest and half the town."

"What house guest?" Mary asked. Albert made no comment, giving Karla the inkling that he already knew the man was there.

"Roger Randall. He's writing an Audubon book. He stays in the Jefferson Davis room. And I'm in the Andrew Jackson suite, living a Scarlet O'Hara dream." Karla's giggle provoked a smile from Albert.

"Has Agatha been cooperative?" Mary asked.

"She hasn't jumped through hoops, but we've managed. Everyone was upset that you didn't come after the funeral."

"I have no reason or interest in visiting The Azaleas."

"They're your kinfolk." Southerners put a lot of emphasis on kin, but Mary seemed to have cut all ties with her father's family. "And Pierre seemed anxious to go. You own the place."

"Not for long, I hope."

Mary had everything her heart desired. Karla had nothing. Mary had Albert's full attention in a way that Karla did not. Karla had to struggle to overcome and neither Mary nor Albert had any idea the pain and agony caused by the daily battle for survival. Karla swallowed her dislike for the owner of The Azaleas. "The plantation is a magnificent place," Karla said. "And I have a good prospect."

Mary lifted thick black lashes. "Who?—"

"A neighbor, Bale Franklin—" The name caused a fear to leap into Mary's eyes. She looked quickly at Albert, then away.

Albert, quiet and studious, head cocked to one side, said nothing. Karla thought he would've liked his pipe, but smoking wasn't allowed. After the mention of Bale Franklin, Mary clammed up. Her silence spoke volumes.

The waitress set a silver tray of miniature sandwiches—watercress, cream cheese, cucumber—little squares of exotic delight with no bread crust.

The surrounding people laughed and talked and clinked silverware, soft waves that lapped at the edges of Albert's table. The longer Karla munched on a tidbit, waiting for Albert or Mary to say something, the more resentful she grew. Why drive all the way here

THE AZALEAS

to sit in this uncomfortable blank space?—Silence spreading like a cancer—what the hell was Albert thinking?

Restraint took tremendous effort and Karla honestly tried, forcing herself to sit and say nothing, a nothing growing bigger and bigger, filling the space under her rib cage, swelling her lungs until she felt the lift of her breasts, and finally, unable to hold *nothing* in any longer, she burst out, "So what's going on, Albert?"

"We'll talk business later, my dear."

"Not later! Now! I don't have time for later! You do know a certain Rainbow Corporation holds a first mortgage payable upon Danielle's Turner's death? As we speak, they're juggling paperwork." Karla turned to Mary. "Did your mother have life insurance?"

She shook her head, negative.

"It takes ninety days to foreclose." The lawyer said and he should know. "You'll have the plantation sold before then." The confidence in his voice was scary. Unless Bale Franklin came through, Karla's chances of finding a buyer were about as good as her winning the national lottery.

"Did you know about the mortgage?" Karla asked.

"Not until yesterday," replied Albert. "That was one reason I wanted you to come."

"Heaven's sake!—you could've told me over the phone! Anyhow, I already knew about the mortgage. How come you didn't? I thought you were Danielle Turner's lawyer."

"Jeremiah Jones took care of that particular transaction," he said, poker-faced, not giving away any clues.

"Your mother was told the $300,000 she received upon your father's death was life insurance money, right Mary?"

"Yes— and Aunt Agatha bullied Mama into paying off the bank."

"So, Albert, here's the hitch. When Hank Turner died he had no insurance. When Hasker and Blount had The Azaleas for sale there was no mortgage on record. I checked every entry in the entire courthouse and as of this morning there was no recorded lien against The Azaleas. Elsa herself told me, 'if it's not recorded, it didn't happen.'"

"You missed it. It's there now."

"It can't be!"

"But it is"—

"Did you know anything about that, Mary?"

"No, I don't know."

Karla didn't want to believe her, but she did. Mary was shy and reticent, head always ducked a little to one side as if to avoid a striking hand. She was beautiful, elegant and well-bred and at one time in her life she'd been hurt badly. She was afraid of somebody, or something, or maybe afraid of life. Sometimes it took extreme courage just to live through the day.

Albert said. "I have a copy of Rainbow's incorporation papers. The partners are Bale Franklin and James Watson."

"*What?*"

"Franklin and Watson—the developer and the sheriff—a touchy situation— I brought you back to discuss strategy."

The two most influential men in West Feliciana Parish sitting back, biding their time, waiting to legally steal the plantation! How they must've laughed behind Karla's back, leading her around, toying with her, answering her dumb questions, telling her nothing! The very idea! Ambitious, untrustworthy bastards! She'd show them!

"Unless Franklin and Watson buy The Azaleas outright, the only way they'll get their mitts on this plantation is over my dead body."

"That's the spirit!" Albert said enthusiastically.

A waitress brushed the crumbs around Karla's plate into a miniature silver dust pan.

"We could've talked on the phone," Karla insisted. "Have you forgotten you equipped me with a super deluxe Sky Pager that can reach me underwater if necessary?"

"I thought it best to discuss our business in person." His eyes lingered on Karla's scowling face, a long, languorous look that almost made her think he was smitten, vanity on her part. "The police have made some headway in finding out who shot Mary."

"Yeah?—" Big deal—"who—?" Right now Karla greatly regretted that the killer had been such a poor shot. "And how about Lebron?—is it important to find out who shot Lebron?"

"One of the college students arrested confessed that a man promised to pay their beer tab if they created a distraction. A practical joke on a friend, the man said—seemed harmless enough to the college kids. Free beer—a big bonus they hadn't counted on. Like the boy said, a win-win situation until the shooting started."

"Wait, wait—wait! What man paid those boys to create a disturbance? Do the police know who?"

THE AZALEAS

"They're coming up with a composite. They'll find him."

"And Mary was accidentally in the line of fire? That doesn't compute. Somebody wants her out of the way—any idea who, Mary?"

"No."

"Maybe—" Karla spoke slowly, watching Mary's face for any reaction—"Bale Franklin."

The little muscles around Mary's eyes tightened and her fine nostrils flared slightly. "Who?—"

Come now! Mary had to do better than that. A man with a legal claim to her inheritance couldn't be forgotten as easily as that.

"Bale Franklin, the neighbor—Remember him? He's the one that hung around The Azaleas all the time when you were young."

"I don't even know that man." Her face gave her away. She was a lousy liar.

"How about Aunt Agatha?—you think she'd shoot you over The Azaleas?"

Albert sat back staring into space and let Karla turn the screws.

"I hardly think Aunt Agatha would resort to murder to keep The Azaleas," Mary replied.

"Have the cops found the sniper?" Karla asked.

"What do you think?" Albert replied.

"Truthfully?—I think Mary knows lots more than she's letting us know. I believe she does have information she's keeping under wraps, not sharing. The only one in the dark around here is me, and frankly, for the record, if anybody is keeping a record, I resent that."

Mary protested. "Oh, dear, that is unfounded—"

"Albert, do you remember the man taking pictures of the tourists? He had his camera on the sidewalk, Jackson Square and the cathedral in the background, so those tourists could take the picture home and tell their friends, 'See, there I am in New Orleans.'"

A quick light came into the cool, gray eyes. Their social orbits might not jibe, but they definitely flew in tangent where their work was concerned. "What about it?"

The hovering waitress removed empty plates and brought new ones with thin wafers and strawberry jam.

"If we could get those negatives from him—"

"That's police business."

"The cops probably had ten murders that day. You think they'd spare a detective to investigate a stray shot that didn't kill anybody and didn't make the front page of the *Picayune?*"

Albert reached into his jacket pocket, withdrew a white envelope, and handed it to Karla.

Six five-by-six-inch black and white glossies spilled on the table. The photos showed the cathedral from a distance, up close and at a right angle. "You had the pictures all along!"

"Well, I didn't think this the proper place— the police do have a detective on it. Saint Louis Cathedral is the oldest in the country, a historical landmark. Bishop Carvel is in an uproar. Mayor Nagin's Catholic contingency is not happy. Unless the police come up with a suspect, Mayor Nagin—" Albert pointed with his chin across the room and Karla craned her neck and saw His Honor drinking tea— "will lose the Catholic vote in the November elections and he doesn't intend to let that happen."

"Does everything in this city become political?"

"Pretty much—the sniper didn't shoot from the tower window. The shutters are nailed closed." With the tip of his fancy pen, Albert tapped the enlarged photograph.

"How high you reckon the cathedral roof is?"

"Ninety feet, more or less; fifteen feet down from the top, there are two arched windows. They look functional."

"Hmm—" Karla scrutinized the photographs: three close-ups showing mama, papa and the little girl Mary Bravelle had thought so cute. The fourth and fifth pictures, taken further away, showed Jackson Square and the Cathedral. The round clock on the tall spire was clearly visible: 12:05 p.m. "That's the time we boarded the buggy. We returned to the cathedral five minutes late, remember? One-ten—the judge threw a fit because Sam wasn't there. You went to find Sam. I saw Lebron and jumped; Pierre helped Mary from the buggy. The only people left seated were the judge and the driver."

"The police established the time of the shooting as 1:12 p.m.," Albert said.

"Two minutes between the time we returned and the shooting," Karla commented. "Look!" she tapped a photo. "That window is cracked open a little."

"Yes, it is."

Mary leaned forward. "Let me see. What is it?"

THE AZALEAS

Karla ignored her—"That extra line there could be an arm parallel to the window frame."

"Possibly—"

Mary extended a trembling hand. "May I see?"

Karla studied the photos. "Did the police find the bullets?"

"A .223 caliber shell in the gutter—It grazed Mary's shoulder and ricocheted off the cobblestone street. And the .223 the doctor took out of Lebron's side. Both matched. Shot from the same rifle."

Albert inclined his head and he and Karla went over the prints slowly, millimeter by millimeter. There was nothing there—nothing at all.

"I looked with a magnifying glass," Albert said. "Zilch—"

Karla held the cathedral picture at an angle, scrutinizing for an arm or a gun barrel. The light slid down the glossy surface, highlighting windows, shutters, louvers, ledges, cornices and pigeons. "*Nada*—" She had expected the photos to solve the mystery. Dummy! Nothing ever came that easy.

"Please," Mary said. "May I take a look?"

Mary owned The Azaleas, was Midas rich and Vogue chic. Her pleading delighted Karla in an odd way. She passed the photos without comment.

"Oh, look. This one has the little girl. Remember her, Karla? She was so adorable." Mary's gaze lingered on the photograph.

Karla ignored Mary's obsession with children. "The sniper shot twice. I believe he hit Lebron accidentally."

Albert spread jam on a scone and took a nibble. "A pro would've taken into consideration the wind coming from the river. It's stronger up high by the steeples. He didn't compensate for that."

"The sniper didn't drop onto the cathedral roof from a helicopter. He didn't scale the outside walls, not with all those tourists gawking. He had no ladder. He shot from a high window. Any idea how he got to the belfry?—"

"Inside job—the police theorize that the sniper went into the twelve o'clock mass, hid and then made it to the top using inside stairs."

"The sniper had to know about the buggy ride," Karla said. "That narrows it down to somebody in your inner circle, Mary. Who knew you were going on that horse and buggy tour?"

"I don't know," she replied, sounding all weepy. "This is police business—"

Please don't start with the tears. "The person who took a shot at you is at The Azaleas and will probably take a whack at me if I'm there trying to sell it. I consider my safety very much my business." Karla's voice, sharper than intended, brought an immediate apology to Mary's lips. Karla continued, less brashly for after all, none of this was Mary's fault. Shit just happened. "Who sat on the church pew with you?"

"Nobody—Pierre and I had the front pew to ourselves."

"Who sat behind you?"

"Aunt Agatha. Mildred Persou, my high-school French teacher. Jeremiah Jones of Twin Oaks, the nearest neighbor, Jimmy Watson—"

"The sheriff came to the memorial?" Jimmy Watson hadn't mentioned that, though Karla should've guessed he attended Danielle Turner's memorial service. How else would he know about the shots from the cathedral?

"Sheriffs never miss a funeral," Albert said. "It's the ideal opportunity to shake hands and secure future votes. When election time comes again, a little voice in the back of the voters' head reminds them 'oh, he came to mama's funeral.' It's very effective."

"I haven't voted in years," Mary said.

Maybe the rich didn't need to change things. Karla never missed an opportunity to pull the lever and dump a corrupt, do-nothing politician from his cushy seat.

"Albert, how did you get the Rainbow papers? When I got too close to finding out about Rainbow Corporation, the clerk of court's office shut down the information pipeline—they cut me off. I was going back today to—"

"Sometimes there are certain advantages to being a lawyer—"

A stirring drew the tea-drinkers' attention. Two violinists took their seats. A young woman in a white strapless gown extended creamy arms and with slender fingers began plucking a harp. The vibrations sounded like water gurgling in a creek.

The music drew aside a veil and made beauty visible. At times the sounds plunged into shadows then sprang back, sunshine bursting over a cloud. The notes scaled to a bold projection before playfully sliding to a lyric base. The fingers plucking the strings did so with sureness, delicacy and great expertise. The melody rose and filled the room, drifted past the ceiling and reached for the heavens, each note clear, light and joyful.

Albert's and Karla's gazes met and they connected, touched the same stone. The music transported them to an unseen oasis, a place they both knew. Karla's ear registered each note. Maybe God didn't intend for her to learn whole notes and half notes, only to feel with all her heart and find the secret places. If she still had her piano, she could've gone home and played the exact melody.

Albert said, his voice silky, "Massenet's classic love song—*"Meditation de Thais."*

Karla surveyed the room. Women in boring little black numbers and the men in gray or black, listened casually. The rich didn't like color. Maybe they had everything and didn't need a bright splash to cheer their lives. Maybe they didn't need big sounds, either. They never hollered and hooted and slapped their thighs. Their conversations murmured along like expensive car engines that never coughed or backfired.

Karla's piano was gone, her pearls, borrowed, her red dress had the price tag tucked into the bosom and was going back to the store first thing in the morning. No point kidding herself. She had no place in this high-society bunch, major league players, all of them. Mayor Nagin at one table, Angela Hill of WWL-TV at another; other faces Karla recognized from their frequent pictures in the *Picayune*.

Karla loved red, funky jazz and Lucky Dogs. She belonged in the minor league or maybe even further down, to a bush team. She'd walked in here pumped full of artificial confidence by the well-intended Mimi. She could swing. She could hit a home run. Strike one! Strike two! She fidgeted in her red Felice dress, surrounded by the muted grandeur, waiting for the inevitable strike three.

And then it came breezing across the room, decidedly, no hesitation in the stride and a face wreathed in the crooked smile she knew so well. It came with the intent and the rush of a baseball zinging across home plate.

Richard the sonofabitch! Lovable, tall, lanky Richard slid into the empty chair at Albert's table as if he'd been invited. He sent Karla's heart pounding and stirred her blood. Her brain sent impulses to her legs—*get up and get out, get up and get out*—but her rubber knees refused to translate the thought into action. Richard's eyes found hers, and she was trapped.

He stood a breath away, leaned and kissed her cheek as he would a long-lost friend, sending tingles from Karla's spine to her toes.

"A vision in red," Richard said huskily. "I felt you come in."

"Hello, Richard," Karla replied, ice in her voice and fire in her heart.

Albert looked smug and superior, as if he'd just won a big poker pot. "Hello, Richard. You know Karla. May I introduce you to Mary?"

Richard said, "Hello, Mary," and to Albert, "I have to hand it to you, old man. She's gorgeous." He clarified the situation for Mary. "Karla is an old flame of mine," he said lightly. "Still burning bright—"

"He has memory lapses," Karla murmured. "He's married."

Richard leaned close and whispered. "Where have you been?"

"Busy." Her whereabouts were none of his business.

Albert said, "Karla and I have formed a partnership. She's selling Mary's plantation and doing a great job."

Richard's hand dropped possessively on Karla's shoulder. "Aha! A business woman, now! You look like a million bucks." Karla wrenched away. "You—" Karla's eyes bright and cold like diamond icicles tripped him. Disconcerted, he asked, "Have you moved?" She ignored the question. "Have you left the Quarter? I asked Mimi, but—" *Mea culpa* was written all over his face.

Karla would've given her right arm to see the angst on his face when he rang the apartment chimes and nobody answered, his distress when he couldn't find her. He had lost her forever—doomed to spend his life removing gall bladders and replacing heart valves without Karla at his side. She dimpled her cheek and favored Richard with a coquettish smile. She fluttered her eyelids with premeditated and vicious intent. "How's your wife?"

He ignored the question.

Karla cut her eyes at Albert. "Albert made me a proposition I couldn't refuse."

Her employer grinned sheepishly, royally entertained.

A mean gleam burned in Richard's eyes. "Listen, Albert. This has gone far enough—"

"Ah, no," Albert replied gently. "This is just beginning, Richard."

THE AZALEAS

"What's gone far enough?" Karla asked. "What's beginning?"

"A private matter," replied Albert.

"Everything with you is always a private matter!" Karla said.

The merriment in Albert's eyes caused Richard to bristle like a porcupine.

If Karla danced with Richard, got next to him close and personal, she'd discover what was going on. Richard would hold her tight, and she'd feel his long thighs against hers, the shirt studs pressing against her breast, his hot breath in her ear. His insides would melt like a block of ice in summer heat, and she'd know what the hell was going on.

The harpist reached the end of her rendition, stood and bowed. Albert, Mary and Richard took a minute to clap politely. No stomping or table slapping allowed at the Windsor Court Tea Salon.

"Give me a good guitar any day," Karla said defiantly, not applauding the performance. "Harps aren't popular with musicians at the Parrot Bar or anywhere else in the Quarter for that matter. The instrument is much too big to lug around. I like music I can tap my foot to."

So there! Childish, of course—a bratty fit.

The uptown wife came from the ladies room, all sunshine smiles and white, straight teeth. She kissed Albert on both cheeks. She warmed to Mary and gushed in Karla's direction delighted to meet her; loving the red dress. The roar in Karla's ears prevented her hearing the entire garbage. *It was like 'he's mine now. I can be nice to you. You're no problem.'* Richard's wife had no idea what a big problem Karla could be. If Karla made up her mind to get Richard back, wifey would be in big trouble. And Karla could do it, too. Had Richard told his wife he couldn't live without Karla? Or was that his little secret?

The wife laid a possessive hand on Richard's arm and with a slight touch led him away like a well-trained puppy. He glanced back over his shoulder, a hang-dog look.

"What a nice man," Mary said. "His wife is lovely."

Karla turned away, choking anger and frustration. Would she ever get completely over Richard? Would her heart always lurch when she saw him?

"Stop that." Albert touched her wrist and drew her hand away from her head. She'd been unconsciously twisting a blonde curl round and round her finger. "You'll ruin your pretty hairdo." His voice was paternal. He reached in his pocket and handed Karla his handkerchief. He never lacked handkerchiefs. "There's a wee bit of a smudge right there—"

Karla snatched the handkerchief. "I have to go—" She pushed up the red satin sleeve. Mickey Mouse strapped to her wrist by a worn leather band grinned 7 p.m. She groaned and looked helplessly at Albert.

"You never know. You may start a trend." Albert's reassuring squeeze and spontaneous laughter did little to bolster her confidence. "Only you," Albert said, "Only you."

And somehow that made the watch, the dress and the hours spent primping, all right. She had packaged herself differently, but she was still her old self and Albert would never let her forget it.

CHAPTER 10

Charity Hospital loomed in the dark, the lower windows black, upper ones black and white lit squares down and across like a crossword puzzle. Karla walked past nurses, interns in scrubs, women toting bags and half-asleep children waiting at the bus stop. The dregs of humanity gathered there, sick, weary, disheartened folks standing in clusters, slumped on the wooden bench, sitting on the ground, waiting for the streetcar, waiting for the bus, waiting for a ride from somebody.

"Side door, Miss," a cop said as Karla walked past. "Front door gits locked after nine." He noticed the fancy dress and high heels. "Whatcha doin' here?—boyfriend git stabbed?"

"No. I have a friend."

He grinned knowingly. "Oh, yeah—an uncle—I'll walks you to the Emergency. You goes in through there."

Karla was glad for the escort. In contrast to the darkness in front, the Emergency entrance blazed with lights. Concrete steps worn smooth by a zillion running feet led to the door. The loading dock exploded with activity. Two ambulances discharged their cargo; two sped away, sirens blaring and lights blinking. Three cops with deadly hardware encircling their waists stood swapping gumbo and jambalaya recipes. Green scrubs on break smoked cigarettes. They looked worn out.

"Elevator is iffy," the cop said—"Safer to walk up."

Four flights and she found herself inside the post-Katrina Emergency Room. The glaring fluorescents enveloped sorrow and depression. Katrina residue streaked brown the once-white walls. Dirty beige spilled onto the worn brown tile floors. People with anxious faces the color of earth or coffee or charcoal sat on brown Naugahyde chairs, waiting. Pine-Oil disinfectant couldn't overcome the moldy, musty smell left by flood waters.

The receptionist slid the bullet-proof glass. She was big and black and tired. "Yes?"

Before Karla could answer, a woman shoved ahead. "She jes' got here. I's been waiting since seven. Ain't nobody else—"

"Go back to your seat or I'll call security and he'll take you back." The receptionist never lifted her eyes from the paperwork before her.

"I'm dying with this instant reflux! It's scorching my mouth til I'm breathin' flames and I needs some medicine to put out—" the woman pursed her lips and blew a hot breath in the receptionist's face.

The receptionist paid no attention to the complaining woman. "Next! Ceasar Illinois! Next!"

The Reflux case pointed a purple fingernail at Karla and said to the others sitting comatose, waiting— "See? See? There ain't no justice."

Karla ignored the tirade and stepped to the window, "I need to check on Lebron. He's in—"

"Lebron who?—" The woman on the other side of the glass didn't look up for Karla, either. She treated everybody equally. Like shit.

Lebron who? Karla had no inkling what Lebron's last name was. She never asked and he never volunteered that information.

"Anyhow, take a look at that clock. Visiting hours long over. Come back in the morning."

"But I won't be here tomorrow."

A nurse entered through a rear door. "Ceasar?—Ceasar Illinois? You're next. This way, please!"

Another waiting patient recognized Ceasar, half-asleep, slumped in a chair. "Hey, bro!—" He shook Caesar by the shoulder. "Wake up! They's calling your name. Watcha doin' here?—you been knifed?" Ceasar half-turned, exposing a pink, raw face—"Oh, jee-sus!—Sweet jeesus! Scalded? Your ole woman done scalded you? You devil, you been dissin' her?"

Karla kept to the business at hand, opened her evening bag and slipped $10 under the bullet proof partition. "Lebron had surgery." The money caught the woman's attention and she raised one eye. "I have to see Lebron tonight. I'm gone tomorrow."

"How old is this Lebron?" she asked.

"I don't know—twelve, maybe."

"He come through Emergency?"

"Sunday afternoon."

She punched keys. "Here's a Lebron. Lebron Washington—came in Sunday—ninth floor. Elevator's down the hall to the left."

Karla waited for the doors to open, listening to the impatient woman heckling the receptionist once again. "You gotta let me in. I'm dying."

"When your number comes up—"

A sudden burst of frenetic activity, a tremendous racket, spun Karla around. A half-dozen green scrubs pushed a gurney with a mountain of flesh on it, bottles swaying, plastic tubes dangling and coiling. A red-headed nurse straddling the man's middle punched his chest with her fist. *Whop...whop...whop.* "Hold it, man! Ready! Ready! Go! Go!" The scene was straight ER TV. And then the defeated sigh; the somber voice: "This one's dead."

"Don't stop here, pal," the receptionist said. "He ain't my paperwork. Take him straight to the morgue."

"I'm on fire—" the Reflux woman screamed. "Whatcha gonna do fer me?"

"Stewart! Stew!—" The receptionist paged someone over a loud speaker. "STAT to front desk!—" Without raising her head, she replied, "I tell you what I'm gonna do for you. I'm gonna get you outta my face, that's what I'm gonna do." The Stewart she paged appeared instantly, as big and burly as any nightclub bouncer. "Take her down to the first-aid station," the receptionist said. "Tell them to give her a couple of Tums. She ain't gonna die from Reflux."

Karla followed the nurse and the scalded Caesar down a long corridor that smelled moldy and damp. The corners were dark with mildew. In places where the fluorescents cast their yellow glare, the fungus disappeared, reemerging a few feet away, the colors and patterns repeating like a great abstract painting.

The expensive medical equipment had been soaked and the beds blown away. The brown water poured through the windows and down the hallways sweeping everything in its path. In the aftermath of Katrina a temporary facility had been set up in Metairie. Who knew Metairie? It took a bus to get there and no buses were running.

Somewhere in Big C's cavernous bowels, a brown file with an identifying red tag held Karla's life's record, the traumas: birth, killing pneumonia, a bout with hepatitis, a broken nose. Except there were no longer any records—the flood waters destroyed them.

The sick and maimed, women about to give birth, men stabbed in bar fights continued to come to Big C. They stood outside and waited for someone who knew, who cared, and who wouldn't abandon the have-nots. The legislature in Baton Rouge argued whether or not to reopen New Orleans Charity Hospital. Month after month the debate went on, life hanging in the balance, people dying on the streets.

Eventually, doctors drifted back to the old place, setting up practice as best they could in their old cubby holes, working on the fourth floor because the bottom three were uninhabitable, not knowing who was going to pay them or when, but they'd taken an oath.

Karla walked down the long hallway, cubby holes on either side manned by young interns in brown-spattered white coats, who arrived after the hurricane. They came from Nevada, Illinois, Texas, filled with book knowledge, lacking experience. "We are here to help." They soon discovered this grist mill didn't offer the option of second opinions, specialists, or transfers to better facilities. Life for the poor began and ended here.

Karla stepped into the elevator. The doors slid closed. She crossed her fingers.

On the ninth floor, several medical carts were parked against the wall; no personnel in sight. After a few false starts down dead-end hallways that ended in "Positively no admittance beyond this point," she found her way to ward 948 and pushed open the door. Her eyes adjusted to the darkness. She discerned six hospital beds, lumps of various shapes and sizes on them.

"Pssst! Lebron!—" She whispered, so as not to wake the dead. "Hey, kid!"

From the bed nearest the wall came a fumbling sound, then a light. Lebron's bed looked like a full-mast ship. The rigging of ropes, pulleys, slings, and hinges kept both plaster-encased legs spread up and apart like sails in the air.

"Hi, Kid. I came to see you."

He gave Karla a weak, tentative smile, lacking its usual kick. "Mmm—"

She leaned over and straightened the top sheet. White bandages, white sheets, white pillow cases—in the midst of all that white, the little round face looked like a black bowling ball. An IV dripped into one arm. A urine bag disposed liquid at the other end. "How are you feeling?"

"Mmm—"

"Lousy, I bet. You can't talk, eh? We'll there's nothing important to say. Just that I'm really sorry you're in such a mess and I love you." His eyes filled with tears. Karla wanted to put her arms around him, hold him against her breast and console the broken little body. "Don't think you're going to lie there forever, being waited on hand and foot, getting fed three squares a day. You need to get well, get out of that bed and kick ass."

He held up the fingers of one hand and the thumb of the other and the tears spilled down his cheeks.

"Ah, it's all right, sugar. Six days?" Negative shake—"Six weeks? Damn! Don't listen to those suckers. They exaggerate. Doctors are always looking for business. It's their trade. You'll be out long before that. They have no idea how tough you are. Have the guys from the Parrot Bar been to see you?"

"Mmm—" A yes nod. Thank God, Karla could count on the musicians. Lebron's mother, Violetta, probably wouldn't show.

The boy on the next bed raised his head. He didn't look as banged up as Lebron. "A man came to see Lebron and tole him his gramma died. He asked Lebron if he knew where Willis was. The Gramma wanted Willis to know she's done gone to her reward."

A sob caught in Lebron's throat, and he coughed and cringed in pain. He closed his eyes and concentrated on breathing, whistling harshly through his nose.

"Don't cry, Lebron. She's lots better up there where the big pearly gates are. I'll tell Willis I promise. I know where he is."

Lebron sniffled and couldn't move his arms high enough to wipe the tears from his cheeks. Karla found Albert's handkerchief in her evening bag and patted and blotted the little round cheeks.

"There. Everything is going to be okay. Real okay— everybody in the Square misses you. Those other boys—they can't hold a candle to your tapping." The familiar impish brightness seeped back into the hazel eyes. "That's a boy, Lebron. Wait 'til you see what I brought you. You'll really perk up then." She reached in her bag and handed Lebron a Nintendo Game Boy, compliments of Whitmore Realty Expense Account.

His eyes lit up like a neon sign, sending a pang to her heart that brought back the thinly buried memory of standing in the drizzling rain, her nose flat against a Christmas window ablaze with lights and golden ribbons, aching for a Barbie, impossible dream. Childhood incidents didn't leave scars. They left spurs that pricked and goaded.

Lebron weakly clicked buttons with his left hand, using fingers he could barely move. Figures jumped across the miniature screen.

"You hang onto it, hear? Don't let anybody steal it. Put it under your pillow when you sleep."

She started to tell him she'd seen Willis but had a change of heart. Willis in chains would be no great inspiration to Lebron in pulleys and ropes, both bound against their will.

She dug in the purse for a red Marksalot. "Can I autograph your cast?"

He nodded.

"Any particular spot?—"

He didn't care. He was all into the Game Boy. She wrote in big letters from his thigh to his ankle 'Get well quick—Karla 10/09/2007.

"Lebron," Karla interrupted his playing, "did you by any chance see anybody on the cathedral roof that day?"

Negative shake—

"One of the other boys saw something, maybe?"

Negative.

"Can I catch them on the Square tomorrow?"

A nod—

"Some time after ten?"

Another nod—

THE AZALEAS

"If the boys help me find the man who shot from the cathedral roof, my boss will pay them big money." A disappointed look came into Lebron's eyes. "You, too—you're the chief. The chief always gets paid." Karla would rather have the FBI after her than a gang of hungry black boys who've been promised a bonus.

"Big money" caught the ear of the boy in the adjacent bed. He propped on one elbow.

Lebron made circling motions with the one wrist he could move.

"You want me to turn around?" Karla asked.

He nodded and she made a slow circle. He looked tired.

"Are you ready for me to leave?"

He repeated the motion again.

The boy in the next bed said, "He wants you to twirl around fast so he can see your underwear."

"You rascal—" Snatching the red skirt, Karla spun on her pointed red shoes. The dress swirled softly around her like a silk parachute. For a moment, before Lebron's wide-eyed look warned her someone with authority had entered the ward, the boy's face beamed approval. Karla expected to make excuses to a nurse or a doctor. Instead, there stood Albert, the familiar wry smile pulling down his lower lip.

"What in God's name are you doing here?" she asked.

"Enjoying the floor show for starters—" His smoldering gray eyes appreciated her impromptu performance. "Checking on Lebron—Taking you home."

"Maybe I'm not going home. Maybe I'm going dancing 'til the sun comes up." If she did or didn't have a date was none of his affair. No reason why her business should be his. She didn't want Albert meddling in her life. Just because she worked for him didn't mean—

Lebron beckoned to Albert and pointed to the leg casts.

The self-appointed interpreter in the next bed translated. "Mister, he wants you to sign, too."

With the red felt pen, Albert wrote down the other leg, 'Get Well Soon—A. M. in a neat, precise, left-hand slant that put Karla's scrawl to shame.

"How did you find me, anyway?" Karla asked, petulant.

"Simple." The throaty vibration in Albert's voice caught her attention. At times something about him made her think—wild amusement danced in his eyes. "I know the way your mind works."

Scary thought had it been true, but Albert was only teasing, indulging his aggravating nature. Karla burst out laughing.

"That's much better." His eyes scanned her from head to toe. "My dear, you looked so stunning tonight, I said to myself, 'Albert, you'd be a fool to let Karla waste that magnificent dress,' particularly—" he clicked his tongue against his teeth, "since I probably paid for it."

Oops! No fooling the old goat. "You said I could use the expense account for whatever I thought necessary." He chuckled good-naturedly, as if he'd just been the butt of a good joke. "We never discussed exactly what 'necessary' meant, and it seemed to me necessary not to appear at the Windsor Court in blue jeans and a tank top. But don't get all uptight about it. The dress is going back tomorrow."

"Don't be silly. That red dress was a perfectly legitimate expense. And we'll take advantage of it and dance until daylight, if you wish."

How could Karla refuse? He was ultimately the keeper of the till and if for that reason alone, she had to humor him. On the other hand—

He noticed her indecision and laughed out loud. "What can it hurt? I promise I won't step on your toes. And you can lead, if you like—wouldn't matter to me."

Karla didn't want to lead. She wanted to close her eyes, fall into the arms of a handsome man and swirl around the dance floor, but pickings were slim and Albert stood there, the man of the moment. Her red silk taffeta rustled fun and frolic. They'd go to dark, crowded, smoky clubs that smelled of whiskey and sex. If she could get him to unbend and relax, get past being so stuffy, she bet Albert could be a real hoot.

"Okay. You can lead," she said, "but first tell me—"

"Anything, my dear—"

"Did you dump Mary or is she going to resurface somewhere?"

They dragged into Cafe du Monde at 5 a.m., Albert holding onto Karla's elbow, keeping her steady. A familiar comfort enveloped a place that stayed open twenty-four hours a day, seven days a week, regardless of weather, war, crime, natural or man-made catastrophe. A place not even Katrina could close down was like the Rock of

Gibraltar, solid and unsinkable, a noisy tribute to endurance and survival.

"Let's go to La Madeline's," Albert suggested. "And get a full breakfast."

A cool, damp mist rolled in from the river. A distance away a foghorn blared. The smell of fresh ground coffee beans tickled the air. Delivery trucks rattled on their way to the French Market. Within the hour all the open-air stalls would be filled with fresh produce. Across the street, the man from River Palace uncoiled a hose and washed the sidewalk. In the Square, through the dissipating gray, Andrew Jackson emerged on his rearing horse, bronze tinged in sunrise gold.

Karla dropped into a chair. Sometime during the night, she'd removed the red shoes, lost the red shoes; she was barefooted. Albert stood behind her. "A shot of black coffee with lots of sugar, then whatever you want," he said.

She wrapped both arms around his neck. He gently disengaged himself and sat across the table. She leaned and traced his jaw line with one finger. "Albert—" giving him her best demure, coy look— "what is it you want?"

"I want to make sure you get home all right."

He couldn't have been a better escort. They went from Snug Harbor to Cafe Brasil to Tipitina's on Napoleon. The jazz musicians and piano players were back from Memphis, Houston, Indianapolis and other god-forsaken cities they had evacuated to. Glad to be home, they said. This is the place.

"Hey, Karla!" the gangly piano player at Tip's called when he spotted her entering, clinging to Albert's arm. "Come do a set on the house!"

"Can't do, George— I'm dancing tonight, right Albert?"

Albert was like a butterfly, light on his feet, polished shoes skimming the floor. The rhythm flowed through his body and moved his hips and shoulders and knees. They whirled and twirled, his hand a light touch on her waist, her wrist. They backed away, came close, shoulders touching momentarily before sliding apart.

From Tips they took a cab to Mid-City Lanes Rock N' Bowl, howling noise and bodies jumping to Rocking Doopsie, Jr. They didn't miss the House of Blues. Albert said he wasn't fond of the House of Blues.

"I don't like anything that springs into being full-grown and complete. Time is essential to the development of character."

"If an owner throws enough money at a club, he can buy character."

"That's not necessarily correct," he said, "Same thing with people, you know. The ones that emerge overnight totally polished and on top of the world don't last. First little crisis and they crumble because they haven't developed the interior resources it takes to have true integrity." He studied Karla, an appraising look.

"Am I developing?" she asked, suddenly self-conscious.

"You are true to yourself, and that's a rare trait."

Did that mean yes or no? Karla decided to keep the evening upbeat and not pursue the answer.

They left Blues and hop-scotched through the Quarter, stopping at the tourist traps where bored women stripped down to G-strings, their audience predominantly National Guardsmen. One club had a new act where a big tropical bird untied knots and undressed the stripper. Albert and Karla walked arm-in-arm through the warm, humid night, down Bourbon and up Royal, a handsome couple taking in the sights like tourists. They strolled the Quarter, the wonderful seedy, steamy Quarter, where nothing ever shut down and people walked the streets at all hours and the biggest concern wasn't criminals in shackles, but penny-ante pickpockets. They sat in the patio at Pat O'Brien's and listened to the piano player and watched the fountain with the red and green and blue dancing waters. At some point Albert hailed a cab and they drove to the plush Fairmont Hotel, to a proper dance floor, with a proper orchestra that did more than rattle brass and toot horns. Everybody wore resplendent evening clothes. Albert held Karla close, and she nestled her cheek on his shoulder, closed her eyes, and pretended he was Richard. Actually, Albert was a much better dancer than Richard. Albert could tango, mambo, samba, jitterbug, and waltz. She concluded that at one time in his life he must've taken dance lessons.

She drained the last sip of coffee and said to Albert, "You're a groovy dancer."

"Thank you. You're no slouch yourself."

She ran her finger along the soft flesh of his bottom lip. He trapped her hand in his. "Are you a good kisser?" she asked.

"Some women say that I am."

"I don't know if you're a good kisser."

"That's right."

"Would you like to kiss me?"

He motioned to the waiter. "More black coffee—"

Obviously, he had no interest in kissing Karla. Maybe he never mixed business with pleasure, or pleasure with business. Maybe he didn't like women all that much. She closed her eyes. If Albert had been Richard, this night would've been so different! A night with Richard was like a melt-down in a hot furnace that left one limp and helpless. They'd be in her apartment by now, intermittently sleeping and making love until cocktail time. Richard's hot kisses left purple marks on her neck he called "love notes," and some mornings she had enough of them to write a symphony.

"I know what you're thinking." Albert's silky purr jolted her back to reality. "All evening long I've known every thought in that curly head of yours." He turned his chair around and straddled it, his arms crossed over the back like an interrogator in a Grade B movie.

"Really?—you can read minds? Then you must know I'm speculating—" A hiccup the size of a walnut interrupted— "Are you gay?"

He threw back his head. His loud, gutsy laugh drew the attention of the other early-birds. "C'mon. Drink this." He held a cup to Karla's lips and didn't admit or deny his status.

"You know what? I think you're an alien—landed here on a spaceship or an angel like in that television series—I can't remember the name—where a holy one comes from Heaven to straighten our miseries—you seen that show?" She leaned across the table, waiting for a reaction that didn't happen. "I don't think you're human."

"I am human."

"Who said?"

"I said." He reached across and dusted the powdered sugar off Karla's chin and the front of her dress. His hand touched her breast and a surprising and unexpected tingle made her look away.

"How did you manage to get sugar in your hair?" His fingers lingered in the tangles, his face close to hers, his breath warm on her cheek. The alert, reckless look in his gray eyes elicited a feverish surge from Karla she never in a million years anticipated and her cheeks flamed. His hand slid down the nape of her neck. Heat radiated from his fingertips. "You be careful out there in the country."

"It is dangerous, isn't it?—not at all safe like the city. I could've gotten killed a dozen times already. What would you do if I had a fatal accident? Drowned in the swamp? Died from a horrible bug bite?"

A rueful little smile played on his lips. "I'd miss you. And my heart would be sad."

"You don't have a heart."

He took both her hands in his and placed them flat on his chest. "Sure I do. Feel it."

Indeed, his heart was pounding. "Albert—" The fingers holding Karla's hand tightened, but the merry, dancing light in his eyes told her he didn't intend to fall prey.

He just wanted her to do his dirty work and sell the damned plantation so he'd look good and rack up extra Brownie points with Mary. If she got killed in the process, her death would make little difference in his grand scheme. Hadn't one man—or did he say two—bit the dust already? "Tell me—am I insured?"

For a moment he said nothing, and then he let her hand drop and laughed so long and loud, three waiters edged toward the table. "Of course you're insured, my dear—double indemnity."

"What's that?"

"If you die in an accident, the policy pays twice the face value."

"If I get bumped off—" dumb question, but she had to know— "who's the beneficiary?"

"Three guesses," he said, giving a playful punch to her chin, "and two don't count. Let's go get a proper breakfast." He reached in both jacket pockets— "Here, put these on," and handed Karla her red spike-heeled shoes.

CHAPTER 11

After lunch the next day when her head quit throbbing, she headed back to The Azaleas. She drove along the winding river road, top down on the Mustang, hair blowing in the wind. Plantation homes tucked in oak groves faced the Mississippi levee. The houses looked like grounded steamboats, big, white and imposing. Every one had a resident ghost, a cemetery where the bodies left their tombs at night, a step where some unfortunate stood and took a last breath.

The houses withstood wars, floods, epidemics and family feuds. New owners electrified the chandeliers and the incandescent bulbs glowed like candles; carpeted the floors, and the pine boards beneath creaked, "I'm here;" air-conditioned the rooms and lost the cold air through transoms designed to let in the river breeze. No matter how hard each succeeding generation altered, adapted and modernized, the houses resisted. Their strength was their history, and that couldn't be swept aside.

Before leaving the city, on an impulse, Karla pulled into the H&B real estate office. As usual, the place jumped and buzzed like Mission Control, phones ringing, screens flashing. Messengers and secretaries clutching file folders and trailing tape scurried through the rooms. She sneaked past the receptionist and found Gloria still inhabiting her old cubbyhole with only enough space for her desk, swivel chair and two straight-backs for customers. She kept her clients on the move, hot on the trail. 'Too much sitting and relaxing,' she said, 'gives them cold feet.' Piled books, papers, folders, maps covered her work space. She hadn't seen the desk surface in years. She had so many million dollar award plaques she couldn't hang them all, so she'd given up displaying them and stacked them on the filing cabinet.

Karla knocked timidly, and Gloria put a hand over the phone mouthpiece, gave a big, surprised smile and waved in Karla as she warned the caller, "Okay. It's up to you, but the deadline is 5 p.m. today. Tomorrow will be too late." Her tactics hadn't changed. She hung up and swung the chair around. "Well, bless my buttons. Look what the cat drug in. How are you, honey?" She pushed the intercom button. "Zoe, hold my calls for ten minutes, will you?" giving Karla a little slice of her precious time.

Karla handed her a business card. Gloria glanced at it quickly. "Well, I'll be. Karla Whitmore, Broker. Congratulations. Albert Monsant called—"

"He said you gave me a good recommendation. Thanks." She didn't look Gloria in the eye. Gloria was shrewd enough to know Karla didn't acquire her license in a conventional way.

"So! You be real careful, honey. Albert dabbles in real estate, sets up these overnight companies and his associates either end up millionaires or—" she stopped herself.

"Dead?—"

"The last one did."

"If something goes wrong, who takes the fall?"

"Take a guess. What's Albert got up your sleeve?"

"Selling The Azaleas, a plantation in St. Francisville—"

"Gracious! I remember that anvil. Who can forget it? Too damned heavy to move— between the bitch-woman who lived there and the other one flying off the wall, they managed to screw up every deal." She shook her head, bobby pins stuck in the piled red hair. "And when I did find a buyer, they killed him."

"They *what?*—"

"The West Feliciana sheriff—James Watson—I'll never forget his name, said Convert McKenzie failed to negotiate a curve in the middle of the night and flipped his Mercedes. His official report said speeding and alcohol, a one-car accident. If McKenzie had been from New Orleans, I could buy that, but the man was a Baptist deacon from north Louisiana, and you know those folks prayer-meet every Wednesday night and place Gideon Bibles in their spare time. Liquor never touches their lips, not as anyone can tell, anyhow. The sheriff's version of the accident didn't compute, as far as I was concerned. You be careful. My advice is to get the hell out of Dodge. No property is worth getting killed over. Don't waste your time—that stupid ghost hanging around. The place is spooky." She laughed drily. "It may work if there's been a recent death in the family and the corpse doesn't return to terrify buyers and stop the sale."

Karla almost clapped with glee. "There has been a recent death—Mrs. Turner's, the owner. Her daughter Mary is hot to sell."

"Motivation is 90% of the deal. If the involved parties are committed, you can work around terms, price, and deadlines. They'll toe the mark and stay with it to the bitter end. On the other hand, if they're ambivalent and lukewarm, any little excuse and they wriggle off the hook."

"I have a determined seller."

"You're way ahead of the game, then."

To Gloria real estate was a contest, each transaction a challenging bout. Sometimes she delivered the knock-out punch; other times she was sent to the ropes. Either way she climbed back into the ring next day. She loved the game too much to quit.

"I really, really need to make this sale. My whole future depends on it," Karla confessed.

"That's too bad, honey, because the chances are—" she saw Karla's sad-sack face and stopped herself. "Oh, it'll be hard, but you can do it, babe. You can do it." She shifted in her chair. "But you just broke the first rule, and you can't break the rules."

"What rules? What did I do?"

"You appeared too anxious, too eager—a position of weakness. The seller and the buyer will walk all over you. You're so fired up to close, the first thing the seller will do is cut your commission to make the deal work. The buyer will go around you directly to the owner, knowing he can come back and settle with you for a lesser fee. This is a tough business, darling. The weak are separated like chaff from wheat in no time at all. What about your commission? How much is it?"

"My part is 10%." She didn't need to know all the details.

"And Albert keeps the other 90%," Gloria said knowingly. "That's the cost of letting him bankroll your company. He pays himself handsomely. And how will you spend your share?" Gloria asked a gleam in her eye.

"Well—I'll put a down payment on a place of my own, buy a new car and a baby grand piano. Take piano lessons. Definitely take piano lessons. Have the hump on my nose straightened. Lend Mimi and Bilbao the down payment so they can buy the bar. Probably put some aside for Lebron—"

"Didn't know you had a kid—"

"Oh, no—Lebron is a young friend of mine. He's in the hospital right now. He caught a stray bullet in the Quarter."

"Too bad," Gloria said. "But you can't let friends get in the way. In this business you have no personal life. The customer is always first. You're at their beck and call twenty-four seven. If you're not available instantly, away they fly to somebody else. They have no loyalty!" sounded grueling—"You can't be too eager. You can't have a life. And above all, you can't count on the commission. Don't even think about the money. Think about the details, all those loose ends that must be tied up to reach a closing. Don't lay awake spending money you don't have until the check is in your hand."

Karla had already spent several nights deliriously over-spending her cut. Her dreams were papered in C-notes.

"So what's your specific problem?" Gloria asked.

"Where to find a buyer, Gloria—three million!—that's the sale price. I don't know anybody with three million."

"Who does? Nobody I know has three million. What they must have is good credit and a pipeline to the bank. It's hard to finance those old historical places with conventional loans. The ratio of 30% land, 70% dwelling is all out of kilter. The land is always worth a helluva lot more than the run-down house. Who's the owner again?"

"Danielle Turner."

Gloria spoke into the intercom. "Zoe, look in the 2003 cabinet. Bring me the Daniel Turner file. Could be under A for Azaleas—" Gloria had a memory like a steel trap when it came to houses. She might not remember the owner's name, but she never forgot his address.

The file came, and she dug through papers. "Well, they wanted five mil six years ago, so it has either gotten rundown, or the owner has had an expectation adjustment. The price reduction is a step in the right direction. Overpriced stuff hangs on the market, gets shopworn, and it's always the Realtor's fault. The owner will bad mouth you all over town." She rifled through the file.

"Is there a copy of a mortgage to Rainbow Corporation in that file?" Karla asked.

Gloria moistened thumb on tongue and flipped documents. "No. Here's one to Feliciana Bank stamped paid. And I guarantee you I had a copy of every scrap of paper connected with The Azaleas."

Karla believed Gloria. She was thorough, seldom overlooked anything and rarely made a mistake. Elsa of the clerk of court's office had said, 'If it is recorded, it happened.' When Karla checked, Daniel Turner's mortgage was not recorded. Twenty-four hours later, the mortgage *was* recorded. Funny, though, that Mary didn't know about it—neither had Albert, initially. Now, Gloria insisted that in 2003 the mortgage didn't exist.

"How could that be?" Karla asked.

"Who knows? Someone with an in at the courthouse or somebody trying to get their grubby little hands on somebody else's land. Life's dirty." Greed, the great motivator at work again— "Here," Gloria lifted a legal page faded yellow, "is a detailed list of everything that stays with the house." She by-passed my extended hand and gave Zoe the list. "Copy, please," and to Karla, "Double check every item. You don't want to sell chandeliers that aren't going to be there, or the gilded mirror that's walking out the back door." Gosh! Could that happen? "Market the dwelling with the furniture in place and the decor intact. The hardest thing in the world to sell is faded wallpaper where former ancestors once hung, gouged flooring no longer covered by oriental rugs, or rooms gone dark with missing Tiffany lamps. I know, honey, I know. I've been trapped by every one of those things."

"Okay. I can do that."

"Sell the sizzle, not the steak. I know this steak is real tough. Sell the illusion of a slow-paced and elegant life where stress and road rage don't exist. Sell lazy Sunday afternoons on the veranda, mint Juleps and rustling taffeta, postcards of a more graceful era. The house takes on a magic hard to resist." Her deep, throaty laugh filled the cubicle. She enjoyed her work more than anyone Karla knew. "I bet that old house needs new plumbing, electrical, roofing." Karla's silent nod confirmed her diagnosis. "And remember, men are from Mars and women from Venus. A woman prospect has a different agenda than a man. A woman will nosy in the closets thinking of her own things and whether or not her stuff will fit on those shelves. She'll comment on the housekeeping and the god-awful drapes. A man gets the sight-seeing over with in a big hurry. He's uncomfortable trespassing in another man's castle. He has to be walked through quickly, before he thinks twice and bolts."

"Okay." Karla dug for her pad and made a note. Gloria nodded approval.

"Most buyers come from within a hundred miles of the property. Seldom does a prospect drop in from outer space," Gloria unselfishly shared her expertise. "An interested buyer knocks the house apart, runs down the architecture, points out every flaw and defect, finds a dozen things that couldn't under any circumstances be corrected and therefore merits a reduced price. After trashing the place to the max, he'll demand to go up in the attic to confirm that the roof timbers are termite-eaten and ready to collapse any moment. He'll crawl on his hands and knees under the house and find the teeniest little leak, then tell you with a straight face that in his opinion this house is a *piece of shit*. When you reach that point, the deal is 90% clinched. The rest is nit-picking negotiations about money." Her knowledge bowled Karla over. "And you're going to need devious strategy, not illegal, mind you, but cunning."

"Like?—"

"You have a prospect?"

"Yes—the man who holds the mortgage—he wants to wait it out and foreclose."

"Aha! Classic example—the only thing that will push a man like that over the edge is another buyer coming into the picture. When he's about to lose what he wants, he'll yield. It's like poker, darling, but with higher stakes."

"But I don't have another buyer."

"You don't need a real buyer. A bluff one will do." She saw the blank look on Karla's face. "You bring in somebody else to make an offer, load the contract with impossible contingencies so that it won't fly, and shake up the real prospect."

"You can do that?"

"Any day of the week—" She opened her desk drawer. "Here. Take my card. You run into any big stumbling block, you give old Gloria a call. I've already made every mistake in the book, there's no sense in you re-inventing them." Four lines on her phone were blinking, the callers on hold.

"Thanks three million."

"Anytime, sweetie— I always thought you had what it took. If you'd stuck around long enough, you would've rose like cream to the top, but you lacked patience. This business requires endless patience and perseverance, sweetie. Tell yourself that over and over. Make it your mantra. Patience and perseverance—if you've got that—"she punched line one—"everything else falls into place." As Karla retreated, she heard Gloria say, "Listen, John, I just came across the most fantastic place—exactly what you've been looking for. Find your wife and let's go out there in the next hour or so. You don't want to miss—"

Encouraged by Gloria's words, Karla sailed into The Azaleas filled with new enthusiasm. The best buyer for the plantation was Bale Franklin. He fit Gloria's formula— an interested, highly motivated party, a nearby neighbor who could dial for dollars STAT. No point wasting time. She must bluff Bale into a purchase. But how?—she felt like a beginning swimmer thrown into the deep end of a pool.

After seven tries, she had Bale on the line. His cell phone had caller ID. He'd ignored her calls, but taking her cue from Gloria, she persisted. "Would you like to walk through The Azaleas tomorrow morning or later in the afternoon?" The question, learned at the H&B training session, required a choice between two options that excluded an outright "no." If he answered "neither," Karla would drown right on the spot.

"I can get there Friday at noon."

Karla gasped. She'd done it! Next, she had to tackle Agatha.

Not knowing how to cushion the blow, circumvent the consequences, she informed Agatha directly: "I have a prospect coming to see The Azaleas Friday at noon. I'd appreciate it if you'd let me walk him through the house, and if there's any questions I can't answer, I'll certainly ask for your help."

Agatha said, "Of course, dah-uh-lin'," but when Bale's pickup truck approached, she rushed to the veranda and stood next to Karla. "Bale?—Bale are you this darlin' girl's prospect? How could you lead her on like that, you silly boy?—"

By the way she looked at Bale, Karla could tell Agatha didn't think he was silly or a boy. Her small head enlarged by the bouffant hairdo reared like a cobra ready to strike.

The Catahoulas ambled toward Bale and rubbed against his legs, friendly, wagging their tails. "Down, boys—Down!—" He patted their flanks, pulled their long ears and pushed them away. "It's all in a day's work, Agatha. Hi, Karla—"

"Why, you don't need to go through this house." Amazing, how a little five-foot woman could block stairs ten feet wide. "My! You've been in and out of it all your life."

"Let Karla do her job, Agatha. That's what Mary hired her for." The space between them was charged, heavy like the air before lightning leaps across the sky. "Come on. Let's get this over with."

Bale and Karla quickly walked through every room, except Hank Turner's, that door was locked, and the Jefferson Davis room where Roger Randall toiled over the Audubon manuscript. Bale insisted disturbing the writer wasn't necessary. The tour took twenty minutes, faster than a Chinese fire drill.

Agatha couldn't contain her satisfaction. "See, darlin'? He knows the house. Why, he played here when he was a little boy. His mother did all our sewing—such a fine seamstress, too. No one better in the whole parish—"

The thinly veiled animosity coming through the placid Southern drawl sent Bale clumping down the steps. He wasn't just fleeing the house. He was running from the past, from Agatha, from memories bitter and sweet and still hurting.

This showing had been a complete disaster, a waste of time. Unless Karla got a second chance, she might as well cross Bale from her buyer's list. A private word with him, if they could get away from Agatha nipping at their heels, might save the day.

He said, "Thanks for showing me the place," like a polite guest who had suffered through a boring party and couldn't wait to scram.

"You want to buy this plantation?"

"No," he replied. "I already told you. I'm waiting for Rainbow to foreclose. I intend to get The Azaleas from the corporation."

"Why didn't you tell me you and the sheriff are partners in Rainbow?"

If Karla's knowledge shocked him, he didn't let on. "I figured you'd been to the courthouse and got the scoop from Jimmy."

THE AZALEAS

"I went to the courthouse, all right, but Jimmy dished out very little." She changed tactics. "You found your truck."

"Yes, I did."

"It was the only way I could get back to the house. Why did you leave me out there?"

"The cows were deeper in the swamp than I anticipated. It took longer to find them."

That simply didn't ring true. Karla temporarily swallowed her disbelief. "The chain gang unnerved me."

"I can understand that. I didn't expect—Listen, Karla—"

She looked up hopefully. Maybe he'd had a change of heart. Maybe he'd make a reasonable offer on The Azaleas.

"We're having a dance at The Hills tomorrow night. Would you like to come?"

The question caught Karla off guard. "With you?—like a date?"

"Yeah—that's right."

"I—" She'd get to meet the gentry, each and every one a prospective buyer—the Harpers and the Joiners and the Meyers and the Sawyers—old families with their names on drugstore fronts and bank certificates. Hadn't Gloria said most buyers came from a hundred-mile radius of the property? Karla drooled at the thought of potential owners lined like lollipops in a candy shop—red, luscious, sweet lollipops with green ribbons trailing to the bank.

She groaned inwardly. Albert had insisted she keep the red dress, but she'd left it in the city at Jung Su's Dry Cleaning. Such stupidity! But the powdered sugar and champagne stains required attention, and she hadn't envisioned big soirees in the dark and silent country where black nights unrelieved by street lights and blinking neon signs, swallowed life; where instead of music and laughter suddenly bursting through an open bistro door, dogs bayed at the moon, one first yelp soon joined by a chorus.

Party time and her one fine dress miles away in the city. Albert might not like it, but what else could she do but buy another one? He might not care. He didn't seem upset the red dress came from the expense account. She'd expense another one. Two prime-time outfits!

"I'd be delighted to go to the party with you."

"Pick you up around nine?"

"Oh, I can—" She bit her tongue, stifling the need to drive to the clubhouse in her own car. With concentration she could reach magnolia standard. "Why, suh, I'd be most charmed."

Her fake drawl brought a burst of laughter. He removed the baseball cap that had 'The Hills' written across the beak, and doffed it in her direction.

A Jaguar XJ8 is a mighty fine car, and Bale Franklin had one. Obviously, money wasn't a roadblock here. Bale could pay for The Azaleas if he wasn't so hell bent on stealing it. Albert said foreclosure took ninety days. Karla hummed merrily. If everything worked out the way she anticipated, Bale wouldn't be able to wait until foreclosure. The sale would become a now or never situation.

Bale looked like a movie star in his tuxedo. He definitely qualified for tall, tanned and terrific, Triple T all the way, plus handsome, rich, not married. The song in Karla's heart drowned her resolution to give up men. Giving up men was like going on a diet, hard to starve more than a few days and the more one abstained, the more one thought about food.

He drove like a race driver, ignoring the speed limit, taking the curves on two wheels. Converse McKenzie flashed across Karla's mind. Had he flipped his Mercedes on this road?

She looked up and offered Auntie Emmy's Almighty a silent prayer. The stars were giant sequins sprinkled across the sky. A bright moon splashed the dark oaks silvery.

Bale reached over and took her hand. "You're humming."

"I always hum when I'm happy. Thanks for asking me."

"My pleasure—you look beautiful."

"You like?—came from Le Chic in town."

Clothes could become an addiction. After Bale left the plantation, she drove into St. Francisville, found Le Chic, the "in" boutique, and refusing every little black outfit the sales clerk paraded before her, settled on a silver lamé sheath, ankle-length, two deep slits up the sides, a form-fitting bodice, a low-cut back and rhinestone spaghetti straps—a Roaring Twenties flapper dress guaranteed to make a splashy entrance. On an impulse she bought a sequined, close-fitting cloche with a long silver feather curling down one side. A single rhinestone band stretched across each stiletto-heeled shoe. She

THE AZALEAS

thought with amazement that this was twice in two days she'd been totally coordinated from head to toe. Shopping without looking at price or pinching pennies gave the spirit a big lift.

Albert wouldn't be at the ball, ready to lift an eyebrow, purse his lips and put a damper on her party. Albert floating about alert and watchful was like having your mother chaperone the senior prom. No matter how nice, she could ruin the evening just by being there. Turning off the cell phone gave Karla a twinge of guilt, quickly overcome. She planned to enjoy herself, uninterrupted. First thing in the morning she'd check with Albert.

Across Thompson Creek the Jag topped a rise. The clubhouse lights, bright and gay like a Christmas tree, came into view then doubled in the mirror-image created by the lake.

The day time pickup owners emerged at night from Mercedes, Cadillacs, Lincolns, Audi's and BMW's. The arrivals hailed one another and cat-called back and forth. The familiar cold knot formed in Karla's gut. Bale Franklin offered his arm, and she half-expected a fanfare as they entered the wide hall swarming with people who knew each other. The tinkling laughter and the soft Southern drawls filled the rooms and Karla's heart with dread. A man grabbed Bale by the arm.

"Be right back, honey." He disappeared to the tune of Blueberry Hill, a real oldie played by a live band.

With a big glued-on smile Karla worked her way to the bar for a nip of courage.

"Margarita?—" Peter, the bartender with the cotton head had an elephant memory.

The heavy-set man on Karla's right draped an arm over her bare shoulder. The skinny one on her left crowded close and said something that didn't get past the roar in her ears.

"Get out of my way, Darrell," the heavy-set one said. "You're impeding my forward progress—look, honey, there's lots better than Bale Franklin sittin' right here next to you. You just tickle me with that fine feather—" he ran his fingers over the cloche's silver plume—"and let me pay for that drink." The burst of laughter traveled the bar like a wave at a football game.

"Careful there, boys—she's with the boss man." Peter placed a Margarita on the counter.

Karla grasped the glass stem. "Thank you." She took a big gulp. Tequila warmed her insides like a summer sunrise.

This goldfish bowl made Karla feel vulnerable and exposed, but by damn she could swim with the best. Mimi told her so. She wished Mimi were here, giggling and poking fun, inventing family histories for this crowd, standing on Peter's bar in her G-string and pasties, wowing the customers.

Bars were Karla's natural habitat. Playing the piano in a dark club or sitting on a swiveling stool was second nature to her. She leaned and adjusted her stocking. The mirror behind the bar reflected grinning faces—boozers watching.

"Everybody wants to pay the tab tonight," Peter said. "When Mr. Franklin throws drink 'til you drop bashes, all these souses show up." Peter tended bar, but he ate no humble pie. Neither subordinate nor inferior, he waited on customers in a cool, detached, amused way.

"Thank you, Peter."

"Any time—"

Men swarmed around Karla like a school of minnows, setting off the other women's sonar. They swirled in, slipped possessive arms around their spouses and significant others, and reestablished ownership. In overly gay voices, the uplifted, powdered faces wanted to dance, now, see the gardens, now, get a bite to eat, now. They dragged away their flopping, helpless men— fish caught on an eyelash and hooked on a smile.

"Give them credit," Karla said to Peter, "a good man is hard to find and harder to keep. Right?—"

Peter replied with a laugh and a fake drawl. "Amen, *sistah*."

"There you are!" Bale made his way to the bar.

What a relief! Hanging on his arm was like flying the standard on a yacht—instant identity. She gulped Margarita dregs. Bale held her hand firmly as they worked their way through the guests. Everyone had a tidbit to share with Bale, a joke to make him laugh or a little private aside. His easy, gracious manner differed from Albert's restrained and tense ways like night from day. Relaxation settled on Karla's shoulders like a warm and comfortable shawl. What a fun night!

She stood by Bale's side, her arm through his, dutifully smiling when introduced. Before long the barracudas began circling, beautiful, self-assured Southern belles born knowing how to bat an

THE AZALEAS

eyelid and show a dimple. One coquettish glance made a man feel wanted, treasured, important—*macho*. "Bale, honey... Bale, dahlin'... Bale, sweetheart..."

Karla abandoned Bale to his adoring harem and sought refuge in food. She crossed the ballroom where the miniature white lights strung everywhere gave the room the look of a starry galaxy. Tables ringed the dance floor. For a centerpiece each had a flickering hurricane lamp, the base twined with fresh ivy.

At the buffet table, a white-hat chef carved Virginia baked ham at one end; at the other, his twin tackled roast beef. Platters of plump shrimp, stuffed mushrooms, cheese crackers, bourbon balls came out of the kitchen with assembly-line regularity. Veggie trays—broccoli, cauliflower, cherry tomatoes, thin cucumber wheels, carrots, radishes cut into red petals—splashed the table with color. Fruits arranged like flowers—pear magnolias, hibiscus from red apple wedges, black-eyed Susans fashioned from yellow plums with raisin centers. Cheeses, yellow, orange, white, squares, cubes, rectangles and crescents like new moons rose in golden mounds. Desserts occupied a different table—Mississippi Mud, rum cake, pecan pie, and thin-layered Dobash with cream filling—and the *piece de resistance*—a big Basked Alaska, a replica of the Hills clubhouse, with white icing and a green coconut flake lawn.

"Turn the lights out!" A woman cried. "Kids!—Come see! Come see the cake on fire!"

The children, delegated to a back room, came rushing forth like pyromaniacs. They danced around the Baked Alaska cake until the blue and yellow flames died and Dorcas and Laura served the thick slices. Afterward, the kids' cherubic faces smeared with icing, the nannies shepherded them into the TV room.

The inclusion of all ages contributed to a Southern party's success. Everyone came, from great-gramma if she could still breathe, to the young mother who excused herself to breast feed a newborn. Guests brought nannies and designated drivers. Those from a night away stayed at The Hills or at the St. Francis on the Lake.

"We won't go hungry here tonight, will we?" Roger Randall appeared at Karla's elbow, and piled goodies onto his plate. He looked distinguished in his tuxedo. Karla reached and straightened the crooked tie.

In the midst of new people, Roger took on the status of old friend. "Hi, handsome—where have you been hiding?"

"That corner—over there— Watching you make waves—"

"I'm on my best behavior. Great bash, isn't it?"

"Very nice—"

"But no fun without your wife—"

"Oh, it's fun," he said. "Just not the same—"

"Will you dance with me?"

"My pleasure, but I must warn you, I have two left feet."

Roger steered her to the dance floor. He wasn't a ten nor a zero, more a five, average. Everything about Roger was outstandingly average. He didn't crush Karla close or hold her too loose. Her cheek rested comfortably against his, not warm, not cold— just right. He held Karla's hand firmly, but easily.

"I know why your wife loves you," Karla whispered in his ear.

He grinned sheepishly. "Because I'm so sexy?—"

"Better than that—because you're like an old slipper, easy on the feet."

"I'm taking that as a compliment—"

"Meant to be—" She kissed his cheek. "For Myra—"

"I'd have to explain that—"

The music stopped and they edged back toward the food.

"So there you are—" Bale took Karla's hand with a brusque motion, and a look in his eye she didn't appreciate. He'd seen her kiss Roger. So what? Jesus! Were all men molded by the same cookie cutter?

Roger said, "Great party, Bale," and to Karla, the local parting, "See ya later, alligator." He drifted unobtrusively through the dancers momentarily stopped while the band regrouped and started again.

"I've been chasing you down," Bale said.

"You didn't look lonesome," Karla replied.

Her eyes followed Roger. He had the habit of quietly retreating, then just as silently re-surfacing. He faded into a shadowy corner and melted easily into a crowd. Yet something about him, something Karla couldn't quite put her finger on, convinced Karla that whenever Roger vanished, he didn't completely disappear.

"You had plenty company," Karla said.

"I always do," he said. "But who did I bring to my own party?" He placed his hand on Karla's chin and lifted her face until her eyes met his.

"Me," Karla whispered, suddenly shy— a new and uncommon sensation.

"I suppose we must dance." He reluctantly led her to the dance floor. "I'm not very good at this."

He was right. He had no rhythm, no moves. His arm weighed heavily on Karla's waist. He had two left feet. His hand clasped hers, palm damp.

"You won't have to suffer long," he said. "One of the boys will come rescue you."

The tension in his thighs came through the material of Karla's new dress. "Maybe I don't want to be rescued."

A woman enveloped in diamonds and perfume swayed close and asked, "Honey, are you by any chance a Whitmore from Geo'gia?"

"Not a chance."

Bale grinned and jerkily turned in the other direction.

"Alabama, maybe?—"

"Sure. That sounds good. Why not?—"

No doubts plagued Southerners, sure of their pedigree. They were part of this land, this nobility. Everybody here knew what regiment their great-great-great grandfather served in during the Civil War. They talked about Robert E. Lee as if the general dozed in the adjacent room, ready to awaken at any moment and join the festivities. This connection, this sense of lineage, contributed to the aura of royalty. Every person here descended from somebody. These people would never stray, by accident or design, too far from their history, their land, or their roots.

Generations ago the Yankees won the war and the Confederates went through the motions of surrender. Here in West Feliciana Parish, isolated from the real world, too remote to be affected by urban flight, relocating industry or mass migrations, life remained static. The South didn't have to rise again. The South had never fallen.

A stout gentleman and his dancing partner stopped while he informed Karla he'd served in World War II with General Jonathan Whitmore. "Are you related?"

"Uncle John? Sure. I'll claim him." An outright lie, but it brought the old man pleasure.

With a smile and a relieved look, Bale ceded Karla to a skittish gentleman with white hair and a matching goatee who looked like the Kentucky Fried Chicken Colonel. The music came to an end, and within seconds the band started again with Ricky Martin's "Living la Vida Loca." Karla figured the Latin rhythm was too much for the old man and he'd make an excuse and move away. Wrong. A wild gleam came into his eyes; he twitched his shoulders, moved his hips and tripped the light fantastic.

"Go, Kevin! Go!" The other couples cheered him on, encouraging his antics.

"Drop dead with a heart attack, you will!"

"What a way to go!" His eyes shifted heavenward and he spun Karla around.

The second number, "Roses are Red," a Bobby Vinton oldie, found Kevin's head purposely nestled against Karla's bosom. They glided past Sheriff Jimmy Watson and a stunning blonde, big green eyes and blue eyelids. One more twirl and the sheriff tapped the old gentleman on the shoulder.

Karla breathed relief. "Thanks. I owe you. Dancing cheek to chest was getting to me."

"You should've seen the expression on your face."

"Oh, dear—did it show?"

"The trick is to smile, no matter what. Even when they're killing you, you keep on smiling." His hand on Karla's hip was like the rudder on a ship. He steered her closer. "Are we still on for the Angola Rodeo?"

"Wouldn't miss it for the world, except, of course, if The Azaleas sells—then I'm outta here. By the way, Mary was touched that you went to her mother's memorial service."

"The Turners are an old Feliciana family. I couldn't do less." He reeled Karla out then back.

Head tilted, arms around his neck, she said, "C'mon, help me out here. Why didn't you tell me about Rainbow Corporation?"

"What's there to tell?"

"That you and Bale Franklin are partners, for starters."

"I figured you'd stumble across that info soon enough."

THE AZALEAS

"That mortgage is dated 2003, but in 2005 it hadn't been recorded."

He pretended a big, fake frown. "Where did you get that idea?"

"In 2005 Hasker and Blunt tried to sell The Azaleas, and they have copies of every scrap of paper concerning the plantation. Why, they even have a bill of sale for slaves going back to the early 1800s, but they have no Rainbow mortgage."

"I don't recall anyone from H&B coming to talk to me. They could've missed the mortgage," he said, unruffled, favoring Karla with a crooked smile.

"And when I checked the other day, I missed it, too?"

"It's not hard to overlook an instrument." No wonder the FBI had so much trouble pinning anything on him! Sheriff Watson was as smooth and slippery as an eel.

"But today it's there, big and bold, for all to find. Why?"

"Why what?—"

"Why don't you buy The Azaleas?"

His hand slipped from Karla's waist to her backside. "I'm not in the house buying business." He crushed Karla close and blew the cloche feather away from his chin, "especially not with the IRS and the FBI poking their nose into every nook and cranny of my life. Sell The Azaleas to Bale."

The robust man with graying beard who enthusiastically tapped Jimmy Watson on the shoulder interrupted. "Listen, you may be sheriff, but you can't monopolize the only fresh face we've had here in years—my turn."

"You're such a party pooper, Edgar." The sheriff feigned an injured tone. "I don't think you can handle this girl. She just poked me with a pretty sharp dart." He stepped gallantly aside, cocked his thumb back as if it were a trigger and shot an imaginary bullet in Karla's direction. He didn't look at all guilty.

The old gentleman smelling of English Leather aftershave and bourbon whiskey shuttled Karla away.

"Why, hello, Edgar," Karla raised her voice above the clamor. "I'm in town to—"

"I know. Everybody knows."

"So does everybody know who'd like to buy The Azaleas?"

"Bale Franklin—" The man's name sprang from the tip of every tongue. Karla must pursue Bale with more vigor. Use a different attack mode, entice and lure, if outright conquest wasn't possible.

"Who else?—"

"Jeremiah Jones. Over there." He motioned toward the wheelchair drawn to a table where a lively card game was in progress. Jeremiah Jones had gone on the fateful Quarter buggy ride. "His land abuts the east boundary."

Agatha leaned over Judge Jones, encouraging his play. Elegant in a pale yellow dress with a short Chinese-style jacket, Agatha rested a hand familiarly on Jeremiah's shoulder, her guard down. Her party make-up didn't differ from her stay-at-home face. The same bouffant hairdo in place this morning had been beauty parlor teased and freshly reworked into this evening's gleaming helmet. Relaxed and smiling, an unexpected happiness softened her face. Sam in a black cotton tee-shirt, baggy pants and ill-fitting black jacket stood behind the Judge.

"Isn't Jeremiah Jones too old to be buying more land?"

Edgar looked at Karla as if she'd arrived on an alien space ship. "What's the matter with your way of thinkin', girl? One's never too old to acquire more land—having land—why land's more permanent than money, more valuable than gold. I'd rather have land than a fickle woman any day. Women come and go, but land is forever."

Properly chastised, Karla swallowed the next question. When was enough land enough? Obviously never—

She skipped from arm to arm, partner to partner, making mental notes of every name she gleaned. The band struck an enthusiastic "Macarena," and the dance floor whirled with bright colors. The blaring music spurred the dancers faster, faster. The frenzy soared to a degree where the partner no longer mattered and the dance itself became an orgasm of purely selfish enjoyment. In his wheelchair Jeremiah twisted to and fro from the waist up, shoulders hunching up and down, fingers snapping in time to the music, legs hanging dead.

Karla whirled by him. "C'mon, Judge! Let's take a spin!" She snatched the cards from his hands, placed them face-down on the table, and pulled his wheelchair.

Sam sprang to the Judge's rescue.

"Leave him alone!" Karla reached for Jeremiah's hand and two-stepped around him. "We're taking a turn!"

THE AZALEAS

The Judge twisted and turned in his chair, tentatively at first, not sure what was happening here. "Listen, Karla—"

"Oh, come on! Loosen up. At the Jazz Fest in New Orleans there's one whole section roped off for wheelchair dancing. Turn those wheels!"

He tipped the chair on its two wheels and spun wildly, a wide grin on his face, Karla twirling in tandem. The other dancers grouped around, clapping to the music, calling encouragement. Judge Jeremiah couldn't move his legs, but his upper body felt the music, swaying and jerking to the rhythm.

"Whew!" Karla said when the number drew to a close. "What a workout! You must've been a great dancer! Here, Agatha, you can have him back. Don't let him sit out the next number!"

Karla escaped to the powder room, locked herself in a toilet stall, wrote all the names she could remember on a crumpled cocktail napkin and stuffed the paper into her evening bag.

The women flushing toilets and primping before mirrors said a lot to each other, and a few polite words to her. Their icy looks skimmed past the butterfly on Karla's shoulder taking in every detail while pretending not to notice.

"Known Bale long?—" A blonde freshening her lipstick asked.

"No." Karla powdered her nose, "a couple of days."

"I've known him since high-school," the blonde said. "Every woman here would give her eye teeth to be in your shoes."

"Is that right?"

Until the clock struck twelve and the Jaguar turned into a truck, Karla was Cinderella— beautiful, popular and wanted—a heady feeling. The imaginary dictionary settled on her head like an invisible weight. She threw back her shoulders, lifted her chin, and sashayed from the powder room. She bumped into Agatha and her blue-haired friends. "Hi, y'all," Karla said. "Isn't this a grand party?"

Agatha replied, "Yes, darlin'. Bale always has magnificent parties."

With the obvious bad feeling between them, it surprised Karla to see Agatha at Bale's party, yet she seemed perfectly at ease, enjoying herself, as if each section of her life operated in different compartments and hate and distrust were locked away for the evening. City people Karla could read instantly. Country gentry left her puzzled. One needed a degree in psychology to understand them.

"My, but you look positively ravishin' in that dress," Agatha said, her voice dripping honey, "doesn't she, girls?"

Karla twirled for their reaction and was rewarded by cries of "Beautiful!" "Looks tremendous on you!—" "Only the thin and slim can get away with that outfit!"

Two little boys streaked past and a grandmother reached with a practiced arm and grabbed their shirttails. "Robert! Cade! What are you doing here? Where's Latisha? She's supposed to be watching you. Go to the back room and watch TV. Are you sleepy? Go upstairs if you're sleepy. Go right this minute or else we'll go straight home and you'll miss the fireworks."

At midnight the boom! Boom! Boom! Boom!—brought the sleeping children outside, yawning and rubbing their eyes. Red flares burst in the sky. Multicolored star showers trickled down. While the children's eyes scanned the heavens, the cars lined the driveway, motors purring, open doors awaiting passengers.

"Good night—" "Great party, Bale—" "Glad to have you here, Karla— you're always welcome. You must come—Bale, be sure to bring Karla to Myron's party next week." Bale walked with his guests halfway to their cars, and sometimes all the way, a Southern departure.

It was almost dawn when Bale and Karla arrived at The Azaleas.

"What a fabulous evening," she said.

Her hesitation at the front door was caused by logistics. She had no right to invite him into The Azaleas, but the evening had been too fulfilling to leave him standing on the veranda petting Catahoula curs. She extended her hand and he took it, drew her close and kissed her, slow and idling at first, then encouraged by her response, he shifted into overdrive. They removed their shoes and tiptoed down the hallway, laughing silently, stopping dead still when an old board creaked. They sneaked upstairs to the Andrew Jackson room like two teenagers afraid of getting caught. The door groaned when Karla pushed it open.

"Remind me to send some WD-40 over in the morning," Bale whispered.

Upstairs this old house had no overhead lighting. Karla groped for the long chain on the Tiffany bedside lamp and jerked it. A circle of light flooded the room. She gasped aloud, and Bale took a quick step back.

THE AZALEAS

Albert, fast asleep, slumped in the Queen Anne chair.

"You had no right—" fury choked the words.
"Had I known—"
"Who let you in? I'll kill them. I'll wring their necks with my own two hands."
"The chambermaid—"
"What chambermaid? They don't have a chambermaid."
"Her name is Laura."
"Oh." That stopped Karla short. She supposed Laura who brought the breakfast tray was a chambermaid.

They were going through the line at McDonald's, 5 a.m., black coffee and biscuits, still dark outside. "How much did you pay her?"
"Standard fare—nothing much—"
"If she values her life, that bitch better not come near me from this day on."

Bale had backtracked from the bedroom as if the place was on fire. Circumstances reduced Karla's shrieking fit to hissing whispers so she compensated by kicking Albert's shins, pummeling his chest and shoving against him. Strength fueled by adrenalin, furious, she physically pushed him through the door that needed WD-40 the same way she needed oiling. She heard thumping footsteps on the stairway and realized both men were descending together. Their short, quick laughter intermingled. Red bombs exploded in Karla's head. The nerve, the nerve, the very nerve!

Like a spurned suitor, Albert returned before daylight, pelting the second-story window with gravel scooped from the flower bed. He wouldn't stop even when Karla threw open the sash and gave him the bird. Screw him.

Pebbles struck the window like hard rain. Shit! He'd break the 18th-century glass pane with wavy imperfections, impossible to replace, and she'd have an even bigger situation on her hands. She ran downstairs. Goddamn if the idiot didn't think the situation hilarious, grinning like a court jester at Carnival. By the time coffee warmed her guts, the urge to kill overpowered her. Thank God the knife in her hand was plastic, else she might commit murder.

"If I may say something—" he began.

"Shut up."

"I'm going to say it anyhow. I have to know where you are. Be able to reach you. Never— you hear me? Never turn off your cell."

What gall! Where did he get the authority to scold her like the father she never had? Angry and resentful as she was and intended to be for many days to come, an unbidden feeling that somebody cared where she was or what she did tempered her retort. "I'll turn off my goddamn phone any time I want to."

"Then I'll show up."

"I hate bullies," Karla puffed angry steam. "And you, Albert, are a bully of the worst kind. A control freak— Come here. Go there. Don't turn off the phone. Leave me alone! For God's sake, leave me alone!"

"Don't get those feathers ruffled again." His gray eyes studied Karla's face, a deep, serious look in their depths, and something else, too, something more she couldn't understand. She had little use for him other than as her ticket out of poverty. She resented being his tool. As soon as she was able, she'd even the score, walk away. The instant she had that first check in her hand, she'd tell this sucker in no uncertain words, in language a fish monger could understand, exactly where to go and where to stuff it.

He set a cigar box on the table. "The tap dancing boys sent this." She glanced down without touching. With her luck, a time bomb could be ticking in there. He let the box sit between them, no rush. Why should he rush? He had nothing better to do than to poke his nose in other people's business and all the time in the world to appreciate their reaction. Albert opened the lid. Nothing but junk in the shoe box—rocks, twigs, pigeon poop, four silver tabs from canned drinks, two strings of Mardi Gras beads, six doubloons, and a crumpled triangular piece of black cloth no larger than a dollar bill.

"Where did you get this?" She momentarily forgot her resolve to stare through Albert as if he didn't exist and poked through the jumble. She placed the cloth and the four silver tabs side by side on the table, studying them closely. The mounting excitement made her guts growl or maybe it was the coffee.

Albert asked, amused. "How much did you pay them?"

Karla glanced up quickly. "The tap-dancing boys?—"

He nodded.

"Nothing yet, but I'll take care of them."

THE AZALEAS

Albert intertwined his fingers, made a tent with the index ones, and placed them in his chin cleft, a studious habit.

Thoughts chased each other through Karla's mind: "Black cotton—could come from anybody's tee-shirt." She held up the torn cloth, smelled it, made a face, and handed it to Albert.

He held the scrap up to his nose. "Mildew?—"

"Perfume—Georgio or some of that industrial strength stuff that lingers forever. How come the police didn't find this?" she asked.

Albert shrugged.

Karla took another sniff. "Oh! I know what this is. It's that horrible Old Spice stuff old men use. Can I keep this?" No way could he drop her in this puzzle and expect her not to put the pieces together. She turned her attention to the aluminum can tabs. "The sniper drank four cokes? Four beers?—"

"Four soft drinks—maybe the tabs weren't his. He also favored peanut butter crackers," Albert said, rattling two cellophane wrappers.

"Doesn't make sense, Albert—if you scaled a cathedral to kill somebody, you wouldn't take a picnic with you."

"What we must do is get The Azaleas sold. Let's wrap our part and leave the rest to the police."

His words infuriated Karla. "I can sell the plantation if you'd quit meddling. You just knocked for a loop the man ready to write a check and buy your precious Mary's plantation—"

"Bale Franklin?—" Albert blinked rapidly when he said the name and a rush of merry devilment swept depth and intensity from his eyes, and the irises went gray and flat, the familiar mocking eyes Karla knew. The wry sneer returned to his lips and he laughed softly. "My dear, though it might seem appropriate at the time, it's not good form to clinch a deal—um—*that way.*"

The coffee spilt. The biscuits went flying. She reached across the table and slapped his face.

CHAPTER 12

Three days later, frustrated, unable to sleep, Karla crept down the stairs, sat on the cool veranda and watched the day unfold. Since the night of the ball, a long, extended quiet like a post-partum depression, enveloped the plantation. Agatha went to New Orleans. Without the captain at the helm, the household drifted aimlessly, a boat without a rudder. After stirring trouble, Albert skipped back to the city, leaving Karla floundering. Since the bedroom fiasco, Bale disappeared. She had no idea how to resume their relationship, personal or business.

She'd never sell this place. If only she had one-tenth of Gloria's real estate expertise! She took stock: Cross out Bale Franklin. Scratch Roger Randall closeted in the Jefferson Davis room churning out x-number of Audubon pages a day. He loved the little bungalow he and his wife built. Forget Sheriff Watson, busy dodging the federal people. His plate had more on it than he could handle. Not one person at the ball jumped at the chance to buy The Azaleas. Karla's list of buyers abruptly dead-ended. Zilch! Zip. Goose egg!

If she didn't sell this plantation, how much did she owe Albert? Two dresses, two months' rent, one Nintendo—she couldn't believe that stupid game cost $100!—four tanks of gas. It made no difference. She couldn't pay. She'd dug herself into a hole so deep not even a mole would keep her company.

Could she overcome? Didn't look likely— Reality meant welfare and food stamps and the monthly eenie-meenie-minie-moe decisions,

THE AZALEAS

pay this one, dodge that one, string along the rest. The preliminary confidence Albert imparted vanished. The initial enthusiasm carrying her to this point lost its punch. Faith in her abilities seemed a gossamer dream, vivid and real in the night, impossible to recall in the morning. Why had she let Albert talk her into this? Allowed him to lift her so high? The fall would kill her. And she was crashing.

Failing to sell The Azaleas eliminated the gold pot at the end of the rainbow and destined her life to remain forever unchanged. Same song, second verse, could be better, but it's gonna be worse.

Back and forth—back and forth— the wicker rocker motion did little to comfort her.

Pink dawn colored the eastern sky. Blurry feathers dispelled the night blues. Daylight skimmed the oak tree canopy and through her tears each leaf glistened like a prism. She cried for a rosy future fast slipping away, for a past she'd rather forget, for Richard who loved her but married somebody else, for Lebron's mangled body and lack of opportunity, for life lived trapped by circumstances. Wasn't that how everybody began and ended? Trapped by circumstances?

As she sat there mulling her fate so irrevocably linked to the success or failure of The Azaleas sale, the rising sun warmed the land and evaporated the dew. The morning mist melted, and the clipped lawns emerged, deep green and bristly like AstroTurf.

Chirps and tweets came from the green branches. The singing birds, country sunrises and soft breezes seemed an exotic paradise, a strange Eden. City life was turbulent and noisy from daybreak to daybreak with little room for quiet space. Would her inner life ever reach this gracious state of natural harmony?

She wanted what Roger had, the closeness, the intimacy that kept his family in the circle of his embrace even when miles apart. Wasn't she entitled to that? Did Aunt Emmy's Everlasting God, Almighty Counselor, the One in which her faith was grounded, intend for Karla to wander forever alone?

Her former McDonough High classmates were married with children. Some had gone through two or three husbands already. Mimi at the Parrot Bar had two cute tykes and a merchant marine husband with glowing red hair she adored. Bilbao came home every other month, and Mimi counted the days until he arrived and immediately began the sweet, agonizing countdown to the hour of his departure.

Women tired with housekeeping often told Karla they envied her freedom, misery in their voices as they griped about being tied down to husband, house and kids, mired in the long, slow boredom that strangled their hopes and ambitions. But they didn't bolt. And if they did, before long they landed back in the same situation. The need for love was the hidden drive that propelled the world.

Karla wanted to be loved. She deserved a man's love. She could earn that love, if only—concentrating on not thinking about Richard was like counting sheep to overcome insomnia. The ploy never worked.

Unlucky in love, that's what she was—damned unlucky in love. Maybe she'd never have anybody, only herself. The thought was daunting. She didn't like herself that well. Maybe no one else liked her either. That depressing idea unleashed tears. Afterward, she felt much better, refreshed, as if she'd opened a soda bottle and let the fizz spill over.

At the sound of approaching steps, Karla squeezed her eyes shut and ran her knuckles across her cheeks, rubbing them dry. No need for anyone to see the real estate agent at this low ebb. Agents were cheerful, upbeat people. Heaven forbid she destroyed that myth.

The screen door slammed. Karla didn't look up. The steps came closer.

"Here." Dorcas handed Karla a mug with Heineken written on it, not official Azalea china.

She settled her big bottom into a rocker, sipped coffee and looked straight ahead at the rolling landscape, giving Karla time to gather herself. She rocked back and forth, the wicker creaking under her weight, coffee smelling strong. After a decent interval, Dorcas gave Karla a sideways glance and said, "You is up mighty early."

As if the cook's voice officially signaled daytime, the two Catahuola dogs emerged from the cool recesses under the house and draped themselves on the front steps.

"I couldn't sleep. What kind of birds are those?"

"The one trillin' ag'in and ag'in is a mockin' bird. They's always stuck on one note— them flying 'round is blue jays, feisty lil' birds. They'll swoop down and peck a squirrel or a cat. They don't care if it's ten times bigger'n they are. Them others peckin' the ground is common wrens. We're all birds, you know. Which one are you?"

THE AZALEAS

Karla gave the question some thought. "Part mocking bird, part jay, a lot of wren with a dash of parrot—"

"I ain't never seen no parrot."

"The Parrot Bar across the street from where I live has a neon parrot hanging over the door, pink and yellow and green. Inside there's a live one on a stand. She has beautiful green feathers. Her name is Mimosa, and she can talk a blue streak."

"Oh, yeah— I heard 'bout them polly-talkin' birds. What do this one say?"

"Basic stuff like 'Come here, you shithead.'"

Dorcas cackled. "My! My! Girl!—you been doing some stirrin'. We ain't had this much action here since—I ain't rememberin' since when."

"Action without results is like spinning a car wheel in a mud puddle. It gets you nowhere. I'm no closer today to selling The Azaleas than I was the first day I got here."

"You done showed it to Mr. Bale."

"He doesn't want to buy it," Karla replied, impatient and frustrated. "He's waiting to steal it."

The whole town pointed a collective finger at Bale, and Karla couldn't get him to budge. From somewhere inside her head came a little refrain 'Patience and perseverance, patience and perseverance. Make that your mantra.' Gloria! In the confusion this last few days Karla had forgotten Gloria. She'd call her right away and ask for help. Hopefully, Karla's SOS would be spiked on the spindle with the glowing orange slips demanding immediate attention.

"Bah! Mr. Bale wants it all right."

"Why doesn't he buy it, then?"

She waved the question aside. "That's white folks' business."

"But black folks know all white folks business, so why don't you tell me?"

She probably would've, if Agatha hadn't bustled through the door right then.

"Oh, there you are, Dorcas. We need you in the kitchen, honey, not out here gossiping." Agatha never raised her gentle, cultured voice, but Dorcas had been brought to task.

An injured Dorcas rolled her eyes. "Mo'ning, Miss Agatha. Welcome back. I ain't doin' no gossipin'." She hoisted herself from the chair and lumbered inside.

"Good morning," Karla said. "It's a beautiful day. How was the big city?"

Everyone here nosed into everyone else's business, a procedure so matter of course that Agatha didn't question how Karla knew about Agatha's trip to New Orleans.

"One of those frustrating days," Agatha replied, "spent at the Bureau of Vital Statistics dealing with incompetents. Preacher Frank needs an original birth certificate with an official seal. I'm working on getting him a little state pension, food stamps, welfare—maybe he'll be lucky and die before he has to resort to those indignities. All we have is a birth record on a prescription pad. Dr. Lucius did things like that. He delivered Preacher in the slave cabin and wrote on the paper, Baby boy born to Morgana Felder on The Azaleas Plantation 4/12/1916, father unknown. Preacher even got in the Army twice with that paper. But now it won't do. It's nothing but more and more red tape." Was Agatha legally documenting Preacher Frank's existence, preparing the old man for the time when he must say goodbye to The Azaleas?

She took care of her servants. She scolded them as if they were her children and participated in their life as if they were family. And they were family, more family than her absentee niece, Mary Bravelle, or the distant cousins who seldom visited. Agatha's household help gave her life meaning and purpose, and that, Karla realized with startling clarity, was what a life needed—meaning and purpose.

When the plantation sale forced Agatha to move into a little house in town with no room for her servants, she'd die. Any move beneficial for Mary Bravelle was detrimental for Agatha Turner. On the see-saw of life when the balance tilted up for one player, it went down for the other. "I'm sorry," Karla said.

"No need be," Agatha replied in her honey-dripping voice. "We're staying put right here. We're not going anywhere." Hard-boiled as a picnic egg, she quietly worked on Plan B. Maybe her business in New Orleans extended past the search for Preacher's birth certificate.

Frying bacon and sausage smells coming from the kitchen derailed Karla's thoughts and made her mouth water—scrambled eggs fresh from the hens, grits dripping melted butter, biscuits made with real milk and sifted flour. Dorcas snubbed plastic substitutes and any product that began with Lite. The cholesterol level zoomed off the charts.

THE AZALEAS

Clem and Laura served breakfast in the small dining room between the butler's pantry and the colonnade leading to the kitchen. Roger came downstairs early. After three days of staring at the computer screen non-stop, he'd gone cross-eyed and taken a break.

"I took a little tour," he said, "along the Audubon Trace. I went through the Myrtles and met their resident ghost. I stopped at Audubon House and half-dozen others," Roger continued. "All except Rosedown—The New York owner wanted $12.50 just to ride through the place, and instead of beautiful girls in hoop skirts conducting the tour, you got an audio-cassette."

Agatha said bitterly, "He's destroying everything we spent years building. The Tourist Commission and Historical Society are trying to stop him. One rotten apple can spoil the whole barrel. Dividing up the land! Selling lots! Trashing the place!—"

If Bale Franklin bought The Azaleas, that was exactly what he intended to do. Would Agatha roll over and die? Maybe so, maybe not—a steel edge tempered her vapors. She belonged, Karla believed, to the elitist group—survivors.

"And to add insult to injury," Roger continued, "He's auctioning the antique furniture to the highest bidder and replacing it with reproductions."

"The museum in Dallas bought the bed Robert E. Lee slept in for $450,000—" Agatha said. "I'd like to see that no-good Yankee reproduce that." Only Agatha's good breeding kept her from spitting on the floor.

Antique beds held no charms for Karla. The short, narrow one she slept on should be delegated to a torture chamber. She shut out the conversation and concentrated on her own personal, financial, life-threatening problem—finding a buyer for The Azaleas.

Jeremiah Jones could buy it. The old man owned the adjoining land on the east. He and Karla had danced around the subject of The Azaleas often enough, but she never gave him a full sales pitch. That omission needed to be corrected right away. She excused myself and made haste to reach the neighbor's house.

Two humongous moss-draped live oaks guarded Jeremiah's plantation front door. Their imposing presence gave the two-story white brick house its name, Twin Oaks. The heavy brass knocker brought the Judge's man, Sam, to the front door.

"G'mornin', Miss," he said, holding the door open, big feet doing a shuffle step. His face was a wreath of vacuous smiles and twitches. "Hello, hello, hello, hi there, hello—"

"Hello, Sam. Your boss in?—"

"In the den playing with the gun— He likes to play with the guns. I'm not good with guns. Judge says I'm too stupid to learn how—"

He led the way, chattering, and Karla followed, observing him from the rear. He had a peculiar build, long, heavy legs and a thick waist. His trousers were slung low on fatty hips that dipped from side to side as he walked. His rounded shoulders hunched forward, and his arms swung vigorously back and forth as if he needed that motion to balance his steps.

Vast rooms with 16-foot ceilings and two-foot wide baseboards flanked the brick-floored hallway. Crown molding impossible to replace trimmed the walls. In some spots where the faded wallpaper had worn, the cheesecloth backing was exposed. Karla peeked right and left at the antiques, silver, porcelain, carpets. These country Southerners knew how to live and live well.

All this space and Jeremiah Jones resided in the den next to the kitchen. He reminded Karla of Mrs. Nordham, the feeble old woman she sat with for a time. Mrs. Nordham had a forty-room mansion on St. Charles Avenue, but she ate, slept, entertained and watched TV in her bedroom. Auntie Emmy, in her final year, moved a bed next to the pot-bellied stove in the kitchen and seldom left that spot. Even Agatha spent most of her waking hours in her office-den, sitting at the tall secretary writing those endless notes that defined a Southern lady, playing solitaire or watching TV. As their houses emptied and their friends died, old people narrowed their range of motion and pulled the walls in closer, seeking warmth in the familiarity of a few well-worn things.

At home, dressed in a plaid cotton shirt open at the neck, Jeremiah appeared frailer, thinner than when dandy in a tuxedo or suited in flamboyant green as he was the day of the carriage ride. That Sunday afternoon Karla had been so preoccupied with her own entanglements, she hadn't noticed the sloping shoulders or the sunken rib cage.

"Check all those trophies!" Karla exclaimed, looking around the room.

THE AZALEAS

Big antlered deer with beady glass eyes looked down from the walls. They shared space with a menacing moose head, a creature with curlicue horns, multi-colored ducks on the wing and bass caught forever in wide-mouth gasp. A six-foot blue and gold marlin leapt across the fireplace mantel. The room looked like the Wild Life and Fisheries Museum that used to be on Carondelet Street before the city turned the building into one more courthouse.

Two glass cases filled with rifles, shotguns and pistols flanked the fireplace. Floor-to-ceiling shelves crammed with books lined the walls.

The room was warm and comfortable, with a worn Oriental rug, end tables, desks, family pictures, reading lamps, newspapers and magazines piled in baskets, a game table with a chess set ready to go. The drapes were tied back from the big windows to let in light and fresh air.

"Good morning, my dear." The judge's wheelchair was drawn to a card table. He worked on a broken-down rifle, the barrel, stock, and trigger placed neatly before him. He was running an oily rag tied to the end of a straightened wire clothes hanger through the gun barrel. "How's my favorite dance partner?" Attuned now to the slow rhythm of the country words, so different from the New Orleans gumbo sounds, his soft, southern drawl fell easy on Karla's ears. "To what do I owe this pleasure?"

"Were you a great white hunter?" Karla stood before the nearest gun cabinet, checking a double-barreled silver pistol.

"Still am," he said, "With the help of gadgets and widgets. You're looking at a Derringer pistol. Next to it, a Smith & Wesson— I collect guns. That one is a single-barrel Remington, and a bolt action—"

"I don't know anything about guns," Karla interrupted.

Quarter residents kept their guns a private affair, stashed under the mattress, in a drawer beneath their underwear, or on the top closet shelf behind a wig box. In West Feliciana, shotguns rode on racks across the truck rear windows. Every house had a gun rack or cabinet. Home owners propped guns near doorways. "Do all the men around here hunt?"

"We have a few crackerjack women, too. Good, good shots—"

"What are you doing with that one?" Karla pointed to the gun in pieces on the card table.

"Cleaning the barrel—deer season opens next week and I will be ready."

"Really?—and how do you—" She stopped herself. Alluding to his condition was rude. In the Quarter everyone co-existed with the physically crippled and maimed, not to mention the mentally deranged. No one ever referred to their afflictions.

"How do I get to the deer stand? I have a rig with a pulley that hoists me up. When I fish, Sam straps me into a chair, so the big tuna won't haul me overboard. If you love something enough, you can find ways to compensate, conquer obstacles."

He didn't stop what he was doing. Karla leaned closer for a better look. The judge smelled like a cross between 3-in-1 oil and—and—she sniffed discreetly. Aha! Goose bumps rose on her arms. Old Spice, old man's after shave. "Can you shoot a .223 caliber bullet with that gun?"

The question caught the Judge by surprise. "I thought you didn't know anything about guns?"

"I don't. I just know that Mary Bravelle and Lebron were shot with .223 bullets."

"The police are busy, are they?"

"Albert says the crime is just about solved. They know who did it."

If that disturbed him, he gave no indication. "Good work."

Guns and aftershave made Judge Jeremiah a suspect, but the crippled legs provided an iron-clad alibi. Besides, he'd been in the buggy with the rest of them. She circled to other subjects. "And when you're not outdoors, you're in front of the fireplace with a good book?"

Behind the thick, horn-rimmed glasses, the amber eyes were clear and sharp. "Sam, bring us a pot of coffee, please, or lemonade if you'd rather."

Karla supposed the old man figured he might as well serve refreshments since it seemed she planned to stick around for a while. "Coffee is fine."

The Judge had an active library. The well-worn covers on his books peeled away from the spines. Some sat crosswise on top of others. Many lay horizontally instead of occupying vertical slots. In this library the owner didn't order books by the yard to fill the shelves. The books weren't all one size in matching leather with gold titles, forever new because nobody opened them. Judge Jones used his library.

"You like to read?" he asked

"I love to read."

"I'm a history buff. Civil War, mainly. Who do you read?"

"Everybody— I like Joseph Conrad and Graham Greene."

"When I stray away from my own turf, I find them very good companions."

"Sometimes when I read Conrad, I think I'm sitting on a boat deck, listening to Marlowe tell his sea-faring stories."

"A good book will do that to you."

"I have a first edition Lord Jim."

"Why, that's not possible."

"Yes, yes, it is. Bilbao, a merchant marine friend who likes to read books about the sea, found Lord Jim in a musty little hole-in-the-wall bookstore in Hong Kong. He picked it up for a song, read it, and brought it home to me. He gives me books. Jacques Frerer who owns the Librairie on Royal Street identified it as a rare first edition, very valuable. I tried to give it back to Bilbao, but he just said, 'don't bother me with all that. If it's that valuable, sell it to Jacques and pay your rent. I'm always having trouble—" She stopped herself. Only a dumb bunny flaunted financial disabilities.

"Dear Jacques—an old friend— we don't see each other much anymore. How is he?"

"You know Jacques? It's a small world! Arthritis gets him sometimes, but he keeps plugging. After Katrina things are slow, very slow, but he opens the shop for a few hours every day."

"He would. Yes, indeed, he would. Let me show you this." He steered the wheelchair toward the rear bookcase and grasped a long pole with a clamp at one end. He knew exactly where to reach— "A first Lofcadio Hearn. Jacques got it for me. You've heard of Lofcadio?"

"From Jacques— Hearn lived in the Quarter before going to Japan. His New Orleans stories are more fascinating than the Japanese ones, but he's better known for those."

The old man and the girl sat for a long time discussing books, his hand moving lovingly from one volume to another. The Judge rumbled on, his words flowing like a tail attached to a soaring kite. He knew his literature—classic, contemporary and local. His deep, rich voice retelling facts and anecdotes transported both of them to another world, another dimension. Together, they took flight to places so real in their imagination that they could see, taste and touch them. After making a full circle they returned to his Civil War Collection. He knew the history of the Felicianas, from the big scenario to the little one-acts and skits. He had a repertoire of Felice stories.

"When the Yankees overran The Azaleas, burning everything they didn't steal, Felice hid her newborn son, Henry, inside a turkey roaster and saved the Turner line. You've seen her green orb yet?"

"No, but I felt her raise the temperature in the living room."

"She moves the lamp, too—the one on the left side of the couch."

Sam brought the coffee. His clumsy hands shook as he poured, missed the cup, and filled the saucer.

"Here, Sam. Let me," Karla pried the pot from his hand. The strength of his grip reminded her of the Down syndrome child who once hugged her with such hidden force it took his mother and two men to disentangle his arms from round her neck.

"You've had a chance to go through the historical district and down to the landing?" Jeremiah asked flipping book pages filled with plantation history.

"No, I haven't done a thing except work, but I will take a tour before I leave. This is the most beautiful town I've ever seen."

"Yes. If only we can keep it that way."

"Progress is hard to stop, but St. Francisville seems to have managed."

"It hasn't been easy. People like you make it almost impossible."

"Me?" She fended the subtle accusation. "What have I done?"

"You look for the highest price a place can bring without regard or consideration to what it will be used for. Bale Franklin will buy The Azaleas and develop it into an extension of The Hills. We'll have a monstrous modern house on every acre and a strip mall fronting the highway with McDonald's and Pizza Hut. That's considered progress." He sounded more resigned than bitter.

"The Azaleas is barely being kept up now."

"Upkeep is a big problem," he agreed. "These places are big and cumbersome. We've resorted to spring and fall tours, letting people tramp over our houses for $10 a head in order to pay the help.

THE AZALEAS

You're right, young lady. It's a losing proposition." He looked away, sadness in his eyes.

Karla sat silently for a few moments, at a loss as to what to say or do. The facts were true and ugly. The plantations were doomed. The upkeep gobbled the reserves, remodeling and updating cost a fortune, maintaining the lawns and gardens required a gold mine. Progress was a whiplash cutting a bloody gash across their lives. Progress dismantled their homes, the last painful drubbing.

"So have you performed the miracle yet?" the Judge asked.

"I haven't turned water into wine, healed the sick, or sold The Azaleas, if that's what you mean," Karla replied gently.

The Judge said in a lighter voice, "Felice watches over The Azaleas. We just have to rely on the old girl. She won't let her plantation be sold."

"She'll come about," Karla said. "It's time."

The judge nodded. "Timing is everything," then asked, "how's Agatha?"

"Fine at breakfast—"

"Cantankerous as usual, I suppose."

"You didn't hear that from me."

"Well, if she had married me, we'd both be happier now, but no, she had to spend her life guarding The Azaleas that should've been hers, but isn't."

In the course of selling a property, a real estate agent waded into everybody's life. "You asked her and she turned you down?"

"More times than I have fingers to count on—and all those years acting as sentinel, what did she accomplish? Nothing— Three days after Danielle Turner's death, the daughter has the place for sale."

"Those decisions aren't mine," Karla said, refusing to accept that guilt trip. "I'm hired to do a job."

"And I'm told you're very good at it. Then I'm told you have no clue as to what you're doing. Which is it?"

"A little of both—"

"Agatha will never let go a plantation that's been in the family over a hundred years. You have no idea what a toll it has taken, spending her life looking after her brother's property."

"I understand what you say, Judge, but look at it from this angle. Mary Bravelle is the Turner's only child and she has no children.

Agatha has no children. Sooner or later that plantation is going to pass from Turner hands to somebody else's."

"Then let it be later," Judge Jones replied quickly. "I'll do everything in my power to keep Agatha from losing The Azaleas."

"But it's not hers to keep or lose, Judge. You know what you should do?" Karla offered him a happy solution. "Buy The Azaleas and join spreads."

"You said that once to me already."

"This time I'm dead serious."

"The answer is the same. It's too late for that."

"You have heirs?"

"My nephew will take over when I pass."

"You have 1,200 acres and Agatha has 640." Between these two childless people they owned a Texas-size spread. What good was land to someone six-feet under? "Then there's the matter of the mortgage you fixed up."

His eyes snapped. "What about it?"

"Albert found it unusual that Danielle Turner hadn't asked him to do the work. He took care of her legal stuff. "

The Judge took off his horn-rimmed glasses, wiped them with a handkerchief, and put them back on. Lawyers were trained to be silent. Jeremiah didn't fill the void.

"According to Mary Bravelle, her mother received $300,000 life insurance when Hank Turner died. Agatha coerced her into using the money to pay off the bank and save The Azaleas from its creditors."

"So I understand."

"But there was no insurance money. Rainbow Corporation lent the money."

"You're following a very complicated paper trail."

"I know, and I intend to get to the end of it."

"Be that as it may—"

He wasn't going to offer any better explanation, and Karla certainly didn't want to alienate the old man. She wanted to butter him up so he'd buy The Azaleas. She changed tactics. "When The Azaleas sells and Agatha is rid of that life-long baggage, you should propose to her again." Karla recalled the way Agatha's hand had rested on the Judge's shoulder at Bale Franklin's party. "I bet she'd say yes."

"Too late now—too much water under the dam—"

"It's never too late to snatch a little happiness."

He chuckled. "What makes you think there's any fire left in the oven?"

"The sparkle in your eye—the way you took those card players for a thousand easy bucks the other night. The tender, crotchety way you look after her—"

His voice turned gruff. "Didn't work out for us, but that's life. I'll still do everything I can for her—everything in my power. And that, young lady, includes keeping you from selling The Azaleas."

Jeremiah Jones was the worst kind of adversary—a man Karla liked. "I respect your position, Judge, but I'm here to do a job and I intend to do it— nothing personal."

"Yes," he repeated, "nothing personal." They sounded like two polite boxers putting on gloves before entering the ring aiming for a knock-out punch.

CHAPTER 13

The Mustang rounded an S-curve. The land rose, fell and rolled gently toward the swamp and the Mississippi River. Louisiana State Penitentiary—*Angola*—owned 18,000 acres, more land than all the remaining plantations lumped together.

Roger Randall drove the Mustang. "I think we'd better stop and put the top up."

The red convertible drew more attention than necessary. The radio on 97.6 Cajun Station blared. The white scarf tying Karla's wild hair blew in the wind. Jackie O sunglasses hid her eyes.

Highway 66 snaked through the Tunica Hills. Coming from pancake flat New Orleans, the rolling inclines felt like Rocky Mountain highs. Tree branches hung across the highway, bathing the road in shadow and light. They met few cars or pickups on the way. This was not a recreational destination.

Roger braked and pulled over to the roadside ditch. Block letters on a crude hand-painted sign nailed to a pine tree trunk said, "Freedom ends here." Earlier, they'd passed a poster meant to cheer: "Don't despair. You're almost there;" and a cynical one: "Welcome to the rest of your life."

Roger fiddled with the latches, fastening the convertible top.

Albert's arrangement for Karla to visit Willis carried one stipulation. Roger must go with her. She didn't understand why, but she'd learned not to argue with Albert. After she scalded him with hot coffee, she never expected to hear from him again. Next thing

THE AZALEAS

she knew, he'd pulled the right strings and Fed-Exed prison visitor passes, one for Karla and one for Roger. Maybe the writer planned to count birds while Karla relayed to Willis the news that his grandma, Lura Mae, died last week.

Roger swapped his usual tee-shirt, jeans and Reebok for a pale blue cotton shirt with starched collar and cuffs, a gray suit, maroon tie and black shoes polished until light danced on the toes. His face was shaved and hair combed neatly. He went from rumpled and comfortable to spiffy and trim—a nice-looking guy able to pass for a lawyer or an accountant.

At the gate a uniformed guard armed with a rifle emerged from a glass cubicle. "Good afternoon," he said. "Mind stepping out for a sec?—"

Karla and Roger left the car doors open. The guard popped the trunk Karla had vacuumed, Albert having warned her beforehand prison authorities sifted through dust. The guard opened the glove compartment, moved the seats back and forth and looked under them.

"Great wheels," he said, admiring the Mustang Shelby. "May I see your purse, please?"

He dug through Karla's tote bag, removed her wallet, rifled through it and handed it back, then glanced perfunctorily at Roger's. Satisfied that they weren't bringing in a knife or a nail file inside a chocolate chip cookie, the gate sentry slapped a visitor card on the windshield and waved the car through. "Parking lot on the left—car gotta be locked."

A creepy feeling came over Karla as they drove into the prison compound. The blue sunlit sky with fluffy cotton clouds lost its glow. The green fields and yellow mums lining the road faded gray like an old photograph stuck in an album and forgotten through the ages.

Roger sensed her mood. "You sure you want to do this?"

"Yes. I'm okay." Inmates, mostly black, marched to the fields, hoes over their shoulders.

"Soybeans," Roger said.

Mounted sentries carrying rifles led long, straggling human columns and guarded the rear.

"Don't they wear black and white stripes?" Karla asked, looking at the convicts in blue jeans and white tees.

"Only in movies—"

"This is a huge place."

"Originally three plantations occupied this land," Roger said. "Slaves from African Angola worked the cotton. The plantations fell on hard times and were sold, but the name Angola stuck. In 1901 the prison began buying the land. You okay?"

"The guard at the gate clipped my wings. I get the feeling one can't soar in here."

"No doubt about that."

"He snuffed my liberty."

"Temporarily," Roger replied. "Think of the 6,000 men whose liberty is gone forever."

"They're never released?"

"Seldom—and those who are, usually return."

"Gruesome."

Roger pulled into a parking lot.

"What will you do while I visit Willis?" Karla asked.

"Don't worry about me. I'll pass the time. I'll have a chat with the warden."

"Oh, sure—the warden is going to stop his life and rap with you."

Roger rumbled his easy laugh. "Never can tell—"

They entered a building. Roger flipped his wallet open and held it to a guard's nose, palm up. The man took off, running down the hall as if his tail were on fire. Roger looked at his watch. "See you in thirty minutes. Is that time enough?"

"Probably twenty minutes too long," Karla replied, wondering what Roger had in his wallet that lent wings to the guard's feet.

A uniformed woman led Karla down a hallway. Friends and relatives crowded into the air-conditioned visitor's room. The early arrivals drew the available chairs into close circles, talking in whispers to jailed relatives. At a small table on the far end, a woman and a teenage boy sat with an inmate. The man and the woman smiled and touched. The boy looked away. Some folks made a line for hotdogs, hamburgers, cold drinks and ice cream sold from a make-shift concession stand. The atmosphere resembled a subdued company picnic, fun with deference to corporate authority.

Willis came in, skittish, eyes darting left, right. Karla had probably spoken to Willis a dozen times in her life, on occasions when he passed by with Lebron or his grandmother, Lura Mae. Auntie Emmy greatly respected Lura Mae for doing her best to raise Violetta's boys.

THE AZALEAS

'Whether those boys turn out or not, Lura Mae done her best and that's all a body can do,' she often said while warning Karla in the same breath to keep a distance. Now Lura Mae had crossed life's great divide and joined Auntie Emmy in the 'great reward' promised to all who made it to the other side.

"Hello, Willis."

"Why you here?—whatcha want?" He snapped at Karla, sullen, brooding.

Why was she entangling herself in his sorry life?

All the chairs were taken, so Karla and Willis leaned against the concrete block wall. "How are you?"

"How do you think I am? Pissed off, that's how I am." He folded his arms across his chest. One bicep had the tattoo snake; Karla couldn't decipher the drawings or lettering on the other. "They gotta get me outta here."

Karla didn't know what to say to him. Polite conversation usually started with the weather, a harmless enough topic, but for a man who saw little outside sky, shooting the breeze could turn into a stormy situation.

With calloused, scarred fingers, nails bit to the quick, Willis reached into his shirt pocket, drew a cigarette pack, plucked a Winston and lit it from the butt of the old one. He asked again, openly resenting Karla's company— "Whatcha doing here, girl?"

"I worried about you after the guard conked you on the head with the shotgun the other day. I thought he'd killed you."

"Asshole!—He jes'stunned me. I come-to soon 'nough. He's on my list. When they get me outta here, he'll get what's coming to him. Let him have his fun now. He won't miss his reckonin'."

Willis scared Karla. Prison made him angrier, more vengeful. If Angola released Willis, he'd wander the city streets, a real live menace. "Lura Mae died."

His face didn't change expression. "Took her long 'nough."

"She waited and waited for you to show up." His grandmother hung on forever. Every time she heard a knock on the door, she lifted her head from the pillow and whispered, 'Willis?'

"Good thing she's gone," Willis said. "She couldn't last fifteen more years." He blew a cloud of smoke. "She go peaceful?"

"In her sleep, the neighbor said. They buried her in the cemetery behind the AME church."

"Grampa buried there, too." Childhood remembrances tempered his angry voice.

"And Lebron got shot accidentally and he's in Big C, improving some. Joey went to LTI."

He took a long drag on his cigarette. "Great family, huh?—"

With his consistent history of robbing and shooting and assault with a deadly weapon, Willis didn't make Karla feel safe or comfortable. "Unless you get an attitude adjustment you'll be in here for a long time."

"Oh, I'll get out," he informed Karla, cocky as hell.

"You could be released early for good behavior. Start over."

"Don't weave me a fairy tale, Miss White Princess. There ain't no startin' over. Fifteen years is life." His lips curled into an ugly snarl. Stars imbedded in his front teeth glinted gold. "I'm black, and the law works one way for black, one way for white—"

"That's not so—"

"What do you know?—"each word a bullet.

"Auntie Emmy and I lived in your same block. I've been just as hungry as you have and I didn't hold up the corner grocery."

"Take a look at your skin. That's the difference."

"Because I'm white?—you think because I'm white I got more breaks than you did?"

"Don't think it, know it for a fact."

Talk of attitude! Did the world owe him a living any more than it did Karla?

Willis was a ticking time bomb. "White boy standing on the corner, no cop bothers him. Black guy on the same corner, minding his own business, disturbing nobody, and next thing he knows he's in jail. Can't make bond—no money for a lawyer—here come a public defender who don't give a shit, who ain't even opened the folder 'fore he gets to the trial room, and poof! Fifteen years." Willis blew smoke through his nostrils. 'Too bad,' the lawyer says. 'Didn't have enough time to prepare—' To him fifteen is jes' a number, not a life. It ain't him gonna rot in here—"

"But you brought it all on yourself. You committed the crimes."

"Look around this room. You see any white people here? You think white people behave better'n black people? No way. Honkies don't get arrested. It ain't fair."

THE AZALEAS

"Dammit, Willis!—Get hung up on fair, will you? I had no father. My mother didn't even try to live straight. I'm climbing past all that. I'm not going to sink in that muck. I owe it to Auntie Emmy and when you do these terrible things, you should think of Lura Mae and cringe in shame."

He stepped away from the wall, flicked cigarette ashes. "Fuck you, bitch!" under his breath, so as not to draw the guard's attention, but Karla heard.

The dry tongue she ran across her parched lips felt like sandpaper. She needed a drink from the concession stand, but didn't dare walk across the room. "Lura Mae never gave up on you. You could get time off for good behavior—"

"Jesus, woman!—"

"Get to be a trusty and they'd let you out in the fields, and you wouldn't be confined all the time. It must be terrible, being locked up day and night."

"You ain't got no idea—you can't even imagine," and then, as if to show Karla how really tough he was, he said, "I volunteered to ride a bull next Sunday."

"At the Angola Rodeo?—you're a city dude! You'll get killed."

"I'll fall off that bull for sure; get banged on the head, a recurrence of the old injury from the deputy's shotgun butt. Whole world watching from the stands, on their feet, taking in the action, shrieking the way women do—"

"I'm going to be there, and I won't shriek."

"Like you didn't shriek when you sailed over that barbed wire fence?"

"I thought he'd killed you."

"Warden sure don't want 'Prisoner Killed at Rodeo' headlines. Ruin his whole picnic. He makes a lot of money on rodeo Sundays and gets all that slick publicity about how good Angola treats its prisoners." His eyes were the same odd hazel color as Lebron's, except that Lebron's were soft and lively. Willis's, hard as agate marbles, were sharp and conniving.

"Don't be stupid, Willis. Nobody escapes from Angola and lives to tell about it." There were a hundred different ways to nab a fugitive—fingerprints, DNA, Retina ID, FBI Ten Most Wanted List, television's America's Most Wanted, every police station alerted, road blocks, blood hounds and helicopter searches, and the biggest trap, the endless muck, the sucking swamp. How insane could Willis be? "You're signing your own death warrant if you blow from here."

He removed the cigarette from his mouth, his bottom lip curled under. He waved smoke to one side and looked Karla straight in the eye. "I'd rather be dead outside," he said, "than alive in here."

CHAPTER 14

That night, her mind laden with heavy thoughts, sleep didn't come. Karla tossed, turned, pulled the sheet to her chin, kicked it off; plumped the pillow. No sale for The Azaleas. Bale Franklin out of her life; Judge Jones ready to block a transaction, if she ever reached that plateau.

She was broke and getting broker. Reckoning time was around the corner. What excuse would Albert buy? How could she avoid paying back the money she'd spent from the expense account? At least she hadn't embezzled their Escrow. They had no Escrow.

And Sam—big, stupid Sam—set off Karla's alarm system. Whenever she came near him, her goose bumps activated and they never failed her. What was it with Sam? Something... something— and then a phantom Willis stood before her, huge and black and threatening.

Oh, to have somebody to talk to! Somebody with a comfortable shoulder to cradle her head! Another soul to share her angst, to hold and cherish her and tell her everything would be all right.

Exhausted, she sat up in the Mallard bed, her thoughts in turmoil. There was no point thrashing all night. Like a sleepwalker led by a subconscious pull, she slipped on a robe and opened the bedroom door. A deep silence enveloped the hallway, dark except for the one lamp casting its yellow glow on the stair landing. The wood floors felt cool under her bare feet. The grandfather clock tick…tick…ticked…breaking the midnight quiet.

She stepped into the hallway, looking right, left, no idea what she intended to do. Suddenly, a plan jelled in her mind. She'd slip into Hank Turner's sacred chamber at the head of the stairs, the only room in the house without a name, off limits to every tour, undisturbed by man or ghost since Hank Turner's death.

She tiptoed back to her bedroom, opened the top dresser drawer and fumbled underneath the underwear for the ring with forty-six keys. Certainly one should fit the lock to Hank's forbidden door. She slipped a pencil thin flashlight into the robe pocket. On second thought, she grabbed her trusty Swiss army knife. The corkscrew always came in handy.

By the flashlight's narrow beam, she checked the keyhole in the ornate brass plate. Looking over her shoulder, watching the hallway and holding her breath, she tried the skeleton keys. After a dozen attempts, one slid in easily. The mechanism clicked. The knob turned and Karla pushed. The door didn't budge. She put her shoulder against the solid oak panel and shoved. Nothing happened.

An unexpected noise stopped her. She wedged into a corner dark in shadow. The pendulum on the grandfather clock swung back and forth, each tick louder than a pealing church bell. The noise came again—a toilet flushing, faulty plumbing endlessly gurgling. She waited until the last gushes faded like the tail end of a long sigh. Silence again. She faced the door once more, aiming the flashlight up and down. A deadbolt installed too high for her reach kept the door locked tight.

What could she climb? The marble-top tables were too heavy to move. The carved oak chairs were massive. At the end of the hall, tucked under a small console home to an old-fashioned rotary telephone, sat a footstool. She carried it over to the locked door, stood on it and began with the keys, trying first this one and then that one, moving them over on the ring this way and that, and in confusion working the same ones twice. Balanced on the footstool, straining to reach the deadbolt, she went through all the keys several times. The door never opened.

What could be in that room?—something of great value?—the secret to the mysteries that enveloped this plantation—? The reason

Danielle Turner left and never came back?—the cause of the rift between the sisters-in-law?

The handicap in selling The Azaleas was not the house, but the people who lived in it. If Karla could find out what made them tick, what motivated them, what secrets held them in the throes of their passion, she could sell this plantation. Somewhere a buyer existed for The Azaleas. The house, well-constructed and pleasing to the eye, posed no problem. It needed maintenance and repairs, but money took care of roof and paint and re-habbing. Money, however, couldn't conquer feuds, mental hang-ups or bad blood. Those emotions created a stumbling block of monumental proportions that Karla's limited experience couldn't overcome.

Balanced barefooted on the stool before the unyielding oak door, reluctant to admit defeat, she cast about for a solution. An idea struck her and she crept back to her room and carefully raised the window. A light breeze blew the curtains against her face. She stepped onto the balcony built more for show and symmetry than for actual use. Back pressed against the wall, she inched toward Hank's window.

The moon, slightly fuller and yellower than last night, turned Karla's terry cloth robe ghostly white. She glided through gold and black patches, the flashlight clutched in her hand.

The windows to Hank's room were dark. She pulled on the sash, pried the lock with her Swiss army knife, grabbed the casing and jiggled—a total waste of energy. The window was wedged tight, permanently sealed by fifteen coats of paint.

A sudden wind came from nowhere, sharp as a double-edged razor. The hair on Karla's arms stood on end. Electricity shooting from her fingers crackled on the iron latch. Driven by the swirling wind, leaves hit the window panes like sharp darts. A violent gust knocked Karla to her knees. Her arms flew up to protect her head. She clung to the balcony railing, struggling against the gale now coming from all directions. She'd be sucked in a whirl and hurled through space like Dorothy from Kansas.

The same suffocating sensation Karla experienced when standing before Felice's portrait descended over her. She gasped for breath. Her lungs couldn't fill with air. She struggled against the enveloping black shroud.

"Hail Mary full of grace—" and she wasn't even a practicing Catholic.

The wind abruptly died as suddenly as it had originated. An eerie calm oozed through the night. An eternity passed before Karla dared look around. The only traces left of the whirlwind were broken limbs, a littered lawn and a gray mist rising like drifting smoke.

Karla's hands shook when she tried the window again. It slid open easily. She stepped into Hank Turner's room.

Darkness enveloped her. The flashlight beam skimmed along the floor and reached a dark bulk. The narrow yellow band revealed an antique bed with an ornate wooden rolling pin across the foot board. Karla had seen a bed like that in Sebring Antique's on Royal Street where she sometimes helped old Mr. Sebring. In olden times, women removed this pin and rolled the feather mattress flat before turning in for the night.

Hank Turner's room had two overstuffed chairs and a huge armoire, easy to open. Khaki pants, suits, shirts and slacks hung inside, exactly as he'd left them. The pencil-thin light slid around the room and fell on a shelf filled with books. Karla checked the urge to read the titles. She had no time to waste.

A Confederate flag was tacked to the wall behind a planter's desk. Two Civil War muskets were mounted on either side. A closer look at a silver-framed photograph of a man and a woman revealed a younger Agatha. Karla presumed the tall, lanky man with his arm casually around the woman's shoulders was brother Hank. His brown eyes stared dreamily ahead, a shy smile on his lips. He had a poet's sensitive face, not a farmer's rugged sunburned features. An oval wooden frame held a picture of a young Mary Bravelle. Karla found it odd that Danielle, Hank's wife, was excluded from this photo gallery.

The desk's roll top pushed back easily—inkwell, pens and writing paper arranged neatly. Karla slid open a drawer, empty except for the one leather-bound book, a ledger. Instead of the long columns of numbers she expected, the beam fell on reams of close, faded writing, the strokes all slanted the same way, a date at the top of each page. *Today the sheriff—*

A diary! Hank Turner's diary!

As Karla gloated over this most fortunate discovery, goose bumps rippling on her forearm made her freeze. Her finger eased off the flashlight button. In the dark, she fiddled with the Swiss Army knife and opened the longest blade.

THE AZALEAS

Heaviness weighed the ominous silence. An expectation hung in the air, a haunting anticipation. Who? What? She hunkered down like a soldier in a foxhole.

Waiting without moving was sheer torture. Time marked by heartbeats stretched each second into an eternity. Her ankle itched and her nose twitched. She stifled a nervous sneeze.

No sound broke the eerie silence, no creak, no movement. Maybe she'd imagined the unseen menace. Her goose bumps were pretty good radar, normally on target.

The thought occurred to Karla that Felice could be the unseen presence in this room. She had opened the window. She could very well be in here doing whatever she floated around doing. Karla found the notion of Felice in the same room comforting. Tonight, she'd acted more like an ally than a foe. Karla believed Felice agreed the time had come for the owners to let go The Azaleas and move on. The ghost in the red brocade dress wanted, at long last, to rest in peace.

With that reassurance, Karla grabbed the leather volume, quickly stepped through the window, and carefully closing it behind her, inched down the balcony to her own room.

She drew a chair to the secretary-desk, turned on the Tiffany lamp and opened the book, wondering as she did so, why Agatha had left the diary in Hank's desk drawer all these years. Why wouldn't she put it up somewhere for safekeeping? Hank's handwriting, neat and precise, covered the first page and every succeeding page; each line crowded against the previous one, the words huddled close as if to draw comfort from one another.

1/1/93

James's party lasted two days. It was good to get away from the problems of the plantation. Precious Mary was the most beautiful of all the girls. The boys swarmed around her. She'll give me gray hairs. Danielle, as usual, endured the outing. She has never liked the country or our country ways. Agatha had a good enough time.

James tells me he's sending his boy off to Tulane University to become a lawyer. James will pass on his post as sheriff to his boy. The Watsons have been in the sheriff business for as long as I can remember.

James is apologetic about the sheriff sale coming up in ninety days unless some miracle takes place. It's his job to conduct the bidding. My heart bleeds at the thought of losing everything my ancestors worked for. I can't stand it. I weep in private. I can't sleep. I get up and pace this room, ten paces from the door to the window, back and forth, back and forth. I count the steps, count the days like a condemned prisoner awaiting execution. I can't bear to look at the dried up fields or the house or the oak trees. It makes me cry. Danielle is right. I am weak. The Happy New Year looks bleak. God help us.

All of January and February the entries varied yet were the same—bills stacking up, despair growing. Karla could sympathize with that: living from hand to mouth, putting on a front, keeping a stiff upper lip. Hank had retreated to his room, finding solace in books and poetry. Danielle complained and was unhappy. His beautiful daughter was the only bright spot in his sad life. Agatha toiled by his side, fending off creditors who brazenly knocked on their door.

3/1/93

He came today. The appraiser from the bank— George Voltaire, his name was. Agatha called him Mr. Vulture. He looked like a scavenger, going through our rooms with his measuring tape, eyeing all our possessions. The Federal Land Bank will foreclose on the land mortgage. Production Credit will come and take away the equipment, "chattel" as they call it. How easy it was to sign those papers! Your name here and here! We'll buy the new combine. You pay the note when the crop comes in. I suppose the furniture and anything valuable will go at auction.

I'm glad Danielle wasn't here when the Vulture came. She's been in New Orleans for the last three weeks. The plantation means nothing to her. Sometimes I believe she'll be glad when it's gone and I'm free of it. True, I'm not a farmer, but this is my home place and I have a love and understanding for it.

Mary is here with me. She can't be skipping school and going off to New Orleans on a holiday. She has her classes. She's a cheerleader for the basketball team. Agatha and I go to the games to watch her. We don't care which side wins. She's popular with her classmates. I'm afraid she likes to flirt. There's something about the way Mary looks from downcast eyes that reminds me of Danielle. Her mannerisms are like her mother's. Mary is full of life, enthusiastic, expectant. Agatha is a better mother to my child than my wife is.

THE AZALEAS

3/10/93

Edgar Gavin came by today—Edgar! The old man Karla danced with at Bale's party!—

*He's talking to me about filing bankruptcy, Chapter 11, reorganization of assets. I'd have to present a plan Edgar said. Something that Judge Jones—*Jeremiah, the next door neighbor!—*would consider workable. Subdivide the land and selling lots is the prime possibility. But it has to be done quickly. The judge would set a time limit. The sale couldn't drag forever.*

How easy it is to give the other fellow advice! Edgar is filled with my desolation. His sympathy overflows and spills over me like cactus prickles. He sighs as if he truly understands my misfortune.

Edgar is a good friend in time of need. He is doing all he can to help me, because I am one of them, a part of this society, a son of the South. If I go under the reality exists that one of them might be next. Yet through the concern in Edgar's eyes surfaces a restrained, universal satisfaction. Better me who never was a farmer, who let the place get down to this, than him.

He's convincing me to work the system and buy time. Time for what?—More misery—Will things change, be different six months from now? Or will it simply be a bigger debt, a different bank, another bad crop, a new dead end?

How it shames me to go in the feed store and know I can't pay Bill Waters what I owe him. Yesterday, with great reluctance and profuse apologies, the dear man cut off my credit. I understand his position. Prudence is a precursor to survival. I'm not the only one he's carrying on his books.

Without fertilizer there's no point in planting beans.

When I go to mass, I feel like a thief. I can't pray. The priest knows I haven't paid my pledge to St. Francis in two years. He has never mentioned it, but the accounting comes in the mail: Tax-deductible contribution, 0.

I can't hold my head up. I see a neighbor downtown and cross the street. What can I say to him—to anybody? What do we have left in common?

The other option, Edgar says, is Chapter 13. All the land would be auctioned to pay the creditors, except the house on 10 acres. Whatever the auction brought, it would be split among those I am indebted to, and they'd have to write off the balance. I, myself, would have to write off the balance of my life.

I don't know what to do. I don't know what to do.

Rich people's problems were no different than poor people's problems. They were simply bigger in scope. The vultures repossessed Karla's car and her piano. A knock on the door of a fancy house might be more refined than the banging on a rented tenement, but the dread that wrung one's guts at the sound of that rap was no different.

4/15/93

Income tax! The IRS demands its share of nothing! Pine beetles struck the Loblolly pines. The trees trunks are splotched with scaly white circles and can't be sold for lumber. The Agriculture Department inspector gave me sixty days to cut the trees. The department aims to control pine beetle infestation. Why couldn't they control it before it hit my pines? The bright side is that we'll have plenty of firewood this winter. That's funny. I'll have to tell Agatha. It was her idea to plant the pines. We'll harvest the timber in ten years, she said, cash crop, easier than soybeans.

The burden of the farm weighed heavier and heavier on Hank Turner's mind and heart. He fled the house at night, walked the driveway and the road aimlessly, without destination, sometimes until the rose-pink sky told him the sun was rising. There was no purpose to his walks. They offered no solution.

Karla flipped through the rest of the diary, quickly glancing at each page, the situation going from bad to worse. And then on the final page, she read:

10/11/1995

I'll kill that Franklin boy. What pleasure to feel his neck bones snapping beneath my grip— Danielle has taken Mary away to New Orleans. Mary will get over it, her mother says. I know my daughter. She is willful and headstrong. She has her grandfather's bull-headed streak.

Danielle is not coming back, I know. She packed her clothes. Her dresser drawers are empty. My wife is gone. She has taken our child.

Monday the plantation goes, too. What have I left?—Nothing but ashes— oh, my heart. My heart—

That was the last entry in the book. Karla closed it softly. Bale and Mary! What was it Albert said? 'I got Mary out of a little scrape when she attended Newcomb back in 1995. She was sixteen when she broke her daddy's heart. Eighteen when Albert rescued her from what he called 'a little scrape'. Did that scrape involve Bale, too? Did Bale get Mary pregnant? What grist for this gossip mill!

The plantation didn't get sold at the sheriff sale Monday. Monday the entire town was at the church mourning Henry Turner V, known as Hank to all his friends and neighbors.

Karla sat at the desk, hugging the diary to her chest, pondering what she had read about this other world, this plantation kingdom so different from the closed, narrow life of the Quarter.

The farmers had abandoned cotton for soybeans, hoping to improve their lot. They'd mortgaged their land to plant their crops. They'd freed slaves and bought combines and reapers, replaced cheap human labor with expensive machinery, yet things grew worse.

Karla's Mickey Mouse watch said 2 a.m.—should she return the diary now, or risk taking it back later? In the morning, the awakened household would tread hallways and bang doors. From his cabin, Preacher Frank could spot her on the balcony. She'd better return the book now while everyone snored in their antique beds and the lights were off. Safety came with darkness.

She pushed back the chair, legs scraping across the wood floor. The leather-bound diary dropped from her clutch with a soft plopping sound. She leaned to retrieve it and—

The strangle grip came before she heard the first sound. The thick arm around her throat choked her and she gasped for breath. A coarse hand slapped over her mouth. She sank her teeth into the tough flesh. One hard jerk yanked her up, feet clean off the floor. She flopped around, biting and kicking, aiming toward the groin, never reaching higher than the knees. Karla and the assailant wrestled, overturning the chair, banging against the desk. Her head slammed against the Louis XIV armoire, hitting the wood with a resounding wallop. She saw stars, blue and red and yellow, green with golden halos around them, and her legs turned rubbery. Light flashes zigzagged across the room.

Darkness closed in. She slid slowly to the floor.

CHAPTER 15

Karla's head pounded like a drum at Mardi Gras. She gingerly felt the goose egg where her head hit the armoire. The brass knob had cut a gash. Her fingers came away sticky—blood!

She held onto consciousness by sheer will power, fighting the impulse to let go and drift into a gray and comfortable twilight zone.

A terrifying thought sifted through the gauzy layers of mental cobwebs. The attacker might be lurking in the darkness, coming after her again.

Instant panic brought Karla to her senses. She sat up with great effort.

The Queen Anne chair, the floor-to-ceiling mirror, the dresser reeled past. The walls wavered. Light patches chased after dark shadows.

She crawled to the bed and pulled the slim chain on the bedside Tiffany lamp.

The thug who strangled her had dumped her briefcase. He'd turned on the laptop and the icons glowed purple and red. Papers were strewn over the bed and floor.

She found her cell and with cross-eyed concentration hit 1#, Albert's programmed number. The fourth ring activated the recorder and she moaned, "Help.... please....help."

Through rising nausea, she saw the broken desk lamp. Staring blankly at the shattered porcelain, she thought incoherently. *This is an*

THE AZALEAS

antique lamp, a valuable lamp, Agatha's lamp, how would she ever pay for it, how much is it worth, this antique lamp.

Despite the excruciating pain forcing her eyes shut, she made her first rational decision. *Get the hell out of Dodge.* Gloria was right. No job was worth getting killed. She'd pack and move out. The Azaleas, as far as Karla was concerned, was history.

Dizziness impeded any effort requiring coordination. The pain behind her eyes made her see double. Opening the armoire took tremendous effort. By the time the doors swung open, cold sweat drenched her body. She struggled with her suitcase, grabbed jeans, shorts and tops; threw in underwear and socks. The sequined flapper dress hung limply from a hanger. She rolled it up like a camping blanket and stuck it in a suitcase pocket.

The diary! Where was the diary? The book fell from the chair to the floor. With her toes she searched through priceless, shattered porcelain and glass. The strangler had taken the diary. Try explaining that to Agatha!

A rattling stopped Karla cold. She ceased her frenzied searching. The strangler! Was he still in the room?

The rattle came again—from the outside.

She looked through the window expecting the strangler to push open the sash and swing inside. He had long legs. Why long legs? The impression persisted he had to lean over quite far to harm her. He certainly wasn't tiptoeing to reach her neck, and when she tried to kick him, she never hit above his knees. And something else—what, what, what? Did she hear a noise? Did he make a sound? No. All the grunting and huffing came from Karla. He was a dark hulk, a shadow. Something else…something else….She was too upset to think straight.

Get a grip. Get a grip. Get out. Leave this room, descend the stairs; walk down the hallway, open the front door; get to the garage and the car.

The window rattled again. The man moved a hand, beckoning her to draw near. Close to hysteria, Karla retreated. A face plastered itself against the window. The wavy glass distorted the image the way a trick carnival mirror warped a reflection. She wished she had her NOPD regulation Billy club.

The man outside pried the window open. His legs came through.

Karla put her head down and charged like a rodeo bull.

He wrapped his arms around Karla. "Hey! Hey! Steady now. It's me. Roger. Get that briefcase and let's get you out of here."

Roger, the writer!

Karla trusted no one. Roger, too, could be engineering something big and disastrous and she'd be dragged into it by association, when all she wanted to do was live a clean life, make some decent money, avoid bodily injury, and end up in the arms of a good man who would love and cherish her, an agenda that looked less and less possible each passing day.

Go through the window and join Roger? Go through the bedroom door and down the steps alone? Roger would protect her against the strangler, but who would protect her against Roger?

Her hesitation consumed precious time.

With shaking hands she stuffed papers into the briefcase. Hours of research! Why did she need them? Each page weighed a pound. She half-stuffed the PC, as heavy as a concrete block, into the case. The zipper seemed coated with lead.

Roger pushed her gently and they both tumbled through the window onto the balcony. The rickety boards creaked under their weight. The rotted boards needing replacement no longer concerned Karla. No chance remained for her to sell this snake pit.

The evening air revived Karla a little and the dizziness subsided, but not the pounding in her head. Would the aftermath of a concussion erase things that happened yesterday? Would she lose memory of the childhood she never had? Maybe a blood clot would shoot into her brain and paralyze her for her remaining days. She'd need a wheelchair, which meant changing apartments, because Earl, the landlord, didn't spend money on handicap accessibility. Federal regulations covered accessibility. At an FHA seminar the HUD man threatened dire consequences to any owner whose building didn't have adequate ramps. She made a mental note to talk to Earl about accessibility.

"Your car in the barn around back?—" Roger asked.

"Yes."

The mild-mannered writer turned into an "in charge" guy. "Let's go."

"Why? Where?—"

"Albert called. I'm a friend of Albert's," he explained, as if that cleared the slate for all that was to follow.

"Where's Albert?"

"In Switzerland— He'll be back shortly. I'm to take you at once to the St. Francis and you're to wait for him there."

Switzerland! What in the hell was Albert doing there again? Did he go every week? Had Pierre been right? Niece! More than likely a mistress—

Roger leaned over the balcony railing and looked both ways. "Can you jump?"

God Almighty! Jump from a two-story balcony? "I can jump."

He threw the suitcase over the railing. It hit the ground with a soft thud.

"Don't throw the laptop!" Karla cried, one leg over the railing, having second thoughts, chickening out. Did she really need this?

"Go!"

And then surprisingly she was over the side, landing on the balls of her feet, legs buckling, going down, springing up again and supporting her weight, too frightened and numb to feel anything.

Roger jumped right behind her. "Can you walk?"

"I don't know."

He grabbed Karla by the waist and slung her over his shoulder. He carried the suitcase and PC, half-crouching under her weight. Her head bobbing, a moment of clarity, and she wondered at Roger's strength. They reached the rear of the house, hurried past the lean-to filled with the crop-dusting planes' bulky outline.

He set her down when they entered the barn converted into the garage. Hay smells clung to the loft. She teetered, lost her balance and braced herself against a splintery wall plank.

"Okay there?"

"No."

"Follow me."

They worked their way toward the end stall where the Mustang was corralled for the night. Karla heard mice squeak, scurry from dark corners, little feet pattering. Three strange creatures with their tails wrapped around a rafter, hung head-down, staring at Roger and Karla with huge glowing eyes circled in black.

"Can you drive?"

"I dunno."

Roger threw Karla's bag into the back seat. "Hurry...Hurry... I'll see you later. I'll be right behind you."

She jumped in, turned the ignition. The engine purred. Good car...nice little car. She turned on the headlights. The yellow beam flooded the barn and she saw him. Saw the big bulk that had to be him. He came toward her like King Kong.

"Roger! Roger!"

"Go! Go!"

She slammed the car into reverse and sped away from The Azaleas, down the gravel drive, onto the paved road, away from there, far away from there, far, far away.

She sped through a night black as tar. No moon; no stars; no neon signs; no streetlights. The only glow came from the headlights as the high beam cut through the darkness.

She drove up a hill and the headlights shone on the yellow double lines marking the no-passing zone on the approaching S-curve.

The speedometer glowed 90 mph.

She placed her foot on the brake. Pumped—pushed again. *Ohmygod!* She half-stood, both feet on the brake pedal, the wind rushing past her face. *Ohmygod!* Wide awake now, alert, all pain forgotten.

An oak tree, wide as a football field, came toward her.

Gloria's customer, Convert McKenzie from North Louisiana, had run off the road and hit a tree! That tree! *Ohmygod!*

She turned the steering wheel with all her might, missed the trunk, and cut a swath through a rutty field.

CHAPTER 16

Karla awakened in a flood-lit emergency cubicle. Her eyelids fluttered. Roger hovered anxiously over her.

A voice said, "She's coming to."

Roger asked, "Are you okay?"

Confused and exhausted beyond reason, Karla truly didn't know what shape she was in. "What time is it?"

"Five in the morning—"

"The car?—" The Mustang Shelby, Albert's pride. "Is the car all right?"

"This girl is fine," Roger said. "She's worrying about the car." He gave Karla a brotherly pat on the shoulder that made her wince. "Wrecker towed the car to the garage."

"Totaled?"

"Half, maybe—one side—the passenger door came off. Damned good thing you had on the seat belt. If you'd been thrown out—" the words hung in the air.

Facts wriggled through Karla's wooziness. "Somebody tampered with the brakes." She tried to sit. It hurt to breathe. Moving her neck was painful.

"Born under a lucky star, that's what you are," Roger said. "Lots of bruises but no broken bones, only a sprained ankle—"

An ace bandage was wrapped tightly around her right foot, her brake foot.

"The grass field you plowed through slowed the car down. You had to be going pretty fast."

"Roger, this was not an accident. Did you call the law?"

He looked sheepish. "No."

"Somebody tried to kill me and you just ignore it?"

"Well, not exactly."

"Not exactly!—what does that mean?"

"It means he'll be dealt with in due time."

"In due time may be too late for me. You are aware that somebody wants me dead. Why?"

"Perhaps you get in the way."

"In the way of what?—"

The nurse came with paper work and crutches and Roger didn't answer Karla's question. She signed half dozen places. An orderly brought a wheelchair.

"I'm not getting in that thing."

The aide looked bored. He'd heard that balk a thousand times before. "Hospital regulations, no options— you're being transferred to a room."

"I'm not staying here!"

"Twenty-four hours for observation, then you can go," the nurse said.

"Roger—"

"Listen to her, Karla. These people know what they're doing." Roger helped her into the wheelchair.

"Roger, who's paying for all this? I don't have hospitalization."

"Don't fret over it. Let Albert worry about the bills."

"Does he know?"

"Yes."

"Is he coming?"

"Tomorrow—"

"Did you tell him about the car?"

"Yes."

"Was he mad?"

"Albert? Of course not— what's one car to him. He'll get you another one."

"Did he ask how I was?"

"Yes, he did. He was very concerned."

Roger left Karla attached to IVs and machines that beeped heart rate, blood pressure, and vital signs. She endured pricks and probes from the hospital staff all day while she stewed about the strangler, worried about the car, and cursed an employer who obviously didn't give a damn or he would've arrived by now.

Something serious was taking place here. Roughing her up was one thing, but tampering with the car brakes with intent to kill was murder, an out and out criminal act. And they'd done it before!

At 11 p.m. the duty nurse disconnected the life-monitoring gadgets so Karla could sleep more comfortably.

"So I'm not going to die, right?" Karla tugged at the skimpy hospital gown held together with strings and Velcro.

"Not on my shift. Your vitals are normal. The bruises will be blue and sore, but that'll go away in time."

"I can go now?"

"Doctor doesn't make rounds until 7 a.m. He orders the discharge—tomorrow, about noon, usually."

Karla had too much to do to wait for paperwork. When the nurse left the room, Karla stood. The effort left her weak and breathless. Her bandaged right foot felt as big as a football and throbbed painfully. She couldn't set it down. She hopped forward on her left, hanging onto the bed railing for balance and support. Each movement brought a fresh wave of pain. She stood like a stork on one leg, and opened the locker door. Her jeans and tank top were neatly folded at the bottom, sandals placed on top.

She shed the hospital gown and crammed the wad into the locker. She struggled into her jeans. The bandaged foot wouldn't slide through the narrow pant's leg. With one leg in and one leg out, she pulled the tee shirt overhead and down to her thighs and trussed the outfit into place with her wide belt.

With one swoop she raked her earrings, navel stud and Mickey Mouse watch from the top shelf, amazed that someone hadn't lifted them. On second thought, the trinkets were probably not worth the risk.

Grabbing metal crutches leaning against the wall, she fitted them under her armpits and swung across the room. She pushed the door ajar and peeked into the hall.

A cold, impersonal light bathed the corridor in a bluish green hue. She breathed alcohol and iodine and other antiseptic smells perfectly at home here, the way that rank and humid odors were natural in the French Quarter.

The nurse at the control desk, her back turned, rummaged in a desk drawer, and called to an unseen person. "You seen that Sweet-and-Low?—"

"Somebody moved it to the second shelf under the EKGs."

She stooped to find the fix for her stay-awake coffee and Karla quickly hobbled to the elevator and pushed the Lobby button.

Except for a few people asleep in uncomfortable plastic chairs, the lobby was empty. The hospital glass doors opened automatically. Confederate Jasmine perfumed the cool night air with a lemony scent. An immense harvest moon, round and orange like a Gulf Oil sign, hung low in the sky, its shimmering light touching the trees, the flower beds, the street.

An old station wagon with "Brown's Transportation Service" written on the side was parked on the curb, Mr. Brown asleep inside. She shook him awake. He sprang and opened the back door and Karla rested her leg full length on the seat.

"Take me to the St. Francis Hotel."

When the cab arrived at the entrance, she realized she had no purse, no wallet, no money. Her only I.D. was the plastic hospital bracelet encircling her wrist.

"How much?—" she asked the driver. "What's your name?"

"Three dollars—name's Henry Brown."

"It's worth ten to me, Mr. Brown, if you take this as temporary security." She unstrapped the Mickey Mouse watch and dangled it before him. "Come by at noon and I'll have your money."

Mr. Brown appraised his half-dressed fare. "You escaped the hospital 'fore they killed you?"

"More or less—how about it?—"

She hated to give up her Mickey Mouse watch.

The St. Francis Audubon Hotel night clerk eyed Karla suspiciously. She could tell what he was thinking by the look on his dried prune face. A single half-dressed woman checking in at midnight was running from trouble. He didn't want any altercations brought to his business place at this bewitching hour.

If this desk idiot gave Karla any lip, she'd yell discrimination and threaten lawsuit. That shook them and got them moving every time. Lacking the energy to make a scene, she took a leap of faith. "Albert Monsant reserved a room for me."

She waited, leaning on the crutches, looking over the counter as he punched keys. If this ploy didn't work, she'd have to sleep under a bridge.

"You name, please?"

"Karla Whitmore."

She held her breath as he typed her name. "Room 145—"

Well, hallelujah! The old goat came through.

She bolted the door to room 145, found a razor in the bathroom, slit the jean leg from knee to ankle, wriggled her bandaged foot into the jeans and lay on the bed dressed, prepared in case someone barged in. It had been a long, endless day. All the years she'd lived in the dangerous French Quarter, no one ever physically attacked her. Six days in St. Francisville and she'd almost been snuffed, not once, but three times. Karla's life may not have amounted to much so far, but it was her life, the only one she had, and she was very attached to it.

She needed a drink.

She rubbed her sore neck. The dark hulk in the garage-barn was the same one who tried to strangle her in the bedroom. Of that she had no doubt. She'd bet the savings she didn't have that he was also the one who tampered with the car brakes.

She needed a drink.

When she saw her face in the bathroom mirror she knew why the desk clerk looked so anxious. Her fingers gingerly touched the blue-black bruise spreading like a five o'clock shadow from her neck to her jaw line. She dumped the ice from the bedside pitcher into the washcloth, tied the four corners and pressed the makeshift pack against her jaw. The cold eased the soreness.

She needed a drink. A Margarita—several Margaritas—enough Margaritas to go blotto—

She opened the room door. Music and laughter came from the lounge. The human noises comforted her. People were talking, clinking glasses. Life hadn't completely gone down the tube.

Great big Audubon prints hung on the hallway walls—birds in flight, birds on limbs, birds close up. Roger shouldn't have any trouble finding enough material for his book.

Crutches weren't easy to maneuver. She gained a new respect for the disabled who swung their way on Quarter sidewalks.

Her eyes took a minute to adjust to the lounge darkness. Men sat at the bar. Couples huddled in the shadows. One big group had pulled several tables together, beer bottles everywhere. They laughed and hooted making the rowdy racket she'd heard from her room.

A man rose on unsteady feet, teetered to the juke box and inserted coins. A woman clung to his waist. They wobbled to the dance floor, four sheets to the wind. At the Parrot's Bar, Bilbao would've bounced them quicker than it took to say, "Outta here!"

The barman asked, "What'll it be?"

"Whatever the lady wanths, ith on me," the sot sitting on a bar stool replied.

Too tired for any new shit, Karla cut him off. "Thanks, but no thanks. Margarita on the rocks—"

The aggravating son-of-a-bitch kept hanging on her, touching her sore shoulder, her hurting leg. She took her drink and hobbled to the upright piano sitting in the corner.

Finding the piano was as though she'd discovered a landmark. The familiar instrument didn't have to be the same make and style as her repossessed one, or the same as the one at the Parrot's Bar or anywhere else in the world. It was sufficient for it to be what it was, a piano. The same as it was enough for Van Gogh's Sun Flowers to be sunflowers. They could hang anywhere, and the moment of recognition brought acknowledgment and inner place. Auntie Emmy had her Twenty-Third Psalm. 'Yeah though I walk through the valley of the shadow of Death—' Whenever Auntie Emmy read those words, she was home.

Karla leaned the crutches against the piano and Margarita in hand sat on the bench.

A tune played in her head. She set down the drink and picked a note or two. The melody flowed of its own volition as if her fingers were directed by an unseen muse. She added a few scales and left-hand base chords. Halfway through, she realized the piece was the *Meditation de Thais*, the same one the harpist at Windsor Court played the afternoon she went there to meet Albert and Mary. Was that

THE AZALEAS

yesterday or a week ago? Hours that didn't touch familiar landmarks and days without rhythm stretched and contracted until they lost their meaning and only accomplishments mattered. Decades could be boiled down to "before the war," or "after mama died," and nothing counted in between.

The man at the bar called in a snickering voice. "Hey, girl!—we ain't into that high-brow stuff! How about a little Professor Longhair!—"

Karla's fingers shifted to jazz, easy, without effort, as if going back to a native tongue after struggling with a foreign language. The syncopated beat filled the semi-dark room. She reached the end and the people at the big table pounded the surface, sending beer bottles toppling and spilling. "More! More!"

The bartender refilled Karla's empty glass.

"More! More!" That voice she recognized. She hadn't seen Bale come in. He waved at her from a side table. She played a few more pieces for the crowd then hobbled over to Bale's table.

He looked at her crutches and bruised face. "You got into trouble again? What happened?"

"Minor accident, y'know—one of those little St. Francisville mishaps—"

"You're okay?"

"Sure. I'm like a bad weed—can't kill a bad weed—it keeps cropping up."

He laughed and admired her piano playing. "That was some show. I had no idea—"

"By ear," she explained. "I can't read a note."

"A talent such as that—"

"Yeah—well—" She didn't want to go there. That third degree was too familiar. The next predictable question was why didn't you study music?—followed by why didn't you take lessons? And then, the nugget always got thrown in—Mozart began playing and composing when he was four. Mozart had parents. The parents had money. He had a piano, a teacher. Karla had Auntie Emmy and glasses filled with different water levels that when struck with a flat knife produced distinctive tinkling sounds. And later, a bamboo stalk with the holes cut into the wood that whistled various tunes depending how hard she blew and which openings her fingers covered and closed. And she made it all the way up to the Green

Choir at St. James AME church, the only member with golden Shirley Temple curls. Putting that childhood into words made it sound like one long litany of need and that wasn't so. She never missed what she didn't have.

They finished their drinks and Karla asked, "What brings you here?"

"You—" Darkness hid his face, but shadows didn't affect Karla's hearing. His voice was husky and husky she understood.

"Why?" She'd given up men. Like an alcoholic she'd sworn abstinence. She looked at Bale's handsome face and knew how easy it was to start down the path to destruction.

"I heard you'd left—"

"Jesus Christ! Already?—"

"Yep—"

"What day is this?"

"Saturday—" He saw the frown on her face. "The wee hours of the morning, Saturday," he said.

Where did she lose twenty-four hours?

Ever since the night Albert put the damper on their lover's delight, both Bale and Karla had done their best to keep the flame from flaring. Their unfinished business was like kindling waiting for a match.

Bale rubbed Karla's hand gently, reassuringly, as though he knew the thoughts going through her head. "It'll be all right," he said.

"Someone tried to kill me," she said. "They tampered with the brakes on my car."

"You're joking me."

She held up the bandaged foot. "Does this look funny to you? I couldn't slow down for the S-curve by your place. The same curve where Converse McKenzie got killed!"

"It's a dangerous curve," Bale said.

Why of all times did Bale come now? He'd had other opportunities and by-passed them. He hadn't spoken to her in days. He'd completely vanished from her life. Why did he resurrect now?

"Let's get out of here," he said.

They left the lounge, arms intertwined. She leaned heavily against him, limping down the hallway, past the frowning desk clerk and into the king-size bed in room 145. Bale offered an inviting arm and cradled Karla in its crook.

She admonished herself not to think of Richard whose passionate love-making lifted her into another world, made her forget time and place. Or of Albert, who warned her about doing exactly what she was about to do, mixing pleasure with business.

God's sake! Couldn't she simply relax, enjoy the moment, give Bale her undivided attention and get the greatest possible delight from this unexpected encounter? How many months since she'd been with a man? Did she care to count the days?

At first Bale was tentative, unsure where Karla's hot spots were, but she helped him by placing his hand here or there, careful to avoid contact with her aching foot. They found their rhythm. Entanglement with another body demanded total physical and mental involvement. Carried on kinetic waves and throbbing energy, she let go and soared. Sometimes a man took you to those heights. Most times he didn't. Bale could and did.

They lay panting, their bodies fused as though they'd gone through a smelting furnace that extracted impurities and left refined metal. Slowly their grip on each other slackened. They breathed easier, slept.

She curled in a warm, happy cocoon, her body damp with musky-smelling sweat oozing from every satisfied pore.

"What are you thinking?" Bale traced a circle around Karla's navel and touched the diamond stud. "When did you do this?"

"A while back on a dare."

"And this?—" He rubbed the butterfly on her shoulder.

"A forever that didn't work out—"

He said, "Ah," and made no comment. She respected him for that.

"How's your ankle?"

"Throbbing—really, why did you come?"

Was he involved in the conspiracy to get rid of her? Did he come to make sure she had been successfully eliminated?

"Because it is hard to disentangle you from The Azaleas, and right now you and I are at odds where the plantation—"

"At odds?—not at all—you want to own it and I want to sell it to you."

"Let's not get off on that tangent. It'll ruin a beautiful night."

He kissed her and then his lips were warm against her breast and they made love again.

Karla nibbled his ear and murmured, "Why do you really want The Azaleas? There's more to it than the expansion of The Hills."

He was silent for a long, dreadful moment. She wished fervently that she had controlled her nosiness and halfway hoped he'd ignore the question. Outside thoughts intruding into their cocoon would ruin perfection.

His voice was just above a whisper. "Mary and I were married once."

As if she'd be jolted by a cattle prod, Karla flopped over in the circle of his arms. She pressed her stomach flat against his, flesh to flesh, warm and damp. "You're kidding me."

"We were married for seventy-two hours." His fingers tangled in Karla's hair. He absent-mindedly rubbed her goose egg.

"Ouch."

"Sorry. That's a big bump on the back of your head."

"So you were married and?—"

"Divorced—" He pulled his arm from under Karla's shoulders and slammed closed the window into his life.

He couldn't leave Karla dangling like the Friday segment of a soap opera! Did he get Mary pregnant? Were they in high school? "Why?"

"Didn't work out, that's all."

"Were you too young?"

"Just kids," he replied. "Life is so intense when you're young."

"And her mother took her away." Karla knew that from Hank's diary.

"Yeah—and then her father Hank—"

"Killed himself—"

"How'd you know that?"

"Preacher Frank told me. He doesn't really believe that. He says Hank didn't have the guts—"

"Mr. Hank lost his will to live, that's what happened."

"He had big problems."

"Problems are challenges to overcome."

"His wife and daughter left and the plantation was about to get repossessed."

"So the story goes."

"And this mysterious $300,000 turns up and Rainbow holds a mortgage—"

"The plantation was not repossessed. Leave it at that. Agatha blamed me for Mr. Hank's death."

"Because?—"

"Because Mary and I—forget it—" a heavy silence followed, more eloquent than any spoken word. "It's all in the past; makes no difference now."

"So when did you get married?" Karla asked with unrestrained curiosity.

"A few months after Danielle took her away, I followed Mary to New Orleans. I couldn't live without her. We drove across the border to Mississippi and got married by a justice of the peace who asked no questions. That was on a Wednesday. Danielle had me put in jail. Albert handled the annulment and bailed me out, too."

Interesting to learn that at one time Albert carried on a regular practice like other normal lawyers did. Even more interesting that he'd mentioned Mary's divorce from Bravelle, but not from Bale.

Bale continued, as if he'd opened a dam that flooded memories. "Mary was 17, under-age. I should've known better than to take a minor across the state line for immoral purposes. That's what the law said I did. The whole thing turned nasty and ugly. We were the town gossip until something juicier came up. I give Albert credit. He presented a good argument on my behalf. I was 22, legal age to qualify as an adult, fresh out of LSU, and our elopement was a mutual consent affair. The matter was finally resolved, and Danielle shipped Mary off to France for good."

"What kind of lawyer is Albert? Civil or criminal or what?—"

"He started out like all the other attorneys with an uptown office, catering to the Garden District clientele—divorces, wills, real estate—a little bit of everything. I met him when he handled our divorce. Then he disappeared. Gossips said it was a love affair gone sour. There was talk he shot a man. Some people swore there was a duel at dawn beneath the oaks at Audubon Park, but that's far-fetched." Talking about Albert instead of himself made Bale more at ease. "I heard he was traveling in Europe, some said South America. Whatever happened, he disappeared for ten years. People say Albert left a Southerner and returned a Renaissance man. He must've made a fortune, because he opened that elite office and takes only selected clients. He discreetly backs various enterprises. He's into art and literature, antiques, real estate. You name it and Albert has his finger in it."

"I think Albert fronts for somebody," Karla said, "for an organization. Everything he does is cloak and dagger."

When she was through with The Azaleas, she intended to find the previous real estate agents Albert had hired and have a good long talk with them. Hopefully, they hadn't vanished into thin air, but with her luck—

"It wouldn't hurt to be extra careful," Bale advised.

"I told Albert I thought he ran an undercover organization and he laughed. 'We sell properties difficult to move, places nobody else wants to tangle with,' he said. 'You think they'd hire us to sell a run-of-the mill chalet when a hundred other agents would do as well? We have our niche. It's difficult, but remunerative.'" The explanation made sense at the time. Everything Albert said made sense at the time. Only when she looked back and dwelled on it did the logic get skewed. "Have you gotten over Mary?"

"Absolutely— Life has a way of not stopping. It keeps keeping on, you know. But the whole thing sticks in my craw. Life would've been so different if—" He could not forget. Whatever the problem was, it threw a long shadow on the gold dust of his success. "I made a vow. I swore one day I'd own The Azaleas."

"And you're almost there."

"You betcha—"

"You want to hurt Mary because you still love her."

"What are you, an amateur psychiatrist? I want revenge because revenge is sweet."

In a warped way, Karla envied Bale's clear path. He had been wronged and he had a plan to get even with the wrong-doers. She lacked such a strategy. She couldn't settle her score. There was nothing tangible she could take away from Richard. She could destroy his marriage, but in the process she'd destroy herself. She'd become the other woman, the home wrecker. Auntie Emmy deserved better than that.

"One never gets over a true love." Karla spoke from experience.

Bale rubbed her back, gentle circles below the shoulder blades.

In the touch, in the despairing motion, Karla found the answer. She and Bale were both jilted souls carrying torches.

"You know what, Bale?" She burrowed closer. "I don't think God answers prayers."

"I don't bother with God."

The pitch and yaw Karla felt under the bed was Auntie Emmy rolling over in her grave.

"My Auntie Emmy said God answers us in ways we don't understand because we can't see the whole picture and He can. Does that make sense?"

"Not a bit. The only philosophy that works is that God helps those who help themselves."

Karla wasn't overly religious, but living under Auntie Emmy's roof, she had acquired faith through osmosis. Survival wouldn't have been possible otherwise. Belief in a better life seeped in through the cracks in the wall. Poor people clung to the promise of a higher plateau reached through a pearly gate—not gold or silver, but pearls. Karla imagined that gate a thousand times—a big archway, with gigantic pearls glued over every inch of it. The round, smooth surfaces caught the sunlight and gleamed so bright and so far that when Auntie Emmy read the scriptures and looked up, she said "Hallelujah!" and was comforted.

"You never saw Mary again?"

"No."

"She's in town. Do you want to see her?"

"Absolutely not," he protested quickly, much too quickly.

Restless, Karla rose and hobbled to a little terrace, a flagstone square with three potted geraniums. She stood naked in the moonlight.

Bale followed. "On top of everything else you don't need to catch cold," he said, draping a white sheet over her shoulders. "Want a smoke?" he asked.

"Sure."

He handed her a joint instead of the Marlborough she expected. She inhaled long and deep, exhaled slowly. "Good stuff."

"None better. Comes from the sheriff's own stash—"

"How come he gets away with everything?"

"Because he's sheriff, that's why."

"The Feds will get him."

"Not in a million years."

"What makes you so sure?"

He said, "I know what I know," and didn't elaborate further.

The sweet grass smell lingered in the air. "I'll make a deal with you," Karla said. "Offer to buy the plantation for three million less credit for the $300,000 mortgage held by Rainbow. It probably won't fly, but—"

"Oh, I'll end up with The Azaleas, be sure of that. I'll work out my own deal."

No doubt existed in Karla's mind that Bale Franklin would do just that. He had drive and determination fueled by ambition and resentment. He was a man with something to prove, and men like that couldn't be stopped.

Albert was specific on one point: no sale, no commission, and therefore no pay. During this romantic interlude, Karla was thinking pay check and Bale was thinking revenge. Something didn't compute in this crazy equation.

Bale stubbed his joint and flicked it behind a bush. Karla retrieved the butt before the warty desk clerk found it and raised a big fuss over nothing.

"What the hell," he said. "Write it up. Offer her a million."

Thirty cents on the dollar! Albert would never let Mary take that, but negotiations had to start somewhere.

CHAPTER 17

A pounding on the room door broke the sweet silence.

Karla bolted upright. The sudden movement sent a sharp pain from ankle to knee.

Bale slipped on his trousers. "What the hell?"

"Open up!" The harsh voice had an official tone. "Open up!"

Bale turned the door knob without removing the chain lock. He looked through the crack. "What the hell you want, Bubba?"

The shotgun-wielding deputy who had struck Willis!

"You got that woman meddling with The Azaleas in there?" the deputy asked.

Karla pulled the sheet over her head.

Bale wasn't in the least intimidated. He was one of them, another thread in their interwoven lives. "That's none your goddam business."

Bubba shifted his stance, straining to look into the room through the slightly ajar door.

"It's my business if the sheriff's got a 10-57 APB out on her."

"Get the hell outta here, Bubba. Leaving a hospital is not a crime." Bale looked over his shoulder to make sure Karla was still in the bed. "And she's not missing, for God's sake."

"Hospital's lookin' for her. She escaped and Henry Brown says he brought her here and she ain't had no money to pay, so she gave him a Mickey Mouse watch."

"You go tell Jimmy I have Karla Whitmore in my possession—"

Possession! Karla couldn't believe her ears. Did Bale say *possession?*

"I'm to bring her in," Deputy Bubba insisted.

"Tell that bastard to meet us for breakfast. We'll see him there, okay?" Bale closed the door in Bubba's face and got back into bed. "I apologize. The sheriff has no finesse."

He reached for Karla as if the interruption was nothing more than a parenthesis in a life paragraph. He threw his arm across her waist. "Don't let Jimmy Watson get to you."

The sheriff did get to Karla in the worst way. And so did Bale and Bubba and the whole country crowd. Suddenly, she yearned for Albert and his cynical observations that put everything in perspective, his magical ease for fixing everything, his cool detachment that elevated him above the fray.

Another rap on the door, a different knock, diffident, tentative—

"What is this?" Bale asked. "Grand Central Station?—"

The hotel bellboy held Karla's battered suitcase in one hand, the briefcase in the other, her leather purse and the Mickey Mouse watch clasped on the handle.

"Henry Brown wants his fare money."

Bale placed two twenties in the bellboy's outstretched hand. "That should take care of everybody."

"My clothes!—"

"Car towed to the wrecker lot. Henry Brown said he brung you here. He figured you'd need your suitcase so he went and got it for you."

"Tell him I said thanks."

Bale sighed. "I can see this party is over."

"Give me a few minutes," Karla replied. "And we'll go get breakfast."

❦

"Sunday breakfast at the St. Francis before the Angola rodeo is a tradition of long-standing," Bale explained as he and Karla waited in line for a table.

The dining room overflowed with people on their way to the wildest show in the South.

THE AZALEAS

Waitresses with laden trays skirted tables. Men in blue jeans, boots and ten-gallon hats sat with women wearing tight pants and gold jewelry. Children and teenagers occupied premium seats. Crystal and silverware clink-clanked like casino slot machines. Conversations rose and fell— accordions compressing and expanding, a melody. The morning sun streaming through the glass touched a knife, a fork, a tray and sent diamonds sparkling in the air. Past the ringing cash register, paying customers emerged with a toothpick clamped between their teeth, reward for their patronage. People waiting to be seated sighed impatiently and groaned. They rose on tiptoes to check lingering diners homesteading tables.

A large party sitting at three tables pulled together rose and left. Through the gap their departure created Karla saw a familiar silver head. The man moved a little to one side and there was no mistaking the profile, the pink baby skin and the white quizzical eyebrows. Across from Albert sat Mary, a navy blue jacket carelessly flung over her bandaged shoulder, arm in a matching sling. Stuck to her side like a refrigerator magnet was Pierre Rousseau.

"They came in a big white limo last night," Bale said. "Heralds blowing trumpets couldn't have made a greater impression. By the time the limo turned into the St. Francis parking lot, everybody knew Mary Bravelle and her pimp count had arrived."

Karla wasn't born yesterday. Bale came to her last night when galled he couldn't have Mary. He used Karla's body for love-making meant for another.

She should've resented him, but she didn't. Until the door banging began, the night had been a satisfactory oasis in her arid desert love life.

As if Albert felt eyes boring holes into his back, he looked over his shoulder and beckoned Karla and Bale to join him.

Bale looked away, pretending not to notice, but nothing so subtle worked with Albert, already on his feet and crossing the dining room. He grasped Karla's forearm, held her at arm's length and ran his gaze over her like a man checking his car after a fender bender, looking for dents and damages and future claims. He noted the blue-black bruises on her face. "A little mishap?—"

Jesus! He made her so mad. What happened to somebody else was nothing. If this bruise had been on his pretty pink face, he wouldn't be calling the injury a little mishap.

Maybe she'd hit him with workman's comp. She had earned it. If he fired her, she'd march herself right down to the unemployment office, put in a claim and show this bastard a thing or two.

Albert pumped Bale's hand as if he were a long-lost friend. Like a shepherd herding strays, he led them to his table.

"Bale Franklin, Pierre Rousseau." Albert made the introductions.

The men eyed each other warily. "*Bonjour, monsieur*," Pierre replied, dumb foreign words.

Nobody shook hands or went into the European kissy-kiss routine.

Bale said, "Mary," softly, as if testing the word for size, for depth, holding the two syllables on his tongue, tasting, playing with them. "How are you?"

"Hello, Bale," she replied, lowering her lashes and looking quickly away. She slipped her hand into Pierre's.

In the short time Karla had known Mary, Karla had classified her as a wimp, a weeping willow, an uppity Elle, a bowl of Jello and other adjectives along that nature, but she'd never seen her do something deliberately cruel. Her clasping Pierre's hand drove nails through Bale's heart.

Karla knew the scene, knew the thoughts chasing each other across Bale's mind. The past had a way of overcoming the present. Bale looked at Mary and saw her in her cheerleader outfit, shaking her pom-poms; in the car, parked in the dark woods, melting into him; at the justice of the peace, by his side, listening to the official say 'repeat after me.'

And she was holding another man's hand.

The simpering smile never left Pierre's face. He fawned over Mary while discreetly eyeing Karla, an invitation for later. The rascal Count was either secure in his position as Mary's prime suitor, or too dumb to know he was slipping from the throne.

The tension climbed like a red mercury column registering fever in an old-fashioned thermometer. Could a wife of 72 hours mean that much to Bale? Karla followed every little move, every expression on Bale's face. Yes! The memory of three perfect days was a touchstone that sustained imperfect years.

Bale balled his big, working-man hands into fists and shoved them in his pants pocket as though it took all the control he could muster to keep from punching Pierre.

Karla shot a look at Albert, who had rescinded the marriage, annulled the couple's love life, destroyed their happiness, and now sat calmly and watched the sparks rekindle.

Albert, too, was smitten with Mary. Damn that Mary! She sat, demure and helpless, surrounded by three adoring men. The phlegm of green jealousy closing Karla's throat tasted bilious.

Amusement danced in Albert's eyes, as if he'd anticipated this meeting, foresaw this reaction, and everyone present was a marionette playing to his tune.

Bale's bid to buy The Azaleas burned a hole in Karla's tote. Bale had signed it while she sat naked on his lap. Karla didn't give a damn how she got it. She got it, and the bottom line was what counted. Albert didn't have to know everything.

"Sell out crowd," Albert appraised the hungry multitude.

Karla dimpled her cheek and gave Pierre her rosiest, most promising smile. It wouldn't take much to lure Pierre away, give Bale and Mary enough time to get together and reconcile their differences, then everybody could move forward with The Azaleas sale.

Handing Mary the man Karla had just slept with wasn't a generous or open-minded gesture on Karla's part. It was a calculated move, a necessary next step. Until Mary and Bale resolved their problem and got their act together, Karla couldn't sell the plantation. It suddenly dawned on her that Albert probably knew this. Had he known all along, from the beginning?

Sam's big hulk filled the doorway. He maneuvered Judge Jeremiah Jones's wheelchair, avoiding tables and chairs.

"Full house today," the Judge bellowed as he rolled to Albert's table. "Pity inmates can't vote or Jimmy would have them all here for breakfast."

Everyone laughed, including Agatha at his elbow, looking comfortable in a silk cowboy shirt and tailored pants.

Agatha's gaze skipped over Bale. With a sudden, gasping breath, color draining from her cheeks, she acknowledged Mary's presence.

The judge felt Agatha's pressuring hand as it gripped his shoulder. He peered over his horn-rimmed glasses. "Mary! So you decided to come after all! What a grand surprise! Why didn't you let us know you were coming? Are you here for the rodeo?" The Judge's voice retained its authoritative boom, but Karla got the definite impression the man was babbling, filling empty air for Agatha's benefit, giving his neighbor and life-long love time to muster her charm and engage her wit, the Southern battle armor.

The Judge bent over Mary's hand, bringing her fingers to his lips as if she was the closest and dearest thing to his heart, saying standard stuff like, "You're still as beautiful as ever." "You're like good wine, better every year it ages," and so forth and so on. All lies, but pleasant to the ear. "You're still our little princess."

Agatha visibly reacted to "princess." Her left eye went into an uncontrollable tic, the lid falling heavily then springing up, down and up, down and up, a motion that for some ridiculous reason made Karla think of kids jumping on a trampoline.

As if from far away, Karla heard Mary say, "Aunt Agatha. It's been so long. How are you?"

Addressed directly, Agatha's southern upbringing kicked into gear. "Good morning, my dear," she replied with icy politeness. "I am well. And you?"

Agatha made haste to escape the conversation, the confrontation of a life gone sour. She urged the Judge to hurry so they could find a table.

"And what about you, Albert?" asked the Judge. "We haven't seen you in these parts in a coon's age."

"It has been a while," Albert replied in his smooth, unruffled manner. "With me it's always business as usual. So little time for pleasure— The Azaleas brings me here."

That pronouncement was the antidote Agatha needed. She reared her helmet-coiffed head. Her eyelid quit ticking, and her eyes gleamed like hurricane lamps in a dark night. A smile plastered itself across her lips.

"You're always welcome in our little neck of the woods," she said, dragging every syllable to the breaking point.

This drawn speech, the slow-motion words, was the dead calm before a hurricane. The gathering storm was sensed by Sam, who rattled, "Hello, hello… hello," and gave the Judge's wheelchair a big push.

Sam's voice activated Karla's goose bumps. The black hands with acorn-size knuckles rested on the wheelchair. The big, thick fingers could strangle. Karla saw the Band-Aid on his hand. A preposterous notion sprang full-blown into her head. "Somebody bit you?"

His hand jumped as if she'd touched it with a blow torch. "I have a Band-Aid, see? The Judge put the Band-Aid—"

"That's enough, Sam," the Judge snapped. "Nobody cares about your Band-Aid."

Oh, but Karla did care. Sam's Band-Aid was a matter of life and death as far as she was concerned.

The strangler's thumb had been on one side of her mouth, the index finger on the other, a visor-like hold that crushed her jaw. She had struggled against the grip, sank her front teeth into the connecting flesh between the fingers. "Let me see?" she took a step closer. "You smell good, Sam."

"Old Spice in a white bottle, a smooth white bottle. It smells good. It feels fresh like cold water. It tastes good, too, but boss says I can't drink it."

Were a Band-Aid and a whiff of aftershave sufficient evidence, probable cause, whatever the police lingo was for attempted murder?

A teenager behind the Judge said, "C'mon, now! We all gotta eat!" and circled the wheelchair, giving Sam a dirty look. The Judge grabbed both chair wheels and rolled impatiently forward. "Let's move on."

Up to this minute Karla had thought of Agatha as steel wool, soft to the touch but tough enough to scour. But now Agatha walked away on zombie feet, looking old and tired, a survivor of too many skirmishes with the big battle still ahead.

Karla stared at Sam's broad back. He was wearing a black cotton tee shirt. A cloth fragment matching that description was in the shoe box in her room. Could it possibly belong to Sam? Could she get into his room, rummage through his drawers and find a ripped tee with a torn piece missing? Not likely. No matter how simple Sam was, he'd have sense enough to burn the shirt. Or somebody would conveniently dispose of the tee for Sam. These people stuck together.

If by some miracle she did get her hands on the tee shirt, she had Sam nailed. That thought brought little consolation. Sam wasn't the brains of this outfit.

She'd report Sam to the sheriff. What good would that do? Better to notify the FBI or NOPD or the IRS, or the CIA. The alphabet ran through her mind.

"This way—" The impatient waitress waved the wheelchair group onward. "Please! This way! Do you want your table or not?" Her tips depended on turnovers, and the Judge and Agatha stymied her livelihood. "This way, please."

As if the group hadn't had enough surprises before the grits and eggs, there came Gloria from Hasker and Blunt beaming like a happy sunrise, smiling brightly at an Asian whose head kept bobbing like an apple in a bucket of water. The red hair piled on Gloria's head bounced as she walked, bobby pins spewing from the French twist.

She'd gotten Karla's call! She'd come to her rescue! Gloria stood in full flesh and glory! With a customer! She didn't drag that Asian all the way here to watch a jail bird ride a bull.

Albert had the waiter re-arrange tables and china. Gloria and Mr. Yen Ito sat down. Gloria didn't believe in wasting time. She came right to the point. "Mr. Ito is from Tokyo. He's here to buy The Azaleas."

An astounded Karla didn't know what to say. She'd asked for help, a nudge to make Bale Franklin cross the line, not for someone to buy the plantation out from under him. Bale pulled his sun-bleached eyebrows into a deep frown. Pierre lit up, already counting Mary's money. Mary, hopeful and confused, turned to Albert. An amused looked played on Albert's face. The devil sparkled in his eye.

Mary glanced at Mr. Ito with curious eyes. The look sent Mr. Ito's head into an Asian yo-yo frenzy. Behind his rimless glasses, the slanted eyes were softened by age wrinkles and sagging skin. Gray hair gave the bowl haircut a dignified sheen. His mannerisms were Eastern, his English Oxford.

"How do you do, madam?" he asked with more head bobbing.

In the fifth grade, after Karla's mother died, a boy in class told her if grave diggers dug straight down and never stopped, they would reach China and she believed him. Every afternoon starting with a spoon and graduating to a shovel, she dug in Auntie Emmy's back yard. She could see herself slipping right down that hole and finding her mother. She probably would've made it, too, except Auntie Emmy went to hang the laundry and fell in the pit and broke her leg. That put a stop to the excavation.

Bale scraped his chair back, a green-eyed scowl on his face, "Karla, lets—"

"There's no need to rush off," Albert said easily. "Here comes breakfast."

The waitress slipped plates and platters onto the table.

Albert explained to Mr. Ito, "Mary Bravelle owns The Azaleas. Agatha Turner lives on the plantation." A sardonic smile played on his lips. "Judge Jones in the wheelchair over there is the next door neighbor to the east and Bale Franklin has the development to the west of the plantation. Pierre Rousseau is Mary's fiancé." Albert slathered butter on his toast. "And I'm the lawyer," he continued, softly, almost teasingly. "And it's my great pleasure to meet you, Mr. Ito," then almost as an afterthought, "Ah, yes. Karla is the real estate agent."

He acted as if he'd purposely gathered everybody for a great Agatha Christie finale.

"How are you?" Karla said, resenting Albert and Mr. Ito alike. "Tokyo is a long piece from here."

Two tables away, the Judge leaned from his wheelchair and announced for all to hear: "I was with the 101st Airborne during World War II. We bombed Tokyo."

Mr. Ito smiled from his teeth out and nodded several times in quick succession. "Very much destruction," he said, "to our country and to our people."

The World War II Museum in New Orleans was filled with photographs, a chronology of destruction: Hiroshima, Nagasaki, Osaka and other unpronounceable places. The displays bragged strength and triumph. Artillery and B-54s, tanks and submarines promoted the idea the U.S. was indestructible, invincible, permanent as the stars in the sky.

Mr. Ito said, "A war that takes place on your own personal soil makes a much greater impression than one that is fought far away, brought to you by the CNN television." He bowed his head respectfully. "We treasure our land. We have not much land, you know. We are an island," he smiled politely, almost apologetic.

Mr. Ito didn't sound angry or resentful. On the contrary, the buoyant lightness in his voice contained a triumphant note. What did he have to gloat about?

And suddenly the reason why Mr. Ito was a happy man dawned on Karla. Like Bale he had a plan for revenge. His island nation had a plan. If the USA's everlasting superiority couldn't be conquered with guns and ammunition, it could certainly be bought. The country could be purchased piece by piece, vanquished dollar by dollar, overtaken quietly and legally, acre by acre, building by building, lot by lot, eliminating need for mindless wars."

Judge Jones tapped his inert legs with his ivory-topped cane. "The destruction wasn't all on your side."

Gloria, the pro at keeping sellers and buyers away from each other's throats, stepped in. "Well, gentlemen, that war has long been over. We've Korea, Vietnam, the Gulf War, Iraq and who knows how many official and unofficial skirmishes since World War II. War is men's favorite pastime."

"As far as the South is concerned," Agatha said, her voice thick with drawn vowels, "there was only one war, the battle over land, keeping our land, our way of life. We may not use guns, but we're still fighting that war today."

The subtle warning was not lost on Gloria, who looked at Karla, gave a little shrug and raised an eyebrow.

Gloria bulldozed the war talk and moved forward. "Mr. Ito," she said, "is quite disposed to buy The Azaleas. He's in the market for U. S. investments."

"Wrong location," snapped Agatha. "We live in the past here, Mr. Ito. We don't cultivate change or progress."

Mr. Ito nodded appreciatively. "We revere olden temples, also."

"He's not concerned about the bottom land or swamp," Gloria said. "Land is land, and he has no plans to subdivide the plantation."

He'd leave the plantation intact. He wouldn't carve roads through the pastures, cut the land into lots, and reserve the prime location for commercial development. What was it Judge Jeremiah had said? The country had become a nation of Burger Kings, McDonald's and Pizza Huts. This foreigner would rescue The Azaleas from a cookie cutter fate.

Gloria continued smoothly. "He'd like to take a look at the house sometime this afternoon or tomorrow morning,"

The choice that excluded an outright "no" didn't work with Agatha. "We're at the rodeo today, and tomorrow will be impossible."

Gloria didn't miss a beat. "We wouldn't in any way interfere with anybody's routine. Karla can walk us through."

Getting a prospective buyer into a house owned by a hostile seller required expertise, and Karla had no clue as to whether or not she could manipulate Agatha. Karla knew she should, because that was her job, what she'd been hired to do by Albert and Mary. If Karla couldn't get the customer in the front door, she might as well admit failure—

"I can do that," Karla replied, planning already to stop first in the parlor, hoping Felice would bounce off the wall and blow this Jap with the bobbing head all the way back to Japan.

Albert looked from one person to another, his pale gray eyes sparkling. In many ways Karla's employer was a common hustler, happiest when pulling strings and pushing buttons.

Bale's million dollar bid was in big trouble. If he were to lose the plantation to the Japanese buyer, he couldn't get even with the Turners. Revenge was what he was after.

The house and land were only the means to the end.

If Karla presented Bale's offer to Mary right now, the suspense would end. Nothing was worse than dangling, not knowing. Mary would either say yes, or she'd say no. Until she made that decision, Karla's own life couldn't go forward.

Waiting wasn't Karla's strong suit. Her life didn't overflow with happy waiting memories. She had no joyful anticipations of Santa Claus, overflowing stockings, vacation trip to Florida beaches or a new birthday outfit. Karla's waiting was filled with angst and outright terror: foster parents who hit with leather belts, landlords banging on the door, and bill collectors calling at all hours day and night.

"Albert, I have—"

"It'll keep," Albert replied. He never hurried, never became flustered, never raised hell. No wind was strong enough to ripple his calm surface.

In Karla's old neighborhood, that nirvana state was only achieved with Prozac.

Two tall, willowy girls approached, beautiful, sensuous beings exuding energy and youth, turning every head as they meandered toward their table. The gorgeous creatures belonged to Roger Randall who looked Albert's way and waved a friendly hello.

Karla excused herself and limped over. "Hi, y'all—Hi, Roger—"

"Well, you don't look too much worse for the wear and tear," he said. "Meet Carleen, Bonnie—"

"Hi, girls—your daddy says nothing but nice things about you."

"—and my wife, Myra." Roger introduced Myra with such pride, as if she were a prize and he'd been lucky to win first place.

"Hi, there," Myra said. She was an athletic blonde, even prettier in person than in the snapshot Roger kept in his wallet, a California sunshine girl who'd aged well and gracefully. She had the relaxed, satisfied look of a woman who is loved. Her teasing smile, quick eyes, the casual fingers touching Roger's arm was love's unspoken language—I'm his, he's mine, we're bonded, we're happy, we have no crack in our seams. Nobody or no thing can separate us. We are one.

"We surprised Daddy," Bonnie said. "Mama got up this morning and said, 'Girls, let's ride to St. Francisville and spend the day with Daddy,' and we piled into my convertible and away we went!"

Daddy Roger took obvious delight in being surrounded by his beautiful bevy, yet Karla detected a resigned air in his jovial attitude. He hadn't expected them or planned for their arrival, but they were here and he'd make the best of it, but—

"There's the sheriff," Roger said.

Jimmy Watson made his way with authority through the breakfast crowd. "G'morning good folks—" He tipped his ten-gallon hat and didn't remove it. "Hiya, everybody—there you are, Karla—been looking everywhere for you, honey—even put out an APB. You didn't go about forgettin' the rodeo, did you?"

"No, no. I'm here. I remembered," Karla replied, relieved.

"Rodeo starts at two o'clock, but I have to get there earlier," he said with an important man's self-satisfaction called on an important occasion to utter important words soon forgotten. His chest puffed like a toad's. "I'm in the VIP section just under the press box. Official duties—" he tried to sound bored, but missed by a mile—"you know how that is."

"I'll be fine sitting with all this good company," Karla replied.

She felt reprieved not having to deal with Sheriff Watson. She could concentrate on Willis. Her gut feeling said Lura Mae's grandson imprisoned in Angola Penitentiary, planning to ride a bull in the rodeo had an ace up his sleeve—not good news.

CHAPTER 18

Bale and Karla made their way to the rodeo arena. She limped along on her crutches. "The sun is hot enough to fry an egg on my head," she said.

Art and crafts booths ringed the area, giving the prison a country fair atmosphere. Beneath once-white tents gaunt, hard-looking, tattooed men sold leather belts, velvet paintings, wooden trays and ceramic vases, tangible evidence of their monotonous lives.

Tramping feet stirred the dry earth, and the dust rose and fell in clouds that settled on the artwork, on the clothing, in the wrinkled, squinting faces. Dust filtered into Karla's shoes, made her mouth gritty and her eyes water.

Mostly, the artwork was flat, one-dimensional and lifeless. The colors lost purity and turned murky. The subjects were limited to self-portraits, cane fields, white prison cottages and men in line holding hoes and rakes, a reflection of their circumstances. This display was nothing compared to those around Jackson Square where backgrounds exploded with exuberant color and minute details were drawn with one-hair brushes.

"Some of this stuff is so bad these men deserve to be locked up for their art alone," a woman behind Karla said.

Karla stifled a laugh— the remark was so on the button.

Across a barricade and behind a wire fence, carvings were displayed. Karla spotted a chess set. From where she stood it looked like ivory. She'd surprise Albert with an unexpected gift. No doubt existed in her mind that Albert played chess. He was born to check and crown.

"Buy it! Come buy it!" The man's lips and nose were tight against the wire. His thick, heavy fingers grasped the fence. The crisscross wiring formed a grid on his face, a great popped black eye here, a distended nose there, an ear cut in half. The red bandanna, brown-streaked teeth, and yellow nails were held together by the black wire lines.

"He looks like a Picasso," Karla said.

Bale looked blank and didn't register. Albert would've picked up on the resemblance right away, no explanations needed.

"Are you the carver?" Karla asked the inmate.

"*The* master carver—heh...heh...heh," the man leered, running an incredibly long tongue over hard, thin lips. "None better. Buy the chess set, huh? Woncha buy the chess set?"

Karla leaned across the barricade for a closer look. Immediately, a guard stood before her. "Stay back, ma'am. Those are the bad boys there."

"Is the chess set for sale?"

"Yes, it is. Which one?—"

"That ivory one—"

"Buy it! Buy it!" The convict chanted. "Buy it! Buy it!" He moved like a monkey in jerky little jumps further down the wire fencing so he could see around the guard and catch Karla's eye once again. "Carved rock— better'n ivory—worked on it two years."

Over the loud speaker, politicians and dignitaries ignored by the crowd had their say. Somebody important was introducing the governor, mayor, city councilmen, representatives and the many sheriffs in attendance.

"We've got to go," Bale said. "It's starting."

"How much?—" Karla asked.

The guard said, "Five dollars."

"—Five dollars! Two year's work!—that's too cheap! It took him so much time!" Karla protested.

"Lady," the guard said. "All this man has is time. Gimme five dollars and I'll get the set for you."

Bale reached into his wallet and handed the guard a twenty.

"I ain't got no change."

"We don't want change," Karla said. "Give him the money."

THE AZALEAS

Two clawed fingers poked through the mesh in the fence, grasping for the bill the guard held an inch away from the convict's reach.

"Aw— c'mon. Gimme— Gimme," the caged man begged.

"Listen, it's his money." Karla rose to inmate's defense. "Give it to him or I'll make a scene right here, right now."

"She'll do it, too," Bale said. "And you don't want to upset Sheriff Watson on a beautiful day like this."

The guard pushed the money through the wire fence and gave Karla a receipt. "Stop at that exit booth on your way out and pick up your package. It'll be wrapped and ready to go."

Karla swung her crutch and hobbled up the stairs to her seat. Spectators ready to watch modern day gladiators packed the bleachers. People were kind. They stepped to one side or the other as she moved clumsily forward like a car made heavy by losing power steering.

"One thing for sure," Bale said as they settled down. "The convicts won't disappoint the viewers. They give the rodeo their best shot. They're losers doomed to life, so death doesn't scare them."

"Must be awful to know that freedom lies just beyond that barbed wire fence," Karla said, thinking of Willis spending the next fifteen years in a narrow barred cell where sunlight never reached.

A pall hung over the bright, sparkling day as though more than sun was needed to lift the darkness hovering over prison life. The laughing, shouting crowd was more than the inmates could absorb all at once. They had a stunned look.

Circling the top tier of the arena every 15 feet, splay-legged guards stood armed with rifles and semi-automatic weapons. Any suspicious move by a convict or a visitor could activate the weaponry. The specter of impending doom heightened the senses and gave the afternoon a sharp edge.

Albert, Mary and Pierre, Roger and his family were already settled. Everybody clustered in Section L, the VIP section, directly under the press box, as if they had season tickets to a Roman slaughter.

Jim Watson had the microphone. He bristled with importance, ego pinned to his shirt sleeve. Today ten thousand people visited his jurisdiction. The occasion was a jubilee, and nothing must ruffle Angola Penitentiary's postcard tranquility this hot October afternoon.

"Rodeo fans, welcome to the great parish of West Feliciana. I hope you enjoy your visit to Angola. My hat is off to our outstanding warden and all the administrators who keep this maximum-security prison running as smooth and incident-free as they do, while at the same time preserving and maintaining the beauty of the farm—"

A deafening shout drowned his voice. A hundred horses thundered into the arena, two by two, dust rising from the galloping hoofs, little whiffs like puffs of smoke that quickly turned into a swirling haze that blanketed the area. Through the dusty, brown curtain Karla caught glimpses of zebra stripes and satin patches—blue, green, red, yellow—black and white stripes once again, silver glints from belt buckles and stirrups. The riders went into a high-stepping serpentine routine, doing figure eights, triangles, circles, intersecting, saved from colliding with each other by some inner time-clock that made them pull the reins at the last second. They crossed, merged and divided, waving and dipping the flags they carried as the horses cantered to one side and then the other.

Relatives—cousins and mamas and papas, aunts and uncles, spouses, children—came to see their loved ones moving about, unfettered, putting on a show. They had a connection to the inmate, and in their eagerness to catch a glimpse, they pushed forward aggressively.

The noise reached a feverish pitch. The roar came in drumming waves. The rumble shook the stands. The pounding hooves vibrated the hard ground. Music blared from across the way, a Sousa march played by a brass band, the notes drowned in the overriding racket.

Karla had never been to a rodeo. The horses she'd seen belonged to rich guys who stabled their mounts at Audubon Park. The uptown gentry perched on English saddles and trotted demurely on park trails or on the Mississippi River levee. And at Mardi Gras the NOPD Equestrian Unit astride huge Tennessee Walkers appeared at midnight, four abreast, steadily coming forward, never stopping, forcing drunks and revelers off the Quarter streets. The moving hoofs and muscular flanks cleared a path for the garbage trucks coming behind picking up trash. Carnival's success was measured in tonnage.

Over the loud speaker a voice boomed, "And there you have it, ladies and gentlemen—the Grand Entry—a big hand for the Rough Riders, our own trusties, Angola's only true cowboys!" The spectators responded with wild clapping and hooting. "They work with horses and livestock throughout the year! They look after our little farm here. We grow vegetables, soybeans and cotton, and raise beef cattle and draft horses. These trusted men oversee the operation. Let's give them another round of applause!"

The Grand Entry riders had barely cleared the arena when a chute opened and a bareback rider bounced forth on a bucking bronco. The horse's four hooves left the ground, back arched and mane flying. Instantly, the rearing horse pitched the cowboy.

The announcer raved, "Most of the contestants are from urban areas and have never been closer to a horse than they are today!"

That certainly held true for Willis. Where is Willis? Had he come to his senses and abandoned his sure-death plan?

"There come the pick-up men," Bale said.

Three riders quickly approached the bucking horse. One leaned from the saddle and snatched loose a tight leather strap tied around the horse's middle. As if by magic the horse stopped bucking and galloped toward the exit gate.

Four clowns in oversized tennis shoes, baggy pants and red suspenders left their perch on the wall and moved into the ring, doing cartwheels and slapstick motions distracting the audience.

Another horse swinging its head wildly from side to side lurched and bucked its way into the arena, immediately ejecting the rider from the saddle. The man landed flat on his back with a thud that drew an extended *ooooooh* from the sympathetic crowd.

The med-techs propped against the ambulance blocking one gate, shifted from one foot to another, waiting for the first victim.

The third, fourth, fifth rider entered the arena, flipped off the horse, and walked away. The last desperate rider didn't last a microsecond before he ate dust. The pickup men and clowns concentrated on the horses. "Looks to me they care more about the horses than the men," Karla said.

"Sure, they do," Bale replied. "Good horses are a lot scarcer than convicts."

The crass remark made her stare at him in disbelief.

"There'll always be more convicts," Bale assured her.

The emcee announced a short intermission.

Willis? Where is he?

A drill team of youngsters dressed in shiny cowboy and cowgirl outfits followed, would-be Roy Rogerses and Dale Evanses, their heads too little for the ten-gallon hats slipping halfway down their noses. They looked like grasshoppers perched atop the big horses, the stirrups drawn high so their short, spindly legs could reach. They led their horses through figure eights, circles, diagonals, angles, their little butts bouncing in the saddles.

The young riders finished their routine and trotted off. They took with them all traces of innocence and love, leaving behind convicts with hard and chiseled faces. Once the kids were safely away from the arena, every chute opened and a dozen wild horses, each trailing a rope, came bucking in. Three-man teams tried to grab a rope and hold the horse long enough for one member to mount. The first team to cross the finish line while still mounted won.

Willis wasn't in that group, either—

Other events followed in dusty succession: bare-back riding, wild horse racing, barrel racing, bull dogging, and buddy pickup.

Karla's attention strayed from the main arena, sifting through the crowd darting here and there, searching for Willis. Willis didn't lean against the fence with the other inmates. He wasn't sitting in the heavily guarded section with prisoners dressed all in white, unholy choir. He didn't perch on the wooden barrier next to the pick-up men and the clowns. He wasn't in the press box or down low with the brass band dressed in striped umpire shirts.

"The Brahma bull riding! This event separates the men from the boys!" the announcer cried excitedly.

The crowd clapped and stomped, put their fingers to their lips and whistled.

The first bull burst from the chute, an inmate aboard, one hand clutching a rope tied around the bull's belly, the other high over his head for balance. The killer Brahma had wide, sharp horns. The bull snorted, pawed the ground and charged, lifting his hind legs clear off the ground.

A woman behind Karla said, "Oh, Lord Jesus. Lord Jesus."

Screams and yells rose to a deafening pitch. Karla's fingers dug into Bale's arm and she closed her eyes.

"More guts than brains," Bale said. "He's down. He's okay."

Karla opened her eyes. The rider was running with quick, mincing steps to the safety of the wooden barrier. The stern-faced men standing behind the partition didn't move an eye or lift a hand to help him climb over.

The clowns did cartwheels and waved red flags. The pick-up crew circled the bull, driving the beast back into the chute.

Two, three, four, eight, ten riders, one after another in quick succession tore into the arena, one hand tied to a strap around the bull's middle, the other high, holding air.

"Eight seconds!" the excited announcer yelled. "A man must stay on eight seconds!"

So far no one had. A big gong announced each rider's fall.

Roger came down the steps.

"Hey, Roger!—Rog!" Karla called. "Where you going?—"

He waved and his easy grin lit his boyish face. "You can't go where I'm going!"

He reached the bottom tier, turned, lifted his head and waved at his wife and daughters before vanishing into the crowd.

Karla's goose bump radar activated. Her warning system engaged. She looked around at the others, searching for reassurance. She spotted Pierre and Mary. They'd had their fill of dust and horses and were on their way out. Roger's girls clasping dollars came skipping down the steps, following their dad to the concession stand. Albert was nowhere to be seen.

The emcee announced the final event. "Convict poker isn't for the fainthearted!" the loudspeaker blared. "Take a look at those four men sitting at that card table playing poker!"

The men sat, teeth clenched, neck cordons like taut ropes, unblinking eyes focused on the far gate. Legs spread apart, they planted their feet solidly on the ground beneath them, ready to push up and blast off.

The announcer raved. "You have to know when to hold them and when to fold them in this wild and dangerous event!"

The card players didn't move. They were frozen in place, distracted by nothing or no one. They reminded Karla of the angel in the Quarter who never blinked, no matter how much she was provoked. The stiller the angel stood, the more money she made.

"These inmate cowboys stare danger square in the face while trying to draw the winning hand," the announcer explained— "And now!—Now!"

A gate opened. The spectators leaned forward craning for a better look. The moment before the bull roared from the chute lasted forever.

"There comes the bull!" The announcer was beside himself. "Watch that 2,000-pound bull—that's one ton, people—one ton! The bull will call the players' hands! Deal those cards!"

The man holding the deck carefully set one card face down, one eye on the table, the other on the oncoming fury. He laid down the second card. Before he peeled off the third, the huge beast, black hide glistening under the sun, shoulders dense and solid, charged. The sharp horns hooked the nearest chair. With a powerful toss of his head, the bull lifted chair and player off the ground.

Flapping legs and kicking boots drove the spectators into a whirling frenzy. They jumped to their feet, smelling blood.

The bull arched his powerful neck, swung his head from side to side, unhooked the chair caught on his horn and sent it splintering to the ground. The rider jumped clear. The crowd roared approval.

Grinning and turning cartwheels, the clowns diverted the bull's attention. Beneath the red yarn wigs, the painted white faces with starry freckles and furry eyebrows were dead serious.

The dealer set down a fourth, a fifth card.

Foaming at the mouth, the two-ton animal once again rammed the table. The pointed horns, sharp as knives, ripped an inmate's leg. The man hobbled off, both hands clutching his thigh.

Two down.

The bull made a wide circle and lowered his head. His thick neck swelled, muzzle foaming wet, ears twitching and hoofs thudding.

The third player didn't hesitate. He was on his feet, fast as a missile. He valued the shred of life he had left.

The clowns distracted the bull. The fourth player squared his shoulders, waiting for the onrush. He turned his head—

Willis! Willis! He'd be killed—the end of him!

The bull stopped abruptly, all four legs stiff and straight. Then pawing the ground and snorting thunder, he lowered his big head, hunched enormous shoulders and slowly circled the unsteady poker table. Exhaling steam through distended nostrils he broadsided the convict's chair. The body landed face-up on the ground, left arm across the chest, right arm with the coiled snake dangling to one side.

Bale said, "That fool better get up and run."

THE AZALEAS

The bull lowered his head, shaking lethal horns from side to side. Willis didn't twitch a muscle.

A pickup man, his body dangling from the saddle, reached Willis. The bull snorted, pawed the ground, charged. The man grabbed Willis's boots and dragged. The sharp horns missed Willis by inches, raked two trenches in the churned dirt.

The pickup man raised his right arm and summoned the ambulance.

Clowns went into a high intensity slap-dash act, cornering the bull on the arena's far side, while red capes waved the beast into the chute. Spectators gave a rousing cheer. They had gotten what they came for—blood.

Karla's nerves stretched like guitar strings. One wrong twang and she'd snap.

"Rodeo is dangerous," the voice over the loud speaker said. "Injury is inevitable. The excellent emergency medical attention we have here at Angola makes the difference between life and death!"

The medical technicians spilled onto the field. They slipped a narrow board under Willis, arranged his arms straight at his sides and put a brace around his neck. They tied him down, a leather strap below the knees and one around his chest. They carried him out feet first.

"There goes our crack team of highly motivated, highly trained, fully equipped and licensed medical technicians!" The Emcee babbled. "Did you see that, folks? Did you see them respond in seconds? I'm not talking minutes here! Seconds! More than one trampled cowboy is still walking around today due to their efforts! How about a big hand for the med-techs?—"

The men carrying the narrow board bearing Willis traversed the arena. As the stretcher passed each section the crowds cheered. The sound traveled like a wave, finally cresting and crashing with another disappointed *oooooh* when the men disappeared from sight.

CHAPTER 19

Med-techs loaded Willis into the ambulance. Deputies stood guard, weapons ready. The band stationed near the gate stopped playing, their attention captured by the accident and ensuing excitement. The curious stood for a closer look, the squeamish placed a hand over their eyes, and the blood-thirsty applauded. The doors slammed; the motor engaged. The ambulance sped away, blinking lights and wailing sirens.

For a few moments, Karla sat watching the riders perched on the rodeo rail, the confused, snorting bulls, the rodeo clowns whirling red capes; the crew in overalls picking up splintered remains, a faded spectacle now devoid of glamour and color; a lean and dull emptiness filling the dusty arena.

"Be right back," she said.

Before Bale could react, ask for an explanation or stop her, she grabbed the crutches, hobbled down the bleachers and stomped through the gate, Bale's truck keys clutched in her hand. Lifting them from his pocket wasn't difficult. Nimble fingers were part of a harsh adolescence. Finding the pickup in a parking field the size of the Atlantic Ocean proved a bigger challenge. All white trucks looked alike.

Crazy, stupid, pointless—stop right now, this minute while there is still time. Return the keys to Bale—forget this wild goose chase—oh, there's the truck! The one with the blueprint rolls on the dash!

THE AZALEAS

The truck cab seemed higher than she remembered. She held onto the steering wheel and hoisted herself onto the seat, the crutches falling aside. Reaching, she threw them on the passenger side. She grabbed the shift lever: *neutral—where is neutral?—I've driven this truck before—not this nervous, though—drove it through The Azaleas' back field—the motor turned over—reverse, down or up? R— where's the R?—There!*

Her bulky right foot wrapped in an ace bandage was useless. She moved it over as far as possible and with her good left foot worked the accelerator and the brakes. She backed slowly from the tight parking slot.

No inmates toiled in the fields. No chain-gangs sang as they shuffled toward the tool sheds. On this Sunday afternoon, prisoners, guards, citizens, visitors—everyone was at the rodeo.

Oh, god. Sunday! Today is Sunday. Sunday is my star-crossed day. My auras don't work Sundays. Everything bad happens to me on a Sunday.

A panic knot formed in her stomach—fifty yards to the watch tower—twenty—she spotted the guard holding a rifle, pacing back and forth on a narrow catwalk—ten yards—*slow down, slow down—don't speed past the sentry—slow down—stop.* The catwalk guard leaned over the railing. The one in the entry kiosk slid open the bullet-proof window and gave her a quick glance. She smiled from her teeth out, more a grimace than a happy face. Without leaving his post, he waved her through. Entering was the problem; leaving presented no difficulties.

She was on the highway. The ambulance was nowhere in sight. Even if she drove 100 miles an hour, she wouldn't catch up. Willis must be near death. The ambulance had headed directly from the prison to St. Francisville.

Angola had a hospital. Certainly, the prison had a morgue—and a cemetery, too. Why hadn't the paramedics taken Willis there?

Karla heard the powerful motor roar before she saw the small plane. The pilot was flying low, following Highway 10. The wings dipped, losing altitude. The engine revved and the plane soared again. She kept driving on Highway 10, head cocked, one eye on the plane, the other looking ahead for the ambulance.

Willis wasn't Karla's responsibility. She had no damned business getting involved in this mess. Do the sensible thing. Turn around and park the stolen truck before Bale discovers it missing. How difficult would it be to get back in?

The plane wheels were down, angling toward the earth. She saw Randall Crop Dusting written in bold black letters on the bright yellow fuselage. Where in the world did the pilot plan to set this bird? She eyed the barbed wire fences, the roadside ditches, and the highway. He had to be crazy. He either had to land on the highway or in a field. If he chose the highway, he'd hit a vehicle head-on. If he settled for a field, the plane would bounce across the ruts and surely hit a tree.

The plane was landing! The nose straight down, the wings dipped and Roger's mosquito hawk ducked beneath electric lines. The wheels barely cleared the barbed wire fence.

The ambulance! Coming toward her at great speed, rounding the Highway 10 curve— the same curve where the van transporting prisoners had a flat tire—*when did the ambulance turn around?* The vehicle veered right, left the blacktop, jumped the ditch, the green scummy ditch Karla once fell into—tore through the barbed wire fence, and careened across the field, tires bouncing over furrows.

Karla pulled to the side of the road.

The ambulance rear door flew open. Without slowing the driver made a U-turn on two wheels—a man jumped. He ran like his feet were on fire toward the crop duster.

Willis! That was Willis! He wasn't dead! He was heading for the plane! Lura Mae gone, Lebron in the hospital, and Joey in LTI—Willis hadn't a living soul who could come to his aid—no one who cared if he rotted in jail or died in a field.

Karla knew his family history, his sad circumstances. Residents of the tourist-infested Quarter formed silent bonds that ran deep.

If the ambulance could jump the roadside ditch, Bale's truck could, too. Karla's head banged the cab roof as the front wheels hit the deep ditch, down, up—her neck snapped. The truck tore through the gap in the barbed wire fence.

The plane touched down on the 50-foot wide strip belonging to the gas company, the only stretch cleared of trees and bushes, where nothing could be built because the natural gas pipe that yielded mega royalties ran under the surface. Bale had shown Karla the big valve painted orange one afternoon years ago it seemed. She remembered telling him the cleared area looked like a drug dealer's landing strip. Roger had confided to Karla it was his preferred emergency landing spot.

THE AZALEAS

The airplane propeller whined and stirred the wind. The pilot wearing earphones and a baseball cap looked neither left nor right, intent on the field ahead.

"Roger! Roger!" Karla couldn't believe her eyes.

Her disbelief paled compared to his. "What the—" his yell was filled with fury, with a rage not common in the mild-mannered Roger. "Get the hell away!" and as Karla sat frozen, he pointed a gun at the truck's windshield. "Go! Go!"

A sheriff's car traveling at jet speed approached the cleared strip from the opposite end, The Azalea direction. The car, jolting over the rough grass, headed straight for the plane with no intentions of stopping or veering. A deputy poked halfway through the window, gun pointed.

At first the shots didn't register. They sounded like firecrackers, not particularly dangerous or deadly, but when Willis began doing a jig like a football player crossing the end zone, dancing around gusts of dust raised by machine gun fire, the afternoon took on a dire and sinister twist.

The plane taxied down the bumpy strip, gathering speed. Willis raced to catch it, his long legs eating the distance like a marathon runner, arms pumping, chest thrown forward about to break the tape.

The passenger door came open. Without losing stride, Willis threw his upper body into the plane. The Mosquito Hawk lurched sideways like a wounded bird. Willis's legs dangled, his boots with the tire tread soles kicking air. The crop duster shot a white dust cloud from its tail and pulled up sharply, barely clearing the sheriff car coming head on.

The rat-tat-tat of gun fire pierced the country quiet. Spent casings burped from guns and glistened in the sunlight before plopping to the ground. The barrage hit the crop duster. The explosion sent a screaming ball of red and yellow fire then a single, deafening boom like that of a jet breaking the sonic barrier.

Karla sat in the truck, heart pounding, ears drumming, cold sweat pouring, tears running down her cheeks, a silent scream frozen on her lips. Through the blue and yellow flames, through the purple smoke, a reasonable thought worked itself into her turmoil. *Back away! Back away from the exploding crop duster!* Her left foot missed the clutch. Her trembling hands fumbled with the gear shift.

The flaming plane spiraled downward.

A deputy leapt from the sheriff's car, swinging a machine gun from his hip. "Don't anybody move!" Bubba yelled. "Don't move! Don't move!"

CHAPTER 20

Bubba pulled open the truck door and seized Karla's arm. "Get out."

Red earth exploded and sprayed dirt. The searing heat turned the air thick and wavy. Flames licked the dry grass. Shrill, ear-splitting sounds echoed, bounced and boomeranged.

Karla swallowed the scream stuck in her throat. Pain wrenched her knotted guts.

"Shit! Move, girl! Move!—"

Sunday—is it still Sunday?

Ambulances, fire trucks and cop cars, lights flashing and sirens wailing sped onto the field. The crash site was overrun by men in red suits, blue suits and yellow Haz-Mat suits running here, there—yelling, pulling hoses, taking pictures, hustling in slow motion. From chaos and confusion they created a systematic order. The police cordoned the perimeter with yellow tape. Firemen sprayed the burning plane with retardant chemicals.

Bubba grabbed Karla's crutches, threw them at her, half carried and half dragged her into his official vehicle. He turned in the driver's seat and bellowed, "I'm holding you as a material witness! Two men are dead! You saw it all!"

Karla was too upset to answer. She needed Albert.

Bubba got in Karla's face. "If you don't tell the truth you'll be charged with obstruction of justice." His breath smelled of beer and chewing tobacco. "You had no business there!"

Right! Bubba was absolutely right! Auntie Emmy was right. Following my crazy impulses would someday cause my sudden and unexpected death.

"We're in one fine hell of a mess now. They want to talk to you."

Karla had no idea who "they" were and was too upset to ask. Bubba drove Karla to the St. Francisville courthouse, escorted her into the building, a firm grasp on her arm. Karla supposed he thought she might bolt—a difficult maneuver on crutches. Her second day in St. Francisville, she and Preacher Frank had gone to the courthouse, climbed stairs to the second floor. Now Bubba rudely pushed her into the elevator marked "staff only."

They walked past Deputy Beauty's window, past the door marked "Sheriff." Bubba's heavy boots clumped alongside Karla, each plop, plop, plop keeping time with her beating heart.

They entered a bare room—nothing on the walls, institutional tile floors, an overhead light, one table and two chairs, no windows. In this box, witnesses sweated until they gave the right answers.

The door opened and a man wearing a gray suit, maroon tie and button-down collar entered. "Hi. I'm Stanley Draner." He pulled a chair, sat and set a tape recorder on the table. "I have a few questions for you," he said. "Do you mind?"

"Who are you?" Karla had expected Sheriff Watson or one of his people.

"FBI—" He reached his wallet and flashed a badge.

"Why do you have to record what I say?"

"Easier that way— I can make mistakes taking notes and my memory is shot— any objections?"

"No."

"Okay, then"

Something about this situation didn't sit right with Karla. "I should call my lawyer."

That gave the agent pause. "Yes, of course. If you feel you need to do that."

Karla had nothing to hide, but she didn't trust this man—she didn't trust anybody. Albert could deal with FBI agents much better than she could. "I'll be right back."

She stepped into the hall and punched #1 on the SkyPager, the emergency number, the number that would never fail, the one to dial if she found herself in a dangerous situation. Hadn't Albert said so himself?

THE AZALEAS

Please leave your message—a recorder! Life or death and she got the recorder! Disgusted—what was the use?—she returned to the interrogation room and lied with a straight face. "He'll be here shortly."

"Who's your lawyer?"

"Albert Monsant."

"Nothing but the best, eh?—"

"I didn't know he was that good."

"Has a reputation, he does. Let me put this to you like this and maybe we can get the preliminaries over with by the time Monsant gets here. I'm sure he's expensive and charges by the minute. You tell me what happened, off the record and I'll tell you what we know. We know you took Bale Franklin's truck and followed the ambulance with the escapee—"

"You're only half right. I did take Bale's truck, but I didn't follow the ambulance."

"But you were at The Azalea field—"

"I was on Highway 10 and saw the plane flying low. I stopped to look."

"Why did you take the truck?"

"Because after the ambulance loaded Willis, I thought he was injured or dead."

"You know Willis?"

"Yes. Willis is from my old neighborhood."

"You visited him last Saturday."

That scared Karla. They'd been checking on her. Maybe she should zip her lips and not say another word until Albert arrived, if he ever did. "Yes, I did. His grandmother died. I went to give him the sad news. She raised him. That's when he told me he'd rather be dead outside than alive in prison."

"I see. Exactly what did you see in the field?"

"The plane touched down. The ambulance crashed through the barbed wire. Willis jumped out and ran. The sheriff's car approached from the other way, a deputy holding a gun. The plane took off fast then nosed up, Willis dangling from it. The deputy in the sheriff's car was spraying bullets everywhere and Roger—" she stopped. Was she saying too much? Was the FBI entitled to all this knowledge? Maybe she should chill until—what if Albert never came?

"Did this event look like an accident to you?"

Mr. Draner's words stunned Karla. Did this man think she was somebody's fool? "Of course it wasn't an accident. It was—"

The door opened and Sheriff Watson entered, a scowl on his face. His big day, his day of fame and glory fractured into a million pieces. Pointedly ignoring Karla, he snapped at Mr. Draner. "What are you doing here?"

"Having a little chat with this eye-witness—"

"In my courthouse—under my roof?—in this room?—"

"Sorry. I mistakenly thought the premises belonged to the tax payers."

"Well, you're through."

Mr. Draner didn't argue. He put his pen in his shirt pocket and rose stiffly. "When I return, Sheriff Watson, I'll have subpoenas and court orders with me."

"That's what all you people say. Now get out."

Karla thought the FBI could lord it over a local sheriff, but that wasn't the case here. Mr. Draner left the room and slammed the door behind him.

With the FBI expelled from the room, Jimmy Watson turned to Karla. "What did you tell him?"

"What I saw. Something wrong with that?—"

"Depends on what you think you saw."

"I didn't see an accident if that's what you're driving at. I saw a deliberate and successful attempt to shoot down a crop dusting plane with Roger Randall and Willis in it."

Sheriff Watson sat, propped his elbows on the table, fingers intertwined, raised his clenched hands to his head and pressed two big thumbs to his temples. "I'm going to give you some free advice, and I want you to listen carefully and heed what I'm saying to you. Stay out of this. Steer clear of this business. Go back to the city for your own good."

"And if I don't?"

"Then I can't be responsible for your safety."

THE AZALEAS

CHAPTER 21

A great number of people Karla didn't know gathered at the Grace Episcopal Church cemetery in St. Francisville to lay Roger Randall to rest. Roger and his family lived in Lake Charles, but their ancestral burial ground was this grave site. The Randall dead were returned to their roots and laid to rest next to family.

An eerie hush pervaded the graveyard. Gray moss dripping from hundred-year old oaks added a somber note. A cold drizzle fell from a lead-colored sky. "Angels crying for the dead," Auntie Emmy always said.

Roger was gone, gone through Auntie Emmy's pearly gates to that better hallelujah place.

He was survived, the obituary said, by his wife, two daughters, three brothers, one sister, his mother and many nieces and nephews. At the grave site, the relatives sat under a green canopy, Tinsley Funeral Home written across the canvas. Karla figured the white-haired woman next to Myra must be Roger's mother. A family resemblance existed in the pointed chin, the skin tones and arched eyebrows. The priest cast anxious looks over the crowd, impatient that everyone assembled quickly, anxious that the family's grief be compressed into the shortest possible time span.

"Like father, like son," Karla overheard a man say. He and his wife huddled under a black umbrella. "Remember when his old man crashed in Thibodeaux?" He craned his neck to better view the grieving Randall family.

A woman replied, "The young'uns all moved away, 'cept Roger."

"They got to move where there's work, y'know," the man answered, "There ain't nothin' here—"

"Roger stayed close," the woman replied. "He's not like the others comin' home for special occasions, weddings and funerals and sometimes Christmas."

"They got their own family and business to tend to," the man defended the stay-away siblings.

"It's not so much that as it is—don't you see it, George? They leave for the big cities and come home later, kinda lookin' down their noses at us—as if we'd been left behind by the rest of the world."

"I think you're imaginin' that, Lisa. In the end, don't they all come back? Who's that one that just walked up there to shake Myra's hand?"

They put their heads together and whispered trying to place the family member, associate a name with a face not often seen, identity blurred by time and space.

Water dripped from the umbrella Sam held over Judge Jeremiah. Agatha held her own umbrella. A few steps back Mary and Pierre huddled under theirs. Bale stood in the drizzle, water dripping down his collar. Karla looked twice before she recognized Dorcas in a wide-brimmed straw hat, holding onto Clem in his butler tuxedo. Frank pressed close, his old brown suit reeking camphor. Laura was dressed in white like an angel come down to carry Roger through the pearly gates. The guest list at The Hills ball was present, plus store clerks, bank tellers and farm hands. Everybody came to Roger's funeral except Albert. Karla wondered what detained her employer.

The thin, bony man approaching had shaved his stubble for the occasion. His face looked raw and unsettled. His thin hair was plastered to his head. "You're Karla?" he asked, an accusation more than a question.

"Karla Whitmore." She offered her hand. For a long moment Karla's fingers trembled in the space between them.

"Joe Ferrace—"the man squeezed Karla's hand in a calloused grip. "You don't know me. I'm a mechanic, a good friend of Roger's. I'm the one who kept that lawn-mower with wings in tip-top shape for him."

"He was very proud of his mosquito hawk—that's what he called it."

THE AZALEAS

"A real marvel that machine. You could say we built it from scratch. Put in that big powerful R1340 engine. He said it was for the family's sake. His dad crashed in a little plane with a small engine. Roger wanted that extra safety—not that it did him any good in the end. We stripped the insides and left only the pilot's seat. We had to make it light as a feather, you know."

One seat, meant to carry one man.

"Got that Shelby back in my shop again—"

"My car?—"

"Fixed it first time 'round for Mr. Albert—sweet little machine."

"The brakes?—what about the—"

"Hi, girl—" Karla had no trouble recognizing the surly voice that derailed her question. She took a step back from Bubba who'd grabbed her the afternoon of the chain gang fiasco, who knocked on the motel door with the sheriff's warrant, who dragged her from the crash site. "You jes' keep makin' trouble, don'tya?"

No way could she erase the nightmare forever emblazoned in her mind, every vivid detail stamped into her brain: the flaming ball falling from the sky hitting the ground like a meteor, the acrid smoke enveloping the burning plane. Roger and Willis were two purposely blank spaces in her mind. Her thoughts reached the edge of their life and recoiled. Their fate was more than she could dwell on. "What do you mean?"

"I mean if you'd stayed put at the rodeo like the other twenty-thousand people did, and hadn't stole Bale's truck and gone off ambulance chasin'—" he stared at Karla with suspicious eyes, shoulders hunched like a coyote waiting to pounce.

Joe Ferrace said, "This ain't the place, Bubba."

"If I'd been guilty of anything, the sheriff would've arrested me. Go ask him." Karla stepped away, not wanting any more trouble, particularly at Roger's funeral.

"I ain't gotta ask him nuttin'. He's too busy over there pumpin' hands and gettin' votes. He'll not miss a one and he'll be re-elected next November by a landslide."

Jimmy Watson worked the crowd as if he were at a fund-raiser, one that didn't cost $100 a plate and was much more effective. With a serious and mournful face, he gave those within reach a big hand clasp or hug. He high-fived his closest supporters and offered condolences to friends and family.

"How do you spell relief?" A man asked, elbowing the sheriff.

Relief from what, Karla wondered.

A deputy crowed for his boss, "We done it again!"

A corpulent man slapped the sheriff's shoulder, "Sent them packing, didn't ya, boy! Feds can't pin nothin' on you, eh?—Clean slate! How much did that cost you? A pretty penny, I bet!"

Sheriff Watson's funeral face melted into one big smile.

"What's he so happy about?" Karla asked Bubba.

"One-upping the Feds, what else? They are some persistent bastards. I reckon they'll send in the big guns next time."

"Who are the big guns?" Karla asked.

"The IRS that's who—"

"Why did the FBI close the investigation?"

Bubba said triumphantly, *"In-suf-ficient* evidence!"

Odd, that suddenly, in the midst of the ensuing confusion over the plane crash, the FBI dried up and disappeared. "I'd think $300,000 in a paper bag in a garbage can was plenty of evidence."

"Those shitheads," Bubba replied with confidence, "will never be able to pin-point one thing on our sheriff."

Those gathered congratulated Jimmy Watson—another investigation, another dead end, no conviction, a big waste of taxpayer's money—as if every citizen had taken part in duping the Feds and the town had triumphed anew. Strangers had no business meddling here. The residents righted their own wrongs, or wronged their own rights. Whatever the case, outsiders were not welcomed.

Agatha raised a handkerchief to her eyes and dabbed tears, smearing the kohl rim, her grief genuine. One of their own was gone, an unscheduled, unnecessary, unplanned departure. Southerners were layered like artichokes, each overlapping leaf attached to a central core that united them all. Through the prevailing sadness, they clung to the rituals, the homespun wit. Food trays and sweet remembrances bolstered them through the bad times. They put aside hard feelings and feuds, joined in purpose, sending one of their own on his way.

The funeral gathering reminded Karla of Bale's party at The Hills, without music. The mourners' softly drawled sympathies and condolences, sorrow drawing their faces, pity in their eyes, a theme with no variation, all clones with the same DNA. In a generic fashion these people looked alike, thought alike, and dressed alike. They were one and the same, yesterday, today, tomorrow and forever.

THE AZALEAS

The diversity of the French Quarter was not present here. No flamboyant gays or introverted shopkeepers existed in this world. No outsiders invaded or broadened this spectrum. St. Francisville would roll up its sidewalks rather than tolerate a street like Bourbon. The gaudy strip was too overtly evil for their sensibilities. Anyone who moved to this town better know their roots and pedigree or they'd never make the cut. A hundred years from now if Karla ever returned, the town would be changed somewhat—they couldn't hold progress at bay forever— but the people would not be one whit different. Neither natural nor manmade catastrophes would alter their minds or hearts.

A certain security existed in that type of life. Yet, deep down, Karla thought the everlasting boredom of living day in and day out in such a magnolia-scented rut would obliterate all benefits.

The gathering moved closer to the tent and the coffin, jostling black umbrellas—"excuse me—so sorry—" The whispering came to a close. The rustling and shuffling stopped. The seated family stirred. Carleen and Bonnie sobbed softly. Their mother put an arm around both girls and the three bowed their heads, waiting.

Karla drew closer. *This shouldn't be! This shouldn't be! How quickly things went wrong. A blink and then a crash—life changed forever—never the same again—never—never—*rain drops glistened silver on her clasped hands.

Suddenly Albert came through the crowd, nodding to this one, pressing someone's shoulder, pausing to acknowledge a mourner. He passed by Karla and said, "When this is finished, we have to talk, so don't disappear."

Did he think that little of Karla? Did he believe she wouldn't plant her two feet right here on this ground and endure the entire ceremony, minute by minute, word by word? She might die on the spot, but she wouldn't run. "I'm not going anywhere."

"Good." He reached the tent, hugged Myra Randall and the two girls and sat in a green velvet covered chair.

Why was he seated with the family? He wasn't blood kin and according to custom, the relatives closest to the deceased got the chairs under the canopy.

Yet there was Albert, comfortable in their midst as if he were one of them, seated next to Myra, next to the flags—the American, Louisianan, Dixie and an unfamiliar one with an embroidered G

Karla thought stood for God and later learned the flag was a Masonic one and the G stood for Geometry. The sheriff wormed his way toward the grieving family. He had a greater right than Albert to sit close to the coffin. West Feliciana was his parish and these were his people.

Everyone moved forward and encircled the green tent. Karla hung back. Roger Randall was dead. Minutes made the difference between life and death. If he hadn't slowed down, taken those few seconds to yell at Karla to get the hell away, he might be alive today. He might surely be alive today if the deputies hadn't shot the plane's gas tank and turned the crop duster loaded with chemical into one giant fireball. No one mentioned that, as if that action had never happened.

The priest rose to start the burial rites. Gloria and Wong Ito approached quietly, as though walking on tip-toes, looking self-conscious and displaced. They didn't know the family and didn't pretend grief. Under the black umbrella Gloria held over their heads, they waited with deference, Mr. Ito's head bobbing respectfully and Gloria with a patient, determined look on her face.

The Japanese buyer for The Azaleas had cash in his wallet. In the confusion Karla had forgotten her job, her purpose in St. Francisville. Even though everything else was crashing down on her head, maybe she could salvage The Azaleas sale. The time for caring what happened to the plantation, assessing who the best buyer would be, was over. Now the case became who had the cash first.

A certain freedom came with that decision. She'd been trapped for days by conflicting emotions, cobwebs that snared small flies and let wasps and hornets through. To hell with Bale Franklin— she'd rather split the commission with Gloria on a sure thing, be the buyer Japanese, African or Lilliputian than gamble on keeping 100% of nothing.

The ultimate decision was Mary's. The Azaleas' rightful owner and her consort stood near the funeral tent, head inclined, listening to every word the priest uttered. Though Mary hadn't been home in years, she understood the Feliciana fabric— people born and raised in the South who stayed connected. Those who left were the betrayers. Mary had denied her heritage by hiding in France. Karla wondered if Mary would reclaim her birthright now. If she did, that meant no sale—no sale—no sale. Oh, God. Life was one big bitch.

THE AZALEAS

The priest finished his prayers, and Albert was saying his few words. "I know many of you are wondering who I am, why I have been chosen to eulogize Roger." He reached for the big coffee table book propped near the coffin. The book had moss-draped cypresses on the cover. A long-legged white crane stood in water matted with green lily pads and pink flowers. *Louisiana Swamps* was written on the cover in large bold letters "by Roger Randall" in smaller print, humble, typical of him. "I was his publisher. We preferred to keep our relationship private. We were both more comfortable that way."

Albert, a publisher! A banker, lawyer, Indian chief! Entrepreneur and art enthusiast—Collector of people fallen by the wayside.

Roger's books were impeccable, both in artistic quality and text. Had Albert personally edited each volume? Was there anything the Renaissance man couldn't do?

"Roger was a good son, a loving husband and father, a trusted friend." Albert touched the coffin, "an Air Force colonel; a defender of freedom. He loved to fly." A note of reminiscence crept into Albert's voice. "And he knew his planes. He could fly a jet and he could fly his little crop-duster. It is fitting that his final hour was in the cockpit. He wouldn't have wanted it any other way." Myra stifled sobs. The girls wept aloud. "We've all seen Roger loop-de-loop over the fields as he dusted the crops. I've seen him come straight down," Albert raised his arm, his hand forming the nose of a plane, "and nearly touch the ground—" his hand came within inches of the draped coffin—"before he swooped into the sky again." With one big arc Albert's arm went over his head then fell to his side. "That is why this was such a tragic accident. This should never have happened to Roger, not to a pilot of his caliber."

Accident! Is that what Albert believed? Is that what the sheriff told him? Was that the official story? Roger died in a plane crash through his own fault? Unbelievable!

Albert couldn't be that dense. Would somebody come investigate? FAA?—CIA?—FBI? The deputies shot the plane's gas tank. An accident?—really! And Willis?— The last thing Karla saw before the explosion was Willis's dangling legs kicking in blue space, wriggling to get into the plane. No one showed any concern about poor Willis. Where had they sent his body? To the city dump?—

These people had their own justice. They created fictional stories based on variations of truth. They confused the investigators. Once the plot was concocted, the entire population stuck together like a bad marriage where the husband and wife hated one another's guts, but when an outsider intruded, the couple united and attacked. The town knew the sheriff was corrupt, yet they unanimously sent investigators packing.

Willis was dead, too. At the AME Church in New Orleans friends and neighbors would gather one afternoon next week for a dismissal service. Instead of a coffin, there'd be a photo of Willis, maybe his first-grade school picture, or a digitally altered mug shot, the stripes and numbers deleted. Flowers would fill the sanctuary, their sweet smell mingling with women's perfume and men's aftershave. The White Choir, Blue Choir and Green Choir would chant "Amazing Grace," and "How Great Thou Art," the singers swaying and wiping tears, the congregation raising their arms, waving their hands and bursting into spontaneous, "Amen, brother! Amen!"

Willis's mourners would lift collective voices and praise the dead. They would remember Auntie Emmy and ask each other, "Why ain't Karla here?" because Auntie Emmy's adopted child had been raised right, reared to show respect, particularly last respects. Louisiana Training Institute might transport Joey to the church, bring him in shackles and sit him in the last pew. Lebron, in traction at Charity Hospital, wouldn't make it to his step-brother's memorial. Neither would Karla. Her heart was there, but her business here demanded closure.

Albert, speaking in his deep, commanding voice drew everyone's attention in a way the soft-spoken priest had failed to do. "We are here to rejoice in the life of Roger Randall. We may never learn the full details of his tragic accident—never know why—" Albert paused and looked steadily at Sheriff Watson. "He'd landed his Mosquito Hawk on that field a hundred times before."

The sheriff's eyes were downcast, weighed by pain. He missed his real calling. He should've been on stage.

"These books," Albert held up *Louisiana Swamps*— "are Roger's legacy. Words live on long after we are gone. The photographs capture the moment forever. Roger's heart and soul are between these covers."

The somber congregation held back tears. Some cried openly. Dry-eyed, Karla resolved right then to buy every book Roger ever wrote. She'd ask Jacques at the Librarie to hold them and she'd pay for them on time, a dollar a month if she had to.

Albert's speech ended, the priest sprinkled the coffin with holy water and the Catholics located their rosaries, fingered the beads and prayed in unison. Their words rose and fell soft and tender like the gentle rain nourishing the earth.

Karla looked for Gloria and Ito and couldn't find them. She edged slowly toward the parking area wanting to get away from the crowd. She didn't want people swirling around her, pounding her with questions she couldn't answer.

She walked to her rented Chevy. A restraining hand closed over her elbow.

"We have to talk," Bale said.

"There's nothing to talk about," Karla replied wearily. "I'm sorry I borrowed your truck."

"Well, it's not the first time you've borrowed my truck. I'm not worried about that. I'm worried about you."

"I'm okay, and I'd be even better if you'd buy The Azaleas and I could get back to New Orleans." Her remark was a wild dart and she never expected it to hit the bull's eye.

"The Azaleas will be mine," Bale assured Karla, "one way or another."

"But not for $1 million when Mr. Ito will pay $3 million." Even to her own ears her voice sounded flat, dull, a robot going through the motions.

"Well, he won't get The Azaleas. I'll have the plantation on my own terms."

Out of the jumble of words, Karla understood that. A sale was what she had originally come to St. Francisville for. She'd lost her purpose in the confusion surrounding the plantation. Her heart and emotions had gotten in the way of her intentions. She had done exactly what Albert said she should never do, mix business with pleasure.

Bale opened the car door for Karla and walked away. In the side view mirror, Karla saw Gloria approaching, determination in every stride. Mr. Ito lagged behind, unable to keep pace. Gloria waved a paper over her head. "I have a contract...I need signatures...we must get together...there are certain clauses—" Gloria was running. The effort left her breathless.

"Come to The Azaleas," Karla said, thinking suddenly that the bigger the crowd, the less Albert could tangle with her. He was circumspect before others. Discretion went well with his cloak and dagger personality.

Two contracts for The Azaleas were in the mill, but between twixt and twain a thousand things could go wrong. Mary might pull the place off the market. That was her prerogative. Mr. Ito might have his bid so ridden with contingencies it could leak like a sieve. Bale might make his own arrangements with Mary, cutting out all third parties, and that included Karla, the real estate agent, in which case her job was history and her debt tripled—*food Stamps and SSI here I come.*

THE AZALEAS

CHAPTER 22

The Azaleas was deserted. The others were still at the cemetery. Karla limped across the veranda and entered the house. Folks here never locked their doors like they did in the Quarter. Her apartment door had a regular lock, a dead bolt, a chain latch, plus a peep hole.

Laura must've tidied the Andrew Jackson room. The furniture was back in place, the desk lamp, tipped over and broken when the strangler attacked Karla, the only missing item. Had it been a week or a year since she first arrived and met Agatha looking through those very windows overlooking the lawn?

The unconquerable curiosity that got Karla into so much trouble pulled her to Roger Randall's room. Everything was as he had left it: typed pages stacked on his desk, wadded paper strewn on the floor, clothes flung across the bed, shoes exactly where he dropped them. Four conservative ties, blue and maroon with little diagonal stripes hung from a chair back. Piled in one corner were camera bags, tripods, lenses and assorted photography paraphernalia; in another corner, Audubon books. His wife hadn't come for his personal belongings. She'd probably do that after the funeral. No one had closed the windows. They were open, and a breeze fluttered the curtains. Roger liked to work by natural light, liked the fresh air redolent with sweet country smells.

Karla wandered aimlessly, restlessly, reaching for a roll of undeveloped film and quickly putting it down, lifting a clothespin holding receipts from the gas station, the grocery store, and drugstore. He must've had the same arrangement with Albert that Karla did—save all the receipts and turn them in against the draw. A rock inscribed—*Carleen 1998 I love you Daddy*—weighed miscellaneous papers. An in-box and out-box both a disordered jumble, a panel of Audubon bird stamps—clutter everywhere, mark of creativity.

Walking around a dead man's room, feeling his spirit still lingering over his belongings raised goose bumps on Karla's arms. Roger Randall's body was gone, but he hadn't departed yet. Karla could sense him standing there, looking over her shoulder.

She opened the armoire and took a quick step back. Lights on three computer screens with multi-colored screen-savers weaving a crazy design blinked red and green. Did a writer need this much electronic gear? Curious, Karla pressed the Enter key. *Enter Code Enter Code Enter Code* flashed on and off. Not a password, but a code. Very James Bond, this whole business. Was this some sort of surveillance system? Could Roger have been spying on somebody?

Was the whole house wired and everything that was said and done monitored from this room? A crazy thought flashed through her mind, but she doused the preposterous idea quickly. Roger had no reason to spy on her. Even though Albert kept close tabs by Sky Phone and that amazing telepathy of his, going to this extent seemed an over-kill. No, it wasn't Karla Roger was after. Who, then? Agatha? That thought came and went, too. The cantankerous woman posed a threat to no one but herself. Scratch the help. They were of no consequence. The Judge next door?—Karla didn't know enough about surveillance equipment to understand whether this system would reach a mile down the road to Twin Oaks.

Leaning heavily on her crutches, Karla stood twirling a corkscrew curl with one finger while staring at the wire jungle and blinking screens. She pondered the code, having no idea how to break in. She punched keys at random. Nothing happened.

*Creak…creak…*The sound of a door opening slowly brought her up short. She inhaled sharply, caught a whiff of Old Spice, disgusting aftershave, and faced the intruder. "Hello, Sam."

He lumbered toward Karla, long arms dangling below his knees, pinkish palms up, and didn't answer. He swung his head from side to side. Under huge front lobes, his sunken eyes had a deranged, glazed look, a frightening, terrifying glare.

"What is it you want?" Not words, but whining like a stray cat's meowing, a strange, eerie sound coming from a tightened throat and through her nose. The high pitch made Sam flinch and he blinked his eyes several times in rapid succession as if to clear his vision.

Panic wiped reason from Karla's mind. "You!—" A one-word explosion— "You! You! You!—" She jabbed a crutch at him, hopping back with each word, angling toward the open window. "You tried to kill me! Twice! In my bedroom! The brakes in my car!—"

He stood an arm's length away, looking confused, stopped by the loud and unexpected dint of Karla's sonic wail. She smelled his rancid body odor and the sweet, spicy nauseating aftershave. She knew his strength. She must escape. "You shot Mary from the Cathedral roof!"

He raised his arms and cracked the knuckles of each incredibly huge hand. Each joint snapped like a rifle shot.

"Stay away!" She pointed the aluminum crutch as if it were a Star Trek power lance. Sam took a step toward her. She poked him in the stomach with the rubber tip. His powerful hands grabbed the crutch and bent the aluminum stick in half.

Karla reached behind, her fingers clawing air, looking for something to use as a weapon. *I'll clobber him in the head— I can't knock him out—he's too big, too solid. Reason with him? Will he listen? Can I distract this demented fool long enough to escape?*

"So tell me what the hell I did!" Her voice, shrill as the calliope on the River Queen when the pipes hissed their steam whistles, upset him. His eyes jumped and his hands twitched. He grunted and boxed his ears.

Talk softly. Softly—don't shriek. Shrieking freaks him out.

She forced herself to control her voice. "Don't let them do this to you, Sam. They put you up to killing Mary so they could steal The Azaleas. The Judge fixed that bogus mortgage that wasn't recorded until Danielle Turner died! He's a part of this, too! And Agatha! Agatha who doesn't want to move—you know don't you Sam, that when the whole deck comes tumbling down, they're all going to point a finger at you, Sam," she poked an index finger in his direction. "At you—"

One giant, lumbering step and the bear arm wrapped around Karla's neck. He cut the air to her wind pipe. Barely able to breathe, she struggled on. "The law will get you for this, Sam. This is worse than cutting my brake lines. This is murder, premeditated murder," a fit of coughing and gasping stifled her voice. "You'll go to Angola for murder!"

"Shut up! Shut up!"

"You're the fall guy—the patsy. Who put you up to this?"

"Shut up!"

"Look in that armoire! Go ahead! Look in there before you kill me! You know what's in there? Surveillance equipment! Televisions, bugs, computers—this whole house is wired. The Judge's house is wired. The sheriff knows everything—he's coming to get you." Tugging at the heavy arms, she struggled on, breathless. "This is—murder. They're taking you to—you know Angola, Sam?"

Angola hit a nerve. Sam jerked Karla up and down as if she were a rag doll. Every bone in her body hurt.

"Lock you up forever—" her breaths came in painful pants. "Throw away the key."

He looked sluggish, confused, like a programmed robot running out of power. Suddenly, he stepped toward the armoire, dragging Karla along, one arm choking her, the other reaching for the wooden door. Her head woozy, her breath a wheeze, Karla half twisted—kicked Sam in the groin with her good foot—a grunt and he doubled over but didn't let go. The more Karla struggled, the tighter his grip. With one last superwoman effort, she sank her teeth into the rancid flesh of his hand, a sense of deja vu coming over her. She'd done this before.

Karla's head pounded; her legs throbbed. She felt life ebbing from her body. There had to be something—

"Hello, Judge!" A desperate, last ditch ploy— Sam's head snapped in the direction of the door—a moment of indecision— Karla broke free, jumped like a jack rabbit across the room. She crashed through the open window onto the second floor balcony.

CHAPTER 23

Karla raised her bruised and aching body and crawled from behind azalea bushes where she'd fallen in a crumpled heap. Arriving vehicles were parking in the driveway and the lawn. Mourners slammed car doors. Their shoes crunched the gravel as they made their way to the house and the main parlor, anxious to share drinks and food, tears and tales about the deceased.

Karla ran her hands over her face, smoothed her wild hair. She'd lost the black denim jacket she wore over a black tank, she didn't know where. She tugged at the top and brushed dirt from her pants, striving to make herself presentable, passable, before limping to the veranda steps and into the parlor. Looks didn't count for much at an inquisition, and she was sure this hour would turn into just that. The mourners and the curious who circled death would pounce on her like vultures scouring garbage—

The room was packed. Myra Randall stood next to the fireplace. Even in desolation and grief, her composure didn't allow for a public breakdown. She received hugs, kisses, shoulder pats, handshakes and condolences with a stoic, determined attitude.

Agatha, a crow in black, sat in the wing-back chair. She chattered endlessly as if her nerves were the spring that released her tongue. At the mention of Roger, she moaned softly and dabbed her cheeks. The Azalea dowager had graciously offered to host the funeral reception. She wouldn't take no for an answer. Why go to a public hall when Roger was almost family?—

This reception placed Agatha in the spotlight, a place she seldom occupied anymore, so she reveled in the occasion. Anyone walking into the parlor would've thought Agatha the closest and most distraught of relatives while Myra who loved Roger the most, kept a smile on her lips and the pain to herself.

Karla searched for Roger's daughters and for his mother, but didn't see them. His brothers and sister milled about, taking turns standing next to Myra, putting an arm over her shoulder, visible family support through the sad ordeal.

Felice looked down from her place above the mantel. As the mourners did a slow two-step from the widow to the bar, to friendly knots of people, Felice's black eyes shifted from one side of the room to the other. Did anyone but Karla notice that?

Laura, the upstairs chamber maid, unaware of Felice's darting eyes, excited to have The Azaleas once again filled with people, danced on her toes and passed pimento-filled celery stalks, and mini stuffed tacos. Dorcas waddled about the room bearing a canapé tray and finger sandwiches. She took furtive glances at the portrait and ducked her head.

Clem, helped by Peter, Bale's bartender at The Hills, served Margaritas and frosty daiquiris, Scotch and Kentucky Bourbon. Many of the grieving ones were already drunk, an acceptable condition at this sad time.

Sam stood behind Judge Jeremiah's wheelchair. He spotted Karla and looked quickly away. A lightning bolt went through Karla, electrifying the hair on her arms and raising goose bumps. Sam deliberately placed both big hands on the Judge's shoulders.

Hiding behind his employer! Using the old man as a human shield! He wasn't going to get away with attempted murder on Mary, on me, on Roger—Roger! Did Sam kill Roger, too? Did he have something to do with the crop-duster's crash? Tampered with the Mosquito Hawk the way he did with the brakes on my car? He was in the barn that night. Had Roger walked in at the wrong time?

The Judge, drink in hand, was deep in conversation with Bale. Whatever they discussed fully absorbed both men. Neither noticed Karla.

A self-conscious Mr. Ito looking displaced bobbed like a cork in shallow water. Gloria, next to him, punched her palm pilot. How rude! Roger was dead! The man deserved a few minutes of respite from business as usual.

Karla's head hurt, her temples pounded. She couldn't stand in the hallway forever. Sam had already seen her, and soon the others would, too. She took a deep breath. *Enter the living room, offer condolences and get it over with—walk away as soon as possible.* Feeling like Marie Antoinette on her way to the guillotine—how long that trip must've been! — Karla screwed her courage and stepped into the parlor.

The swirling mourners surrounded her, their movements a grotesque waltz, their faces enlarging as they drew near, shrinking as they walked past. They danced in her direction then glided away—white wrist below a black sleeve, a perfume whiff, a bearded face approaching and retreating, a spilled drink, whiskey smell—death.

Jumbled thoughts raced through Karla's mind. Agatha and the Judge and Sam and the sheriff and Bale and—where was Mary? Albert? — Off with Mary someplace? The unexpected pang couldn't be jealousy. Why would she be jealous? Albert was a meal ticket, a way to conquer poverty, a practical anesthesia to deaden the pain that was Richard. Her employer had failed on all three counts.

Was Bale talking to the Judge about buying The Azaleas? About undoing the bogus mortgage? About his plans to steal the place?—Ito wanted The Azaleas—a Japanese! These Southerners would never let a foreigner live in peace among them—

Tonight Karla had almost been killed once again. That's what happened to Albert's agents. That's why they didn't last. She had news for Albert. She'd quit this job before anybody erased her. Life was too precious. She knew how to live in poverty. Being a rich corpse held no appeal.

Roger was dead. Bonnie and Carleen had no father. He'd never see Carleen play basketball again. How proud he was of his girls! The first day Karla met him, he showed Karla the pictures and away he went—

Her commission for selling The Azaleas was $30,000. She needed $30,000.

Sheriff Jimmy—big, ole Sheriff Jimmy Watson, shaking everybody's hand—these people better take a closer look at their sheriff. The man manipulated events. He was evil. And Bubba, too—mean, deputy Bubba, more than mean, sadistic.

Poor Willis! Dead in the field! Burnt to a crisp! No newspaper mentioned his name. No television broadcaster reported his death. Authorities wiped him off the face of the earth as if he never existed. Could Karla be vanished with the same slight effort? She clamped her jaw to keep her teeth from chattering. *Don't fall apart now, girl. Don't sink under the heavy weights. Don't trip this close to the finish line.*

The sheriff swaggered toward Karla, a cold look in his eye. *Sayonara.* This was it. He'd arrest her, concoct a story, fabricate a trumped charge and throw Karla in jail. Feed her to the alligators.

Her knees turned to jelly. Her gut feeling was to turn, run, escape to the French Quarter with its big city attitude and little neighborhood problems.

The sheriff put one hand on her arm—the room swam in strange, quivering waves. A huge roar filled her ears.

"Karla! Karla, dear—" Through the tumbling confusion in her head, Karla saw Myra leave her post by the fireplace, walking quickly through the crowd. The ebbing voices turned into a murmur. Roger's widow embraced Karla. "Roger said so many nice things about you." Turning to Jimmy Watson, who'd quickly dropped Karla's arm and taken a step back, Myra said in the quiet, sweet voice of mourning, "You must let me have Karla for a few minutes—" and drawing Karla along, she placed Roger's friend safely by her side. When mourners approached to offer condolences, Myra graciously introduced the last dear person to see Roger alive. Instead of a meddling outsider, Myra turned Karla into family, one of them, and courtesy forbid stoning by the mourners.

The remaining evening blurred. When the artificial smile plastered across her face began slipping, and shaking one more warm and sticky hand would surely make her scream, Karla said, "Thank you, Myra," and took her leave without hugging or kissing her savior. The widow had received a thousand pats and empty gestures. Karla's sincere thanks came from deep in her heart.

Myra nodded and said, "I'll talk to you later. Will you check on the girls?"

"Sure," Karla worked her way toward the hallway. The girls had probably escaped to the kitchen or an upstairs bedroom.

Mary Bravelle came from the direction of the bar. She eyed Karla with the big, melancholy eyes that held no secrets. She wanted to unburden her soul, make peace and start anew.

THE AZALEAS

Relief through absolution?—go to a Father Confessor. "Where's Pierre?"

"I don't know." Mary dropped onto the piano stool.

"You'd better not sit there. Felice doesn't like that."

Mary looked at the portrait and quickly rose. "The famous Felice," she said. "When I was little she rattled through the house and broke window panes and smashed china. Did she really do those things or was that a child's over-wrought imagination? Does she still fly off the wall?"

"On occasions," Karla replied. Felice looked down upon the women. Her black eyes shifted. The goose bumps on Karla's arms felt the size of baseballs. "Very much so—"

"The house is much smaller than I remembered. When I lived here the rooms seemed big as football fields," Mary said.

The Quarter had seemed vast to Karla when she was a child— crisscrossing streets bound by the river, the wide Esplanade Avenue, Canal Street and Rampart— endless adventures within the boundaries. The levee that contained the Mississippi was as high as a mountain, and the river itself an endless brown ribbon with no beginning and no end. She didn't remember exactly at what point in her life the streets shrank, the levee down-scaled and her world turned Lilliputian, stifling, closed in.

Gloria approached, impatient, frowning. She was a woman of action, and waiting didn't sit well with her. The funeral, burial and reception seemed a lifetime to her interrupted business cycle.

"Ito," she said directly to Mary, "really does want to buy The Azaleas," and turning to Karla, "it's not going down the pike the way we planned."

"Can we discuss this later?" Roger wasn't fully settled six-feet under yet. His memory deserved more respect.

"*Later* doesn't exist in the real estate business. *Now* is the operative word."

Initially Gloria had started by doing Karla a big favor. Somehow the good intentions backfired. Mr. Ito was ready to gobble American land and willing to pay cash, a circumstance irresistible to any good salesperson, and Gloria was the best. Why waste time with the recalcitrant Bale?

As soon as Bale owned the plantation, he would evict Agatha and her servants. He'd bulldoze the house, a personal triumph, a mean-spirited trump, cut the land into lots and put a Burger King on the highway corner.

Whatever else Albert might fuss about, he couldn't quarrel with results. Two offers in three weeks to buy The Azaleas was good work.

No law said the seller had to accept the highest bid, though most were greedy enough that this was the established practice. Karla had no clue what Mary would do. This sale was a problem of the heart more than real estate. Mary loved Bale. Bale loved Mary. Of that Karla had no doubt. Mary went away to Paris, married somebody else, had lovers, had Pierre. A lifetime of other men hadn't been able to erase Bale from her heart. A sad heart gave her that melancholy look. Between Bale with his low-ball proposal and Ito with his full-price offer, which would she take? Would she decide with her heart or negotiate with her brain?

Who bought The Azaleas ultimately wasn't up to Karla. If Mary wanted to take $1 million from Bale instead of $3 million from Ito, that was unfortunate. Then there was fiancé Pierre to worry about. How much influence did he have on Mary?

The question of loyalty arose. As Mary's representative, Karla's first duty was her client's best interest—no, take that back. Albert had her prime loyalty. He was her employer. She had to be true to him. Let him deal with Mary.

Working for Albert was stressful and challenging. Once this deal was a wrap she could easily associate with any real estate agency, sell houses with three bedrooms two baths down the hall to the left, or three bedrooms two baths down the hall to the right—simple, uncomplicated, boring transactions.

Selling The Azaleas to Ito would net Mary the most money, leave Agatha in residence, and make Gloria happy. Splitting her commission with Gloria was the only drawback, depressing math. Best to stay away from the numbers—what difference did the amount make? She'd never seen that much money in one pile in her entire life.

Mary looked at Karla with big, innocent, trusting eyes brimming with tears, confusion in her heart, unsure what to say, what to do.

"All things considered," Karla said, putting her bank account, her baby grand piano, the down payment for Mimi and Bilbao's bar,

Lebron's education, and all her selfish motives aside. "Mr. Ito is your best buyer."

The approaching Gloria overheard the verdict. "You're top drawer, kid," she said admiration in her eyes.

Suddenly, a sound came from the outside like the rush of a mighty wind and filled the house. The vibrations rattled window panes and set paintings dancing on the walls. Wind gusts fluttered the red velvet drapes. Books tumbled from the bookcases. Whirlwind dust motes rose from the carpet and disappeared into the tingling notes coming from the swaying chandelier.

Over the mantel the ornate gilded frame tilted violently to one side. The brilliant red dress turned into bleeding streaks. The coal eyes and jet hair formed uneven blobs on a face no longer there. The portrait ran muddy brown like the Mississippi at flood time with jetsam surfacing red and yellow and cobalt blue.

An invisible force pushed and pulled against Karla, twisting her arms and stretching her curls vertically, Rastafarian style. Her body went limp.

Laura freaked. "Did you see the way her hair spun out?"

Dorcas held smelling salts under Karla's nose. Her black face inches from Karla she said in a soothing voice, "It's ah right, honey— it's ah right. She's gone back. She didn't like what y'said about Mr. Ito buying the plantation. She ain't wantin' no foreigner ownin' her Azaleas."

"But it's the best—"

"The best don't matter, honey. Ain't you seen her come flying off that wall?"

"Yes, but—"

"Ain't no *but*, Miss Karla. You follow your conscience. You promise Dorcas you'll follow that conscience of your'n."

"What are they talking about?" Gloria asked. "Is Karla delirious?"

"I'll do my best," Karla said.

Karla and Dorcas stared at the portrait. Felice had returned to her gilded frame, her dark eyes calm and still. The red dress was arranged in neat folds. The big ruby ring sparkled on the hand demurely crossed on her lap. She was smiling, looking pleased. Karla had never seen Felice smile before. The illusion must be caused by the light streaming through a window. Nothing else could explain it.

Had no one but Dorcas and Karla seen Felice leave her frame and whip the room into a sudden frenzy? Karla's eyes met Mary's, and Karla noted with relief that although the others had not an inkling what had happened, Mary understood.

And then the bodies moved aside as if Moses had parted the Red Sea, and staring down at Karla through the trough lined with frowning faces was Albert, her employer, a look of utter concern on his face.

THE AZALEAS

CHAPTER 24

Albert helped Karla to her feet. She leaned for support against him, the room circling her head, temples throbbing, and knees weak. "Let's step outside," he said, immediately in command, "get a little fresh air." She clung to an arm strong and hard as granite.

They descended the veranda steps in silence, her arm drawn through his. He walked slowly while she hobbled down the gravel drive, the crutches gone. Sam had bent one in two as if it were a hairpin. Where was the other one?

The sun set a brilliant red and yellow splash. The oak branches vaulting over their heads turned the driveway into a misty gray tunnel, relieved in places by bright uneven light splotches. Through the thick, leafy ceiling drifted subdued laughter, slamming doors, cars starting. The sounds grew dimmer, slowly fading in the background.

Karla's pounding heart settled down. Her breath came easier. Albert had a calming effect. The idea persisted in Karla's mind that when he was present no harm could touch her. He was a master at projecting that myth.

"I have seen the sunset, stained with mystic wonders, illumine the rolling waves with long purple forms, like actors in ancient plays," Albert said.

Karla stared at him, wondering what the hell he was talking about. She looked at the setting sun, not that she cared. Of all things in the world, at this moment the sunset didn't matter one whit.

"Arthur Rimbaud wrote that in the 18th century," he said.

Damn his high-fallutin' rigmarole! She didn't want to listen to bullshit. Whatever he had to say to her, he'd better get with it, because she wouldn't stand still for philosophical or artistic discussions when her life was totally unhinged.

She'd been in the pasture when the prison van had the flat tire and the deputy struck Willis, and she'd meddled in what was none of her affair. Albert had hauled her back to the city and given her a stern lecture and ample warnings. She'd trespassed into Hank Turner's locked room and gotten herself in big trouble, and Albert had sent Roger to rescue her and later came himself to read her the riot act. She'd been in the field when the crop duster crashed, and she definitely had no business there; and he was sure to give her hell about it. She gritted her teeth. *Let the ass-chewing begin.*

"Tell me about this," he said his face suddenly very close to hers. He lifted her chin with the pressure of his index finger. An ugly bruise ringed her neck.

"You weren't up front with me, Albert. You didn't tell me exactly how dangerous this job was, that my life was at stake. That someone—and now I know who that someone is—would try to kill me—not once, but three times. Is any job worth that?"

Confessing her fright and terror brought a great, enveloping tiredness and she sagged against Albert. The moment her body touched his, a rush of adrenalin stiffened her spine. "No fuckin' job is worth getting killed! I quit!"

"Shh—shh. You're all right. You're safe with me."

For a split second, his reassuring words were comforting. Then her mind shifted from neutral to first gear. This comfort was just another pat reply, another ruse. Albert didn't really care. All he wanted was the plantation sold so Mary Bravelle would think he was the most wonderful man in the world. He'd make big money and dole Karla her piddling commission. *Well, it wasn't really piddling—more money than she'd ever seen in one pile in her whole entire shitty life.* "Why does Sam want to kill me? You must know."

He didn't answer. Instead he led Karla away from the driveway toward the shotgun where Preacher Frank lived. They walked past the white clapboard church, past the cemetery with the leaning headstones, black people and slaves buried there. Albert said a quiet resolve in his voice. "Show me where the plane crashed."

THE AZALEAS

"It's too far to walk. We'll have to get Preacher Frank to take us in his truck."

Preacher was snoring, worn out, an empty Jack Daniels bottle on the floor by his cot. He and hired boys had mowed the lawns, raked leaves, weeded flower beds, smoothed gravel and washed the veranda. The mourning citizens of Feliciana Parish would see the plantation at its sparkling best. No point disrupting Preacher's rhythmic snort. The truck keys hung on a peg by the door.

"If I can drive it," Karla said. "It's temperamental."

When the truck refused to start, Albert walked to the front and unlatched the hood, quite a joke because the man couldn't drive much less did he know the difference between a radiator and a cam shaft. He jiggled coils, fiddled with hoses, pulled the oil dip stick, looked at it curiously and slipped it back into place.

Karla knew more about cars than Albert did. "Why don't you kick it?" she asked.

He ignored her suggestion. "Try again."

She turned the ignition. With a cough and a spurt, the motor started. Wiping the palms of his hands one against the other, he climbed into the cab.

"Don't fall out," Karla warned. "The door on that side doesn't shut, and crossing the fields is pretty rough." With newfound left foot dexterity, she pushed the clutch, an iron pedal worn to a shine, and shifted into first. The gear grated and rasped. She held the loose steering wheel tightly. The truck bounced and bumped across the ruts.

"Do you think we'll wrap this up today?" She asked between jolts.

"More than likely—"

"I'm ready to head back to civilization."

"All this fresh air getting to you?—Miss the alley smell of the Quarter?"

"I do—I do."

Albert jumped from the cab and opened the gate.

He's pretty spry for an old man—she drove through, and he closed the gap. They were in Bale Franklin's leased field with the big black cows and the ponds. Highway 10 to the north, the Hills to the west, the swamp starting east of The Azaleas, stretching behind Judge Jeremiah Jones's house to the Mississippi River.

The barbed wire fence in the distance sagged where the wires were cut. A pickup drove by slowly on Highway 10, the driver rubbernecking. Near the gas line strip the crop duster tilted like a crippled grasshopper, one wing gone and the other crumpled, the fuselage charred black, the surrounding earth churned and rutted, tire tracks everywhere. Yellow police tape sealed the perimeter.

"There," Karla pointed. "Over there." The orange gas valve jutted from the ground. "I was standing there—"

"You were that close?"

"Yeah—the plane was coming toward me and Willis was clinging to the side, and it was tipping and dipping as it rose, then—then—" she choked on the words.

"That's okay—that's okay. I get the picture." He left the truck and stood for a time viewing the wreckage, hands in his pockets, the wind ruffling his white hair. He looked like a tired old man.

"The crash wasn't an accident." Would Albert believe her? The man was a mystery: sometimes young and vigorous, other times old and tired. He could be foppish and effeminate, masculine and virile. He could be gentle and poetic, rough and mean. A chameleon—a strange, weird creature—

"I know." Albert walked slowly around the wreck one way, then turned and walked in the opposite direction, Karla trailing. He was careful not to touch anything.

"And Roger was there," Karla said, despising the catch in her voice, "and Willis, too."

"I know."

Was that it? Was that all he intended to say? He didn't plan to explain? "How come you know?" His extended silence angered her. "Don't you think I'm entitled to an explanation?"

His face was grave and stern. "Did it ever occur to you that the less you know the better off you are?"

"I'm not into unsolved mysteries. "I don't care! I want to know! I demand—"

He raised a quirky eyebrow. "Demand?—"

"Hell, yes! Demand!—" Willis was her neighbor. Lura Mae was Auntie Emmy's cousin. In the big scheme of life they were all related. "Yes, yes! I demand to know!"

A crash is a crash is a crash, a picture on TV, an account in a newspaper. Destruction up close and personal was a different thing altogether. This calamity was young girls without a father; a widow, an inmate killed, a good man dead, a conspiracy with evil consequences.

Returning to The Azaleas, crossing the field into the pine forest, Albert said, "Stop the truck."

"Here?"

"Yes. Let's sit on the ground, catch our breath, and let this settle." The truck sputtered to a stop and they got out. Albert leaned against a pine trunk and patted the earth beside him, motioning Karla to sit. "What do you want to know?"

"Everything—I have the feeling something I can't understand has happened here. There's something unfinished—something—I don't know what."

"It's a long story," he replied.

He wasn't getting off the hook. "I have nothing but time. I want to hear what happened to Roger, to Willis."

"Willis," Albert said reluctantly, as if he was beyond his jurisdiction, trespassing on privileged information—

"Willis is dead! He fell out of the plane seconds after the explosion. I saw that with my own eyes. There'll be a funeral at the AME church."

"A memorial—they'll bury that Willis, but won't have a body."

"Not a body!—at least there has to be ashes! Scoop up a handful and send them to the church!"

Admiration colored Albert's voice. "That will be done. Willis was the FBI's inside man. They sent him to Angola."

"A mole!—"

"Well, that's more James Bond than FBI. The Bureau refers to their inside people as 'contacts.'"

"How do you know all that?" How did he discover all these facts if he wasn't associated with *the company*?

"I have ways. Willis is no angel. I'm sure you know that. Willis plea-bargained. Sold his soul to the devil, you might say. He was traded."

Karla was utterly confused. *Willis traded. What the hell did that mean?* "What the hell does that mean *traded?* Swapped like a baseball player?"

A smile crossed Albert's lips. "Something similar, maybe—Willis exchanged for Roger."

"But Roger is dead!"

"Yes. Roger was Willis's outside contact." *That explained the electronic equipment in the armoire.* "Roger is dead. He can't testify. The drug money was never picked up. The evidence is circumstantial at best. The case is compromised—one of their biggest FBI snafus to date, and they do make their fair share. In exchange for not blowing Roger's cover, for not involving his unknowing family, for not plastering the event all over the front page of every paper, the FBI agreed to desist their investigation of the sheriff—that's temporary, I'm sure, but it'll do for now."

"What's the sheriff hiding?"

"Everything from political corruption to payoffs from the alleged drug ring headquartered in Angola Penitentiary. The $300,000 in the trash bin, for example—

"Willis put it there?"

"No. Willis couldn't leave the prison. He tampered with the plumbing, flooding several bathrooms. The warden called the plumbing company. The plumber was FBI. The town crawled with FBI agents—waiting—they knew—someone would slip, make a mistake, and they'd close in. They were a few hours away— maybe minutes—from cracking the drug ring operating in Angola prison and nabbing the sheriff red-handed. The plumber stuffed the cash in the trash can behind the courthouse as agreed— however, Watson is too smart for them. He smelled a rat and never retrieved the money.

"Everything began to unravel from that point on. Lies and scams and bogus affairs have a way of getting out of hand. They develop a life of their own, and in the end someone breaks and the paper castles come tumbling down."

Karla hadn't been wrong. Lura Mae's boy wasn't a seasoned criminal—a petty one perhaps, but not the big ugly kind. He was on the side of good. "And how about the sheriff—is he going scot free?"

"I told you already. I'm afraid so."

"Why?"

"He's got good lawyers. He has the whole town solidly behind him. The investigation is ongoing."

"Which means?"

"That the IRS and not the FBI will nab him—"

"Why would Roger be the one to pick up Willis? Why were you his publisher? What's the connection?" Questions tumbled from her lips.

Albert raised a hand in a slow-down gesture. "My interests," he said, "are diversified."

"Roger!" Karla cried thinking of Carleen who wouldn't have her father rooting for her in the basketball stand. "Tell me about Roger!"

Albert was silent for a long time before he answered. "The FBI came to see me— they frequently talk with lawyers to get leads and information, and I was the publisher of Roger's books. In addition I represented The Azaleas' owner and my associate was living on the premises at the time—or so I thought—"

"I would've been a fool to stay in the house after Sam tried to kill me the second time!"

"—and with those connections and the fact that I'd helped them here and there a time or two before, a federal agent came calling. Roger worked for them —special assignment type of thing—he was a Viet Nam veteran. Many of his friends are still MIA. Roger happened to be at The Azaleas working on his Audubon book—" Karla followed the trail in her mind. "And the federal agents needed someone who could fly to pick up Willis when he busted out. The day Roger and you rode to Angola, Roger made the arrangements with Willis—"

Karla recalled how Roger flashed his wallet and the guard scurried down the hallway. Albert studied Karla, his eyes keen. "What you must remember is that our primary interest, our only interest here is the sale of The Azaleas. The rest is no concern of ours. We concentrate on real estate."

Real estate: land, houses, fence posts—immovable assets that weren't going anywhere. On the other hand—"How does Sam fit into this picture?"

"Jimmy Watson had Angola release him. Don't ask me how—on a pardon, I suppose. Sam strangled a man and got life."

Karla rubbed her sore neck.

"When the Judge's man died, the one he'd had for forty years, Watson recommended Sam—"

"Huh," Karla fit the pieces of the crazy puzzle. "The sheriff used that dumb bastard—"

"That's right. With Sam in place, living at the Judge's house, the good sheriff knew what was going on at the Judge's house and at Agatha's too, for that matter. He was nervous about the affair concerning the bogus mortgage."

"Tell me about that mortgage."

"Contrary to popular opinion, Henry Turner had no insurance when he died—"

"I found that out soon enough."

"He hadn't paid the premium and the policy lapsed. Agatha didn't know that, but the Judge did. He was frantic, knowing no cash was forthcoming to rescue The Azaleas from the creditors. The Judge didn't have the means, so he approached Bale Franklin for a loan. Bale agreed, but only if he could have a mortgage on the land, that way he could at some future date foreclose and own The Azaleas. He formed a front corporation—Rainbow—"

"The sheriff was in on that, too?"

"Always cut the sheriff in if it involves a courthouse record."

"Danielle Turner signed the papers? She knew she owed $300,000?"

"She was never told. Someone forged her signature on the mortgage."

"Wait a minute! Who was the Rainbow check made out to?"

"Danielle Turner."

"Did the endorsement signature on the check match the forged signature on the mortgage lien?"

"It appears so."

"So all these years Danielle Turner thought she owned the plantation free and clear—"

"That's right. According to Louisiana law— Napoleonic inheritance code—Louisiana is the only state with French law—half the inheritance goes to the spouse, half for the offspring, but Mary wasn't 21 yet, so she didn't have to sign. Danielle was her custodian. Danielle knew nothing about the bogus mortgage and neither did Mary. Upon Henry Turner's death, Danielle Turner was duped into thinking she received $300,000 insurance policy proceeds, and coerced by Agatha to turn over the money so she could pay the plantation debts, which she did. Danielle's files contained copies of the paid bills. The only document missing was the mortgage lien. Danielle thought she owned the plantation free and clear."

"Hasker & Blount found no recorded mortgage."

"Bale was reluctant to record a bogus mortgage. I suppose his conscience bothered him—that is, until you began poking your nose into their shady business. Then the sheriff looked the other way while the back-dated document was entered into the public records. With a recorded lien, the debt to Rainbow had to be paid in order to transfer a clear unencumbered title which the buyer requests and is entitled to."

"Let me get this straight in my mind: Bale and the sheriff formed Rainbow Corporation funded with Bale's money. The Judge fixed a bogus mortgage held by Rainbow. Rainbow wrote a check to Danielle Turner, supposedly insurance proceeds. Someone forged her name, cashed the check and the Judge gave the money to Agatha who paid the creditors."

"Correct. Agatha settled the debts and saved the plantation. When the FBI began poking into the sheriff's affairs, he was afraid the Judge would get nervous and confess to the falsified document. He wasn't worried about Bale. He was sure Bale wouldn't cave, but nevertheless, the sheriff wanted his name off the Rainbow papers. The only way to do that was to pay Bale his $300,000, dissolve the corporation and make the transaction disappear. To pay off Bale, Sheriff Watson exhorted $300,000 from the Angola drug ring from which the FBI suspects he receives regular installments anyways. Watson knew he'd get his $300,000 back when Bale sold the place, and if he didn't, it wasn't money out of Watson's pocket to start with. If the drug ring refused to go along with the plan, the sheriff threatened to hold a press conference, step into the limelight, expose the Angola corruption and emerge heroic."

"That was the money delivered in a paper bag, deposited in a garbage can behind the courthouse?"

"That's right. The big hitch was that Bale didn't want the money, wouldn't take the money. He wanted the land. Bale and the sheriff had a huge argument. The sheriff was jumpy. He didn't retrieve the trash can money."

"When the man from North Louisiana signed to buy, why didn't Bale record the mortgage then?"

"He was going to, but Converse McKenzie had a fatal accident."

"They tampered with his brakes. They killed him."

"Not so. The man, a non-drinker, partied too long and too hard. He couldn't handle his liquor. He was plastered drunk. Several men offered to drive him home that night. The alcohol content in his blood was three times the legal limit. Converse McKenzie couldn't control his car."

"Who started the ugly rumor of the so-called accident?"

"Scuttlebutt has it that it drifted down from North Louisiana. His friends and relatives couldn't believe their Baptist deacon had fallen to sin."

They sat in friendly silence for some time while Karla processed the data.

"So they were part of the scam for different reasons: the Judge wanted The Azaleas for Agatha. Bale wanted the plantation to expand The Hills and get even with Mary Bravelle, and the sheriff—of course the sheriff who runs the courthouse had to be cut in on the deal, or there was no recording going to take place without his say so."

"That's pretty much it. When Danielle died, Mary entered the picture. If she endeared herself to Judge Jeremiah and he suffered a stroke of conscience—with the FBI in town Jimmy Watson couldn't run any risks. We're lucky Sam turned out to be such a bad shot."

"The sheriff or the Judge or Bale—who set Sam up?—"

"I understand Bale wasn't in on the scheme. The other two didn't tell him. They were afraid he wouldn't go along. He wasn't at the funeral, so that simplified things."

Unbelievable! "How did that grizzly bear get to the Cathedral roof?"

"Simple. Simple solutions always work best. Sheriff Watson and Judge Jeremiah came to the memorial service. Watson showed Sam the stairway to the top floor."

"But Sam was on the sidewalk at twelve o'clock. He lifted the Judge into the buggy."

"That's right. Then, already knowing the way to the roof, the route the buggy would take, what time they'd be back, he sneaked up—"

"Drank four soda pops—"

"—ate peanut butter crackers and waited."

"He snagged his black Jersey on the way up."

"That's right."

"That reminds me. I have to pay the tap-dancing boys a little something—"

"It's taken care of."

"Thanks. Good thing Sam couldn't shoot straight."

"Actually, the men counted on that. Sam's half blind. They knew he couldn't hit the side of a barn. Nobody had intentions of killing Mary—scaring her is what they aimed to do."

"How did Sam get the gun up there?"

"The priests had no reason to suspect Simple Sam whose most difficult job in life was pushing the judge's chair. Nobody checked. He hid the rifle inside his baggy trousers."

"My goodness!—"

"Bale, Judge Jeremiah and Sheriff Watson expected Mary to arrive, bury her mother, leave things as they were and go back to France. When they got wind she planned to sell the plantation, they decided something had to be done to stop her."

"Did you know this beforehand? Did you have this information tucked away somewhere before you sent me to the plantation?"

"Let's just say I knew St. Francisville wasn't the peaceful, idyllic place it pretends to be."

"Will the police arrest Sam?"

"They already have."

"Poor bastard!—the others should go to jail, too—" What was it Willis had said? Two kinds of justice: one for white men, one for blacks. Even if Sam did try to kill Karla three times, he wasn't responsible. He was a stupid dolt, forced to do what he was told in order to preserve his freedom. "Why did they send Sam after me? I had nothing to do with their nasty entanglements."

Albert tweaked Karla's nose. "Because you're so nosey—you kept getting close to their big secret, their bogus mortgage. They didn't expect a real estate agent in residence."

"I nearly got killed!"

"Roger was there, and he promised to look after you. Roger and I go way back and sometimes he did little favors for me here and there. When you found the diary and Sam attacked you and I had that pitiful help!—help!—message on my phone, I called Roger right away and he had the good sense to get you out of there STAT."

"What happened to that diary? Where is it?"

"Back in the desk drawer or in an FBI file somewhere."

"Sam tampered with the brakes. I lost control on the big curve, ended in the hospital, got out and went to the St. Francis Hotel—"

"That's right. And got wrapped up with Bale once again—"

"That's my private business."

Albert raised both hands, palms out. "I'm not prying, honey. What else is bothering you?"

"Mary? What about Mary and Bale? You know the truth. You were the lawyer."

He was so closed-mouth, Karla thought for a moment he would ignore the question and not answer, leaving her up in the air about one more situation. She was sick, sick to death of not knowing what was going on, of not having all the cards face up.

"Bale and Mary go back a long ways. They have a history. Mary conceived a child—"

"Bale's?—" The question popped out, without thinking.

He looked off into space and didn't say yes and didn't say no.

"Let me fill in the gaps, please," Karla said. "Bale got Mary pregnant when she was a senior in high school. Danielle Turner had you arrange the abortion. Being a good Catholic, she found it difficult to live with her decision and took pills to get through the days and nights. Two years later Bale and Mary eloped. Again, Danielle called on you and you handled the divorce. Danielle and Mary moved to Paris, as far away from The Azaleas and Bale Franklin as they could get. Bale dedicated himself to becoming rich. He wanted to make enough money to tell all the people who snubbed him and made his life miserable to go to hell."

"Your version is close," Albert said, as if he'd made up his mind to clear the slate. "Danielle was a devout Catholic. Abortion never entered the picture."

A feather could've knocked down Karla. "What happened to the baby? Put out for adoption?"

"Friends of mine in Switzerland have custody."

"*Your niece*!—Does Mary know? Does Bale?"

"Neither one knows. The doctors were instructed to tell Mary the baby was still born."

"They'll do that?"

"Not often. But in this case the doctor, a family friend, was prevailed upon."

"So Mary and Bale have a baby who is alive and well and they don't know about it?" This business grew more entangled by the minute. "How old is it?"

"Suzanne will be ten years old next February. She was born on Valentine's Day."

"Star-crossed!—Romeo and Juliet move over! Do you see her?"

"Uncle Albert visits Suzanne frequently."

Curiosity spurred Karla. "Did you name her?"

"I did. Felice Suzanne: Felice after that formidable ancestor, that indomitable guardian of the past, of The Azaleas— I thought the name appropriate, but rather cumbersome for a little girl—and Suzanne—" a faraway look came into his eyes, a dream lost, a hope not to be—

"Why, Albert—"

"Suzanne was someone very dear to my heart," his voice soft, almost reverent.

Karla's unintentional prying disclosed that once upon a time Albert had strong feelings for a woman named Suzanne. He wasn't always the cold fish he pretended to be. The revelation made Karla uncomfortable. She moved on. "The Azaleas does have an heiress, somebody the plantation can be passed on to. And the child has a mother and father who are still desperately in love with each other."

"Right on all counts—" The old gleam returned to Albert's eyes.

Karla recognized the spark. "It won't work, Albert. Bale wants to get even with the Turners—all of them—in the worst way. Hate is a stronger motivation than love."

"Love triumphs."

"You don't really believe that."

"Yes, I do, with all my heart."

"Bale can buy the plantation, y'know. The ultimate feather in his cap is to own The Azaleas. He planned to steal it, but Mr. Ito making an appearance changed that. He'll have to pay big money for it now and that's sticking in his craw big time."

"Every negative has a positive. If the Turner family hadn't spurned Bale, he would never have become the Boy Wonder that he is."

"Revenge however sweet, has its price. Drive by The Azaleas ten years from now, and you won't even know the place once existed. He'll erase it from the map."

"Memories can't be erased."

"He still loves Mary." The realization made Karla want to cry out, *"What about me? What about me?"* but she clamped her lips and buried the anguish. She'd been to this junction before. She was a seasoned hand at dealing with rejection. Richard gave her the ultimate lesson. Richard! She hadn't thought of Richard in days! "Ooooh—" A sigh escaped her lips, regret or relief, she wasn't sure which.

The fairy tale ended. She was never going to be Richard's Uptown wife with Mardi Gras balls, cotillions and Junior League. She wasn't going to marry Bale and sip afternoon mint juleps on the veranda. The only thing left to salvage was her pride and self-respect.

She wouldn't let the sale fall apart. All her work wasn't going down the drain, not if she could help it. Bale must up his bid right away, before he had second thoughts. He had to forget, forgive and go with his heart.

"I'm not sending Gloria and Mr. Ito packing. I'll not let a cash buyer disappear for an iffy proposition by a rejected lover." Karla's armor was back in place. She rose, ready for battle.

"Where are you going in such a rush?" Albert asked.

"To find Bale Franklin—c'mon—get up."

CHAPTER 25

The Hills Club House lounge was in shadows, except for light at the far end where Bale, still wearing his funeral suit, tie hanging loosely on either side of his open collar, slumped over the polished mahogany bar. His jacket was slung over a wooden stool. The bar lights splashed silver on the mirrors, on the liquor bottles and on the rumpled hair of Bale's bowed head. He held a glass in his fist.

Karla worked at the Pirate's bar long enough to know when a man was drowning his sorrows, his private grief. Not a good time to butt in. "Bale—"

He stared down into his drink with the intensity of the fortune teller on Jackson Square who made her living peering into a teacup and finding answers to life's big questions in the shriveled leaves.

Karla drew nearer slowly, on tiptoes, a little step at a time as if she were wading into an ice-cold pool. "Bale—"

He motioned with a rubbery arm and said in a thick voice, "Well, if it isn't our real estate agent." He narrowed his bloodshot eyes into slits. "Sit down, honey."

Doubts assailed Karla. Dealing with a sober man was one thing, quite another trying to talk sense to a drunk.

The clunk her brief case made when she set it down on the bar sounded like a cannon. Taking a deep breath she took the plunge. "You have to buy The Azaleas now—this minute! In another half hour, Ito from Tokyo will be the new owner. Can you hear? Are you sober enough to understand?"

Bale tilted his head back, drained the glass and extended it for Peter to refill— "So whadda y'say about that?"

"I say you're drunk and you're going to pass up the one and only opportunity to straighten out your life."

"My life ain't crooked." He shook his fist low over the bar, opened his fingers and slung two rings on the counter as if throwing dice. "Peter, pour the girl a drink."

"No thanks." This was work and working and drinking didn't mix.

Peter's eyes warned Karla the best thing to do was go along with the program— "Margarita coming."

Bale rolled the rings on the bar again, retrieved them, sent them down the counter again, and then again, a mechanical gesture filled with frustration. One was a gold wedding band. The other had little diamond chips, nothing big, nothing fancy, the kind of forever token Quarter couples bought on time from Zales and pawned soon after the divorce. Tequila warmed her gizzard and gave her courage. "You love her."

A fearful scowl came over his face. For a horrible moment Karla thought Bale would hit her. Peter leaned over the bar, a human shield.

Oh God not the wrong place at the wrong time, again! Was this knack for trouble a lifetime curse?

"I don't love Mary Turner!" Bale's words bounced off the paneled walls and echoed in the empty room. "You know what I love? Revenge!—"

From the recesses of Karla's mind came the first conversation she ever had with Bale. They were seated at his table in the dining room across the way, talking about the sheriff and what motivated him. She recalled Bale saying greed was life's greatest motivator, revenge, second. Jealousy came next and hate was an overall blanket that kept the emotions boiling.

Forgetting her fright, her feelings, even her safety, Karla concentrated on The Azaleas. She had one mission: convince Bale to buy the plantation. Put together the deal. Make the numbers work. If he was sober or drunk made no difference—yes it did. If the person who signed a contract wasn't sober, sane and eighteen, the contract could be rescinded. All this work for nothing—

"Love is a greater force than revenge," Karla spouted like a TV pop-shrink. "And you know it!" She removed a blank sales contract from the briefcase, uncapped a pen and filled in the place and date: St. Francisville, West Feliciana Parish; October 24, 2006. "Ito's offer is three million, full price. You must match that or you'll lose—listen, it's not only the plantation you'll lose. You'll lose Mary. She and The Azaleas go together." Liquor dulled his eyes. Karla had seen that blank stupor often enough. "You love her," she said. "You love her."

He turned his head slowly, with great effort, as though his neck had lost its natural ability to swivel. "Where is she?" he asked. "Where is she?" A spark dissipated the dullness in his eyes. They glittered green and hard like her cats. *Sir Gato! How was her cat? She missed her cat!* The rings were tight in his fist. "Gone off with her Pierre?"

"I don't think so. Pierre is history." *Why didn't Bale get it? Men were so dense!* "She loves you. She's always loved you."

"Sure. That's why she married Bravelle and went off to Paris, why she's dragging around that little wuss count, why she's—" his face contorted darkly and the rings clattered down the counter once again. "She...she..."

"She was young, don't you understand? Her mother took her away from the boy she loved. Her father committed suicide. She was a teenager—the divorce— the baby—"

Bale's face turned ashen. "The baby died. They killed it."

It wasn't Karla's place to tell him he was wrong. His baby was alive.

For once in her life, she listened to her better judgment and kept her mouth shut. "What happened— happened. Move on, for God's sake!" *Deja vou!* Where had Karla heard that before? Albert! That's what Albert had said to her when she was mooning over Richard, stuck in a groove like a damaged CD. "Mary can have other children."

He was obstinate. "One of her fancy Frenchmen can father them."

Minutes were ticking away and Karla wasn't making any headway. The time had come to turn the big screw. Thank goodness for Albert. Like a magician pulling a rabbit out of a hat, Albert had drawn a copy of the bogus mortgage from his coat pocket, and said, "This may come in handy in your negotiations."

Karla placed the document next to the sales contract. "Dorcas and Preacher Frank witnessed that they saw Danielle Turner sign—" Bale raised his head and curiosity narrowed his bloodshot eyes. "I expect convincing the loyal cook who's as much a part of the house as Felice or the chandelier, and Preacher Frank old as Methusela to witness that they personally saw Danielle Turner sign the mortgage—tell me, did you do that in case anything went wrong, the rap would fall on them, specially old Preacher—he's expendable, right? He should've died already, so no harm done. Except you made one big mistake—" Karla had Bale's full attention. "Neither Preacher Frank nor Dorcas went with the judge to New Orleans—because the judge never went— so obviously they couldn't have actually seen Danielle sign those papers." Bale winced and Karla went right on. "Preacher Frank and Dorcas simply did whatever the judge told them to do— yessir, yessir. Then when Danielle died and I arrived on the scene, the sheriff took the mortgage over to the clerk of court's office and had Elsa record the backdated instrument. Voila! Danielle is dead, and Mary owes $300,000 she can't pay, and you can grab the property at a conveniently arranged sheriff sale. Nice piece of work, if you—it's not only you—it's this whole corrupt town—can get away with it."

Karla understood the sense of community that existed in St. Francisville. The whole town had been in on scamming Mary. They justified their actions because Danielle had left The Azaleas, taking her daughter with her and causing the anguished Hank Turner to take his life. The Feliciana citizens closed ranks and took care of Agatha, one of their own, the same way the Quarter residents did. Anybody who willingly (not kicking, screaming or handcuffed) abandoned an apartment with a wrought iron balcony overlooking a patio green with banana trees, who deserted the narrow, cobblestone streets in favor of another place was a traitor. Newcomers like Richard—her Richard—were looked upon with suspicion. Richard was an invader and a traitor, and up and down the block Quarter residents in their own clumsy way did their best to protect and console Karla.

"Not 'zactly right," Bale's speech blurred, "but close enough."

Albert was the only person Karla knew who belonged to both worlds. He was as much at home in the Quarter squalor as in the charm and grace of Uptown New Orleans. He could talk with transvestites and prostitutes and weirdos as if he were a friend, an ally, the father confessor of all warped mankind. He was comfortable drinking tea at Windsor Court, chatting with the waiters at Cafe Du Monde or the clerks at Central Grocery. His office was plush and highbrow, but it was Albert who the tap-dancing black boys turned to when in a periodic sweep to "clean up the Quarter," City Hall banned them from their corners. Albert was there for them—for Karla—for everybody.

Karla had Bale cornered and he knew it. Bale and Mary were meant for each other, and life had interfered and warped their love and motives. What should've turned out a beautiful love story, ended up a sordid tale of fraud and revenge— "So," Karla said softly, placing her hands over Bale's, stilling his drumming fingers, "why don't we forget the low-ball offer—it's dead in the water, and you sign right here—" she tapped the bottom line on the contract lying at an angle on the counter, "and we'll go find Mary."

If he signed, Karla had catapulted herself from amateur to pro.

Bale propped his chin on one hand and sat on the stool staring at the paper, reading the fine print or seeing double, who knew. The next phase was the most difficult of all. The make or break step.

What time was it? Bars had no clocks. A customer with an eye on the time didn't drink as much. Karla beckoned Peter for another Margarita. He salted the glass rim, poured lime juice and tequila. She took a sip and counted to 60—one minute—120—two minutes—three—four—fifteen. The first person who broke the silence, who explained, justified, insisted, encouraged or objected lost the deal. If Karla sat there until midnight, she'd never utter the first word, interrupt the long, growing void, or plug in sounds to fill the uncomfortable empty space.

She observed Bale discreetly. On the other side of the silent shield between them, he held his head in both hands, squeezing his temples as if to rid himself of a tremendous headache. He closed his eyes, stepping blind on all the flagstones that paved his life, jumping from one to another, following the erratic path, searching for its end. He squirmed on the stool, swung his knees. The seat rotated left and right.

Karla bit her lip.

His left hand reached as if of its own volition, finger tips extended, knuckles raised. His hand looked like a crab sidling diagonally across the counter. She nudged the uncapped pen and placed it in his path.

CHAPTER 26

In a million years Karla could never have anticipated what happened the next morning. Of all the impossible, overwhelming events of the past three weeks, this one was the most unbelievable—totally mind boggling.

Albert summoned Karla to his suite at the St. Francis Hotel. When she arrived, Bale was already there, pacing like a caged lion. Soon afterward, Mary entered.

"Have a seat," Albert said, motioning to them.

Bale crashed at one end of the couch, Mary, the other. Karla took the armchair nearby.

With his maddening ways, Albert dragged the moment to its fullest potential. He ordered coffee and rambled with deliberate slowness about the weather, the rodeo, the town's colorful history.

"Interesting town," he said. "During the Civil War the fighting in St. Francisville stopped for several hours while Captain John E. Hart of the U. S. S. Albatross was brought ashore and buried in the Episcopal Church—the very same church the Yankees had been shelling hours before—the same graveyard where yesterday we buried our friend Roger. Captain Hart was a Mason and had requested a Masonic burial, and as luck would have it, there were two mounted Confederate Masons on the river levee. When the delegation from the vessel arrived waving a white flag and made their unusual request, the Confederates Masons agreed and made the arrangements to bury one belonging to their order. Captain Hart's grave is still there. Did you know that?"

"That's ancient history," Bale replied, impatient. "Everybody knows that."

Room service knocked on the door, pushed a cart with coffee urn, cold drinks, desserts into the room. "Will that be all?"

"Yes, thank you." Albert turned to his guests, "Sugar or Sweet and Low? Cream?—"

"Black," Karla snapped. Who did Albert think he was? A hostess at a DAR tea?—" She placed the contract on the coffee table, presuming they were assembled to settle that score. Mary had to accept Mr. Ito's offer or Bale's offer. Decision time had arrived. Was it fair to have Bale present and exclude Mr. Ito? What would Gloria have to say about that?

Decision time! Karla's life, like it or not was entangled with that of the two people sitting on the couch. Regardless who bought the plantation, the purchase affected her pocketbook, her future and the final outcome of her wretched life.

Mary and Bale had a big stake in this transaction, too. The Azaleas significantly impacted their lives. Their past was interwoven with that of the plantation. Lingering ghosts cast long shadows across generations. Mary and Bale had been touched by Felice, scarred by Hank Turner, hurt by Agatha and set free by Danielle Turner's death.

The pair sitting on the sofa had not forgotten their youth and the happy, care-free days on the plantation. The specter colored every day, every breath they took. The memories determined the reckless paths they followed. Mary had grown distant and reserved, enveloped in perennial melancholy, harboring painful memories. Bale had taken a different course, a get-even approach that made him the richest man in town and the unhappiest. He could make all the money in the world, but he couldn't forget his love, his true love torn from his side and sent to a far country.

They sat on the sofa, looking straight ahead, not daring a sideways glance, afraid to let their eyes meet and allow one look to destroy the chasm they'd spent years building.

Albert cleared his throat and said, "A lot has gone on here the past few weeks," as if that were news to anybody. "Karla has worked diligently to sell The Azaleas, the cause that brought us to this point."

Bale shifted in his seat, removed an arm cushion and plumped it with a fist. Mary stared ahead, eyes shining with contained tears.

With maddening slowness, Albert placed the two sales contracts side by side on the table. "Mary, you have a $3 million offer from Wong Ito and a $3 million offer from Bale Franklin. Both are cash. No contingencies. No financing." He paused, lips pursed. Fingers intertwined he tapped the dimple on his chin. The words hung in the air like the climax scene of a bad play where the falling curtain brought the only relief.

Bale looked sullen and stubborn. Mary hung her head and fidgeted.

Two full-price offers! Surely, Mary must accept one or the other. Karla's paycheck loomed so close, she could almost touch it. She smelled green and at this point didn't much care who bought the property.

"Mary, my dear," continued Albert, "The decision is yours, so if you'll excuse Karla and me for a few minutes, you and Bale talk this over." He made a 'let's go' motion with his head, and Karla followed him into the adjacent bedroom.

Sitting cross-legged on the king-sized bed sat a young girl. She sprang excitedly, ran to Albert, threw her arms around his middle, raised expressive brown eyes and asked, "Now?"

"In a minute," Albert replied, stroking the black hair pulled into a long braid.

Karla didn't have to ask. The girl looked exactly as Mary Bravelle must've looked at that age. The black hair framing the oval face had ancestor Felice's widow's peak, the same rosy cheeks and dimples. The girl wore blue jeans and a white tee with a yellow smiley face.

"Suzanne, this is my colleague, Karla Whitmore."

The girl kept her left arm around Albert's waist and extended her right hand. "How do you do?" she asked politely, a definite foreign bent to her words, no trace of a Southern drawl.

"I'm fine, thanks— and you?" Karla replied, barely able to contain her astonishment.

"I'm nervous," Suzanne confessed, raising an eyebrow, a mannerism so purely Bale that any trace of doubt disappeared from Karla's mind. "Very, very nervous—"

"Now, Suzanne, there's nothing to be nervous about," Albert reassured the girl. "Your parents—remember, I've always told you, you had parents and that someday—"

"Where's Aunt Greta! I want Aunt Greta! Uncle Hans!"

"They've gone shopping. They'll be here in a little while."

"They love me! I want to go home with them!"

"You will go home with them. I simply want you to meet your parents. I've always told you this day would come, haven't I?"

The little girl's bottom lip pouted, and she drew a shallow breath. "I know. I know. What if they don't like me, Uncle Albert?"

Karla walked over to the window. White swans glided on a large pond. One flapped a feathery wing and made a honking sound. "They'll like you," she said.

Suzanne recognized the theme song blaring on TV and with a child's simplicity turned her attention to the set. "Walt Disney! I love American TV!" She bounced on the bed, flopped on her stomach and stared at the screen, sliding from reality to make-believe in one quick, childish flip.

Karla studied the graceful, snow-white swans, deliberating this new development—hard to believe. Albert approached quietly in that slinky, quiet way he had.

"What in the world do you think you're doing?" Karla whispered, furious. "How do you plan to pull off this crazy stunt? You're not dealing with a *thing* here. You're not even dealing with an adult who has made mistakes and is entitled to reap what was sowed. You're playing with a child's life, an innocent child that can be hurt—traumatized—forever."

"Danielle Turner is dead and out of the way. Bless her dear departed soul. It's time those two in there patched their differences and got together again."

"And if they don't?"

"Love will triumph. Trust me."

Karla didn't trust him. She knew first hand the battle was to the death and greed, hate, jealousy and revenge were formidable black riders not easily overcome. "Love sucks," she replied. "It never wins. I know how things are, Albert. I don't live a pipe dream."

Albert placed his hands on Karla's shoulders and massaged her neck. The tenseness eased and the taut muscles relaxed. "They only way to be a successful cynic is," he said, "to develop a sharp wit that tempers truth. Read Oscar Wilde. He was the master."

A dead child resurrected, estranged lovers orbiting in a colliding path, contracts that could make or break her future—soap opera at its highest level—and she was supposed to read Oscar Wilde? Albert was certifiably nuts. "You're sick."

If the remark offended him, he didn't show it. "Why don't you go find out whether Mary accepted Bale's or Ito's offer?"

"Who?—Me?" Karla was drowning in this grand confusion Albert had created, and this request was definitely not a life line.

"It's your plantation to sell, isn't it?—" a subtle reminder of Karla's duty.

"Okay—"

Albert caught the waver in Karla's voice. "That won't do it."

"Dammit! Leave me be! I can do it!"

The sardonic smile returned to his lips— "Much better, Tiger."

Bale and Mary had left their respective ends of the couch and were clinched in a passionate embrace. Karla cleared her throat loudly and waited for the pair to surface for air. "Hmmm! Excuse me, please!"

They weren't interested.

Bale reached for the papers on the coffee table and waved them toward Karla, kissing Mary and kissing her and kissing her as if he planned to make up for a life deficiency in ten minutes.

Mary Bravelle had scrawled her signature across the seller's line. Dollar signs danced before Karla's eyes. The sale was taking place. She'd get paid legal tender. *Oh, my god, oh, my god.* Mr. Transino at the pawn shop would have a stroke when she walked in to redeem her stuff. He'd never known Karla to reclaim anything before.

Karla ducked into the bedroom, waving the signed contract over her head. "She sold it to Bale! To Bale!—"

The satisfaction the contract brought Karla's employer had nothing to do with money. Money didn't matter to rich people who had plenty of it. What mattered to Albert was manipulating a situation, playing God.

"Suzanne," he said, "Turn off that TV and let's go, Pumpkin."

"Uncle Albert?" Suzanne looked worried, scared.

"It'll be fine." He held the little girl's hand. She hung back, ducking behind his coat. Karla tiptoed behind, walking on egg shells.

THE AZALEAS

This could be a disaster—fly like a rocket or crash and burn like the crop duster.

CHAPTER 27

Oh, how great the city looked! How she missed the wrought iron balconies! The comfort found in solid banks of two-story buildings jammed one next to the other, flanking narrow cobblestone streets. The smells! How she missed the river's misty vapors, the oily ship bilge, fresh-ground coffee beans, rancid oysters and rotting bananas— aromatic integrity of her Vieux Carre! Jackson Square! There was Andrew Jackson—the old scoundrel—still perched on his rearing bronze horse! Laughing deliriously, she kicked a Budweiser can thrown in the gutter, followed its trail as it arched through the air and clattered on the pavement.

She walked past the shop that made pralines, the one that rolled cigars, the Librarie, and the perfume shop where Joella created individual scent for each customer. She skipped around the tables sitting on the sidewalks because this day was clear and blue and beautiful. A crippled man bumped into her, knocking her sideways and she hugged him, insanely happy. She stopped at the Farmer's market, comforted by its bustle and familiarity. The lemon pyramids looked yellower than she ever imagined, the oranges more orange, the apples redder, the peppers greener. Tourists jostled her and said "excuse me," thinking she was one of them because she gawked and smiled and looked overwhelmed.

A long, poignant jazz note swelled and expanded like a balloon being inflated with one great breath until it exploded into joyous sound. Carriage and buggy drivers wearing stove-pipe hats, taxis blaring horns, nightclub barkers, tarot card readers, mimes, caricaturists, the frozen angel—everybody, every wonderful body—standing or sitting in their licensed spot. The tap-dancing black boys—Lebron! She had to go right over to Big C and check on Lebron!

Beethoven's Eroica welcomed her when she pushed open the gate to her patio. She couldn't suppress a little shriek of pleasure. She skirted the shallow pool with silvery leaves floating on the murky water and waltzed down the flagstone path, silky banana fronds caressing her face. She tap-danced up the iron steps two at a time, tipsy with joy, elated to be back in Earl's pseudo-Tennessee Williams *garconniere*.

One quick whirl around the apartment—couch, bed, dinette table, toilet—she flushed and the innards gurgled and gushed the same happy tune—and she was back on the street. "Mimi! Mimi! Hooey! Bilbao! I'm back! Oh, y'all, I'm here! I love you! I'm back!"

Her friends dashed through the Parrot Bar door. They embraced her on the sidewalk and with interlocked arms swept her inside.

"Where's El Gato, Hooey?"

The old black man laughed. "Somethin' done happened to your cat."

Her heart sank. "He got run over?"

"No'm. He's weaned off milk and drinks nothing but beer. Here Cat!" El Gato slithered on rubbery legs toward them. He jumped on Hooey's lap and hurt Karla's feelings. Gato's eyes, shining green lanterns set in the black fuzzy face, were glazed. Hooey picked up Gato by his nape. The cat extended four legs and fur rose two inches. He looked like a black Halloween cutout. "Here," Hooey said, "and good riddance."

Mimi laughed her long cackling familiar sound. "Gato is a star now, you know. A TV man came by and filmed Hooey filling Gato's saucer with beer, and the cat lapping Budweiser—"

"Bud! We're a Miller family!—"

"—and Gato licking his chops, big grin on his silly cat face, and they might run it at the Super Bowl and pay you a fortune."

Karla hugged and kissed the cat and couldn't quit giggling, everybody laughing and talking at once, glad to have Karla back. God, it was good to be home.

"You sold the plantation!" Mimi said. "Girl, that's too wonderful. Albert came and told us. He said to plan a big party to celebrate and he's picking up the tab." She looked at me, a question in her eyes. "He did pay you, didn't he?"

Before she could answer, Bilbao said, "Where's the little red car?"

"He did pay me, and the Mustang got wrecked. Wait 'til I tell you. You'll never believe it. Anyhow, I'm so glad to walk on real sidewalks—even if they are cracked and uneven. Listen, would you believe I fell on my knees and kissed the pavement? Y'all don't know how desolate country roads are! Those wide open spaces make a person all jittery and nervous. And I have great news, Mimi, Bilbao. I have the down payment so you can buy the bar from Earl. Where is that stinking old turtle? He hasn't even poked his head outside his shell to tell me hello!"

"Earl's gone," Hooey said.

"—and we can't let you do that—" Mimi said.

"Gone—gone where?" Karla asked—everybody talking at once. "I can do anything I want. I have money, Mimi! Can you believe that? I have money!"

"Some corporation bought Earl's place," Bilbao said.

"You mean I have a new landlord? They must've paid Earl a fortune to pry him out of there. Did they buy the bar, too?"

"Yes, the bar, too—"

"Oh! Damn!" Mimi's dreams dashed once again!

"We got a letter—" Bilbao started—

"—the corporation said when the company decided to sell we would have first option—" Mimi finished Bilbao's sentence.

"That's great—fabulous!" Karla felt disappointed, though. She wanted her money to rescue Mimi and Bilbao, raise them to the next level. She wanted to be of importance to their life, to have a hand in their success.

Tourists—paying customers— came in the door, laughing and talking loud. They stomped in, snorting and charging like Angola bulls, noisily dragged chairs and appropriated a table. A tipsy woman spilled her drink. Hooey went after the mop. Mimi checked her face in the bar mirror, glued a big mole on her cheek, pressed on long, upturned lashes, and donned a silvery spun-candy wig. She slipped into her spiked heel rhinestone shoes, the ones on the shelf beneath the liquor bottles, grabbed an order pad, and with mincing steps and swaying hips made her way to the table. "Honey—" she batted her eyelashes at the man wearing a Boston University pullover. "Ain't you terribly hot in that heavy thing?" The entire table laughed the loose, goosey laughter of people determined to have fun no matter what. A woman said, "Take it off! Take it off!" but the one next to Boston U, obviously his wife or keeper quickly nixed the idea and Mimi asked, "What'll it be? What's your poison?"

"I'll be back!" Karla cried above the ruckus.

"Where you goin'?—"

Karla buried her face in Gato's soft black fur and waved a hand over her head, "Got places to go, things to do! I'm outta here! See ya tonight!"

CHAPTER 28

Lebron's eyes danced a welcome. "Yo! Miss Karla! You back!"

His legs were down flat. She sat on the bed and hugged him. "You rascal— Look at you! Almost ready to go, are you?"

"I guess so." He puckered his lips, not happy.

"So what's the matter?" A hundred things could be the matter, starting with Lura Mae dead, Joey in LTI, and Willis disappeared from the face of this earth. What else could happen to Lebron? "Okay, come clean. What is it?"

"Ain't nothin'," he replied, obstinate. How well Karla knew that routine! Keep the bad news bottled up. No point sharing something nobody could fix.

"You have to stay here a year?"

"Shit! No way—"

"Lost your tap shoes?"

"Nah—I got 'em."

She looked at the empty bed next to his. "Where's your partner, the interpreter?"

"He gone to the AME cemetery."

"What happened to him?"

"Nurse said it was an unexpected setback," Lebron said in a low voice, eyes downcast. "Infection—*new-monia*—who knows—"

Of course Lebron was worried and upset! Poor baby! Death had swooped down and plucked his friend from the next bed, and no

THE AZALEAS

doctor or nurse—nobody—could stop it. Death was beyond human control. Death struck at random, without notice.

Karla patted Lebron's leg, the once-white plaster streaked brown like the dreary walls, her name smeared down one side, other names, other inks, bleeding and splotching the cast. "Nothing is gonna happen to you, Lebron. You're getting better, you know that. You'll soon be out of here." Her words did little to cheer him. Tears glistened in the hazel eyes. "Aw, sweetie, what is it?"

He sucked in a deep breath and said in a whisper, "Social worker, she been to see me three times."

How relieved Karla was to hear that! Whatever was bothering Lebron wasn't a life or death situation, but a government agency chewing time— "So what?—you haven't done anything. She can't send you away."

He nodded silently, his chin barely lifting off his chest. "Yes'm, she can."

"Where do you think she's gonna send you?"

He kneaded his eyebrows, bit his lower lip and stuck out his pointed little chin, struggling to put on a courageous front. In the end his face crumpled and tears wet his cheeks.

"Aw, Sweetie— Here's a Kleen—" she reached for the bedside table. "—here's toilet paper. Blow your nose and tell me what all this is about."

"My gramma's dead, my mama don't want me, and my two bros in jail." He smiled crookedly, a sad attempt at bravery. "I ain't got nobody."

Karla understood. Love wasn't what Lebron missed, since tender care didn't happen much in the neighborhood, everybody stripped to bare bones, scratching like chickens to get a little corn. The biggest part of his love consisted of fear. Fear of his gramma dying and having nobody to run to when life kicked him in the teeth. Fear for his brothers who played street ball with him and were now locked far away. Fear of abandonment by the ones he cared for. Fear was the halo that encircled and contained his love. Love without fear was a shallow proposition.

"Of course you've got somebody! You've got me and Mr. Albert and Mimi and Hooey and all the guys from Parrot's."

Lebron looked up at Karla, his sweet eyes bruised with hurt. "I'm going to a foster home."

Karla recoiled as if he'd slapped her face. *Foster home*! Mrs. Thorney and the room in the attic and her soft prissy little voice and Karla and the other two starving because she never fed them—*Foster home*! Scrubbing floors and crying every night until sleep's black curtain brought temporary relief. *Foster home*! Five in one year, Karla had before Auntie Emmy came along. *Foster home!*—"You're not going to any foster home."

"Yes, I is in two weeks when I leaves here. The arrangements made. Mama signed papers. I'm a ward of the state." He mumbled the words as though he'd memorized them. "Miss Karla, what's a ward of the state? Is that bad? Can I go to LTI? Robert's there."

How could anybody pile more crap on this poor little mangled body? The cold, unfeeling system that caused such terrible grief should be dismantled. The social worker should be shot.

"What's your SW's name?"

He shrugged. "I dunno. Miss Roxanne or something like that."

Karla leaned over the bed and gave him a big hug. "Don't go anywhere," she said. "I'll be back."

CHAPTER 29

Karla aimed a sugar-powdered beignet and hit the newspaper. The sugar exploded with a little burst of white dust and Albert lowered the front page.

"I'm glad it's not Sunday, Albert," she said.

"Why is that?" He asked as he neatly folded the pages.

"Everything terrible happens to me on Sunday."

"Ah, yes I recall—something about the numbers not lining up or the stars being crossed. May I join you?"

Stupid question—Kara wasn't in a position to tell her employer no. "Sure."

He sat across from her at Cafe du Monde, where weeks ago he'd jump-started her life. As usual, he was impeccably dressed in a gray suit, silk shirt, gray ascot, polished black shoes. Both his clothes and his face were unwrinkled. Stress didn't affect him. He was as placid and serene as if he'd been on a two-week cruise. She was tied in knots.

His gray eyes alertly searched her face. The warmth and vitality in their depths was reassuring. He wasn't going to chew her ass. He was okay with the sale, entanglements and confusion aside. He watched her closely, observing her doubts, her struggles, as if he could peer into the recesses of her mind. "It's not as bad as all that," he said. "What's the matter?"

Post-partum depression—Karla heard about that from her women friends. The big let-down after the baby's birth. Months of anticipation and then poof! "I don't know—"

"Sure you do." He took her hand, palm up and absent-mindedly traced the life lines the way the fortune teller did.

"It's...it's..." should she bring up Lebron? After all, Albert had no responsibility when it came to Lebron. If Albert said no, he couldn't help she'd simply have to rescue Lebron some other way.

He noted her hesitation. "It's not as bad as all that. What is it, honey?"

"I'm worried about—"

"Tell me. You can tell me anything. It's okay."

She took the plunge. "Lebron! I can't let Lebron go into a foster home! I've talked to his social worker. There's all kind of red tape—"

"You need a good lawyer?"

"Would you?"

He snapped his fingers. "Piece of cake—you're doing for Lebron what Auntie Emmy did for you. You know what that is?"

"What?"

"An act of love you don't believe in."

"No it isn't. It's doing what has to be done. And I'm not even sure if taking Lebron is the right thing. Auntie Emmy never had any doubts, any regrets. I'm so scatterbrained. I have this knack for getting myself into trouble—I'm not really sure—I don't know if this would work—"

"Lebron can pretty much take care of himself. All he needs is a place to come in out of the rain—he's a tough little fellow."

"I don't have a mothering bone in my body—"

"Mothering bones are like baby teeth. They come in slowly and with a lot of pain. Don't worry about Lebron. He's a survivor."

Albert would take care of the situation! She'd buy a new couch, the kind that turned into a bed, and Lebron could sleep there. He could have the bottom dresser drawer. She'd enroll him in school—have him learn to read, really read, not the halting struggle over every word, but read page after page like a bird swooping from limb to limb. Marooned in foster homes, reading had been her escape. Books saved her life.

"Thank you."

"What else is on your mind? You cashed your check?"

Of course she'd cashed her check! Right away! And half of it was gone already! Money sifted through her fingers. Snap! Snap! Snap! "Thank you."

"Was it enough? Did you pay all the creditors?"

"Yes! Yes! Sent each and every one a money order marked 'paid in full'—wonderful feeling paying off those vultures with their eighteen percent interest and their late charges!" She looked at him seriously. "I asked the clerk to write 'go to hell' across the money orders, but she said the post office wasn't allowed to use profanity."

"And have you bought a piano?"

"Not yet."

"And why not?—"

She wanted a baby grand piano, wanted to take lessons and learn to play notes written down in black and white. But a piano was so much money—"I'm trying to sort out my life, Albert. It's changed, you know. You've changed it."

His warm hand covered Karla's. He gave her fingers a slight squeeze. "For the better, I hope."

"I don't want to owe anybody anything anymore."

"Nothing wrong with that—"

"There's got to be an easier way." Now that her debts were satisfied and creditors were not barking at her heels, she seriously considered finding other work. Associating with Albert was dangerous. His previous agents found that out—two of them, too late.

"Of course there are easier ways, but easy is boring, wouldn't you say? You've proved your mettle. I'd increase your commission."

"How much more?—Fifty-fifty split?" A leap of faith—from 10% to 50%! Inwardly, she laughed at her boldness—but what the hell—she had nothing to lose.

"And I presume you want hospitalization and retirement benefits, too?"

"Absolutely—even McDonald's and Burger King offer that."

He said, "Hmm," and interlaced his fingers, extended the two index ones and pressed the tips into the dimple on his chin, a habit of his when studying something closely.

She'd overstepped her boundaries and this deal wouldn't fly. He'd be upset and end their relationship and she'd never see Albert again. No other man rode across fields with her in compatible silence, or took Game Boys to the children's ward at Charity or appeared like a genie released from a bottle whenever she needed him most. She'd miss the old goat.

"We'd be equal partners," he mused.

"I did all the field work." Her life was at stake while he played lord and master in his big-time office in New Orleans.

"So you did."

"You found the place to sell."

"We do work well together, you know."

"Up to a certain point—"

"What point is that?"

"The point at which I almost get killed—so far I've been lucky—"

"Your luck will hold out."

"Says who? You?—"

"You think I'd let anything happen to you?" She felt the heat warming her face, "to my partner—? You want me to draw up a contract of some sort?"

"I don't need a contract. I trust you." Crazy thought, but true—she had confidence in him. He had not failed her. "It's not that. I'm worried about something else—I don't know what to do—I have to do something." She'd already dumped her biggest concern—Lebron—on his shoulders. Nothing else was as important. "Gloria. She'll be mad at me forever."

"On the contrary—I talked to her yesterday. She's very happy for you."

"She can't be! Ito wanted to buy the plantation. He had the cash, and I screwed up her sale and butted in with mine."

Albert smiled. "Ito had no intention of buying the plantation."

"What—what are you saying?"

"Exactly what you heard—"

"But Gloria told me—she said—"

"Gloria knew she was dealing with a greenhorn."

That ruffled Karla's feathers. "What do you mean?"

"You couldn't have convinced Bale to buy the plantation unless you were positive that Ito was about to snap it up from under him. You're not seasoned enough to bluff your way."

The remark stung. The past few days she had paid bills, opened a bank account, folded crisp twenties into her new wallet, exulting in her new status due to her ability to put a deal together and make it work. Her self-importance had ballooned. "She went to so much trouble! She took two days out of her own busy schedule! I owe Gloria big time. Should I offer her part of my commission?"

"You don't owe her a thing. She's a pro. Seeing your rise to the next level is reward enough for her." He saw Karla's doubtful face. "Gloria is tops in her field," he said, "If misery wants company, success demands it even more. Success is a lonely plateau."

"I don't believe that." Successful people had money, friends and social status, fine furniture and trips and popularity. "Gloria's appointment book is jammed. She has an endless social life. She stays busy, busy—busy—she doesn't even have spare time to find a husband."

"Maybe she doesn't want one. Husbands require a lot of attention."

"She doesn't have time—"

"To be charitable?—ah, but she does. When you need something done, you look for the busiest person you know." Albert gave the impression he was never busy, yet he was a lawyer and publisher, art dealer, antique collector, rare book trader—

"What you did for Mary and Bale and Suzanne was truly wonderful. You made a fairy tale come true."

"Not really. I righted a wrong that had been bothering me for ten years. At that time removing the infant assured Mary a future. A seventeen-year old with a baby gives up life. Danielle didn't want that to happen to her daughter. She was sure Mary would get over Bale and find happiness with someone else. It didn't happen that way."

"I've never seen two people more ecstatic, thanks to you."

"Don't forget. Thanks to me, too, for the marriage annulment, for the years of distress, for their botched lives. A lawyer does a lot of meddling in the course of a business day. The only absolution is to somehow tip the scale more to the good than the bad, a tricky business sometimes."

"But you did it!"

"Ten long years—there's a lesson in all this—patience and more patience." He sipped his coffee, lost in private thought.

"Gloria told me the same thing. 'Patience and perseverance, she said. Make that your mantra'."

"Now you know. It's the only combination that works, that brings success. Anything else is like a falling star, one big splash and then a fizzle." He sighed audibly. "Bale and Mary, Suzanne and the Ibsens have all flown back to Switzerland. They've agreed to share Suzanne, let her go back and forth, and come to the States for holidays and summers. The Ibsen's have five other children."

"Five children!—and they took in another?"

"They are good people, and the financial arrangement helped them educate their flock. They cared for Suzanne as if she were one of their own, but there was never any question that she belonged to her estranged parents."

"But Suzanne"—

"Children have a way of sensing situations. Suzanne knew the Ibsens loved and cared for her, but that she wasn't one of them. Children are resilient. They adapt."

"Oh, so now you, the man with no children, are the expert."

"I did my damage and repaired the rift I helped create. The rest is up to them. I'm sure they'll work it out."

After a long silence, not an uncomfortable space, but an eloquent quiet filled with unsaid words, Karla asked, "Albert, why did you pick me for this job? I don't fit any of your profiles."

"Oh, but you do. I was looking for somebody with gumption, somebody so far down in the pits the only way out was up."

"Come now! New Orleans is a big city with small town mentality. Gossip travels from the Garden District to the Quarter."

"I thought you had what it took—with a little boost—"

"Come clean! We're going to be partners? We tell the truth—no more lies. You made a bet with Richard. You told him you could make a silk purse out of a sow's ear."

"Did that cad tell you that?"

"Never mind who told me. I heard it."

Albert took a chance on Karla, and she did her part and they both came out okay. He'd made his pile of money, and she got her agreed take. And Bale and Mary were okay and so was Suzanne. And Agatha and Judge Jeremiah were okay. Everybody was gonna live happily ever after—"Except...except—"

Albert chuckled. "I doubt you're going to die an old maid, if that's what's bothering you." He made old maid sound like a terminal disease.

"I had hopes for a while that Bale and I—" She stopped midsentence. Albert wasn't entitled to know every facet of her life.

"Bah! He's not the right man for you. Picture yourself marooned in St. Francisville, that southern oasis from here to eternity, surrounded every single day by country people who refuse to acknowledge a world exists beyond the Mississippi River. They are happy as long as they are intermingling, intermarrying and meddling in each other's business. Sure, their houses are big, but remember they're stuck in them day in and day out. They never leave. And their parties are grand the first six or seven times. Then you know what happens?"

"What?"

"Soon enough you find yourself repeating the conversation you had at the last party—the same thing over and over—why I must have told Agatha a dozen years in a row that the blue Chinese jacket she wore was very complimentary to her complexion. Those people are stuck in a time warp and like it that way. You'd be bored and restless before you knew it. You'd never be happy there, not for the long haul, anyway."

"I would so be happy there." Thinking of Bale and Richard and all the perfectly good men she was destined never to have depressed her. "If only—"

"Spare me! I don't want to hear! Your romance with Richard was doomed from day one. Marriage was never going to happen. I know Richard's parents, his heritage and his history. By now you should be over that fool notion."

"Did you or did you not make a bet with him?"

"Yes I did."

"And who won?"

"Well, up to this moment, I thought I had."

"What right do you have to wager on another human being's life? Am I just a toy to be played with? A trifle to amuse you?—"

"On the contrary—I saw that you had—have—a lot of promise. Otherwise, we wouldn't be fifty-fifty partners."

"Oh." How could she have forgotten something as life-altering as that? Fifty-fifty was a lot more than ten percent. In a few years if she saved and invested well, she could be a millionaire. Albert had said so himself.

"And when you have all that money—" laughter flashed in his eyes, "and can buy anything you want—that's what you want, isn't it?"

She could have anything she wanted: walk into a store and say 'I'll take *that* and *that* and *that*, please deliver.' "Yes! I don't want to ever be poor again. Poor isn't pretty. I want to erase food stamps, foster homes, Santa Bear and Lion's Club eye-glasses forever from my mind. I don't want government assistance! I don't want charity! I want to make my own way."

"Admirable." For a moment Karla thought he was being sarcastic, but she saw he was serious. "If you marry wealth, the riches come and go," he said. "Think about that."

Albert confused her. "You mean when you get a divorce?—might as well divorce a rich man as a poor one. The settlement is better."

"I'm a rich man."

"Is that a proposal?"

He laughed. "I'm not the marrying kind."

He was gay. No wonder she liked Albert so much. Gay men made such great friends. A girl could confide in them. They never groped or lusted after you. They were always involved in their own triangles. Their apartments were decorated in the best taste, and they knew their antiques and were gourmet cooks and had a life. Until gays went over the edge and walked with mincing steps and fluttered their hands when they talked and their voices slid into an affected falsetto, they were okay people.

"And the car—I really hated to wreck the Mustang Shelby."

"It's only a car."

"Yes, I know, but—"

"Check the Royal Sonesta parking garage when you leave here."

"Albert!"

"All fixed. Like new—Joe Ferrace is a miracle worker. Title is now in your name—a bonus for a job well done."

"Albert!"

"And this is yours, too." He reached under the table for a box wrapped in newspaper and handed it to her.

Karla tore the paper and lifted the lid. The carved chess set nestled inside. "Where did you get this?"

"From the guard at Angola—you didn't collect it when you tore out of there."

Karla tilted the box so he could see the chess men. He fingered the queen and examined the workmanship closely. "A real work of art," he said, "Must've taken years to carve."

THE AZALEAS

"The inmates have nothing but time. You like it?"

"It's exquisite."

"It's yours. I bought it for you."

"That's very nice, thank you. And as long as we're exchanging tokens of affection—

He extracted from his pocket a thin, rectangular box, a jeweler's box.

Her fingers trembled as she undid the clasp on the box. "Albert!"

"Well, if you prefer the Mickey Mouse one, I—"

"No! No! This is fine—great—wonderful." Maurice LaCroix of Switzerland—she'd never heard of the brand, but it sounded elegant and expensive.

"Here, let me." He leaned across the table and clasped the thin watch around her wrist. Then putting a hand on either side of her head, he drew her face close. She felt his warm breath on her cheeks. With a swift, abrupt motion his lips were on hers, a hard, bruising kiss that wiped all gay thoughts from her mind.

The waiters clapped and whistled.

Breathless, Karla pushed Albert away. "Why Albert!—" She intended to say something flip, irreverent, a show for the tourists and the waiters. After all this was New Orleans, and everyone came to be entertained in one fashion or another.

Before another word escaped her lips, Albert kissed her again, gently and softly this time, like a lover returned from a long mission.

Her heart unexpectedly beat furiously, and in her head she heard violins playing—what was that music? Meditation de Thais—the Windsor Court music! The sweet notes had drawn Albert and her together that afternoon, and they'd transcended to the next dimension, leaving Mary behind.

When he finally pulled away, his quiet, gray eyes were deep with feeling. "And now that leaves us one more thing to discuss—"

He opened her clenched hands slowly, lifting each finger away from the palm like a flower opening its petals. He brought her hands to his lips. Goosebumps sprang on her arms.

Flushed with anticipation, a whole new world opening before her, she asked, "Yes, what is it?"

He replied lightly. "Your next assignment—"

ABOUT THE AUTHOR

Katie Wainwright, a native of Cuba and a resident of Hammond, Louisiana, owned a real estate agency for many years before retiring to write and travel. The Azaleas, a real estate mystery set in a Louisiana plantation, explores with gentle humor and deep insight the mystique that is the South. She is presently working on Pohainake Parish, a satirical view at local Louisiana politics. Her two previous novels, historical fiction, *Cuba on my Mind* and the sequel *Secuestro*, published by the University of West Alabama's Livingston Press highlighted life in Cuba before and during the Castro revolution. The third volume in the series, tentatively named *Perseverance* is scheduled for release in the fall.